SINGLE & SINGLE

John le Carré

SINGLE & SINGLE

Hodder & Stoughton

Copyright © 1999 by David Cornwell

First published in 1999 by Hodder and Stoughton
A division of Hodder Headline PLC

The right of David Cornwell to be identified as the Author of
the Work has been asserted by him in accordance with the
Copyright, Designs and Patents Act 1988.

10 9 8 7 6 5 4 3 2

A CIP catalogue record for this title is available from the British Library

Typeset in Monotype Baskerville by
Rowland Phototypesetting Ltd.
Bury St Edmunds, Suffolk
Printed and bound in Great Britain by
Clays Ltd., St Ives plc
Bungay, Suffolk

Hodder and Stoughton Ltd.
A division of Hodder Headline PLC
338 Euston Road
London NW1 3BH

Jane's book

Human blood is a commodity
US Federal Trade Commission, 1966

CHAPTER ONE

This gun is not a gun.

Or such was Mr Winser's determined conviction when the youthful Alix Hoban, European Managing Director and Chief Executive of Trans-Finanz Vienna, St. Petersburg and Istanbul, introduced a pallid hand into the breast of his Italian blazer and extracted neither a platinum cigarette case nor an engraved business card, but a slim blue-black automatic pistol in mint condition, and pointed it from a distance of six inches at the bridge of Mr Winser's beakish but strictly non-violent nose. This gun does not exist. It is inadmissible evidence. It is no evidence at all. It is a non-gun.

Mr Alfred Winser was a lawyer, and to a lawyer facts were there to be challenged. All facts. The more self-evident a fact might appear to the layman, the more vigorously must the conscientious lawyer contest it. And Winser at that moment was as conscientious as the best of them. Nevertheless, he dropped his briefcase in his astonishment. He heard it fall, he felt the pressure of it linger on his palm, saw with the bottom of his eyes the shadow of it lying at his feet: my briefcase, my pen, my passport, my air tickets and travellers' cheques. My credit cards, my legality. Yet he did not stoop to pick it up, though it had cost a fortune. He remained staring mutely at the non-gun.

This gun is not a gun. This apple is not an apple. Winser was recalling the wise words of his law tutor of forty years ago as the great man spirited a green apple from the depths of his frayed sports coat and brandished it aloft for the inspection of his mostly female audience: 'It may *look* like an apple, ladies, it may *smell* like an apple, *feel* like an apple' – innuendo – 'but does it *rattle* like an apple?' – shakes it – '*cut* like an apple?' – hauls an antique breadknife from a drawer of his desk, strikes. Apple translates into a shower of plaster. Carols of laughter as the great man kicks aside the shards with the toe of his sandal.

But Winser's reckless flight down memory lane did not stop there. From his tutor's apple it was but a blinding flash of sunlight to his greengrocer in Hampstead where he lived and dearly wished himself at this moment: a cheery, un-armed apple-purveyor in a jolly apron and straw hat who sold, as well as apples, fine fresh asparagus that Winser's wife Bunny liked, even if she didn't like much else her husband brought her. Green, remember, Alfred, and grown above ground, never the white – pressing the shopping basket on him. And only if they're in season, Alfred, the forced ones never taste. Why did I do it? Why do I have to marry people in order to discover I don't like them? Why can't I make up my mind ahead of the fact instead of after it? What is legal training for, if not to protect us from our-selves? With his terrified brain scouring every avenue of possible escape, Winser took comfort in these excursions into his internal reality. They fortified him, if only for split seconds, against the unreality of the gun.

This gun *still* does not exist.

But Winser couldn't take his eyes off it. He had never seen a gun so close, never been obliged to take such intimate note of colour, line, markings, burnishment and style, all perfectly pointed up for him in the glaring sunlight. Does it *fire* like a gun? Does it *kill* like a gun, *extinguish* like a gun, removing face and features in a shower of plaster? Bravely, he revolted against this ridiculous possibility. This gun does not, absolutely does *not* exist! It is a chimera, a trick of white sky, heat and sunstroke. It is a fever gun brought on by bad food, bad marriages and two exhausting days of smoky consultations, unsettling limousine rides through sweltering, dusty, traffic-choked Istanbul, by a giddying early-morning dash in the Trans-Finanz private jet above the brown massifs of central Turkey, by a suicidal three-hour drive over switchback coast roads and hairpin bends under red rock precipices to the world's utter end, this arid boulder-strewn promontory of buckthorn and broken beehives six hundred feet above the Eastern Mediterranean, with the morning sun already turned to full, and Hoban's unblinking gun – still there and still a phantasm – peering like a surgeon into my brain.

He closed his eyes. See? he told Bunny. No gun. But Bunny was bored as usual, urging him to have his pleasure and leave her in peace, so instead he addressed the Bench, a thing he hadn't done for thirty years:

My Lord, it is my pleasant duty to advise the Court that the matter of Winser versus Hoban has been amicably resolved. Winser accepts that he was mistaken in suggesting that Hoban brandished a gun during a site conference in the southern Turkish hills. Hoban in return has provided a full and satisfactory explanation of his actions...

And after that, out of habit or respect, he addressed his Chairman, Managing Director and Svengali for the last twenty years, the eponymous founder and creator of the House of Single, the one and only Tiger Single himself:

It's Winser here, Tiger. Very well indeed, thank you, sir, and how about your good self? Delighted to hear it. Yes, I think I can say that everything is exactly as you wisely predicted, and the response to date has been entirely satisfactory. Only one small thing – water under the bridge now – not a breakpoint – our client's man Hoban gave the impression of drawing a gun on me. Nothing in it, all a fantasy, but one does like to be forewarned...

Even when he opened his eyes and saw the gun exactly where it had been before, and Hoban's childlike eyes contemplating him down its barrel, and his child's hairless forefinger crooked round the trigger, Winser did not abandon the remnants of his legal position. Very well, this gun

9

exists as an object, but not as a gun. It is a joke gun. An amusing, harmless, practical joke. Hoban purchased it for his small son. It is a facsimile of a gun and Hoban, in order to introduce some light relief into what for a young man has no doubt been a lengthy and tedious negotiation, is flourishing it as a prank. Through numb lips, Winser contrived a species of jaunty smile in keeping with his newest theory.

'Well, that's a persuasive argument, I must say, Mr Hoban,' he declared bravely. 'What do you want me to do? Waive our fee?'

But in reply he heard only a hammering of coffin-makers, which he hastily converted to the clatter of builders in the little tourist port across the bay as they fixed shutters and rooftiles and pipes in a last-minute rush to make ready for the season after playing backgammon all winter. In his longing for normality, Winser savoured the smells of paint-stripper, blowtorches, fish cooking on charcoal, the spices of street vendors, and all the other lovely and less lovely scents of Mediterranean Turkey. Hoban barked something in Russian to his colleagues. Winser heard a scramble of feet behind him but dared not turn his head. Hands yanked his jacket from his back, others explored his body – armpits, ribs, spine, groin. Memories of more acceptable hands momentarily replaced those of his assailants, but provided no solace as they groped their way downward to his calves and ankles, searching for a secret weapon. Winser had never carried a weapon in his life, secret or otherwise, unless it was his cherrywood walking stick to fend off rabid dogs and sex maniacs when he was taking a turn on Hampstead Heath to admire the lady joggers.

Reluctantly he remembered Hoban's too-many hangers-on. Seduced by the gun, he had briefly imagined it was just Hoban and himself alone here on the hilltop, face to face and nobody in earshot, a situation any lawyer expects to use to his advantage. He now conceded that ever since they had left Istanbul, Hoban had been attended by a gaggle of unappetising advisers. A Signor d'Emilio and a Monsieur François had joined them on their departure from Istanbul

10

airport, coats over their shoulders, no arms showing. Winser had cared for neither man. Two more undesirables had been waiting for them at Dalaman, equipped with their own hearse-black Land Rover and driver. From Germany, Hoban had explained, introducing the pair, though not by name. From Germany they might be, but in Winser's hearing they spoke only Turkish and they wore the undertaker suits of country Turks on business.

More hands grabbed Winser by the hair and shoulders and flung him to his knees on the sandy track. He heard goat bells tinkling and decided they were the bells of St John at Hampstead tolling out his burial. Other hands took his loose change, spectacles and handkerchief. Others again picked up his treasured briefcase and he watched it as in a bad dream: his identity, his security, floating from one pair of hands to another, six hundred pounds' worth of matchless black hide, rashly bought at Zürich airport with cash drawn from a funk-money bank account Tiger had encouraged him to open. Well, next time you're in a generous mood, you can bloody well buy me a decent handbag, Bunny is complaining in the rising nasal whine that promises there is more to come. I'll flit, he thought. Bunny gets Hampstead, I buy a flat in Zürich, one of those new terraces on a hillside. Tiger will understand.

Winser's screen was suffused with a vibrant yellow wash and he let out a shriek of agony. Horned hands had seized his wrists, dragged them behind him and twisted them in opposing directions. His shriek hurtled from one hilltop to the next on its way to extinction. Kindly at first, as a dentist might, more hands raised his head, then yanked it round by the hair to meet the sun's full blast.

'Hold it right there,' a voice ordered in English and Winser found himself squinting up at the concerned features of Signor d'Emilio, a white-haired man of Winser's age. Signor d'Emilio is our consultant from Naples, Hoban had said in the vile American-Russian twang that he had picked up God knew where. How very nice, Winser had replied, using Tiger's drawl when Tiger didn't want to be impressed, and granted him a tepid smile. Hobbled in the sand, his arms and shoulders screaming bloody murder, Winser wished very much that he had shown respect to Signor d'Emilio while he had the opportunity.

D'Emilio was wandering up the hillside and Winser would have liked to wander with him, arm in arm, chaps together, while he put right any false impression he might have given. But he was obliged to remain kneeling, his face twisted to the scalding sun. He pressed his eyes shut but the sun's rays still bathed them in a yellow flood. He was kneeling but straining sideways and upright and the pain that was entering his knees was the same pain that tore through his shoulders in alternating currents. He worried about his hair. He had never wished to dye it, he had only contempt for those who did. But when his barber persuaded him to try a rinse and see, Bunny had ordered him to persist. How do you think I feel, Alfred? Going around with an old man with milky hair for a husband? – But my dear, my hair was that colour when I married you! – Worse luck me, then, she had replied.

I should have taken Tiger's advice, set her up in a flat somewhere, Dolphin Square, the Barbican. I should have fired her as my secretary and kept her as my little friend without suffering the humiliation of being her husband. Don't marry her, Winser, buy her! Cheaper in the long run, always is, Tiger had assured him – then given them both a week in Barbados for their honeymoon. He opened his eyes. He was wondering where his hat was, a snappy Panama he had bought in Istanbul for sixty dollars. He saw that his friend d'Emilio was wearing it, to the entertainment of the two dark-suited Turks. First they laughed together. Then they turned together and peered at Winser from their chosen place halfway up the hillside as if he were a play. Sourly. Interrogatively. Spectators not participants. Bunny, watching me make love to her. Having a nice time down there, are you? Well, get on with it, I'm tired. He glanced at the driver of the jeep that had driven him the last leg from the foot of the mountain. The man's got a kind face, he'll save me. And a married daughter in Izmir.

Kind face or not, the driver had gone to sleep. In the

Turks' hearse-black Land Rover further down the track, a second driver sat with his mouth open, gawping straight ahead of him, seeing nothing.

'Hoban,' Winser said.

A shadow fell across his eyes, and the sun by now was so high that whoever was casting it must be standing close to him. He felt sleepy. Good idea. Wake up somewhere else. Squinting downward through sweat-matted eyelashes he saw a pair of crocodile shoes protruding from elegant white ducks with turn-ups. He squinted higher and identified the black, enquiring features of Monsieur François, yet another of Hoban's satraps. Monsieur François is our surveyor. He will be taking measurements of the proposed site, Hoban had announced at Istanbul airport, and Winser had foolishly granted the surveyor the same tepid smile that he had bestowed on Signor d'Emilio.

One of the crocodile shoes shifted and in his drowsy state Winser wondered whether Monsieur François proposed to kick him with it, but evidently not. He was offering something obliquely to Winser's face. A pocket tape recorder, Winser decided. The sweat in his eyes was making them smart. He wants me to speak words of reassurance to my loved ones for when they ransom me: Tiger, sir, this is Alfred Winser, the last of the Winsers, as you used to call me, and I want you to know I'm absolutely fine, nothing to worry about at all, everything ace. These are good people and they are looking after me superbly. I've learned to respect their cause, whatever it is, and when they release me, which they've promised to do any minute now, I shall speak out boldly for it in the forums of world opinion. Oh, and I hope you don't mind, I've promised them that you will too, only they're most concerned to have the benefit of your powers of persuasion . . .

He's holding it against my other cheek. He's frowning at it. It's not a tape recorder after all, it's a thermometer. No it's not, it's for reading my pulse, making sure I'm not passing out. He's putting it back in his pocket. He's swinging up the hill to join the two German Turk undertakers and Signor d'Emilio in my Panama hat.

Winser discovered that, in the strain of ruling out the unacceptable, he had wet himself. A clammy patch had formed in the left inside-leg of the trouser of his tropical suit and there was nothing he could do to conceal it. He was in limbo, in terror. He was transposing himself to other places. He was sitting late at his desk at the office because he couldn't stand another night of waiting up for Bunny to come home from her mother's in a bad temper with her cheeks flushed. He was with a chubby friend he used to love in Chiswick, and she was tying him to the bedhead with bits of dressing gown girdle she kept in a top drawer. He was anywhere, absolutely anywhere except here on this hilltop in hell. He was asleep but he went on kneeling, skewed upright and racked with pain. There must have been splinters of seashell or flint in the sand because he could feel points cutting into his kneecaps. Ancient pottery, he remembered. Roman pottery abounds on the hilltops, and the hills are said to contain gold. Only yesterday he had made this tantalising selling point to Hoban's retinue during his eloquent presentation of the Single investment blueprint in Dr Mirsky's office in Istanbul. Such touches of colour were attractive to ignorant investors, particularly boorish Russians. *Gold, Hoban! Treasure, Hoban! Ancient civilisation, think of the appeal!* He had talked brilliantly, provocatively, a virtuoso performance. Even Mirsky, whom Winser secretly regarded as an upstart and a liability, had found it in him to applaud: 'Your scheme is so legal, Alfred, it ought to be forbidden,' he had roared and, with a huge Polish laugh, slapped him so hard on the back that his knees nearly buckled.

'Please. Before I shoot you, Mr Winser, I am instructed to ask you couple of questions.'

Winser made nothing of this. He didn't hear it. He was dead.

'You are friendly with Mr Randy Massingham?' Hoban asked.

'I know him.'

'How friendly?'

Which do they want? Winser was screaming to himself.

Very friendly? Scarcely at all? Middling friendly? Hoban was repeating his question, yelling it insistently.

'Describe please the exact degree of your friendship with Mr Randy Massingham. Very clearly, please. Very loudly.'

'I know him. I am his colleague. I do legal work for him. We are on formal, perfectly pleasant terms, but we are not intimate,' Winser mumbled, keeping his options open.

'Louder, please.'

Winser said some of it again, louder.

'You are wearing a fashionable cricket tie, Mr Winser. Describe to us what is represented by this tie, please.'

'This isn't a *cricket* tie!' Unexpectedly Winser had found his spirit. 'Tiger's the cricketer, not me! You've got the wrong man, you idiot!'

'Testing,' Hoban said to someone up the hill.

'Testing what?' Winser demanded gamely.

Hoban was reading from a Gucci prayer book of maroon leather that he held open before his face, at an angle not to obstruct the barrel of the automatic.

'Question,' he declaimed, festive as a town crier. 'Who was responsible please for arrest at sea last week of SS *Free Tallinn* out of Odessa bound for Liverpool?'

'What do *I* know of shipping matters?' Winser demanded truculently, his courage still up. 'We're financial consultants, not shippers. Someone has money, they need advice, they come to Single's. How they *make* the money is their affair. As long as they're adult about it.'

Adult to sting. *Adult* because Hoban was a pink piglet, hardly born. Adult because Mirsky was a bumptious Polish show-off, however many doctors he put before his name. Doctor of where, anyway? Of what? Hoban again glanced up the hill, licked a finger and turned to the next page of his prayer book.

'Question. Who provided informations to the Italian police authorities concerning a special convoy of trucks returning from Bosnia to Italy on March thirtieth this year, please?'

'Trucks? What do I know of special *trucks*? As much as you know of cricket, that's how much! Ask me to recite the names and dates of the kings of Sweden, you'd have more chance.'

Why Sweden? he wondered. What had Sweden to do with anything? Why was he thinking of Swedish blondes, deep white thighs, Swedish crispbread, pornographic films? Why was he living in Sweden when he was dying in Turkey? Never mind. His courage was still up there. Screw the little runt, gun or no gun. Hoban turned another page of his prayer book but Winser was ahead of him. Like Hoban, he was bellowing at the top of his voice: 'I don't *know*, you stupid idiot! Don't ask me, do you hear? –' until an immense blow to the left side of his neck from Hoban's foot sent him crashing to the ground. He had no sense of travelling, only of arriving. The sun went out, he saw the night and felt his head nestled against a friendly rock and knew that a piece of time had gone missing from his consciousness and it was not a piece he wanted back.

Hoban, meanwhile, had resumed his reading. 'Who implemented seizure in six countries simultaneously of all assets and shipping held directly or indirectly by First Flag Construction Company of Andorra and subsidiaries? Who provided information to international police authorities, please?'

'What seizure? Where? When? Nothing has been seized! No one provided anything. You're mad, Hoban! Barking mad. Do you hear me? Mad!'

Winser was still recumbent but in his frenzy he was trying to writhe his way back onto his knees, kicking and twisting like a felled animal, struggling to wedge his heels under him, half-rising, only to topple back again onto his side. Hoban was asking other questions but Winser refused to hear them – questions about commissions paid in vain, about supposedly friendly port officials who had proved unfriendly, about sums of money transferred to bank accounts days before the said accounts were seized. But Winser knew nothing of such matters.

'It's lies!' he shouted. 'Single's is a dependable and honest house. Our customers' interests are paramount.'

'Listen up, and kneel up,' Hoban ordered.

16

And somehow Winser with his newfound dignity knelt up and listened up. Intently. And more intently still. As intently as if Tiger himself had been commanding his attention. Never in his life had he listened so vigorously, so diligently to the sweet background music of the universe as he did now, in his effort to blank out the one sound he absolutely declined to hear, which was Hoban's grating Russian-American drone. He noted with delight a shrieking of gulls vying with the distant wail of a muezzin, a rustle of the sea as a breeze blew over it, a tink-tink of pleasure-boats in the bay as they geared themselves for the season. He saw a girl from his early manhood, kneeling naked in a field of poppies, and was too scared, now as then, to reach a hand towards her. He adored with the terrified love that was welling in him all the tastes, touches and sounds of earth and heaven, as long as they weren't Hoban's awful voice booming out his death sentence.

'We are calling this exemplary punishment,' Hoban was declaring, in a prepared statement from his prayer book.

'Louder,' Monsieur François ordered laconically from up the hill, so Hoban said the sentence again.

'Sure, it's a vengeance killing too. Please. We would not be human if we did not exact vengeance. But also we intend this gesture will be interpreted as formal request for recompense.' Louder still. And clearer. 'And we sincerely hope, Mr Winser, that your friend Mr Tiger Single, and the international police, will read this message and draw the appropriate conclusion.'

Then he bawled out what Winser took to be the same message in Russian, for the benefit of those members of his audience whose English might not be up to the mark. Or was it Polish for the greater edification of Dr Mirsky?

*   *   *

Winser who had momentarily lost his power of speech was now gradually recovering it, even if at first he was capable only of such half-made scraps as 'out of your wits' and 'judge and jury in one' and 'Single not a House to mess with'. He was filthy, he was a mess of sweat and piss and mud. In his fight for the survival of his species he was wrestling with irrelevant erotic visions that belonged to some unlivable underlife, and his fall to the ground had left him coated in red dust. His locked arms were a martyrdom and he had to crane his head back to speak at all. But he managed. He held the line.

His case was that, as previously stated, he was *de facto* and *de jure* immune. He was a lawyer and the law was its own protection. He was a healer not a destroyer, a passive facilitator of unlimited goodwill, the legal director and a board member of the House of Single with offices in London's West End, he was a husband and father who, despite a weakness for women and two unfortunate divorces, had kept the love of his children. He had a daughter who was even now embarking on a promising career on the stage. At the mention of his daughter he choked though no one joined him in his grief.

'Keep your voice up!' Monsieur François the surveyor advised from above him.

Winser's tears were making tracks in the dust on his cheeks, giving the impression of disintegrating make-up, but he kept going, he still held the line. He was a specialist in pre-emptive tax planning and investment, he said, rolling his head right back and screaming at the white sky. His specialities embraced offshore companies, trusts, havens, and the tax shelters of all accommodating nations. He was not a marine lawyer as Dr Mirsky claimed to be, not a dicey entrepreneur like Mirsky, not a gangster. He dealt in the art of the legitimate, in transferring informal assets to firmer ground. And to this he added a wild postscript regarding legal second passports, alternative citizenship and non-obligatory residency in more than a dozen climatically and fiscally attractive countries. But he was not – repeat *not*, he insisted boldly – and never had been – involved in what he would call the *methodologies* of accumulating primary wealth. He remembered that Hoban had some kind of military past – or was it naval?

'We're *boffins*, Hoban, don't you see? Backroom boys!

Planners! Strategists! You're the men of action, not *us*! You and Mirsky, if you want, since you seem to be so hugger-mugger with him!'

No one applauded. No one said Amen. But no one stopped him either and their silence convinced him that they were listening. The gulls had ceased their clamour. Across the bay it could have been siesta time. Hoban was looking at his watch again. It was becoming a fidget with him: to keep both hands on the gun while he rolled his left wrist inwards till the watch showed. He rolled it out again. A gold Rolex. What they all aspire to. Mirsky wears one too. Bold talking had given Winser his strength back. He took a breath and pulled what he imagined was a smile communicating reason. In a frenzy of companionability he began babbling tidbits from his presentation of the previous day in Istanbul.

'It's *your land*, Hoban! You own it. Six million dollars cash, you paid – dollar bills, pounds, Deutschmarks, yen, francs, liquorice allsorts – baskets, suitcases, trunks full, not a question asked! Remember? Who arranged that? We did! Sympathetic officials, tolerant politicians, people with influence – remember? Single's fronted it all for you, washed your grubby money Persil white! Overnight, remember? You heard what Mirsky said – so legal it ought to be forbidden. Well, it's not. It's legal!'

No one said they remembered.

Winser became breathless, and a little crazy. 'Reputable private bank, Hoban – us – remember? Registered in Monaco, offers to buy *your land* lock, stock and barrel. Do you accept? No! You'll take paper only, never cash! And our bank agrees to that. It agrees to everything, of course it does. Because we're *you*, remember? We're *yourselves* in another hat. We're a bank but we're using *your* money to buy *your* land! You can't shoot *yourselves*! We're *you* – we're *one*.'

Too shrill. He checked himself. Objective is the thing. Laid back. Detached. Never oversell yourself. That's Mirsky's problem. Ten minutes of Mirsky's patter and any self-respecting trader is halfway out of the door.

'Look at the numbers, Hoban! The beauty of it! Your own thriving holiday village – accounted any way you like! Look at the cleansing power once you start to invest! Twelve million for roads, drainage, power, lido, communal pool, ten for your rental cottages, hotels, casinos, restaurants and additional infrastructure – the merest child could get it up to thirty!'

He was going to add 'even you, Hoban' but suppressed himself in time. Were they hearing him? Perhaps he should speak louder. He roared. D'Emilio smiled. Of course! Loud is what d'Emilio likes! Well, I like it too! Loud is free. Loud is openness, legality, transparency! Loud is boys together, partners, being one! Loud is sharing hats!

'You don't even need *tenants*, Hoban – not for your cottages – not for your first year! Not *real* ones – ghost tenants for twelve straight months, imagine! *Notional* residents paying *two million a week* into shops, hotels, discos, restaurants and rented properties! The money straight out of your suitcase, through the company's books, into legitimate *European* bank accounts! Generating an immaculate *trading record* for any future purchaser of the shares! – and who's the purchaser? *You are!* Who's the seller? *You are!* You sell to yourself, you buy from yourself, up and up! And Single's there as honest broker, to see fair play, keep everything on course and above board! We're your friends, Hoban! We're not fly-by-night Mirskys. We're brothers-in-arms. Buddies! There when you need us. Even when the rub of the cloth goes against you, we're still there –' quoting Tiger desperately.

A burst of rain fell out of the clear heaven, laying the red dust, raising scents and drawing more lines on Winser's clotted face. He saw d'Emilio step forward in their shared Panama and decided he had won his case and was about to be lifted to his feet, slapped on the back and awarded the congratulations of the Court.

But d'Emilio had other plans. He was draping a white raincoat over Hoban's shoulders. Winser tried to faint but couldn't. He was screaming *Why? Friends! Don't!* He was blabbering that he had never heard of the *Free Tallinn*, never met anyone from the international police authorities, his whole life had been spent avoiding them. D'Emilio was fitting something round Hoban's head. Mother of God, a black cap. No, a ring of black cloth. No, a stocking, a black stocking. Oh God, oh Christ, oh Mother of Heaven and Earth, a black stocking to distort the features of my executioner!

'Hoban. Tiger. Hoban. Listen to me. Stop looking at your watch! Bunny. Stop! Mirsky. Wait! What have I done to you? Nothing but good, I swear it! Tiger! All my life! Wait! Stop!'

By the time he had blurted these words his English had begun to labour as if he were interpreting from other languages in his head. Yet he possessed no other languages, no Russian, no Polish, no Turkish, no French. He stared round him and saw Monsieur François the surveyor standing up the hill, wearing earphones and peering through the sights of a movie camera with a sponge-covered microphone fitted to its barrel. He saw the black-masked and white-shrouded figure of Hoban posed obligingly in the shooting position, one leg histrionically set back, one hand folded round the gun that was trained on Winser's left temple and the other clutching a cellphone to his ear while he kept his eyes on Winser and softly whispered sweet nothings in Russian into the extended mouthpiece. He saw Hoban take one last look at his watch while Monsieur François made ready, in the best tradition of photography, to immortalise that very special moment. And he saw a smear-faced boy peering down at him from a cleft between two promontories. He had big brown unbelieving eyes, like Winser's when he was the same age, and he was lying on his stomach and using both hands as a pillow for his chin.

CHAPTER TWO

'Oliver Hawthorne. Come up here immediately if you please. At the double. You're wanted.'

In the small south English hilltown of Abbots Quay on the coast of Devon, on a sparkling spring morning that smelt of cherry blossom, Mrs Elsie Watmore stood in the front porch of her Victorian boarding house and bawled cheerfully at her lodger, Oliver, twelve steps below her on the pavement where he was loading battered black suitcases into his Japanese van with the assistance of her ten-year-old son, Sammy. Mrs Watmore had descended on Abbots Quay from the elegant spa of Buxton in the north, bringing her own high standards of decorum. Her boarding house was a Victorian symphony of furled lace, gilt mirrors and miniature bottles of liqueur in glass-fronted cabinets. Its name was the Mariners' Rest, and she had lived there happily with Sammy, and her husband Jack until he died at sea within sight of his retirement. She was an abundant woman, intelligent, comely and compassionate. Her Derbyshire twang, lifted for comic effect, resounded like a bandsaw over the plunging seaside terraces. She was wearing a rakish mauve silk headscarf because it was a Friday, and on Fridays she always did her hair. A mild sea breeze was blowing.

'Sammy darling, jab your elbow in Ollie's ribs for me and

tell him he's wanted on the telephone, please – he's asleep as usual – in the hall, Ollie! Mr Toogood from the bank. Routine papers to sign, he says, but urgent – and he's being very polite and gentlemanly for a change, so don't spoil it or he'll be cutting down my overdraft again.' She waited, indulging him, which with Ollie was about all you could do. Nothing stirs him, she thought. Not when he's inside himself. I could be an air-raid and he wouldn't hear me. 'Sammy will finish loading for you, won't you, Samuel, of course you will,' she added by way of further incentive.

Again she waited, to no avail. Oliver's pudgy face, shadowed by the onion-seller's beret which was his trademark, was locked in a ferocious pout of concentration as he passed Sammy another black suitcase for him to fit into the back of the van. They're two of a feather, she thought indulgently, watching Sammy try the suitcase all ways on because he was slow, and slower since his father's death. Everything's a problem for them, never mind how small it is. You'd think they were off to Monte Carlo, not just down the road. The suitcases were of the commercial traveller's sort, rexine-covered, each a different size. Beside them stood an inflated red ball two feet in circumference.

'It's not "Where's our Ollie?" – it's not like that at all,' she persisted, by now convinced the bank manager had rung off. 'It's "Kindly have the goodness to bring Mr Oliver Hawthorne to the telephone," more like. You've not won the lottery, have you, Ollie? Only you wouldn't tell us, would you, which is you all over, being strong and silent. Put that down, Sammy. Ollie will help you with it after he's spoken to Mr Toogood. You'll drop it next.' Bunching her fists she plonked them on her hips in mock exasperation: 'Oliver Hawthorne. Mr Toogood is a highly paid executive of our bank. We can't let him listen to a vacuum at a hundred pounds an hour. He'll be putting up our charges next, and you'll be the one to blame.'

But by then, what with the sunshine and the languor of the spring day, her thoughts had taken their own strange turn, which with Ollie they tended to. She was thinking what a picture they made, brothers almost, even if they weren't that similar: Ollie, big as an Alp in his grey-wolf overcoat that he wore all weathers, never mind the neighbours or the looks he got; Sammy, haggard and beaky like his father, with his cat's tongue of silky brown hair and the leather bomber-jacket Ollie had given him for his birthday and Sammy had hardly taken off since.

She was remembering the day Oliver first arrived on her doorstep looking crumpled and enormous in his overcoat, two days' beard and just a small suitcase in his hand. Nine in the morning it was, she was clearing breakfast. 'Can I come and live here, please?' he says – not, have you got a room? or can I see it? or how much for a night? – just 'Can I come and live here?' like a lost child. And it's raining, so how can she leave him standing there on the doorstep? They talk about the weather, he admires her mahogany sideboard and her ormolu clock. She shows him the parlour and the dining room, she tells him the rules and takes him upstairs and shows him number seven with its view of the churchyard if he didn't find it too depressing. No, he says, he's got no objection to sharing with the dead. Which is not how Elsie would have put it, not since Mr Watmore went, but they still manage to have a good laugh. Yes, he says, he's got more luggage coming, mostly books and stuff.

'And a disgraceful old van,' he adds shyly. 'If it's a bother, I'll shove it down the road.'

'It's no bother whatever,' she replies primly. 'We're not like that at the Rest, Mr Hawthorne, and I hope we never will be.'

And the next thing she knows, he's paying a month in advance, four hundred pounds counted onto the washstand, a gift from Heaven considering her overdraft.

'You're not on the run, are you, dear?' she asks him, making a joke of it, but not quite, when they're back downstairs. First he puzzles, then he blushes. Then to her relief he cracks a five-star sunny smile that makes everything all right.

'Not now I'm not, am I?' he says.

'And him over there's Sammy,' Elsie says, pointing to the half-open parlour door because Sammy as usual has tiptoed downstairs to spy out the new lodger. 'Come on out, Sammy, you've been spotted.'

And a week later it's Sammy's birthday and that leather jacket must have cost fifty quid if a shilling, and Elsie fretted herself sick about it because these days men got up to everything, never mind how charming they were when they needed to be. All night long she sat up beating her brains to guess what her poor Jack would have done, because Jack with his years at sea had a nose for them. He could smell them as soon as they came up the gangway, he used to boast, and she was fearful that Oliver was another and she'd missed the signs. Next morning she was halfway to telling Ollie to take that jacket straight back to where he'd bought it – would have done, in fact, if she hadn't been chatting to Mrs Eggar of Glenarvon in the checkout queue at Safeways and learned to her astonishment that Ollie had a baby girl called Carmen and an ex-wife called Heather who'd been a no-good nurse up at the Freeborn, into bed with anybody who could work a stethoscope. Not to mention a plush house on Shore Heights that he'd made over to her, paid and signed, not a penny owing, some girls made you sick.

'Why did you never tell me you were a proud father?' Elsie asked Ollie reproachfully, torn between the relief of her discovery and the indignity of receiving sensational intelligence from a competing landlady. 'We love a baby, don't we, Samuel? Baby-mad we are, just as long as they don't bother the lodgers, aren't we?'

To which Ollie said nothing: just lowered his head and muttered, 'Yeah, well, see you,' like a man caught in shame, and went to his room to pace, very lightly, not wanting to disturb, which was Ollie all over. Till finally the pacing stopped and she heard his chair creak, and knew he'd settled to one of his books piled round him on his floor although she'd given him a bookcase – books on law, ethics, magic, books in foreign – all sipped at and nibbled at and put down again on their faces, or with bits of torn paper stuck in to mark the place. It made her shudder sometimes, just to wonder what a cocktail of thoughts he must have churning away inside that shambling body of his.

And his binges – three there'd been till now – so controlled they scared the wits out of her. Oh, she'd had lodgers who took a drop. Shared a drop with them sometimes, to be friendly, keep an eye. But never before had a taxi pulled up at daybreak, twenty yards down the road so as not to wake anyone, and delivered a deathly pale, mummified six-foot-something hulk who had to be nursed up the steps like a bomb casualty, with his overcoat hung round him and his beret straight as a ruler across his forehead – yet was still able to fish out his wallet, select a twenty for the driver, whisper, 'Sorry, Elsie,' and with only a little help from her, haul himself upstairs without disturbing a soul except Sammy who had waited all night for him. Through the morning and afternoon, Oliver had slept, which is to say Elsie heard no creak or footfall through the ceiling, and listened in vain for the knocking of the water pipes. And when she went upstairs to him, taking a cup of tea as an excuse, and tapped on his bedroom door and heard nothing, and fearfully turned the handle, she found him not on his bed but on the floor and on his side, still wearing his overcoat, with his knees drawn up to his tummy the same as a baby, eyes wide awake, staring at the wall.

'Thank you, Elsie. Just put it on the table if you would,' he said patiently, as if he had more staring to do. So she did. And left him, and back downstairs had wondered whether she should call the doctor but she never did – not then, and not the other times that followed.

What was burning him? The divorce? That ex-wife of his was a hard-nosed tart by all accounts, and neurotic with it, he was lucky to be rid of her. What was he trying to drink away that the drink only drove deeper down in him? Here Elsie's thoughts returned, as latterly they always did, to the night three weeks ago when for a terrible hour she had believed she was going to lose her Sammy to a home or worse, until Oliver rode up on his white horse to rescue them. I'll never be able to thank him. I'd do anything he asked me to, tomorrow or tonight.

Cadgwith, the man called himself, and waved a shiny visiting card at her to prove it – P. J. Cadgwith, Area Supervisor, Friendship Home Marketing Limited, Branches Everywhere. Do your Friends a Favour, said the fine writing underneath, Earn Yourself a Fortune in your Home. Standing where Elsie was standing now, with his finger on the doorbell at ten o'clock at night, and his slicked-back hair and copper's polished shoes glistening in the fisheye, and a copper's false courtesy.

'I'd like to speak to Mr Samuel Watmore, if I may, madam. Is that your husband, by any chance?'

'My husband's dead,' said Elsie. 'Sammy's my son. What do you want?'

Which was only the first mistake she made, as she realised when it was too late. She should have told him Jack was down at the pub and due back any minute. She should have told him Jack would give him a good leathering if he so much as put his dirty nose inside her house. She should have slammed the door in his face, which Ollie afterwards told her she'd a perfect right to do, instead of letting him walk past her into the hall, then almost without thinking, calling out, 'Sammy, where are you, darling, there's a gentleman to see you,' a split second before she glimpsed him through the half-open parlour door, on his tummy with his bottom in the air and his eyes closed, wriggling behind the sofa. After that she had only bits of memory, the worst bits, nothing whole:

Sammy standing in the centre of the parlour, dead white and his eyes closed, shaking his head but meaning yes. Mrs Watmore whispering, 'Sammy.' Cadgwith with his chin back like an emperor, saying, 'Where, show me, where?' Sammy groping in the ginger jar for where he'd hidden the key. Elsie with Sammy and Cadgwith in Jack's woodshed where Jack and Sammy used to make their model boats together whenever Jack came home on leave, Spanish galleons, dinghies, longboats, all hand-carved, never a kit. It was what Sammy had loved doing best in the world which was why he went and moped there after Jack died, till Elsie decided it was unhealthy for him, and locked the shed up as a way of helping him forget. Sammy opening the shed cupboards one by one, and there it all was: heap upon heap of sales

27

samples from Friendship Home Marketing, Branches Everywhere, Do your Friends a Favour, Earn Yourself a Fortune in your Home, except that Sammy hadn't done anyone a favour or earned himself a penny. He'd signed himself on as agent for the neighbourhood and he'd stored everything away for treasure to make up for his lost dad, or perhaps it was a kind of gift to him: costume jewellery, eternal clocks, Norwegian rollneck pullovers, plastic bubbles to enlarge your TV image, scent, hairspray, pocket computers, ladies and gentlemen in wooden chalets who came out for rain or sun – seventeen hundred and thirty quids' worth, Mr Cadgwith reckoned back in the parlour, which with interest and loss of earnings and travel time and overtime and the date added in, he rounded up to eighteen hundred and fifty, then for friendship's sake down again to eighteen hundred for cash, or up again to a hundred a month for twenty-four months with the first instalment due today.

How Sammy had ever put his mind to such a thing – sent away for the forms and faked his date of birth and everything, all without anyone in the world to help him – was beyond Elsie's comprehension but he had, because Mr Cadgwith had the documentation with him, printed up and folded into an official-looking brown envelope with a button and a cotton loop to fasten it, first the contract that Sammy had signed, giving his age as forty-five which was how old Jack was when he died, then the impressive Solemn Undertaking to Pay with embossed lions on each corner for extra solemnity. And Elsie would have signed everything on the spot, signed away the Rest and whatever else she didn't own, just to get Sammy off the hook, if Ollie by the Grace of God hadn't happened to shamble in from his last gig of the day still in his beret and grey-wolf coat to find Sammy sitting on the sofa looking dead with his eyes open – and as to herself, well, after Jack went she thought she'd never weep again in her life, but she was wrong.

First of all Ollie read the papers slowly, wrinkling his nose and rubbing it and frowning like somebody who knows what he's looking for and doesn't like it, while Cadgwith watched him. He read once, then frowned more fiercely still and read again, and this time as he read, he seemed to straighten up or shape up or square up, or whatever it was that men did when they were getting ready for a scrap. It was a real coming-out-of-hiding that she was watching, like the moment in a movie she and Sammy loved, when the Scots hero strides out of the cave with his armour on, and you know he's the one, although you knew it all along. And Cadgwith must have spotted something of this, because by the time Ollie had read Sammy's contract a third time – and after it the Solemn Undertaking to Pay – he had gone a bit poorly looking.

'Show me the figures,' Ollie ordered, so Cadgwith handed him the figures, pages of them, with the interest added in, and everything at the bottom of the page printed red. And Ollie read the figures too, with the kind of sureness you only see in bankers or accountants, read them as fast as if they were just words.

'You haven't a bloody leg to stand on,' he told Cadgwith. 'The contract's a lot of codswallop, the accounts are a joke, Sam's a minor and you're a crook. Pick up and piss off.'

And of course Ollie's a big fellow, and when he's not speaking to you through a wad of cotton wool he's got the voice – a strong, upright, officer-class voice, the sort you get in courtroom melodramas. And he's got the eyes too, when he looks at you properly instead of at the floor three yards ahead of him. Angry eyes. Eyes like those poor Irishmen had after years in jail for things they'd never done. And being tall and big, Oliver stood close to Cadgwith, and stayed close to him all the way to the front door, looking attentive. And at the door he said something to Cadgwith to help him on his way. And though Elsie never caught his words, Sammy heard them plainly, because over the next weeks while he was recovering his sparkle he repeated them at any odd moment like a motto to cheer him up: 'And if you ever come back here, I'll break your dirty little neck,' in a nice low measured, unemotional voice, no threat intended just information, but it kept Sammy going through his recovery. Because all the time while Sammy and Ollie were in the woodshed packing up the treasures to send back to Friendship Home Marketing, Sammy went on muttering it to keep his spirits up: 'If you ever come back here, I'll break your dirty little neck,' like a prayer of hope.

*   *   *

Oliver had finally consented to hear her.

'I can't talk to him now, thank you, Else, I'm afraid it's not convenient,' he replied, manners perfect as always, from inside the darkness of his beret. Then he stretched himself, one of his writhes, arching his long back and shoving both arms down behind him, and his chin tucked in like a guardsman called to order. Standing his full height this way, and his full width, he was too tall for Sammy and too wide for the van, which was red and upright and had UNCLE OLLIE'S MAGIC BUS painted on its side in pink bubble writing defaced by bad parking and vandals.

'We've got a one o'clock in Teignmouth and a three o'clock in Torquay,' he explained, somehow cramming himself into the driving seat. Sammy was already beside him clutching the red ball, banging his head against it, impatient to be off. 'And the Sally Army at six.' The engine coughed, but that was all. 'They want bloody Take That,' he added over Sammy's howl of frustration.

He turned the key a second time, without success. He's flooded it again, she thought. He'll be late for his own funeral. 'If we haven't got Take That, we're not to bother, right, Sammy?' – twisting the key a third time. The van's engine hobbled reluctantly to life. 'So long, Else. Tell him I'll phone him tomorrow, please. Morning. Before work. And stop playing silly buggers, you,' he ordered Sammy. 'Don't bang your head like that, it's stupid.'

Sammy stopped banging his head. Elsie Watmore watched the van zigzag down the mid-levels of the hillside to the harbourfront. Then round the roundabout twice before Oliver took the ring road, fumes pouring from the exhaust. And as she watched she felt the anxiety rise in her the way it always did, she couldn't hold it back and she wasn't sure she wanted to. Not on account of Sammy, which was the strange thing, but of Ollie. It was the fearing he'd never come back. Every time he walked out of the house or drove off in his van – even when he took Sammy down to the Legion for a game of billiards – she found herself saying goodbye to him for good, the same as when her Jack went off to sea.

Still daydreaming, Elsie Watmore relinquished her sun-spot on the front porch and, returning to her hall, dis-covered to her surprise that Arthur Toogood was still waiting on the telephone.

'Mr Hawthorne's got performances all afternoon,' she told him disdainfully. 'He won't be back till late. He'll tele-phone tomorrow if it's convenient to his schedule.'

But tomorrow wasn't good enough for Toogood. In immense confidence he had to give her his ex-directory home telephone number. Ollie should please to ring him at whatever hour, never mind how late, Elsie, are you with me? He tried to make her tell him where Ollie was per-forming, but she remained aloof. *Mister* Hawthorne may have said something about a grand hotel in Torquay, she conceded airily. And a disco up the Salvation Army hostel at six. Or maybe it was seven, she forgot. Or if she didn't forget, she pretended to. There were times when she had no wish to share Ollie with anyone, least of all a randy small-town bank manager who last time she had gone to him about her loan suggested they sort the details in bed.

*   *   *

'*Toogood*,' Oliver repeated indignantly as he drove round the roundabout. '*Routine papers. Friendly chat.* Stupid tit. Damn.' He had missed the turning. Sammy let out a great honking laugh. 'What's there left to sign?' Oliver demanded, appealing to Sammy as if they were equals, which was how he always spoke to him. 'She's got the bloody house. She's got the bloody money. She's got Carmen. All she hasn't got any more is me, which is how she wanted it.'

'Then she's lost the best bit, hasn't she?' Sammy shouted hilariously.

'The best bit's Carmen,' Oliver growled, and Sammy held his tongue for a while.

They crawled up a hill. An impatient lorry carved them into the kerb. The van wasn't very good at hills.

'What are we giving?' Sammy asked when he judged the moment safe.

'Menu A. Bouncy ball, magic beads, find the birdie, windmills of the mind, puppy sculpture, origami, thuds and get out. What's wrong now?' – for Sammy had let out a horror-film wail of despair.

'No spinning plates!'

'If there's time we'll do plates. Only if there's time.'

Spinning plates were Sammy's best thing. He had practised them night and day and, though he had never succeeded in getting one spinning, he had convinced himself he was a star. The van entered a grim council estate. A threatening poster warned of heart attacks but the remedy was unclear.

'Watch out for balloons,' Oliver commanded.

Sammy was already doing so. Pushing aside the red ball, he was standing in his seatbelt, his arm flung out. Four balloons, two green, two red, drooped from an upper window of number 24. Bumping the van onto the verge, Oliver handed Sammy the keys to start unloading, and with the skirts of his grey-wolf coat flapping round him in the crisp sea breeze strode up the short concrete path. Pasted across the frosted glass front door, a lacklustre streamer read HAPPY BIRTHDAY MARY JO. Smells of cigarette smoke, baby and deep fried chicken issued from indoors. Oliver pressed a bell and heard it chiming above the war-whoops of demented children. The door was wrenched open and two tiny breathless girls in party frocks stared up at him. Oliver removed his beret and performed a deep Oriental obeisance.

'Uncle Ollie,' he declared with immense gravity – though not enough to scare – 'Magician Extraordinary. At your service, ladies. Rain or shine. Kindly take me to your leader.'

A shaven-headed man appeared behind them. He wore a string vest and had tattoos on the first knuckle of each broad finger. Following him into the living room, Oliver took a reading of stage and audience. In his short recent life he had worked mansions, barns, village halls, crowded beaches and a promenade bus shelter in a force eight gale. He had practised in the mornings and performed in the afternoons. He had worked poor kids, rich kids, sick kids and kids in care. At first he had let them push him into a corner with the TV set and the *Encyclopaedia Britannica*s. But these days he was able to speak up for himself. Conditions this afternoon were tight but adequate. Six adults and thirty children were crammed into a tiny living room, the kids on the floor in a half-circle facing him, the adults in a group photograph on one settee, men on the lower deck, women perched above them on the backrest with their shoes off. Unpacking, Oliver did not remove his grey-wolf coat. Swooping and rising, lugubriously piecing together with Sammy's help the birdcage with the vanishing canary and the Aladdin's lamp that filled with priceless treasure when you rubbed it, he used its folds for cover. And when he sank to his haunches to address the kids at their level – for it was a principle with him never to talk down but only upwards or along – and his massive knees rose up beside his ears, and his spongy hands dangled ponderously forward of them, he resembled some sort of praying mantis, part prophet, part giant insect.

'Hullo, you lot,' he began in a surprisingly mellow voice. 'I'm Uncle Ollie, man of mystery, skill and magic.' He was speaking middle low English, not posh but not too many aitches either. His smile, released from its confinement, had become a friendly light. 'And here on my right we have the great and not very good Sammy Watmore, my invaluable assistant. Sammy, take a bow, please – OUCH!'

Ouch for the moment when Rocco the raccoon bites him, which at this point Rocco always does, sending Oliver's huge frame bounding into the air and down again with unlikely ease while, under the pretext of restraining him, Oliver surreptitiously works the clever spring in Rocco's tummy. And when Rocco is brought to heel, he too has to be formally introduced, then make a flowery speech of welcome to the children, singling out Mary Jo the birthday girl, who is frail and very beautiful. And from here on it is Rocco's job to demonstrate to the kids what a truly awful magician his master is, which he does by poking his snout out of the grey-wolf coat and exclaiming, 'Oh boy, you should see what else is in here!' then flinging out playing cards – all aces – and a stuffed canary, and a packet of half-eaten sandwiches, and a lethal-looking plastic bottle marked BOOZE. And having trashed Oliver as a magician – though not quite – Rocco trashes him as an acrobat, by clinging to his shoulder and squealing in fright while Oliver with unlikely grace rides the bouncy red ball round the tiny arena of the living room, arms outstretched and the skirts of his grey-wolf coat billowing behind him. Almost but never quite, he crashes into bookcases and tables and the television set and squashes the toes of the nearest children, to the clamour of Rocco's backseat warnings that he is exceeding the speed limit, has overtaken a police car, is headed for a priceless family heirloom, is riding the wrong way down a one-way street. There's a shimmer in the room by now and a shimmer in Oliver's bearing also. His flushed head is thrown back, his rich black locks fly behind him like a great conductor's, his fluid cheeks are glazed with strenuous pleasure, his eyes are clear and young again and he is laughing and the children are laughing louder. He is the Prince of Shimmer, the unlikely rainmaker in their midst. He is a clumsy buffoon and therefore to be protected, he is a nimble god who can call down laughter, and enchant without destroying.

'Now, Princess Mary Jo, I want you to take this wooden spoon from Sammy – give her the wooden spoon, sport – and Mary Jo, I want you to stir this pot very very slowly and with tremendous concentration. Sammy, offer her the pot. Thank you, Sammy. Now. You've all of you seen inside the pot, haven't you? You all know the pot is empty except for a few boring loose beads that are no good to man or beast.'

'And they all know it's got a false bottom too, you fat old fool,' Rocco yells to huge applause.

'Rocco, you are a nasty smelly little furry ferret!'

'Raccoon! Raccoon! Not ferret! Raccoon!'

'Hold your tongue, Rocco. Mary Jo, have you ever been a princess before?' A minuscule shake of Mary Jo's head tells us she has no previous experience of royalty. 'Then I want you to wish a wish, please, Mary Jo. A very big, splendid, very secret wish. As big as you like. Sammy, hold that pot very still now. *OUCH!* – Rocco, if you do that again I'll –'

But Oliver decides on reflection to give Rocco no second chance. Grabbing him by head and tail he bends Rocco's midriff to his mouth and takes an enormous cathartic bite out of him, then to peals of laughter and cries of fear spits out a convincing lump of fur conjured from the recesses of his coat.

'Tee hee, didn't hurt, didn't hurt!' Rocco yells above the applause. But Oliver ignores him. He has gone back to his act.

'Boys and girls, I want you all to see inside that pot and watch the boring loose beads for me. Will you wish a wish for us, Mary Jo?'

A demure nod advises us that Mary Jo will wish a wish for us.

'Stir slowly now, Mary Jo – give the magic a chance – *stir* the boring loose beads! Have you wished, Mary Jo? A good wish takes time. Ah. Superb. Divine.'

Oliver leaps back dramatically, fingers splayed to protect his eyes from the splendour of his creation. The birthday princess, decked overall, stands before us, a collar of silver beads round her neck, a silver diadem on her head. Oliver weaves his hands through the air around her, careful not to touch her because touching is taboo.

'Oncers all right for you, squire?' the shaven-headed man enquires, counting twenty-five pound coins from a chamois-leather bag into Oliver's open palm.

Watching the coins collect, Oliver remembers Toogood and the bank, and his stomach turns without his knowing why, except that there is a stink of the unnatural about Arthur Toogood's behaviour and it is getting stronger all the time.

'Can we play billiards Sunday?' Sammy asks as they drive again.

'We'll see,' says Oliver, helping himself to a free sausage roll.

Oliver's second engagement of that same Friday afternoon took place in the banqueting hall of the Majestic Hotel Esplanade in Torquay, where his audience consisted of twenty upper-class children with voices from his childhood, a dozen bored mothers in jeans and pearls, and two supercilious waiters with grimy shirtfronts who slipped Sammy a plate of smoked salmon sandwiches.

'We absolutely adored you,' said a fine lady, writing out a cheque in the bridge room. 'Twenty-five pounds seems frightfully cheap. I don't know *anyone* who does *anything* for twenty-five pounds these days,' she added, putting up her eyebrows and smiling. 'You must be booked up the *whole* time.' Uncertain of the purpose of her question, Oliver mumbled something unintelligible and blushed scarlet. 'Well, at least *two* people rang for you during the show,' she said. 'Unless it was the same man twice. *Desperate* for you. I'm afraid I told the switchboard to say you were *in flagrante* – was that awful?'

The Salvation Army building at the bottom of the town was a contemporary red-brick fortress with curved corners and arrow-slit windows to provide the Soldiers of Jesus with an all-round field of fire. Oliver had dropped Sammy at the foot of West Hill because Elsie Watmore didn't want him late for his tea. Thirty-six children sitting at a long table in the assembly room waited to eat potato chips out of paper boxes brought by a man in a beaver-lamb coat. At the head of the table stood Robyn, a red-headed woman in a green tracksuit and flyaway spectacles.

'All raise your right hands like so,' Robyn ordered, whipping up her own hand. 'Now raise your left hand like so. Put them together. Jesus, help us enjoy our meal and our evening of games and dancing and not take it for granted. Let us not get out of order and let us remember all the poor children in hospital and elsewhere who are not having any fun tonight. When you see me or the lieutenant wave our arms like so, you'll stop whatever you're doing and freeze because it will mean *we* have something to say or *you* are getting out of order.'

To clumping nursery music the children played pass-the-parcel, galloping elephants and statues-when-the-music stops. They played sleeping lions and a long-haired Venus of nine became the last remaining lion to stay asleep. Draped at the centre of the floor, she kept her eyes pressed shut while boys and girls reverently tickled her without visible effect.

'So it's on your feet for Take That!' Oliver cried hastily as Robyn gave a roar of fury.

The children punched air, made conventional signs of ecstasy. Soon the strobes and the din were giving Oliver a headache, which they always did. Robyn handed him a cup of tea and bawled at him but he couldn't hear her. He thanked her in mime but still she didn't leave. He yelled 'Thanks' above the uproar but she went on talking until Oliver lowered the volume and tipped his head sideways to her mouth.

'There's a man in a hat needs to speak to you,' she screamed, unaware the music had gone quiet. 'A green one and the brim turned up. Oliver Hawthorne. It's urgent.'

Peering into the flickering haze Oliver made out Arthur Toogood at the tea bar in the custody of the beaver-lamb coat. He was wearing a curly trilby and an upholstered ski-jacket over his suit. The strobes were making a podgy devil of him while he grinned and flapped his rainbow hands to show he wasn't carrying an offensive weapon.

CHAPTER THREE

The hospital supervisor clutched his hands in Oriental supplication and regretted that the refrigeration was deficient. A spectral doctor in a bloodstained white overall agreed with him. So also did the Mayor, who had put on a black suit, either out of respect for the dead or in honour of the English diplomatic visitors from Istanbul.

'The refrigeration will be replaced this winter,' Her Majesty's Consul translated for Brock's benefit, while the assembled company listened and nodded without comprehension. 'A new apparatus will be installed regardless of expense. A British apparatus. It will be personally inaugurated by His Excellency the Mayor. A date has already been appointed for the ceremony. The Mayor has great regard for British products. He has insisted that only the best materials be purchased.' Brock acknowledged this intelligence with a hobgoblin's twinkly smile of complicity, while the Mayor energetically confirmed his commitment to things British, and his people, crowded uncomfortably round him in the cellar, nodded in energetic agreement. 'The Mayor wishes you to know that it is a particular sadness to him that our friend is from London. The Mayor has been to London on a visit. He has seen the Tower of London and Buckingham Palace and many other attractions. He has great respect for British continuity.'

'I'm glad to hear that,' said Brock gravely without lifting his white head. 'Kindly thank the Mayor for his trouble, will you please, Harry?'

'He asked who you are,' said the Consul in a lower voice when he had done this. 'I said Foreign Office. Special line in dead Brits abroad.'

'That's quite correct, Harry. You spoke well. I thank you,' Brock replied courteously.

But a deal of authority in the voice despite its meekness, the Consul noted, not for the first time. And that Merseyside twang not always quite as homey as it meant to be. A man of layers, not all of them savoury. A predator in disguise. The Consul was a timid soul who hid his sensitivity behind a wispy, offhand elegance. When interpreting he frowned into the middle distance in the manner of his father, a distinguished Egyptologist. 'I shall puke,' he had warned Brock as they drove up the hill. 'I always do. I've only to see a dead dog at the roadside to bring up instantly. Death and I simply aren't made for one another.' But Brock had merely smiled and shaken his head as if to say it takes all sorts to make a world.

The two Britons stood one side of the galvanised iron bathtub. The hospital supervisor and the chief doctor and the Mayor and all his Corporation stood above them on a raised stage on the other, their smiles bravely hoisted. Between them, naked and with half his head blown off, reclined the late Mr Alfred Winser. He was in the foetal position, on a bed of ice pellets from the machine in the main square just down the hill. A part-eaten ring of sugared bread, somebody's unfinished breakfast, lay amid several cans of fly spray on a trolley at his feet. An electric fan whined uselessly in one corner, next to an ancient elevator which the Consul assumed was used for conveying bodies. Sometimes the wheels of an ambulance went past, sometimes a pair of busy feet, bringing hopeful news of the living. The air inside the mortuary stank of putrefaction and formaldehyde. It nipped at the Consul's larynx and turned his stomach like a slow key.

'The post mortem will be conducted on Monday or Tuesday,' the Consul translated, frowning vigorously. 'The pathologist is heavily engaged in Adana. He's the best in Turkey, et cetera. They always are. The widow must first make the identification. Our friend's passport isn't enough. Oh, and it was suicide.'

All this to Brock's left ear in murmured confidences while Brock went on studying the corpse.

'I beg your pardon, Harry?'

'He says it was suicide,' the Consul repeated. And when Brock showed no further sign of having heard, 'Suicide. Honestly.'

'Who does?' Brock asked, as if he were a little slow about these things.

'Captain Ali.'

'Now which one's that, Harry? Refresh my memory if you'd be so kind.'

But Brock knew very well which one. Long before he asked the question his innocent blue eye had singled out the grinning, lethargic figure of the local police captain in a pressed grey uniform and gold-rimmed dark glasses of which he was clearly proud, lounging with a couple of plain clothes acolytes at the edge of the mayoral party.

'The Captain says he has made extensive investigations and is confident the post mortem will bear out his findings. Suicide while drunk. Case complete. He says your journey was unnecessary,' the Consul added, in the forlorn hope that Brock would see this as their cue to leave.

'Suicide by what means now exactly, Harry, please?' Brock enquired, resuming his patient study of the corpse.

The Consul put this to the Captain. 'A bullet,' he responded to Brock after a staccato exchange. 'He shot himself. Through the head.'

Brock again lifted his gaze, first to the Consul and then to the Captain. His eyes, being wrinkled at the corners, imparted at first sight benevolence. But to the Consul they were also unsettling.

40

'Well, well. Yes. Thank you, Harry, I'm sure.' Brock seemed at first uncertain whether to continue, then took the plunge. 'Only if we're to view the Captain's theory seriously, Harry, which I've no doubt we are, maybe he will start by telling us how a man shoots his brains out with his hands cuffed behind his back, which is the only way *I* can see to account for the sores on our friend's wrists. Will you ask him that for me, please, Harry? I must say, your Turkish is first rate.'

Consul to Captain again, the Captain very active with his hands and eyebrows while his eyes remained blacked out by the gold-rimmed glasses.

'The handcuff marks were on our friend's wrists when he landed at Dalaman airport,' the Consul duly translated. 'The Captain has a witness who can testify to seeing them.'

'Landed what *from*, Harry, please?'

The Consul put Brock's question to the Captain. 'The evening flight from Istanbul to Dalaman,' he said.

'The commercial flight? The standard commercial flight?'

'Turkish Airlines. Our friend's name is on the passenger list. The Captain would be happy to show it to you.'

'And I would be happy to see it, Harry. I'm very impressed by his diligence tell him, please.'

The Consul told him. The Captain accepted Brock's compliment and resumed his testimony, which the Consul translated. 'The Captain's witness is a nurse by profession who sat next to our friend on the flight. She is the best nurse in the region, the most popular. She was so concerned by the state of our friend's wrists that she begged him to let her take him to a clinic as soon as the plane landed and have them dressed. He refused. Drunkenly. Shoved her drunkenly aside.'

'Oh dear.'

From his raised stage the other side of the bathtub the Captain was applying his histrionic skills to re-enacting the scene that he depicted: Winser slumped ungraciously in his passenger seat, Winser brusquely waving away the well-intentioned nurse, Winser lifting his elbow to menace her.

'A second witness who rode here with our friend on the bus

41

from Dalaman airport provides similar testimony,' the Consul explained to Brock after the Captain had again held forth.

'Oh he came by *bus*, did he?' Brock interjected happily, in the manner of one enlightened. 'A commercial flight and a commercial bus. Well, well. And him a top lawyer with a major finance house in the West End of London, using public transport. I'm very glad to hear it. I may buy their shares after all.'

But the Consul would not be deflected: 'Our friend and this second witness were sitting on the rear bench of the bus and side by side. The second witness is a retired policeman, the most loved policeman in the community, a father to the peasants, which makes a change. He offered our friend a fresh fig from a paper bag he was carrying. Our friend threatened to assault him. The Captain possesses sworn and signed testimony from both these important witnesses, also from the bus driver and the stewardess on the aeroplane.' The Captain had obligingly paused in case the distinguished gentleman from London had a question. But Brock it seemed had none and the smile on his face betrayed only a wordless admiration. Thus encouraged, the Captain placed himself at Winser's marbled feet and poked a punctilious forefinger at the lacerated wrists. 'Furthermore these marks are not made by Turkish handcuffs,' the Consul announced without the smallest hint of humour. 'Turkish handcuffs are distinctive because they are more humane, more considerate of the prisoner. Don't laugh. The Captain deduces that our friend was arrested in another country, handcuffed, and either escaped or was ordered to run. The Captain would like to know whether there is any record of our friend committing a crime abroad before he came to Turkey. Also whether alcohol was a feature of the offence. He would like you to assist him with this line of enquiry. He has great respect for English police methods. He says that together there is no crime you and he can't solve.'

'Tell him I'm very flattered, please, Harry. It's always nice to solve a crime, even if it's only suicide. However, as regards his line of enquiry, I regret to inform him that, on paper, our friend was lily-white in all respects.'

But the Consul was spared the labour of translating this by a thump on the steel door. The supervisor leapt to open it and a tired Kurd was admitted bearing a bucket of ice and an enema tube. He poked one end of the tube into the bathtub and sucked the other. Melted ice splashed onto the floor and ran away in the gutters until the bathtub had emptied itself. The Kurd dumped the fresh ice into the bathtub and withdrew, his mules slapping the stone steps. The Consul lurched after him, bent double, hand slammed over his mouth.

'I'm not pale. It's just the light,' he assured Brock in a drenched murmur as he slunk back into the room.

As if provoked by the Consul's return, the Mayor burst out complaining in very broken English. He was a stocky man, by build a risen labourer, and he spoke fiercely, as to a group of fellow strikers, gesticulating with powerful forearms, now at the corpse and now at the barred window beyond which lay the town entrusted to his care.

'Our friend was suicide,' he pronounced indignantly. 'Our friend was thief. Is not our friend. He steal our boat. He float in boat dead. Was alcoholic. Whisky bottle was also in boat. Was empty. Which gun make this hole?' he demanded rhetorically, jabbing a stubby arm in the direction of poor Winser's shattered head. 'In this town, please, who has so big guns? Has nobody. Has all small guns. Was English gun. This Englishman drinks, he steals our boat, he shoots himself. Is thief. Is alcoholic. Is suicide. Finish.'

Brock's kindly smile absorbed this onslaught without flinching. 'I wonder if we could go back a little, Harry,' he suggested. 'Assuming you're recovered.'

'Please yourself,' the Consul muttered miserably, dabbing his mouth with a paper tissue.

'Our friend came here on an internal commercial flight from Istanbul, we hear, and public bus from Dalaman. Then he shot himself, right? Now why did he do that, I wonder? What caused him to come here in the first place? What did he get up to when he got off the bus? Did he have friends to meet? Did he book himself a room in one of the town's many fine hotels? Was there a suicide note? Most of our

English suicides like to leave a line or two behind them when they go. Where did he get his gun from? Where is the gun now, I wonder? Or have they failed to show it to us?'

Suddenly everyone was speaking at once: the hospital supervisor, the chief doctor, the Captain and several members of the Corporation, each anxious to outdo the other in the vigour of his denial.

'There was no suicide note and the Captain was not expecting one,' the Consul translated crisply, selecting the Captain's voice from the hubbub. 'Nobody who steals a boat, takes a bottle of whisky out to sea and drinks it, is in a state to write notes. You ask about motive. Our friend was a mendicant. He was a degenerate. He was an escaped prisoner. Here it comes. He was a pervert.'

'That too, was he, Harry? My goodness. What gives them *that* impression, I wonder?'

'The police have taken the testimony of several handsome Turkish fishermen whom our friend encountered on the waterfront in the early evening and attempted to seduce,' the Consul explained in an expressionless monotone. 'All refused him. Our friend was a rejected homosexual, an alcoholic, a fugitive from justice. He decided to end it all. He stole a bottle of whisky, waited till dark, pinched a boat out of spite against the men who had repulsed his advances, took the boat out to sea and shot himself. The gun fell into the water. In due course, divers will be sent down to retrieve it. At present, with so many pleasure boats and cruisers in the harbour, diving would not be appropriate. Where did he have the gun from? The Captain says it is immaterial where he had it from. Criminals are criminals. They seek each other out, they sell each other guns, it is well known. How did he manage to carry the gun on the internal flight from Istanbul? In his luggage. Where is his luggage? Enquiries are proceeding. In this country, that means the next millennium but one.'

Brock resumed his study of Winser's body.

'Only that looks to me like a soft-nosed bullet, you see, Harry,' he objected mildly. 'That's not an exit wound, that's a splat-wound. You'd need a dum-dum bullet to make a hole like that.'

'I can't do splat,' the Consul warned Brock wretchedly. 'It doesn't translate,' and glanced uneasily at the route of his previous escape.

The Mayor was having another tantrum. Perhaps, with the shrewdness of a politician, he was more suspicious of Brock's equanimity than were his underlings. He began strutting up and down the cellar floor, taking the larger, more aggressive view. The *English*, he complained. Why did the *English* imagine they had a right to barge in here asking questions when they were themselves the cause of the town's misfortune? Why does this *English* pederast come to our town in the first place? Why doesn't he go to some other town and kill himself there? – Kalkan? Kas? – why does he have to come to Turkey at all? Why doesn't he stay in *England*, instead of spoiling people's holidays and giving our town a bad name?

But Brock took even this tirade in good part. You could tell by his gently nodding head that he saw the force of the argument, respected the local wisdom and the local dilemma. And this sweet reasonableness gradually had its effect on the Mayor, who first put a finger to his lips, and then, as an exhortation to himself to remain composed, patted the air with his palm, up and down as if it were a cushion he were straightening. The Captain, however, showed no such self-restraint. Arms raised in surrender, though he was surrendering nothing, he thrust a heroic leg forward and orated in proud sentences kept brief for the benefit of the Consul.

'Our friend is drunk,' the Consul translated impassively. 'He is in the boat. The whisky bottle is empty. He is depressed. He stands up. He shoots himself. His gun falls into the sea. He lies down because he is dead. In winter we shall find the gun.'

Brock heard all this with every show of respect. 'So can we take a look at the boat, at all, Harry?'

The Mayor was back, eyes blazing. 'Boat was dirty! Was too many blood! Owner from this boat very sad man, very

angry! Very superstitious of God! He has burn boat. He
don't care! Insurance? He spit!'

*　　*　　*

Brock pottered alone through the narrow streets, acting
the tourist as he paused to examine a display of carpets or
Ottoman artefacts or reflections in a convenient shop
window. He had left the Consul in the Mayor's office, drinking apple tea and thrashing out such technical matters as
steel coffins and the regulations regarding the transportation of the dead once the post mortem had been conducted.
Pleading the necessity of finding a birthday present for a
non-existent daughter, he had resisted the Mayor's offer of
luncheon and been obliged in consequence to listen to
lengthy recommendations regarding the town's many
superb shops, the best being undoubtedly an air-
conditioned boutique belonging to the Mayor's nephew. He
felt no fatigue, no slackening of his habitual quest. In the
last seventy-two hours he had slept at best for six, on aeroplanes, in taxis, on his way to hastily called meetings, Whitehall in the morning, Amsterdam in the afternoon, and come
evening the twilit gardens of a druglord's hacienda in Marbella, for Brock had informants everywhere. People of all
kinds were drawn to him and for all kinds of reasons. Even
on his passage through this little town, hardened shop-
keepers and restaurateurs, calling out to him to buy their
wares, spotted something about him that gave them pause
amid the hubbub. Some even lowered their prices in their
heads. And when, in the act of crossing the road to see who
around him faltered or abruptly changed direction, Brock
gave a cheerful wave and an apologetic 'Next time perhaps!',
they discovered their intuitions in some vague way confirmed by his rejection, and followed him with their eyes
and kept a lazy lookout for him in case he should happen
their way a second time.

Reaching the little fishing harbour with its white-painted
lighthouse, ancient granite mole and bustling taverns, he
continued to display an open pleasure in everything he saw:

the chandlers and jeans shops where, if he had had a daughter, he might have found what he was looking for, the pleasure cruisers and glass-bottomed safari boats, the little trawlers in their fishing-net mantillas, the grimy ochre jeep parked on a red dirt track cut into the hillside behind the harbour. Two figures sat in it, one boy, one girl. Even from sixty yards off, you could see they were as scruffy as the jeep. Brock entered a chandler's, handled a few things, glanced in mirrors and settled for an amusing T-shirt that he paid for with the credit card he used for operational expenditures. Shopping bag in hand, he wandered out along the mole until he reached the lighthouse where, quite alone, he drew a cellphone from his pocket, dialled his office in London and at once the West Country voice of Tanby his lieutenant was providing him with a series of disjointed messages that were nonsense to anyone who did not know their inner meaning. Having listened to these in silence Brock growled, 'Got you,' and rang off.

A narrow wooden staircase led up to the dirt track. Brock climbed it as any tourist might. The ochre jeep had disappeared. Gaining the track he skirted a row of half-built holiday houses and climbed another flight of stairs to an upper level where more houses had been staked but not yet started. This second track was strewn with builders' junk and empty bottles. Brock placed himself at the verge, a prospective buyer getting the feel of the place, picturing the view from the unbuilt houses. Siesta time was approaching. No vehicle, no pedestrian, not a dog. From the village below, two competing muezzins moaned their exhortations, the first peremptory, the second soft and winning. The ochre jeep appeared, throwing up red dust. The driver was a pebble-chinned girl with broad clear eyes and a scruffy blonde mane. Her boyfriend, if that was who he was, sulked beside her in the passenger seat. He wore a three-day beard and one earring.

Brock looked up the road and down the hillside he had just ascended. He raised a hand, the jeep stopped, the tailgate was flung open from within. On the rear seat lay a pile of rugs, some rolled, some folded. Brock sprang aboard and with an agility remarkable for his age flattened himself on the floor. The boy threw the rugs over him. The girl drove the jeep at a stately pace up the zigzag track to a plateau high on the headland and stopped.

'All clear,' said the bearded boy.

Brock emerged from the carpets and sat himself on the back seat. The boy turned on the radio, not too loud. Turkish music, clapping hands, tambourines. Ahead of them lay a redstone quarry, disused and marked dangerous by crumbling noticeboards. There was a wooden bench, now broken. There was a turning place for lorries, overgrown, and a view of six small jagged islands stepping in descending order out to sea. Across the bay white holiday villages nestled in ravines.

'Let's hear it,' Brock ordered.

They were Derek and Aggie and there was no lovers' bond between them, however much Derek might wish it otherwise. Derek was shaggy and thundery in the modern idiom. Aggie was straight-eyed and long-legged, and unconsciously elegant. Derek gave his story while Aggie watched the mirrors and seemed not to hear. They had taken a room at the Driftwood, Derek said, with an accusing eye for Aggie – an upmarket dosshouse with a tavern and a gay Irish barman called Fidelio who could get you anything you wanted.

'The whole town's buzzing, Nat,' Aggie broke in, speaking in a trim Glaswegian accent. 'There's only the one topic from morning till night and that's Winser. Everyone's got a theory. Most people have two or three.'

The Mayor featured in most of the rumours, Derek continued as if Aggie had not spoken. One of the Mayor's five brothers was a big wheel in Germany. Rumour had it that he owned a heroin ring and a team of Turkish construction workers. Aggie once more interrupted.

'He owns a bunch of casinos, Nat. And a leisure centre on Cyprus. Gross turnover like millions. And get this. The rumours say he's in with one of the big Russian mobs.'

'Is he now?' Brock marvelled, and allowed himself a private smile which somehow emphasised his age and apartness.

According to the rumours, Derek went on, this same

brother was actually in town on the day of Winser's death. He must have dropped in from Germany because he was seen driving round in a limousine belonging to the sister-in-law of the Chief of Police for the district.

'The police chief's brother is married to a Dalaman heiress,' Derek said. 'It was her firm provided the limousines that met the private jet from Istanbul.'

'And Nat, Captain Ali rides point for the police chief' – Aggie again, excitedly – 'I mean, they're a sackful of cats, Nat. There's not one of them hasn't got a piece of the other one. Fidelio says Ali actually took Wednesday *off*, just so he could drive the limo for his chief's sister-in-law. Okay, Captain Ali's not exactly a mental Titan. But he was *there*, Nat. At the murder. Part of the action. A copper, Nat! Taking part in a ritual gang *murder*! They're worse than ours!'

'Are they though?' said Brock softly, and for a moment everything stopped, for this was a subject dear to Brock's heart.

'There's this ex-girlfriend of Fidelio's cook,' Derek said. 'Freaked-out English sculptress, Cheltenham Ladies College, three needles a day and living with a bunch of lowlife in a commune out on the headland. Drops into the Driftwood to collect her junk.'

'She's got this little *boy*, Nat,' Aggie cut in again while Derek scowled and coloured. 'Zach, his name is. He's hell in bare feet, believe me. The commune kids, they all run wild, hustling flowers to the tourists and draining the petrol out of their cars while they're away taking a look at the Ottoman fort. So Zach, he's up in the mountains among the goats doing God knows what with a bunch of Kurdish kids, when a whole convoy of limousines and jeeps pulls up below them and the fellows all get out and act a scene from a gangster movie.' She broke off as if expecting to be challenged, but neither Derek nor Brock spoke. 'One man gets shot while the rest of the gang film him. When they've killed him, they throw him in a jeep and drive down the hill and away into town. Zach says it was just great. Blood like real blood and everything.'

Brock's pale gaze was straining across the bay. Billows of

white cloud rose behind the cockscomb ridges. Buzzards circled in the shimmering heat.

'And deposited him in a dinghy with an empty whisky bottle,' he said, completing her story for her. 'Lucky they didn't do the same to Zach. Anyone live up there apart from goats?'

'Rocks and more rocks,' said Derek. 'Beehives. Lot of tyre marks.'

Brock's head turned until his eyes were feasting thoughtfully on Derek's and his good smile seemed cast in iron. 'I thought I told you not to go up there, young Derek.'

'Fidelio's trying to flog me his old Harley-Davidson. He let me try it for an hour.'

'So you tried it.'

'Yes.'

'And disobeyed orders.'

'Yes.'

'And what did you see, young Derek?'

'Car tracks, jeep tracks, footprints. Lot of dried blood. No attempt to clear up. Why bother to sweep everything under the carpet when you own the Mayor and the police chief? And this.'

He dropped it into Brock's waiting hands: one scrumpled bunch of cellophane with the words VIDEO – 8/60 printed in repeat.

'You get out of here tonight,' Brock ordered when he had spread the cellophane on his knee. 'The both of you. There's a six p.m. charter from Izmir. They're holding a couple of seats for you – and Derek.'

'Yes, sir?'

'On this occasion, in the eternal struggle between initiative and obedience, initiative paid off. Which makes you a very lucky young man, doesn't it, Derek?'

'Yes, sir.'

Estranged from each other in all but their work, Derek and Aggie returned to their attic at the Driftwood and packed their kitbags. While Derek went downstairs to pay the bill, Aggie shook out their sleeping bags and gave the room a tidy. She washed the remaining cups and saucers and put them away, wiped down the handbasin and opened the windows. Her father was a Scottish schoolmaster, her mother a general practitioner and visiting angel of the poorer Glasgow suburbs. Both had notions of decency that went beyond the ordinary. Her ministrations completed, Aggie trotted after Derek to the jeep and they set off at speed along the winding coast road to Izmir, Derek driving with an air of injured manhood and Aggie watching the hairpin bends, the valley beneath them and the clock. Derek, still smouldering from Brock's rebuke, was silently vowing he would resign the Service as soon as he got home, and qualify as a solicitor if it killed him. It was an oath he took once a month at least, usually after a couple of pints in the canteen. But Aggie, on a different tack entirely, was torturing herself with memories of the child Zach. She was remembering how she'd picked him up the day he came trotting into the taverna with his money to bargain for an ice – I *pulled* him, for God's sake! – how she had danced with him, skimmed stones with him on the beach and sat with him on the sea wall while he fished, one arm round his shoulder in case he slipped. And she wondered what she thought of herself, the twenty-five-year-old daughter of her parents, worming secrets out of a kid of seven who believed she was the woman of his life.

CHAPTER FOUR

Perched like a royal coachman at the wheel of his over-polished Rover, Arthur Toogood drove at a stately pace down the winding hill while Oliver followed him in his van.

'What's all the fuss about?' Oliver had asked in the Salvation Army forecourt as Toogood helpfully handed up the wrong box.

'There's no *fuss*, Ollie, that's not the tone at all,' Toogood had retorted. 'It's the searchlight. It can happen to anyone,' he insisted, handing up the right one.

'What searchlight?'

'The beam that comes round, takes a look at us, finds no fault and passes on,' Toogood had said heatedly, already dismissive of his own metaphor. 'It's totally random. Nothing personal at all. Forget about it.'

'What's it examining us for?'

'Trusts, as it happens. They're doing Trusts this month. Trusts Corporate, Charitable, Family, Offshore. Next month it will be Securities, or short-term loans, or some other branch of business.'

'Carmen's Trust?'

'Among others, many others, yes. What we call a non-aggressive dawn raid. They choose a branch, look at the numbers, ask some questions, move on. Routine.'

'Why are they interested in Carmen's Trust suddenly?'

Toogood had by now become thoroughly cross with being questioned. 'It's not just Carmen's. It's *all* Trusts. They're doing a general inspection of Trusts.'

'Why are they doing it in the middle of the night?' Oliver had persisted.

They parked in the bank's cramped back yard. Intruder lights beat down on them. Three steps led to a steel rear door. Toogood crooked a finger to type the entry code, changed his mind and made an impulsive grab for Oliver's left biceps.

'Ollie.'

Oliver shook his arm free. 'What?'

'Are you – were you – expecting any movement on Carmen's account? Recently, say, over the last few months – in the near future, for instance?'

'Movement?'

'Monies in or out. Never mind what movement. Action.'

'Why should I be? We're both trustees. You know what I know. What's happened? Have you been playing games?'

'No, of course not! We're on the same side in this. And you haven't – you've had no advance notice of anything? Independently? Privately? *From* anyone? You're aware of no other factor affecting the Trust's position – as of recent date?'

'Not a dickie bird.'

'Good. Perfect. Stay that way. Be exactly who you are. A child's magician. Not a dickie bird.' Toogood's eyes gleamed greedily under the brim of his hat. 'When they ask you their routine questions, say exactly what you just said to me. You're her father, you're a trustee, as I am, bound to do your duty.' He typed a number. The door buzzed and opened. 'They're Pode and Lanxon from Bishopsgate,' he confided, willing Oliver ahead of him into a steel-grey corridor with striplights. 'Pode's small but he's big. Big in the bank. Lanxon's more your type. Heavy fellow. No, no, no, on you go, youth before beauty, or whatever they say.'

It was a starry sky, Oliver noticed before the door closed on them. A pink moon hung above him, cut to pieces by the razor wire coiled along the courtyard wall. Two men sat at a conference table in the window bay of Toogood's office, both worried about their hair. Pode, small but big in the bank, was tweedy with rimless bifocals, and his exiguous hair was drawn over his scalp in tramlines all starting from the same side of his head. Lanxon the heavy fellow was an Old Boy of somewhere, with bud-like ears and a tie adorned with golf clubs, and a news announcer's wig of brown wire-wool.

'You took some finding then, Mr Hawthorne,' said Pode, not altogether playfully. 'Arthur's been chasing round town after you like a man demented, haven't you, Arthur?'

'My pipe bother you?' Lanxon asked. 'Sure not? Take your coat off, Mr Hawthorne. Chuck it over there.'

Oliver removed his beret but not his coat. He sat down. A strained silence followed while Pode fiddled with papers and Lanxon gardened at his pipe, gouging sodden tobacco onto an ashtray. White blinds, Oliver recorded glumly. White walls. White lights. This is where banks go at night.

'Mind if we call you Ollie?' Pode asked.

'Whatever.'

'It's Reg and Walter – never Wally, if you don't mind,' said Lanxon. 'He's Reg.' The silence came back. 'And I'm Walter,' he added for a laugh he didn't get.

'And he's Walter,' Pode confirmed, and all three men smiled awkwardly – on Oliver, then on one another.

You should have grey silky side-whiskers, Oliver thought, and purple noses tweaked with frost. You should have turnip watches inside your topcoats, instead of ballpoint pens. Pode held a pad of yellow legal paper in his hand. Scribbles in more than one handwriting, Oliver noticed. Columns of dates and numbers. But Pode wasn't doing the talking. Lanxon was. Ponderously, through his pipesmoke. He would jump straight in, he said. No point in beating about the bush.

'My particular bailiwick for my sins is bank security, Ollie. What we call *compliance*. That's everything from the night-watchman who's been walloped on the nut to money-laundering to the teller who is subsidising his salary from the cash drawer.' Still no one laughed. '*And*, as you will have

54

gathered from Arthur here, *Trusts*.' He took a suck of his pipe. It was of the short-barrelled variety. In his childhood, Oliver remembered, he had had one not unlike it, made of china clay, for blowing bubbles in the bath. 'Tell us something, Ollie. Who's Mr Crouch when he's at home?'

An abstraction, Brock had replied when Oliver had asked him the same question a hundred years ago in a pub in Hammersmith. We thought of calling him John Doe but it's been done.

'He's a friend of my family's,' Oliver said to the beret on his lap. Dull, Brock had dinned into him. Stay with dull. Don't turn up the lights. Us coppers like dull.

'Oh yes?' said Lanxon, all puzzled innocence. 'What *sort* of friend, I wonder, Ollie?'

'He lives in the West Indies,' Oliver said, as if that defined the friendship.

'Oh yes? A black gentleman then, I dare say?'

'Not as far as I know. He just lives there.'

'Where for instance?'

'Antigua. It's in the file.'

Mistake. Don't make him look a fool. Better to look one yourself. Stay with dull.

'Nice bloke? Like him?' said Lanxon, eyebrows raised high in encouragement.

'I never met him. He communicates through solicitors in London.'

Lanxon frowns and smiles at the same time, indicating reluctant doubt. Puffs at pipe for solace. No soap bubbles appear. Makes rictal grimace which among pipesmokers passes for a smile. 'You never met him, but he made a personal gift to your daughter Carmen's Trust of one hundred and fifty thousand pounds. By way of his London solicitors,' he suggested through a noxious cloud of smoke.

It's approved, says Brock. In a pub. In a car. Walking in a wood. Don't be a fool. It's signed for. Oliver refuses to be swayed. He has refused all day. I don't care whether it's approved or not. It's not approved by me.

'Don't you find that a somewhat unusual way to carry on?' Lanxon was enquiring.

'What way?'

'To make such a large financial gift to the daughter of somebody you never met. Through solicitors.'

'Crouch is a rich man,' Oliver said. 'He's a distant relative, some kind of cousin removed. He appointed himself Carmen's guardian angel.'

'What we call the vague uncle syndrome then,' said Lanxon, and directed a smirk of heavy portent at Pode and then at Toogood.

But Toogood took umbrage at this. 'It's not a *syndrome* of any shape or kind! It's a perfectly normal banking practice. A rich man, a friend of the family, appointing himself a child's guardian angel – that *is* a syndrome, I grant you. And a very normal one,' he ended triumphantly, contradicting himself at every turn, yet carrying his point. 'Am I not right, Reg?'

But little Pode who was big in the bank was too absorbed in his yellow pad to answer. He had found another angle for it, one less amenable to Oliver's line of sight, and he was questioning it earnestly through his bifocals while the reading lamp made his striped pate glisten.

'Ollie,' said Pode quietly. His voice was thin and circumspect, a rapier to Lanxon's bludgeon.

'What is it?' said Oliver.

'Let's go over this from the start, can we?'

'Go over what?'

'Just bear with me, please. I'd like to begin on the day of the Trust's birth and reason forward, if you don't mind, Ollie. I'm a technician. Interested in antecedents and modus operandi. Will you bear with me?' Oliver the dullard gave a shrug of acquiescence. 'According to our records you came to see Arthur here in this very room by prior appointment eighteen months ago almost to the day, and one week exactly after Carmen's birth. Correct?'

'Correct.' Dull as mud.

'You had been a customer of the bank for six months. And you had recently moved into the area after a period of residence abroad – where was that now, I forget?'

Ever been to Australia at all? Brock is asking. Never, Oliver

56

replies. Good. Because that's where you've been for the last four years.

'Australia,' said Oliver.

'Where you had been – what?'

'Drifting. Sheep stations. Serving fried chicken in cafés. Whatever came along.'

'You weren't into your magic, then? Not in those days?'

'No.'

'And you had been non-resident in the UK for tax purposes for how long, by the time you returned?'

We're disappearing you from Inland Revenue records, Brock had said. You resurface as Hawthorne, resident on return from Australia.

'Three years. Four,' Oliver replied, correcting himself for extra dullness. 'More like four.'

'So when you went to Arthur you were by then a UK tax-resident but self-employed. As a magician. Married.'

'Yes.'

'And Arthur gave you a cup of tea, I expect, did you, Arthur?'

A burst of hilarity to remind us how much bankers love the human touch whatever tough decisions they are obliged to take.

'He hadn't got enough in his account,' Toogood rejoined, to show how human he was too.

'It's the antecedents I'm after, you see, Ollie,' Pode explained. 'You told Arthur that you wanted to put some money in trust, right? For Carmen.'

'Right.'

'And Arthur here said – reasonably enough, assuming you were talking of a modest sum – why not just go for National Savings or a building society or an endowment policy? Why go through all the palaver of a formal legal Trust? Correct, Ollie?'

Carmen is six hours old. Oliver stands in one of the old red phone boxes that the councillors of Abbots Quay have insisted on preserving for the pleasure of our foreign visitors. Tears of joy and relief stream down his face. I've changed my mind, he tells Brock between chokes. I'll take the money. Nothing's too good for her. The house for Heather and whatever's left for Carmen. Just as long as it's nothing for me, I'll take it. Is that corruption, Nat? It's fatherhood, says Brock.

'Correct,' Oliver agreed.

'You were adamant that it had to be a Trust, I see.' The yellow page again. 'A full-blown Trust.'

'Yes.'

'That was your position. You wanted to lock up this sum of money for Carmen and throw away the key, you told Arthur – you're a great note-taker, Arthur, I'll give you that – you wanted to be sure that, whatever became of you, or of Heather or anybody else, Carmen would have her nest egg.'

'Yes.'

'There in trust. Out of reach. Waiting for her when she grew to woman's estate, got married or whatever young ladies will be doing by the time she reaches the ripe age of twenty-five.'

'Yes.'

Fussy adjustment to bifocals. Churchy pursing of lips. Two fingertips to coax a tramline of black hair back into position. Resume. 'And you had been advised – or so you told Arthur here – that it was possible to open a Trust with a nominal amount and add to this amount whenever you or anybody else felt flush.'

An itch had formed on the tip of Oliver's nose. He rubbed it fervently with his big palm, fingers upwards. 'Yes.'

'So who gave you that advice, Ollie? Who or what prompted you to come to Arthur that day, one week after Carmen had been born, and say "I want to open a *Trust*?" Specifically a Trust? And talk quite knowledgeably on the subject too, according to Arthur's memo here?'

'Crouch.'

'Our same Mr Geoffrey Crouch? Residing in Antigua and contactable through his London solicitors? It was Crouch who gave you the original advice to set up a proper legal Trust for Carmen.'

'Yes.'

'How?'

'By letter.'

'From Crouch personally?'

'From his solicitors.'

'His London solicitors or solicitors in Antigua?'

'I don't remember. The letter's on file, or it should be. I gave everything relevant to Arthur at the time.'

'Who duly filed it,' Toogood confirmed with satisfaction.

Pode was consulting his yellow page. 'Messrs Dorkin & Woolley, a reputable City firm. Mr Peter Dorkin has Mr Crouch's power of attorney.'

Oliver decided to show a little temperament. Dull temperament. 'Then why did you ask?'

'Just checking the antecedents, Ollie. Just making sure.'

'Is it illegal or something?'

'Is what illegal?'

'Her Trust. What's been done. The antecedents. Is it illegal?'

'Not in the least, Ollie' – defensive now – 'not by any means. Nothing illegal or irregular about it whatever. Except it appears that Messrs Dorkin & Woolley haven't met Mr Crouch either, you see. Well, that's not unknown, I suppose.' He considered the semantic point. 'It's irregular, perhaps, but it's not unknown. He's very reclusive, I must say, is your Mr Crouch.'

'He's not my Mr Crouch. He's Carmen's.'

'Indeed he is. And her trustee as well, I see.'

Toogood was again taking umbrage: 'Why shouldn't Crouch be a trustee?' he demanded, much aggrieved, of the two men from London together. 'Crouch provided the cash. He's the settlor. A friend of the family, part of the Hawthorne tapestry. Why shouldn't he want to make sure Carmen's money is handled in a proper manner? Why shouldn't he be reclusive if he wants to be? I'll be reclusive one day. When I'm retired.'

Lanxon, the heavy fellow, had decided to return to the charge. Propped on one lumpy elbow, he leaned massively over the table, pipe in hand and wire-wool forelock leading, every inch our security officer. 'So acting on Mr Crouch's advice,' he said, half-closing his eyes for extra shrewdness, 'you open the Carmen Hawthorne Trust with yourself and Mr Crouch and Arthur here as trustees and you pay in five hundred pounds of start money. Two weeks later this sum is increased by a further one hundred and fifty thousand pounds, thanks to the generosity of Mr Crouch. Yes?' He had quickened the pace.

'Yes.'

'Did Crouch pay out any other monies to your family, that you're aware of?'

'No.'

'No, he didn't? Or no, you're not aware of them?'

'I haven't got any family. My parents are dead. I've no brothers or sisters. That's why Crouch adopted Carmen, I suppose. There was no one else.'

'Except you.'

'Yes.'

'And he has given you personally nothing? Directly or indirectly? You derive no benefit from Crouch?'

'No.'

'Never did?'

'No.'

'Never will – far as you know?'

'No.'

'Ever dealt with him, had business dealings with him, borrowed from him, even indirectly – through solicitors?'

'No to all of it.'

'Who paid for Heather's house then, Oliver?'

'I did.'

'What with?'

'Cash.'

'Out of a suitcase?'

'Out of my bank account.'

'And how did you accumulate this cash, if I may ask? Through Crouch, perhaps, through his associates, his shady business dealings?'

'It was money I saved in Australia,' said Oliver gruffly, and began to colour.

60

'Did you pay Australian tax on your earnings during your residence there?'

'The earnings were casual. Maybe tax was deducted at source. I don't know.'

'You don't know. And you kept no records, of course?' He cast a knowing sideways glance at Pode.

'No, I didn't.'

'Why not?'

'Because I didn't fancy hitchhiking ten thousand miles with a set of records in my backpack, that's why.'

'No, well, I don't suppose you would,' Lanxon conceded with another glance for Pode, not half so knowing. 'So how much did you bring back from Australia to UK in all, Ollie? How much had you saved up, put it that way?'

'When I'd bought the house for Heather and the furniture and the van and the equipment, that was pretty much my lot.'

'Did you ever follow any *other* occupation out there in Australia at all? Never *dealt* in any – what I might call *commodities*, let us say – *substances* –'

He got no further. Toogood saw to that. Toogood had taken the whole imputation on himself. Half-rising from his chair, he aimed his piglet forefinger straight at Lanxon's heart. 'That's a bloody outrage, Walter! Ollie's *my* valued customer. You take that back right now.'

Oliver stared into the middle distance while Pode and Toogood waited awkwardly for Lanxon to extricate himself, which he did by resorting to ponderous innuendo.

'So meanwhile,' Lanxon suggested, 'it's Ollie and Arthur in charge of the Trust, it's some funny solicitor in London rubber-stamping whatever you decide to do, and it's reclusive *Mr Crouch*, who as usual nobody can find including his solicitors, crouching out of sight in his house in Antigua, West Indies.' Oliver said nothing – just sat and watched him flail, as they all did. 'Ever been there?' Lanxon demanded, louder still.

'Where?'

'His house. In Antigua. Where d'you think?'

'No.'

'I don't expect many people have, have they? Assuming there's a house to go to, of course.'

'That's a travesty, that is, Walter!' Toogood declared, now thoroughly incensed. 'Crouch isn't a rubber stamp, he's a sound financial mind, as good as the brokers any day and sometimes better. Oliver and I agree strategy, we put it up to Crouch via his solicitors, we get his say-so. What could be more shipshape than that?' Swinging round in his chair, he appealed to Pode who was big in the bank. 'All of this was reported to Head Office at the time, Reg. Legal Department looked at it, we passed it *pro forma* to Criminal Intelligence and never heard a peep. Trustee Department looked at it. The Revenue didn't blink, Head Office told us well done and get on with it. And we did. Very effectively, if I may say so. Turned a hundred and fifty thousand into one nine eight in less than two years and rising.' He swung back to Lanxon. 'Nothing's changed except the numbers. The Trust's a regional matter, to be handled locally. By Ollie here and by myself as local incumbent, which is fair and normal. It's only the size of the money that's altered, not the principle. The principle was established eighteen months ago.'

Oliver slowly collected his limbs together until he sat upright. 'What numbers? How have they changed?' he demanded. 'What haven't you told me? I'm Carmen's father. I'm not just her trustee.'

Pode took an age to answer. Or perhaps the delay was in Oliver's mind. Perhaps Pode answered straight out, and Oliver's mind, having recorded what Pode said, ran the tape slowly, over and again, until the monstrosity of the message had sunk in. 'A very large sum of money has been paid into your daughter Carmen's Trust, Ollie. It's so immense that the bank assumed it must be a mistake. Mistakes can happen. Institutional money misrouted in error. A couple of digits transposed. Millions of pounds ending up in some unlikely private account till we get on to the remitting bank and sort it out. But in this case the remitting bank is adamant that the right amount of money was sent to the right account.

To the credit of the Carmen Hawthorne Trust. The donor anonymous because that's what he or she wishes to be. You can't beat down the Swiss when it comes to banking confidentiality. The law's the law for them. The code's the code. "From a customer," and you can sing for the rest. All they're prepared to tell us is the money comes from a well-conducted account of long standing and they've every reason to be confident of the integrity of the client. From there on in, it's a blank wall.'

'How much?' said Oliver.

Pode did not falter. 'Five million and thirty pounds. And what we'd all like to know is, where did it come from? We've enquired of Crouch's solicitors. Not from him, they say. We've asked them whether Mr Crouch might otherwise be able to enlighten us regarding Carmen's benefactor. Mr Crouch is travelling at present, they tell us. They will advise us in due course. Well, *travelling*, that's no excuse these days. So if Crouch didn't send it, who did? And how did he or she come by it in the first place? Who wants to give your infant daughter's Trust five million and thirty pounds in cash, yet not be a trustee, not inform the trustees in advance, and not reveal his or her name? We thought you might be able to tell us, you see, Oliver. Nobody else can, apparently. You're our one chance.'

Pode paused to allow Oliver to speak but Oliver had nothing to say. He had retreated again. He was hunched inside the collars of his overcoat, long black hair swept back, wide brown eyes fixed on something distant, the tip of one large finger wedged to his lower lip. In his head he was watching clippings from the lousy film of his life so far – a flat-fronted villa on the Bosphorus, schools, all failures, a white-walled interviewing room at Heathrow airport.

'Take your time, Ollie,' Pode urged, in the tone of someone exhorting him to repentance. 'Think back. Somebody in Australia perhaps. Somebody from your past or your family's past. A philanthropist. A rich eccentric. Another Crouch. Did you ever buy a share in a gold mine or something? Did you ever have a business partner – somebody who might have struck lucky?' No answer. Not even a sign that he was heard. 'Because we need an explanation, you see, Ollie. A convincing one. Five million pounds sent anonymously from a Swiss bank, well, that's more than certain authorities in this country are willing to swallow without a pretty good explanation.'

'And thirty,' Oliver reminded him. And thought back. And further back, until his features acquired the solitude of a long-term prisoner. 'Which bank?' he asked.

'One of the biggest. Never mind.'

'Which one?'

'Cantonal & Federal of Zürich. C & F.'

Oliver gave a distant nod, acknowledging the rightness of this. 'It's a death,' he suggested in a remote voice. 'Someone's left a Will.'

'We asked that, Ollie. I'm afraid we quite hoped it was the case. Then at least we'd have a chance of seeing documents. C & F assure us that the settlor was alive and well and in possession of his mental faculties at the time of the transfer. They rather imply that they've been back to him and confirmed the instruction. They don't say it in as many words, the Swiss won't do that. But the implication is there.'

'Then it's not a death,' Oliver said, for himself rather than for them.

Yet again Lanxon sprang into the breach. 'All right. Suppose it *was* a death. Who's dead then? Or who isn't? Who's alive now, who might be leaving Carmen five million and thirty quid on his death?'

Gradually while they waited Oliver's mood changed. It is said that when a man is sentenced to be hanged a contentment descends over him and for a while he performs all sorts of minor tasks with precision and diligence. Oliver now acquired that kind of friendly clarity. He stood up, smiled and politely excused himself. He stepped into the corridor and made his way to the men's room which he had observed on his passage to Toogood's office. Inside, he locked the door and gazed into the mirror while he made an assessment of his situation. He stooped over the handbasin, turned on the cold tap and with water from his great cupped hands rinsed his face, imagining he was washing away some version of himself that was no longer operative. There being no towel he beat his hands with his handkerchief which he then tossed into the waste bin. He returned to Toogood's office and placed himself in the doorway, filling it with the folds of his overcoat. He spoke courteously and directly to Toogood, ignoring Pode and Lanxon.

'I'd like to talk to you alone, please, Arthur. Outside, if that's all right.' And he stepped back to let Toogood go ahead of him down the corridor. They stood in the back yard again, under the stars, surrounded by the high wall and the razor wire. The moon had freed itself of earthly attachments and lay luxuriously above the bank's many chimney pots, washed by a milky haze. 'I can't accept the five million,' he said. 'It's not appropriate for a child. Send it back to where it came from.'

'No go,' Toogood rejoined with unexpected force. 'As trustee I haven't the authority, nor have you. Nor has Crouch. It's not up to us to say the money's clean. It's up to the authorities to say it's not. If they don't, the Trust must keep it. If we refuse it, twenty or so years from now Carmen can sue the bank, sue you, me and Crouch to hell and back.'

'Go to the Courts,' Oliver said. 'Ask for a ruling. Then you're protected.'

Startled, Toogood began to say one thing, then changed his mind and said another. 'All right, we go to the Courts. What have they got to work on? Hunch? You heard what Pode said. A well-conducted account, a client of integrity in full possession of his faculties. The Courts will say the authorities are powerless unless they can put up a criminal case.' He took a pace backward. 'Don't look like that. What are you, anyway? What do you know about Courts?'

Oliver had moved neither feet nor body, he had his hands deep in his overcoat pockets and they stayed there. So it could only have been his bulk and the expression on his great moist face in the moonlight that had prompted Toogood to recoil so abruptly: the gathering grimness of Oliver's hollowed eyes against the stars, the despairing anger round the mouth and jaw.

'Tell them I don't want to talk to them any more,' he told Toogood, climbing into his van. 'And open the gates, please, Arthur, or I'll have to smash them down.'

Toogood opened the gates.

CHAPTER FIVE

The bungalow lay in a private unmade road called Avalon Way, huddled below the crest of the hill and out of sight from the town, which was one of the things that Oliver had liked about it: nobody sees us, nobody thinks about us, we're in nobody's consciousness except our own. Its name was Bluebell Cottage and Heather had wanted to change it but Oliver, without giving his reasons, had overruled her. He preferred to re-enter the world as it stood, to be absorbed and hidden away and forgotten. He liked the summer when the trees were in leaf and you couldn't see the bungalow from the road. He liked the winter spells when Lookout Hill iced over and nothing went by for days. He liked the plain boring neighbours whose predictable conversation never threatened him or went beyond the bearable. The Andersons in Windermere ran a sweet shop at Chapel Cross. A week after Christmas they had given Heather a box of liqueur chocolates with holly on it. The Millers in Swallows' Nest were retired. Martin, an ex-fireman, had taken up watercolours, every leaf a masterpiece. Yvonne read tarot cards for friends and was a sidesman in the church. To have their decent ordinariness on either side of him was a comfort and to begin with he had felt the same way about Heather and her pathetic need to please everybody all the time.

We're both fragmented people, he had reasoned. If we put the fragments of ourselves together and have a baby to unite us, we'll be fine.

'Haven't you got any old family photographs or anything?' she had asked him sadly. 'It's a bit one-sided, all my rotten lot and none of yours, even if your lot are dead.'

Lost, he had explained. Left behind in my kit in Australia. But that was all he told her. It was Heather's life he wanted, not his own. Heather's relations, childhood, friends. Her banality, her continuity, her weaknesses, even her infidelities, which gave him a kind of absolution. He wanted everything he'd never had, at once, ready-made, backdated, warts and all. His pessimism was a gigantic impatience that required life to be set like a tea-table for him by yesterday: dull friends with silly opinions, bad taste and all the commonest factors.

Avalon Way was a hundred yards long with a turning bay and a fire hydrant at the far end. Cutting the van's engine Oliver coasted down the dark road and parked. From the turning bay he walked back lightly, favouring the grass verge, scanning empty cars and darkened houses because the curse of stealth was on him and so were memories of other times. He was in Swindon where Brock had trained him in useless, furtive things. 'We're lacking concentration, son,' a kindly instructor told him. 'It's not having your heart in it is the problem. I expect you're one of those do better on the night.' The moon hung ahead of him making a white ladder in the sea. Sometimes when he passed a bungalow a burglar light plopped on, but the denizens of Avalon Way were frugal souls and it soon went out again. Heather's parked Ventura, exaggerated by the moonlight, loomed vastly in the driveway. The curtains in her bedroom window were drawn shut, a light glowed behind them. She's reading, he thought. Bodice-rippers, whatever her book club sends her. Who does she think of when she reads that stuff? How-to books. What to do when your partner tells you he doesn't love you and never did.

The curtains in Carmen's window were of gauze because she needed to see stars. At the age of eighteen months she had already learned how to make her wishes known. The small tilt window at the top, open because she liked air but not a draught. Her Donald Duck nightlight on the table. The tape of *Peter and the Wolf* to send her to sleep. He listened and heard the sea but no tape. From the darkness of a copper beech he made a survey of the garden and everything he saw accused him. The new Wendy-house, or new last summer when Oliver and Heather Hawthorne were buying everything because buying was the only language left to them. The new climbing frame with bits already missing. The new plastic children's slide, warped. The new paddle pool, clogged with leaves, half inflated, dying where it lay. The new shed for the new mountain bikes they swore they would ride religiously every morning of their new life with Carmen riding pillion as soon as she was big enough. The barbecue, let's have Toby and Maud round: Toby her employer at the estate agents, with a BMW, a maniacal laugh and an espousing wink for the husbands he was cuckolding. Maud his wife. Oliver walked back along the grass verge to the van and called the number on his carphone. First he got a languid bit of Brahms, then a shriek of rock music.

'Congratulations. You have reached Heather and Carmen Hawthorne's ancestral pile. Hi. I'm afraid we're having too much fun to take your call at the moment but if you'd like to leave a message with the butler –'

'I'm down the road in the van,' Oliver said. 'Have you got anybody with you?'

'No, I bloody haven't,' she retorted.

'Then open the door. I need to talk to you.'

They stood facing each other in the hall under the chandelier they had bought together at architectural reclaim. The hostility between them was like a heat. Once she had loved him for making magic in the children's ward at Christmas, for his sloppy dexterity and warmth. She had called him her gentle giant, her lord and schoolmaster. Now she was contemptuous of his size and ugliness, and kept her distance while she looked for things to hate about him. Once he had loved her failings as a precious charge upon him: she is the reality, I am the dream. Her face in the light of the chandelier was bruised and shiny.

'I need to see her,' he said.

'You can see her Saturday.'

'I won't wake her. I just need to see her.'

She was shaking her head and grimacing to show that he disgusted her.

'No,' she said.

'I promise,' he replied, not sure what he was promising.

They were speaking in damped voices for Carmen's sake. Heather clutched her nightgown at her throat to block his view of her breasts. He smelt cigarette smoke. She's taken it up again. Her long hair, naturally dark brown, was dyed blonde. She had brushed it before letting him in. 'I'm going to have it cut short, I'm sick of it,' she'd say to get him going. 'Not an inch,' he'd say, stroking it, folding it against her temples, feeling his lust collect. 'Not half an inch. I love it as it is. I love you, I love your hair. Let's go to bed.'

'I've had a threat,' he said, lying the way he'd always lied to her, in a tone to discourage question. 'People I got mixed up with in Australia. They've found out where I live.'

'You don't live here, Oliver. You visit when I'm out, not when I'm in,' she retorted, as if he had propositioned her.

'I need to make sure she's safe.'

'She's safe, thank you. As safe as she can be. She's beginning to get used to the idea. You live in one place, I live in another place, Jillie helps me look after her. It's hard, but she's working it out.'

Jillie the au pair.

'It's these people,' he said.

'Oliver. Ever since I've known you there's been little green men who were going to come and get us in the night. It's got a name, you know. Paranoia. Perhaps it's time you talked to somebody about it.'

'Has anyone funny called? Strange enquiries – people coming to the door, asking questions, offering you unlikely things to buy?'

'We're not in a movie, Oliver. We're ordinary people living ordinary lives. All of us except you.'

'Has anyone called?' he repeated. 'Phoned. Asked for

me.' He caught the flicker of a hesitation in her eye before she answered.

'A man telephoned. Three times. Jillie got him.'

'For me?'

'Well, it wasn't me, was it, or I wouldn't be telling you.'

'What did he say? Who was he?'

'"Tell Oliver to ring Jacob. He knows the number." I didn't know you'd got a Jacob tucked away. I hope you'll be very happy.'

'When did he call?'

'Yesterday and the day before. I was going to tell you when we next spoke. All right, I'm sorry. Go on then. Look at her.' But he didn't move except to grasp her upper arms. 'Oliver,' she protested, pulling angrily free of him.

'A man sent you roses. Last week,' he said. 'You rang me.'

'That's right. I rang you and told you about it.'

'Tell me again.'

She heaved a theatrical sigh. 'A limousine brought me some roses with a nice card. I didn't know who they were from. Right?'

'But you knew they were coming. The firm had rung up in advance.'

'The firm had rung up. Correct. "We're delivering some flowers for Hawthorne and when will somebody be in?"'

'It wasn't a local firm.'

'No, it was a London firm. It wasn't Interflora, it wasn't the little green men. It was special blooms being sent all the way from London by a firm that specialises in special blooms and when will I be in to receive them? "You're joking," I said. "You've got the wrong Hawthorne," but they hadn't, it was us. "A Mrs Heather and a Miss Carmen," they said. "And how about six tomorrow evening?" I still thought it was a joke or a mistake or a selling gimmick, even after I rang off. Six o'clock on the dot next day this limousine rolls up.'

'What kind?'

'A shiny great Mercedes – I told you, didn't I? – and a chauffeur in a grey uniform like one of the ads. "You ought to wear gaiters,'' I said to him. He didn't know what gaiters were. I told you that bit too.'

'What colour?'

'The chauffeur?'

'The Mercedes.'

'Metallic blue, polished like a wedding car. The chauffeur was white, his uniform was grey and the roses were creamy pink. Long-stemmed, scented, just opened and a tall white china vase to put them in.'

'And a note.'

'That's right, Oliver, a note.'

'Not signed, you said.'

'No, Oliver, I didn't say it wasn't signed. I said it was signed ''To two beautiful ladies from their devoted admirer'' on the firm's card, Marshall & Bernsteen, Jermyn Street, W1. When I rang them to find out who the admirer might be, they said they weren't at liberty to reveal the name of the customer even if they knew it. Lots of flowers went out that way from anonymous customers, particularly round St Valentine's Day, which it wasn't, but their policy was the same all year. Right? Satisfied?'

'Have you still got them?'

'No, Oliver. I haven't. I had a little moment, as you know, when I thought they might have been from you. Not because I wanted them to be particularly, but you're the only person I know who's mad enough to make a gesture like that. I was mistaken. It wasn't you, as you were kind enough to tell me in very clear terms. I thought of sending them back or giving them to the hospital, but then I thought to hell with it, at least *somebody* loves us, and I've never seen roses like that in my life and they were sent to us, so I did everything I could think of to make them last. I bashed the ends of the stalks and mixed the little packet of powder into the water and kept them in a cool place. I put six in Carmen's room and she loved them, and when I wasn't worried about mysterious sex maniacs I was completely in love with whoever sent them.'

'Did you throw away the note?'

'The note was not a clue, Oliver. It was written by the

72

firm to the sender's dictation. I checked. So it was no good me puzzling over the handwriting.'

'So where is it?'

'That's my business.'

'How many roses were there?'

'More than anyone's ever given me before.'

'Didn't you count them?'

'Girls count roses, Oliver. It's what they do. It's not that they're greedy. They like to know how much they're loved.'

'How many?'

'Thirty.'

Thirty roses. Five million and thirty pounds.

'And you've heard nothing since,' he asked, after a space. 'No phone call – letter – nothing to follow them up?'

'No, Oliver, nothing to follow them up. I have raked over my entire lovelife, which doesn't amount to a lot, thinking of all my men who might have struck it rich, and the only one I could come up with is Gerald who was always going to win the Irish Sweepstake but in the interim he was on the dole. However, I live in hopes. The days go by but I still look out of the window now and then in case there's a blue Merc waiting to whisk us away somewhere, but it's usually raining.'

He stood at Carmen's bedside, peering down at her. He stooped over her until he could smell her warmth and listen to her breathing. She snuffled and appeared about to wake as Heather grabbed his wrist and marched him into the hall, through the open doorway and down the path.

'You've got to get out,' he told her.

She didn't understand him. 'No,' she said. 'You have.'

He was glaring at her without seeing her properly. He was shaking. She could feel the shaking in his wrist before she let it go.

'Away from here,' he explained. 'Both of you. Don't go to your mother or your sisters, they're too obvious. Go to Norah's.' Norah her friend, the one she talked to for an hour at full rates every time they had a row. 'Tell her you've got to get away for a bit. Say I'm driving you mad.'

'I'm a working woman, Oliver. What do I tell Toby?'

'You'll think of something.'

She was scared. She was dreading whatever Oliver dreaded, even if she didn't know what it was. 'Oliver, for Christ's sake.'

'Call Norah tonight. I'll send you money. Whatever you need. Someone will come and see you and explain.'

'Why don't you do the explaining yourself?' she screamed after him.

It was his secret place not ten minutes' drive from the bungalow at the end of a timber track cut into a hilltop. It was where he had come to practise his balloon sculpture and his plate-spinning and the juggling he couldn't get his hands round. It was where he used to hide himself when he was afraid he would hit her or smash up the house or kill himself out of rage at the deadness of his soul. Sitting up here in the van with the window down he would wait for his breathing to settle, listening to the prickle of pine trees and the mewing of night gulls and the rumble of other people's worries coming up from the valley. Sometimes he would sit all night staring into the bay. Sometimes he saw himself balanced on the sea wall at high tide, kicking off his shoes before jumping feet first into the foam. Or the sea became the Bosphorus, and he imagined a constant criss-cross of small and large boats nearly colliding. Parking in his usual corner, he switched off the engine and stabbed out Brock's number on the green digits of his carphone. He heard the altering tones as his call was rerouted, and knew he had dialled right because he heard a woman's voice reciting the number back at him, which was all she ever did, she was a recorded woman, an unattainable abstraction.

'It's Benjamin for Jacob,' he said.

More atmospherics, followed by the voice of Tanby, Brock's emaciated shadow. Cadaverous Cornish Tanby who drives Brock's car for him when he needs to catch an hour's kip. Fetches Brock's Chinese take-in for him when he can't leave his desk. Fronts for him, lies for him, hauls me upstairs when my feet are lame from drink. Tanby the calm voice in the storm, the one you want to throttle with your sweating hands.

'Well, *there's* a nice surprise at last, Benjamin,' said Tanby, all jaunty. 'Better late than never, I will say.'

'He's found us,' Oliver said.

'Yes, Benjamin, I fear he has. And the Skipper would like a one-to-one with you in this regard as soon as possible. There's a fast train leaving your neck of the woods at eleven thirty-five tomorrow morning, if that's convenient, same place, same routine. And the Skipper says to bring a tooth-brush and a couple of your City suits and bits to match, specially the shoes. You've seen the newspapers, I dare say?'

'What newspapers?'

'Then you haven't. Good. Only the Skipper doesn't want you worried, you see. Everybody you care about is all right, he says to tell you. No losses within the family, not as of now. He wants you reassured.'

'What newspapers?'

'Well, I take the *Express* myself.'

Oliver drove slowly back into town. His neck muscles were aching. There was something odd going on in the big veins leading to his head. The newspaper kiosk at the railway station was closed. He drove to a bank, not his own, and took two hundred pounds cash out of the wall. He drove to the waterfront and found Eric at his usual corner table in the brasserie across the square, eating what he always ate now he was retired: liver, chips and mushy peas and a glass of the Chilean red. Eric had stooged for Max Miller and understudied with the Crazy Gang. He had shaken hands with Bob Hope and slept, he liked to say, with every pretty boy in the chorus. When Oliver was on a bender, Eric would drink along with him, apologising that his years prevented him from keeping pace with Oliver's consumption. And if the need arose Eric would take Oliver back to his apartment which he shared with an ailing young hairdresser called Sandy, and open up the sofa-bed in the lounge so that Oliver could have a nice rest and baked beans for his breakfast in the morning.

'How's tricks, Eric?' Oliver asked, and Eric at once thrust up the clown's hooped eyebrows that he darkened with Grecian Formula.

'They comes and they goes, my son, I'll put it that way. There's not quite the demand these days for a geriatric poof with origami and the bird-noises. I expect it's the recession.'

On a page torn from his diary Oliver wrote out a list of his engagements for the next few days.

'It's my guardian, Eric,' he explained. 'He's had a heart attack and he's asking for me. And here's a bit of extra.' He slipped him the two hundred pounds.

'Now don't you go being too hard on yourself, my son,' Eric warned, stowing the money inside his bright check jacket. 'It wasn't you who invented death. God did. God's got a lot to answer for, you ask Sandy.'

Mrs Watmore was waiting up for him. She looked pale and scared, the way she had looked when Cadgwith came to feel Sammy's collar.

'If he rang once he must have rung a dozen times,' she burst out. '"Where's that Ollie? Tell him he'd no cause to run out on me." Next thing I know, he's on my doorstep, ringing my bell and slamming my letter box and waking up nextdoors.' He realised she was talking about Toogood. 'I can't have trouble, Ollie. Even for you. I'm in debt to my eyes, I've got neighbours, I've got lodgers, I've got Sammy. You're too much, Oliver, and I don't know why.'

She thought he hadn't heard her because he was leaning over the hall table, reading her *Daily Telegraph*, which wasn't usual in him at all. He hated newspapers, would actually make a detour to avoid them. So she thought he must be fobbing her off and was going to tell him to get his head out of that newspaper and give her a proper answer. Then she took a calmer look at him and knew by his posture of alertness and her own intuition that what she had always feared would happen had happened, and that he was finished for her, and for Sammy too, it was over. And she knew, even if she couldn't put her knowledge into words, that all the time he had been with her he'd been hiding from something, not just his child or his marriage, but from himself as well, given what her late husband would have called his calibre. And that whatever it was he had been running away from, it was bigger than his wife and child and it had come to find him.

HOLIDAY LAWYER SHOT DEAD IN TURKEY, Oliver read. Photograph of Alfred Winser, described as Chief Legal Officer to the West End finance house of Single & Single, and looking strictly legal in the horn-rimmed spectacles that he never wore unless he was interviewing a new secretary. Identification of body delayed while a nationwide search is mounted for the widow who, according to her mother, is taking advantage of her husband's absence to have an away-from-it-all holiday of her own. Cause of death still to be determined, foul play not ruled out, vague talk of a resurgence of Kurdish terrorism in the region.

Sammy stood in the doorway, wearing one of his late father's pullovers as a dressing gown. 'What about our billiards?' he demanded.

'I've got to go to London,' Oliver said, not lifting his head from the newspaper.

'How long for?'

'Few days.'

Sammy disappeared. A moment later the voice of Burl Ives came floating down the staircase singing 'I never will play the wild rover no more'.

CHAPTER SIX

For his reunion with Oliver after several years of separation
Brock took all the usual precautions and others that were
less usual but dictated by the discreet crisis that was breaking
over his department, and by his almost religious sense of
Oliver's rarity. It is an axiom of Brock's profession that no
two informants should ever use the same safe house, but in
Oliver's case Brock insisted on a house without an operational history of any kind. The result was a furnished three-
bedroomed brick villa in the backwoods of Camden, with
an all-night Asian grocery store one side and a bustling
Greek restaurant the other. Nobody was interested in who
went in or out of the battered front door of number 7. But
Brock's precautions did not stop there. Oliver might be hard
to handle, but he was Brock's ewe lamb, his prize acquisition
and his Benjamin, as every member of the crew was made
thoroughly aware. At Waterloo station, rather than entrust
Oliver to an unmarked van, Brock had Tanby meet him on
the platform and usher him into a tame London cab, sit
with him in the back and pay the fare in cash like any honest
citizen. And in Camden he posted Derek and Aggie and
two equally unlikely looking crew members on both pave-
ments with the task of making sure that Oliver, consciously
or otherwise, had brought nobody in his wake. In our world,

Brock liked to preach, you did best to think dirty and double it. But with Oliver, if you knew what was good for you, you added the number you first thought of as well.

It was mid-afternoon. Arriving at Gatwick airport the previous night, Brock had driven himself straight to his anonymous office in the Strand and telephoned Aiden Bell on the secure line. Bell was Commander of the inter-service task force to which Brock was currently assigned.

'It's a company town,' he told him, after relaying Captain Ali's suicide theory with appropriate scepticism. 'It's either we make you rich or we make you dead. The town's chosen rich.'

'Wise chaps,' said Bell, an ex-soldier. 'War party after prayers tomorrow. At the shop.'

Then, like an anxious shepherd, Brock called up his outstations one by one, beginning with a shuttered corner flat in Curzon Street, passing to a British Telecom repair van at the edge of Hyde Park and from there to the headquarters car of a mobile squad assigned to a lost valley in the emptiest part of Dorset. 'What's new?' he demanded of each team leader without bothering to introduce himself. Not a peep, sir, came the disappointed answers. Not a whisper, sir. Brock was relieved. Give me time, he thought. Give me Oliver. A church-like quiet overtook him while he set to work transferring his operational expenses to a claim form. It was broken by the buzz of his Whitehall internal line and the glib voice of a very senior, hairless Metropolitan police officer named Porlock. Brock at once pressed a green button that engaged the tape recorder.

'Where the hell have *you* been, Master Brock?' Porlock demanded, all banter, and Brock saw in his memory the naked grin stretched humourlessly across Porlock's pitted jaw and wondered, as he always wondered, how anyone so brazenly corrupt could walk so bold for so long.

'Nowhere I'd like to go again, thank you, Bernard,' he said primly.

This was how they always spoke: as if their mutual aggression were a sparring game, whereas on Brock's side it was a deadly earnest duel that only one of them could win.

'So what's on our mind, Bernard?' Brock asked. 'Some people sleep at night, I'm told.'

'Who killed Alfred Winser then?' Porlock demanded coaxingly, through the same long grin.

Brock affected to search his memory. 'Winser. Alfred. Ah, yes. Well, it wasn't the common cold that killed him, was it, not according to the papers? I'd have thought you boys would be out there by now, come to think of it, frustrating the locals in their enquiries.'

'So why aren't we, Nat? Why does nobody love us any more?'

'Bernard, I am not paid to justify the comings and goings of the distinguished gentlefolk of Scotland Yard.' He was still seeing the taunting smile, talking at it. One day, if I live long enough, I'll be talking at it through the bars, I swear.

'Why are those fairies in the Foreign Office insisting I wait and see the Turkish police report before forcing my nasty attentions on them? There's somebody's hand at work and I've a good idea it's yours, when it isn't busy elsewhere,' said Porlock.

'Now you've shocked me, Bernard. Why would a mere downtrodden customs officer two years off retirement seek to interfere with the wheels of justice?'

'You chase money-launderers, don't you? Everyone knows Single's are laundering money for the Wild East. They're practically listed in the Yellow Pages.'

'So how does that lead us to the random murder of Mr Alfred Winser, Bernard? You're losing me on the causality, I'm afraid.'

'Winser's a related case, isn't he? If you can find out who killed Alfred Winser, maybe you can nail Tiger. I can see that one playing with our Whitehall masters, specially when accompanied by a nice brown nose.' He affected an offensively posh accent, and rendered it with a homophobe lisp. '"Let old Net handle this one. This one is *raight* up old Net's street."'

Brock allowed himself a pause for prayer and contemplation. I'm watching it in action, he thought. It's happening to me here and now. Porlock is coming to the protection of his paymaster, and he's doing it under the arclights. Get back to the shadows, he thought. If you're a crook, act like a crook, and don't sit next to me at weekly meetings. 'I don't chase launderers, Bernard, you see,' Brock explained. 'I've learned my lesson on that one. I chase their money. There *was* one I chased, long ago, it's true,' he reminisced in a caricature of his Liverpool twang. 'Put a lot of very expensive lawyers and accountants on to him, turned him inside out. Five years and several million quid of public money later he gave me two fingers in open court and walked out a free man. I'm told the jury are still trying to read the long words. So goodnight to you, Bernard, and many of them.'

But Porlock had not quite done with him.

'Here. Nat.'

'What is it?'

'Let your hair down. Little club I know in Pimlico. Very friendly people, not all of the male gender. On me.'

Brock nearly laughed out loud. 'You've got this one a bit wrong, haven't you, Bernard?'

'Why's that then?'

'Policemen are supposed to be bribed by crooks. They don't go bribing one another, not where I come from.'

Released, Brock unlocked a formidable wall-safe and drew out a hardbacked, quarto-sized, ruled diary labelled HYDRA in his own hand, opened it at the day's date and wrote as follows in his painstaking courtroom copperplate:

0122 hrs, unsolicited incoming call from D/Supt Bernard Porlock seeking information regarding the state of investigation into the murder of A. Winser. Taped conversation terminated 0127 hrs.

And having filled in the rest of his claim form, he rang his wife Lily at home in Tonbridge, although it was by now two in the morning, and let her regale him with stories of dark doings in the local Women's Institute which she confided in a breathless torrent.

'And that Mrs Simpson, Nat, she marches straight up to the jams table and she picks up Mary Ryder's jar of marmalade and she smashes it on the floor. Then she turns round to Mary and she says, Mary Ryder, if your Herbert ever stands outside my bathroom window again at eleven o'clock at night with his nasty nature in his hand I'll set the dog on him and you'll both be sorry.'

He didn't say where he'd been these last days, and Lily didn't ask. Sometimes the secrecy saddened her, but more often it was like a shared and precious bond of service. Next morning prompt at eight-thirty, Brock and Aiden Bell headed southward in a cab across the river. Bell was a graceful figure with a seeming courtliness that women trusted at their peril. He sported a military-looking suit of green tweed.

'Had an invitation from a bald St Bernard last night,' Brock informed him, in the short-range murmur with which he reluctantly imparted secrets. 'Wants me to go with him to a dirty club he knows in Pimlico so that he can take compromising photographs of me.'

'Nothing if not subtle, our Bernard,' said Bell grimly, and there was a shared moment while they pooled their indignation. 'One day,' said Bell.

'One day,' Brock agreed.

Neither Bell nor Brock was any longer what he seemed. Bell was a soldier and Brock, as he had reminded Bernard Porlock, a humble customs man. Yet both had been assigned to the Joint Team, and both were aware that the first purpose of the Team was to close artificial gaps between departments. Each second Saturday of the month any member not engaged elsewhere was invited to attend these informal prayer sessions held in a glum box-shaped building beside the Thames. The speaker today was a wise woman from Research who treated them to the latest doomsday tally of international crime:

– this many kilos of ex-Soviet weapons-grade nuclear materials sold under the counter to this or that Middle Eastern maverick

– this many thousands of machine guns, automatic rifles,

night vision glasses, landmines, cluster bombs, missiles, tanks and artillery pieces dumped by means of spurious end-user certificates on the newest terror-friendly African despot or narcotyrant
– this many billions of drug money spirited into the so-called white economy
– this many tons of refined heroin shipped via Spain and northern Cyprus to the following European ports
– this many tons reached the British wholesale market in the last twelve weeks, street value this many hundreds of millions, this many kilos impounded, amounting to an estimated .0001 per cent of gross.

Illegal narcotics, she said sweetly, now accounted for one tenth of all world trade.

Americans spent seventy-eight billion dollars a year on their drugs habit.

World production of cocaine had doubled in the last ten years, heroin had tripled. The industry turned over four hundred billion dollars annually.

South America's military élite now made drugs, not war. Countries unable to grow their own crops were offering chemical refineries and sophisticated forms of transportation as a means of getting a toehold in the business.

Uninvolved governments were in a quandary. Should they frustrate the success of the black economy – assuming they were able – or share in its prosperity?

In dictatorships, where public opinion was irrelevant, the answer was obvious.

In democracies a double standard existed: those who preached zero tolerance were giving a free licence to the black economy while those who preached decriminalisation were offering it safe conduct – which was the wise woman's cue to tiptoe into the Hydra's lair.

'Crime no longer exists in isolation of the state, if it ever did,' she declared, with the firmness of a headmistress lecturing her school leavers. 'Today's stakes are too big for crime to be left to the criminals. We are no longer looking at adventurous outlaws who will reveal themselves by clumsiness or repetition. When one containerload of cocaine safely landed at a British port is worth a hundred million pounds, and the harbourmaster is enjoying a salary of forty thousand, we are looking at *ourselves*. At the harbourmaster's ability to resist temptation on an unprecedented scale. At the harbourmaster's superior. At the dockside police. At *their* superiors. At Customs. And *theirs*. At the enforcers, bankers, lawyers and administrators who look the other way. To imagine that these people can synchronise their collaborative efforts without a central command and control system, and the active connivance from others in high positions, is absurd. That's where the Hydra comes in.'

A pop from somewhere as the inevitable visual aid was flashed onto the screen behind her, showing the anatomy of the British body politic laid out like a family tree. Strewn across it were the Hydra's many heads and, in gold, the ley lines that connected them. Instinctively Brock's eye selected the Metropolitan Police, where the bald silhouette of Porlock like an arrogant Roman medallion presided, and the gold lines spewed out of him like fountains of munificence. Born Cardiff 1948, Brock rehearsed: 1970, joined West Midlands Regional Crime Squad, reprimanded for excessive zeal in the performance of his duties, i.e. faking evidence. Sick leave, promoted on transfer. 1978, joined Liverpool Docks Police, secured spectacular conviction of useless drugs gang that was unwisely competing with established rival. Three days after trial ended, took all-expenses-paid holiday in southern Spain with leaders of said rival gang. Claimed he was gathering essential criminal intelligence, exonerated, transferred on promotion. 1985, investigated for allegedly accepting inducements from identified leader of a Belgian drugs syndicate. Exonerated, commended, promoted on transfer. 1992, featured in British tabloid press lunching with two members of an illegal Serbian arms procurement team at a girlie restaurant in Birmingham. Caption: 'PORLOCK THE WARLOCK. Whose side are you on, Superintendent?' Awarded fifty thousand pounds libel damages, exonerated by internal enquiry, promoted on transfer. How do you face yourself in the shaving mirror every morning?

Brock asked him in his mind. Answer, easily. How do you sleep at night? Answer, excellently. Answer, I have a Teflon hide and the conscience of the dead. Answer, I burn files, terrify witnesses, buy allies, walk tall.

The meeting ended, as such meetings were wont to do, in a mood of jocular despair. On the one hand the troops were heartened: anything went, nothing was too much in the war against human wickedness. But they also knew that, if they lived to be a thousand and all their efforts were successful, they would inflict at best a few flesh wounds on the eternal enemy.

*   *   *

Oliver and Brock sat on deck chairs in the back garden of the Camden house under a brightly coloured parasol. A tray of tea and biscuits lay before them on a table. Nice china, proper tea, no tea-bags, low spring sun.

'Tea-bags are made of dust,' said Brock, who had his little fads. 'If you want a decent cup of tea, you've to go for the leaves, not dust.'

Oliver squatted in the parasol's shade. He was wearing what he had travelled in: jeans, chukka boots and a sloppy blue anorak. Brock sported a silly straw hat that the crew had bought him in Camden Lock that morning for a joke. Oliver had no quarrel with Brock. Brock had not invented, seduced, bribed or blackmailed him. Brock had committed no sin against Oliver's soul that had not been committed long ago. It was Oliver, not Brock, who had rubbed the lamp and it was Brock who had materialised in obedience to Oliver's command:

It is mid-winter and Oliver is a little mad. That much he knows about himself, no more. The origins of his madness, its causes, duration and degree, are not within his grasp, not now. They are out there, but for another time, another life, another couple of brandies. The neon-lit gloom of a December's night at Heathrow airport reminds him of a boys' changing room in one of his many boarding schools. Garish cardboard reindeer and taped carols compound his mood of unreality. Snowy lettering dangles from a washing line, wishing him peace and joy on earth. Something amazing is about to happen to him and he is eager to find out what it will be. He isn't drunk but technically he isn't sober either. A few vodkas on the flight, a half of red with the rubber chicken, a Rémy or two afterwards, have done no more in Oliver's eyes than bring him up to speed with the furore already raging inside him. He has only hand luggage and nothing to declare except a reckless ferment of the brain, a firestorm of outrage and exasperation starting so long ago that its origins are impossible to peg, blowing through his head like a hurricane while other members of his internal congregation stand around in timid twos and threes and ask each other what on earth Oliver is going to do to put it out. He is approaching signs of different colours and, instead of wishing him peace, joy on earth and goodwill among men, they are requiring him to define himself. Is he a stranger in his own country? Answer, yes he is. Has he arrived here from another planet? Answer, yes he has. Is he blue? Red? Green? His eye drifts to a tomato-coloured telephone. It is familiar to him. Perhaps he noticed it on his way out three days ago and, unknown to himself, recruited it as a secret ally. Is it heavy, hot, alive? A notice beside it reads: 'If you wish to speak to a customs officer, use this phone.' He uses it. That is to say, his arm reaches out for it unbidden, his hand grasps it and puts it to his ear, leaving him with the responsibility of what to say. The telephone is inhabited by a woman, and he has not expected a woman. He hears her saying 'Yes?' at least twice, then, 'Can I help you, sir?' which suggests to him that she can see him though he cannot see her. Is she beautiful, young, old, stern? Never mind. With the courtesy that is innate in him he replies that, well, yes actually she *could* help him, he would like please to speak privately to someone in authority on a confidential matter. When he hears his own voice in the earpiece, its composure amazes him. I am in command of myself, he thinks. And with the detachment from his terrestrial self now absolute, he is overwhelmingly grateful to be

86

in the hands of someone so capable. Your problem is that if you don't act now you never will, the assured voice of his terrestrial self explains to him. You'll go under, you'll drown, it's now or never, one hates to be dramatic but there comes a time. And perhaps his terrestrial self actually says some of this live into the red telephone, because he senses the alien woman stiffen and pick her words with deliberation.

'Remain exactly where you are by the telephone, please, sir. Don't move. An officer will be with you in one moment.'

And here Oliver has an extraneous memory of a telephone bar in Warsaw where you rang girls at other tables and the girls rang you – which was how he had found himself buying a beer for a six-foot schoolteacher named Alicja who warned him that she never slept with Germans. This evening, however, he draws a small athletic-looking woman with a boy's haircut and a white shirt with epaulettes. Is she the same artful woman who called him 'sir' before he spoke? He cannot tell but knows that she is scared of his size and wondering whether he is a nutter. Standing back from him she takes in his expensive suit and briefcase and gold cufflinks and handmade shoes and red-hot face. She ventures a step closer and staring straight up at him with her jaw out she asks his name and where he has arrived from, and mentally breathalyses his answers. She asks for his passport. He slams his pockets, can't find it as usual, locates it, delves for it, nearly buckles it in his anxiety to please, and hands it to her.

'It's got to be someone high up,' he warns her but she is too busy turning the pages.

'This is your only passport, is it?'

Yes, it is, his terrestrial self retorts loftily. And nearly adds 'my good woman'.

'You're not dual nationality or anything then, are you?'

No, I'm not.

'So this is the passport you're travelling on, is it?' – turning another page.

Yes.

'Georgia, Russia?'

Yes.

'And that's where you've just arrived from, is it? Tbilisi?'

No. Istanbul.

'And was it something about Istanbul you were wanting to talk about? Or Georgia?'

I wish to speak to a senior officer, Oliver repeats. They traverse a corridor crammed with frightened Asians seated on suitcases. They enter a windowless interviewing room with a table screwed to the floor and a mirror screwed to the wall. In his self-induced trance Oliver sits unbidden to the table and marvels at himself in the mirror.

'So I'm going to find someone for you, right?' she says severely. 'I'm going to keep your passport and you'll get it back later, right? Somebody will come as soon as they can. Right?'

Right. Everything absolutely right as rain. Half an hour passes, the door opens, but instead of a full admiral dripping with gold braid a scrawny blond boy in white shirt and uniform trousers appears bearing a cup of sweet tea and two sugary biscuits.

'Sorry about this, sir. It's the season, I'm afraid. Everybody going everywhere for Christmas. An appropriate officer *is* on his way to you. You asked for somebody senior, I believe.'

Yes, I did. The boy stands himself behind Oliver's shoulder, watching him drink his tea.

'Nothing like a nice cuppa when we get back to the old country, is there?' he says to Oliver's reflection in the mirror. 'Got a home address at all, sir?'

Oliver spells out his glitzy Chelsea address while the boy writes it in a notebook.

'How long you been in Istanbul, then?'

Couple of nights.

'That was long enough, was it, for what you had to do?'

Quite long enough.

'Pleasure or business?'

Business.

'Been there before?'

A few times.

'Always visit the same people, do you, when you go to Istanbul?'

Pretty much.

'Travel a lot, do you, in your line of work?'

Too much, sometimes.

'Gets you down, does it?'

It can do. Depends. Oliver's terrestrial self is becoming bored and apprehensive. Wrong time, wrong place, he is telling himself. Nice idea but a bit over the top. Ask for passport back, taxi home, large nightcap, bite the bullet, get on with life.

'What do you do, then?'

Investment, says Oliver. Asset management. Portfolios. Mostly round the leisure industry.

'Where else do you go? Apart from Istanbul.'

Moscow. St. Petersburg. Georgia. Wherever business calls, really.

'Anybody waiting for you in Chelsea, is there? Somebody you ought to ring? – square – say you're all right?'

Not really.

'Don't want people worrying about you, do we?'

My goodness, no – jolly laugh.

'Who've you got then? – wife? – kids?'

Oh no, no, thank God. Or not yet, anyway.

'Girlfriend?'

Off and on.

'They're the best sort really, aren't they? Off-and-ons.'

I suppose they are.

'Less trouble.'

Much. The boy leaves, Oliver sits alone again, but not for long. The door opens and Brock enters, bearing Oliver's passport and wearing full Customs uniform – the only time Oliver ever saw him in it, and as he later learns the first time Brock has worn it in the twenty-something years he has been assigned to less recognisable duties. And it is not till Oliver is several lives wiser that he pictures Brock standing the other side of the mirror throughout the boy's careless inquisition, unable to believe his luck while he struggles into his regalia.

'Good evening, Mr Single,' says Brock, shaking Oliver's

passive hand. 'Or may we call you Oliver so that we don't confuse you with your revered father?'

*   *   *

The parasol was quartered green and orange. Oliver's side was green, leaving his big face sallow. But Brock's straw hat gave off a jaunty glow and his sharp eyes shone with hobgoblin merriment beneath its rakish brim.

'So who told Tiger where to find you?' Brock enquired comfortably, more in the manner of somebody airing a theme than eliciting a reply. 'He's not psychic, is he? Not omniscient. Ears everywhere. Is he? Who bubbled?'

'You did, probably,' said Oliver gracelessly.

'*I* did? Why should I do that?'

'Probably got a new agenda.'

Brock's smile rested contentedly in place. He was taking stock of his prize possession, checking what had happened to it in the years it had been out to grass. You're one marriage and one child and one divorce older, he was thinking. And me still stuck with what I've got, thank God. He was looking for signs of wear in Oliver and not seeing any. You're a finished product and don't know it, he thought, remembering other informants he'd resettled. You think the world will come and change you but it never does. You're who you are until you die.

'Maybe *you* had a new agenda,' Brock countered good-humouredly.

'Oh great. Sure. "I miss you, Dad. Let's kiss and make up. Bygones are bygones." Sure.'

'You might have done. Knowing you. Got homesick. Dose of the guilts. After all, you changed your mind over your gratuity money a few times, I seem to remember. First you dithered. Then it was no, Nat, not on your nelly. Then it was yes, Nat, I'll take it. I thought you might have done a U-turn on Tiger too.'

'You know bloody well the gratuity money was for Carmen's sake,' Oliver snapped from his shade the other side of the tea table.

90

'This is for Carmen's sake too. Could be. Five million of the best. Maybe you and Tiger cut a deal, I thought. Tiger comes up with the money so Oliver does the love. I can see filial loyalties being restored on the strength of a five million down-payment on Carmen. What's the logic of it otherwise? None that I'm aware, not from Tiger's point of view. It's not as if he was burying a bag of fivers in the family allotment, is it?' No answer. None expected. 'He can't go back with a spade and a lantern and dig them up in a year's time when he needs them, can he?' Still none. 'It's not even Carmen's for another quarter of a century. What's Tiger bought himself for his five million quid? His granddaughter's never even heard of him. If you have your way, she never will. He must have bought *something*. Then I thought, perhaps it's our Oliver he's bought – why not? People change, I thought, love conquers all. Perhaps you really did kiss and make up. Given a five million quid sweetener to help the medicine go down, anything's possible.'

In a totally unexpected gesture, Oliver flung up his great arms in surrender, stretched until they creaked, then let them flop to his sides. 'You're being bloody ridiculous and you know it,' he told Brock, without any particular animosity.

'*Somebody* told him,' Brock insisted. 'He didn't just find you from nowhere, Oliver. *Some* little bird whispered in his ear.'

'Who killed Winser?' Oliver countered.

'I don't think I mind, do you? Not when I survey the glorious field of candidates. House of Single's got more scoundrels among its valued clients these days than the entire Rogues' Gallery at Scotland Yard. Could be any one of them, far as I'm concerned.' You're never ahead of him, thought Brock, facing out Oliver's glower: you never fool him, you never deflect him, he's thought out all the worst things for himself long ago. All you do is tell him which ones have come true. Some case-officers of Brock's acquaintance, when they were handling informants, thought they were God in high heels. Not Brock, not ever, and least of all with Oliver. With Oliver, Brock saw himself as a guest on sufferance, liable to be thrown out any time. 'Your friend

Alix Hoban of Trans-Finanz Vienna killed him, according to a certain whisperer I know, and he was assisted by a full supporting cast of fellow hoodlums. He made a phone call while he was about it, too. We think he was reporting progress to somebody. Only we're not telling anyone about all that, because we don't want undue attention drawn to House of Single.'

Oliver waited for the second part of this announcement but, finding none forthcoming, rested his chin in his hand and his elbow on his big knee and fixed Brock with an appraising stare. 'Trans-Finanz Vienna, in my recollection, is a wholly owned subsidiary of First Flag Construction Company of Andorra,' he said through a bunch of heavy fingers.

'And still is, Oliver, still is. Your memory is as sharp as ever.'

'It was me set the bloody company up, wasn't it?'

'Now you come to mention it, I believe it was.'

'And First Flag is the wholly owned fiefdom of Yevgeny and Mikhail Orlov, House of Single's biggest clients. Or has that changed?'

Oliver's tone had not altered. All the same, Brock noticed that it cost him a certain effort to come out with the Orlov name.

'No, Oliver, I don't think it has. There are strains, but formally speaking I would suspect that your good friends the Orlov brothers still rate as Single's number one.'

'And Alix Hoban is still their man?'

'Yes, Hoban is still the Orlovs' man.'

'He's still family.'

'He's still family, that hasn't changed either. He's on their payroll, he does their bidding, whatever else he does on the side.'

'So why did Hoban kill Winser?' Lost to his own dogged line of reasoning, Oliver frowned into his enormous palms, reading from them. 'Why did the Orlovs' man kill Tiger's man? Yevgeny loved Tiger. More or less. As long as they were making a fortune. So did Mikhail. Tiger returned the compliment. What's changed, Nat? What's going on?'

Brock had not planned to arrive here half so soon. He

had wishfully imagined a gradual process where the truth emerged. But with Oliver you never presumed and you were never surprised. You let him pace you and you followed in his trail, rewriting your march-route as you went along.

'Well, I'm afraid it's one of those cases of love turning to gall, Oliver,' he explained cautiously. 'A full swing of the pendulum, as you might say. One of those weather changes that occur even in the best conducted households, I'm afraid.' Oliver offered him no helping hand so he continued. 'The brothers' luck went sour.'

'In what way?'

'Some of their operations came unstuck.' Brock was tiptoeing on hot coals and Oliver knew it. Brock was putting names to Oliver's worst apprehensions, raising unsleeping ghosts from his past, adding new fears to old ones. 'A sizable chunk of hot money belonging to Yevgeny and Mikhail got blocked before it could be recycled by Single's.'

'You mean before it reached First Flag?'

'I mean while it was still in the holding pattern.'

'Where?'

'All round the globe. Not every country cooperated. Most did.'

'All those little bank accounts we opened?'

'Not so little any more. The smallest was around nine million sterling. The Spain accounts were up to eighty-five million. My view is the Orlovs were getting a bit careless, frankly. Staying liquid with sums like that! You'd think they could at least have gone for short-term bonds while they were waiting, but no.'

Oliver's hands had returned to his face, enclosing it in a private prison.

'Plus one of the brothers' ships got boarded while it was carrying an embarrassing cargo,' Brock added.

'Bound for where?'

'Europe. Wherever. What does it matter?'

'Liverpool?'

'All right, Liverpool. Directly or indirectly, it was Liverpool-bound – will you come out of there, please, Oliver? – *you* know how those Russian crooks are. If they love you, you can do no wrong. If they think you've double-crossed them, they'll firebomb your offices, put a missile through your bedroom window and gun down your wife in the fish queue. That's who they are.'

'Which ship was it?'

'The *Free Tallinn*.'

'Out of Odessa.'

'Correct.'

'Who boarded it?'

'Only Russians, Oliver. Their own people. Russian special forces, in Russian waters. It was Russians boarding Russians, all the way.'

'But you tipped them off.'

'No, that's exactly what we didn't do. Someone else did. Maybe the Orlovs thought Alfie had tipped them off. It's guesswork on all sides.'

Oliver's face sank deeper into his hands as he continued to consult his internal demons. 'Winser didn't double-cross the Orlovs. I did,' he said in a voice from the grave. 'At Heathrow. Hoban shot the wrong messenger.'

Brock's anger, when he released it, was a little frightening. It came from nowhere, without warning, and clamped itself across his face like a death mask. 'Nobody bloody double-crossed them,' he growled. 'You don't double-cross crooks. You catch them. Yevgeny Orlov's a lowlife Georgian thug. So's his moronic brother.'

'They're not Georgian. They just want to be,' Oliver mumbled. 'And Mikhail's not moronic. He's different, that's all.' He was thinking of Sammy Watmore.

'Tiger laundered the Orlovs' money for them and Winser was a one hundred per cent willing accomplice. It's not betrayal, Oliver. It's justice. That was what you wanted, if you remember. You wanted to put the world to rights. That's what we're doing. Nothing's changed. I never promised you we'd do it with fairy dust. That's not what justice is.'

'You promised you'd wait' – still from inside his hands.

'I *did* wait. I promised you a year, it took me four. One to get you clear. Another to run the paper trails to earth. Another to persuade the ladies and gentlemen of Whitehall to get their thumbs out of their arses and a fourth to make them realise that not all British policemen are wonderful and not all British officials are angels. You could have gone anywhere in the world in that time. It had to be England. That was your choice, not mine. Your choice to cut and run, your marriage, your daughter, her Trust fund, your country. For those four years Yevgeny Orlov and his brother Mikhail have been flooding what we used to call the free world with every dirty product they can lay their hands on from Afghan heroin for teenagers to Czech Semtex for Irish peace-lovers and Russian nuclear triggers for Middle Eastern democrats. And Tiger your father has been bankrolling them, laundering their profits and making their beds for them. Not to mention what he's been coining himself. You'll forgive me if after four years we grew a tad impatient.'

'You promised you wouldn't hurt him.'

'I didn't bloody hurt him. I'm not hurting him now. The Orlovs are. And if a bunch of villains want to start blowing each other's brains out, and informing on one another's shipments to Liverpool, all they'll hear from me is applause. I don't love your father, Oliver. That's your job. I'm who I am. I've not changed. Nor's Tiger.'

'Where is he?'

Brock laughed contemptuously. 'In deep shock, where else? Inconsolable, crying his heart out. Read all about it in the press releases. Alfie Winser was his lifelong friend and comrade-in-arms, you'll be pleased to learn. They trudged the same hard road, shared the same ideals. Amen.' Oliver was still waiting. 'He's bolted,' Brock said, abandoning sarcasm. 'Vanished from our screens. There's not a bell rung anywhere and we're watching and listening for him round the clock. Half an hour after he heard the news of Winser's death he walked out of the office, dropped by his flat, walked out again and hasn't been seen or heard of since. It's the sixth day now that he hasn't called or faxed or e-mailed or sent a postcard. In Tiger's life that's unprecedented. One day without a phone call from him, it's a national emergency. Six, it's the apocalypse. The staff are fronting for him all ends up, casually phoning his known watering holes, plus anyone he might have gone to earth with, and doing their damnedest not to raise a storm.'

'Where's Massingham?' – Massingham, Tiger's Chief of Staff.

Brock's expression didn't alter, neither did his voice. His tone remained deprecatory, dismissive.

'Mending fences. Roaming the globe. Soothing customers' feathers.'

'All because of Winser?'

Brock ignored this. 'Massingham phones in from time to time, mostly to ask if anybody's heard anything. He doesn't say a lot apart from that. Not on the telephone. Being Massingham. Being any of them, come to think of it.' They ruminated together in silence until Brock spoke aloud the fear that was taking root in Oliver's mind. 'Tiger could be dead, of course, which would be nice – for society, if not for you –' hoping at least to wake Oliver from his daydream. But Oliver refused to be stirred. 'The honourable way out would make quite a change for Tiger, I must say. Except I don't think he'd know where to find the door.' Nothing. 'Plus all of a sudden he turns round and has his Swiss banker transfer five million quid to Carmen's Trust. Dead men don't do that as a rule, I'm told.'

'And thirty.'

'I beg your pardon? I'm a tiny bit hard of hearing these days, Oliver.'

'Five million *and thirty*,' Oliver corrected him in a louder, angrier voice. So which hell have you gone to now? Brock wanted to ask, as Oliver continued to stare sightlessly ahead of him. And if I succeed in getting you out of this one, which hell will you go to next? 'He sent them flowers,' Oliver explained.

'Sent who? What are you talking about?'

'Tiger sent flowers to Carmen and Heather. Last week by chauffeur-driven Mercedes from London. He knows where they live and who they are. He phoned the order from somewhere, dictated a funny card signing himself an admirer. One of the smart West End florists.' Groping around his jacket, slamming pockets, Oliver eventually found a slip of paper and handed it to Brock. 'Here. Marshall & Bernsteen. Thirty bloody roses. Pink. Five million and thirty pounds. Thirty pieces of silver. He's saying thanks for ratting on me. He's saying he knows where to find her any time he feels like it. He's saying he owns her. Carmen. He's saying Oliver can run but he can't hide. I want her protected, Nat. I want Heather spoken to. I want her told. I don't want them contaminated. I don't want him ever to set eyes on her.'

If Brock's unexpected silences drove Oliver mad, he was also reluctantly impressed by them. Brock gave you no warning. He didn't say, 'Wait a moment.' He just stopped talking until he had thought the thing through and was ready to pass judgment on it.

'He *could* be saying that,' Brock agreed at last. 'He could be saying something different, couldn't he?'

'Like what?' Oliver demanded aggressively.

Brock again let him wait. 'Well, Oliver. Like he's a bit short of company in his old age.'

Oliver watched from the shades of his anorak collar as Brock strolled across the garden, tapped on the french windows and shouted, 'Tanby!' He saw a stalky girl appear, tall as himself but fit. High cheek bones, long blondish pony-tail, and that thing that tall girls have of putting all their weight on one leg while they cock the other hip. He heard her say, 'Tanby's up the road, Nat,' in a Scottish brogue. He watched Brock hand her the slip of paper with the florist's name on it. The girl listening while she read the name. He heard Brock's mumble and set it to words from his informed imagination: I want whoever took the order for thirty roses to Abbots Quay last week, name of Hawthorne, and the chauffeur-driven Mercedes to deliver them – the girl nodding in time to Brock's undertone – I want how the car and flowers were paid for, I want origin, time, date, duration of the call, and a description of the caller's voice if they didn't record him which they may have done because lots of firms do. He thought he caught the girl's eye over Brock's shoulder and flapped a hand at her but she was already on her way indoors.

'So what have you done with them, Oliver?' Brock enquired cosily when he had sat down again.

'The flowers?'

'Don't be bloody silly.'

'Sent them to Northampton to her best friend. If they go. Norah. Unmarried dyke.'

'You want her told what exactly?'

'That I was on the right side. I may be a traitor but I'm not a criminal. It was all right to have my child.'

Brock heard the detachment in Oliver's voice, watched him stand up, scratch his head, then his shoulder, then look round him while he appeared to take fresh stock of where he was: the little garden, apple blossom just beginning, the rumble of traffic from the other side of the wall, the Victorian backs, each in its rectangle of garden, greenhouses, washing on the line. Watched him sit down again. Waited as a priest might for his penitent's return. 'Must be hard for a man like Tiger, running and hiding, at his age,' he mused provocatively, reckoning it was time to interrupt Oliver's reverie. 'If that's what he's doing.' No answer. 'One minute he's eating nice food, riding round in his chauffeur-driven Rolls-Royce, all his systems of self-deception nicely in place, nothing rude, nothing bare-knuckle. Then all of a sudden Alfie gets his head blown off and Tiger wonders if he's next in the queue. Bit chilly out there, I should imagine. Bit lonely for a man in his sixties. I don't think I'd like to have his dreams very much, would you?'

'Shut up,' said Oliver.

Undeterred, Brock gave a rueful shake of his head. 'Then there's me, isn't there?'

'What about you?'

'I hunt a man for fifteen years. I conspire against him, hair goes white, I neglect my wife. Fret and worry how to catch him with his pants down. Next thing I know, he's cringing in a ditch with the hounds after him and all I want to do is reach out for him, give him a hot cup of tea and offer him a total amnesty.'

'Bullshit,' said Oliver, while Brock's clever eyes twinkled and measured him from beneath the brim of the straw hat.

'And you're *twice* the man I am, Oliver, when it comes to fine feeling, I've seen it. So when you boil it down, it's a question of who finds him first. You, or the Orlov brothers and their merry men.'

Oliver peered across the lawn to where the girl had stood, but she was long gone. He squidged up his big face, registering a countryman's irritation at the din of city traffic. Then he spoke loudly and precisely, each word cleared well ahead with himself. 'I'm not doing any more. I've done all I'll ever do for you. I want Carmen and her mother protected. That's all I care about. I'll get another name and set myself up in some other bloody place. I won't do any more.'

'So who finds him?'

'You do.'

'We're not equipped. We're small and British and poor.'

'Balls. You're a bloody great secret army. I've worked with you.'

But Brock shook his head in equally stern rejection. 'I can't send squads of my kids round the world on a wild goose chase, Oliver. I can't advertise my interest to every foreign policeman in the phonebook. If Tiger's in Spain I've got to go on my knees to the Spaniards and by the time they notice me he's skedaddled and I'm reading about myself in the Spanish newspapers, except I don't read Spanish.'

'Learn it,' Oliver said rudely.

'If he's in Italy it's the Italians, Germany the Germans, Africa the Africans, Pakistan the Paks, Turkey the Turks, and the story's the same every time. Greasing palms as I go and never knowing whether the brothers have greased them better and earlier. If he's gone to ground in the Caribbean, it's scour every island and bribe every telegraph pole before I get a phone tap.'

'So hound someone else. There's enough of them about.'

'But *you* –' Brock sat back and surveyed Oliver with a kind of rueful envy. 'You can feel him, guess him, live him, just by breathing in. You know him better than you know yourself. You know his houses, his footwork, his women and what he has for breakfast before he orders it. You've got him *here.*' He patted his own chest with one neat palm while Oliver groaned *no, no.* 'You're three-quarters of the way to him before you even start. Have I said something?'

Oliver was rolling his head like Sammy Watmore. You kill your father once and that's it, he was thinking. I'm not doing any of it, hear me? I've had it. I'd had it four years ago, I'd had it before I ever started. 'Find some other poor sod,' he said gruffly.

'It's the old song, Oliver. Brother Brock will meet him any time, any place, nothing up my sleeve. That's my message to him. If he doesn't remember me, remind him. Young customs officer Brock from Liverpool, the one he advised to look for other employment after the Turkish ingot trial. Brock's willing if he is, tell him. Brock's door's open twenty-four hours a day. He has my word.'

Flinging his arms round his chest Oliver hugged himself in some private ritual of prayer. 'Never,' he muttered.

'What's never?'

'Tiger would never do it. Never betray. That's my job, not his.'

'Bollocks frankly, and you know it. Tell him Brock believes in creative negotiation, same as he always did. I've wide powers and one of them is forgetting. It's a memory game, tell him. I forget, he remembers. No public inquisition, no trial, no prison, no confiscation of assets, provided he does his remembering right. All private and between ourselves, and an immunity guarantee at the end of it. Say hullo to Aggie.'

The tall girl had brought fresh tea.

'Hi,' said Oliver.

'Hi,' said Aggie.

'What's he got to remember?' Oliver asked when she was out of earshot.

'I've forgotten,' said Brock. But he added, 'He'll know. So will you. I want the Hydra. I want those less-than-perfect coppers and overpaid white-collar civil servants who signed up with him for their second pensions. The bent MPs and silk-shirt lawyers and dirty traders with smart addresses. Not abroad. Abroad can look after itself. In England. Up and down the road. Next door.' Oliver released his knees, then promptly rearrested them, locking his fingers round them while he stared into the grass as if it were his grave. 'Tiger's your Everest, Oliver. You'll not climb him by walking away from him,' said Brock piously, extracting from his inner pocket a worn leather wallet that his wife Lily had given him for his thirtieth birthday. 'Ever seen this fellow on your travels?' he enquired lightly. And he handed Oliver a black-and-white photograph of a heavy-built, naked-headed man emerging from a nightclub with an under-dressed young woman on his arm. 'Old chum of your dad's from Liverpool days. Currently a very senior bent officer at Scotland Yard with excellent connections across the country.'

'Why doesn't he wear a wig?' said Oliver facetiously.

'Because he's bloody brazen,' Brock retorted savagely. 'Because he does in public what other villains wouldn't do in private. That's how he gets his kicks. What's his name, Oliver? You've clocked him, I can tell.'

'Bernard,' said Oliver, handing back the photograph.

'Bernard is correct. Bernard who?'

'Not given. He came to Curzon Street a couple of times. Tiger brought him down to Legal Department and we fixed him up with a villa in the Algarve.'

'For his holiday?'

'As a gift.'

'You're bloody joking. What for?'

'How should I know? My job was to do the conveyancing. It was got up as a sale at first. We were poised to exchange, then Alfie said there's no money involved, just shut up and sign it over. So I shut up and signed it over.'

'So it's Bernard.'

'Bernard the bald,' Oliver agreed. 'He got lunch afterwards too.'

'At Kat's Cradle?'

'Where else?'

'It's not like you to forget a surname, is it?'

'He didn't have one. He's Bernard, an offshore company.'

'Called what?'

'It wasn't a company, it was a foundation. The foundation owned the company. Arm's length, then another arm.'

'A foundation called what?'

'Dervish, domiciled in Vaduz. The Dervish Foundation. Tiger made a funny joke about it. "Meet Bernard, our whirling dervish." Bernard owns Dervish, Dervish owns the company, the company owns the house.'

'So what was the name of the company owned by the Dervish Foundation?'

'Something flighty. Skylight, Skylark, Skyflier.'

'Skyblue?'

'Skyblue Holdings, Antigua.'

'Then why the hell didn't you tell me at the time?'

'Because you never bloody well asked me,' Oliver came back just as angrily. 'If you'd asked me to look out for Bernard, I'd have looked out for Bernard.'

'Did Single's make a point of doling out free villas?'

'Not that I'm aware of.'

'Did anybody else get a free villa, apart from Bernard?'

'No, but Bernard got a motorboat as well. One of those super-light, long-nosed jobs. We had a joke about not rocking it too hard if he was obliging a lady on the high seas.'

'Whose joke was that?'

'Winser's. Now if you'll excuse me, I'm going to practise.'

Watched by Brock, Oliver stretched, ruffled his head with both hands as if his scalp were itching, and ambled off towards the house.

CHAPTER SEVEN

'Oliver! Step up here, please. Certain very distinguished gentlemen would like to meet you. New clients brimming with new ideas. Just up your street. At the double, if you please.'

It is not Elsie Watmore calling Oliver to arms but Tiger himself on the internal office telephone. It is not Pam Hawsley our fifty-thousand-a-year Ice Maiden, nor Randy Massingham our Chief of Staff and raddled Cassius. It is The Man, live on stage, impersonating the Voice of Destiny. The season is spring, as now, five years ago. And it is spring-time in the young life of our budding junior-and-only part-ner fresh from law school, our Czarevitch, our Heir Apparent to the Royal House of Single. Oliver has been in Single's three months. It is his promised land, his hard-won goal after the buffetings of a privileged English education. Whatever humiliations and deprivals he has suffered until now, whatever scars have been inflicted by a seemingly interminable procession of crammers, tutors and boarding schools of a descending order, he has reached the distant shore, a qualified barrister like his father, a mover and a shaker designate, brimming with the zeal of his young years, wet-eyed, in love with all of it.

And there is much to fire him. The Single's of the early nineties is not just another venture capital investment house, witness the financial columns: Single's is the 'Knight Errant of Gorbachev's New East' – *Financial Times* – 'boldly going where lesser houses dither'. Single's is the 'risk-taker extraordinaire' – *Telegraph* – 'quartering the nations of the new-look Communist bloc in search of opportunity, sound development and mutual profit in the spirit of perestroika' – *Independent*. Single's, to quote its dynamic founder aptly dubbed the Tiger, is 'willing to listen to anyone, any time, anywhere,' in its determination to meet the 'Greatest Challenge to the Commercial World Today'. Tiger is speaking of nothing less than the 'appearance of a market-orientated Soviet Union'. Single's uses 'a different set of tools, is nimbler, braver, smaller, younger, travels lighter' than the hoary juggernauts of yesteryear – *Economist*. And if there are those who say that Oliver should have been packed off to Kleinwort, Chase or Barings to brown his knees, Tiger has a word for them also: 'We're a pioneering house. We want the best of him, and we want it now.'

What Oliver wants of Single's is no less admirable. 'Working alongside my father will be an added dividend for me,' he explains to a sympathetic woman diarist from the *Evening Standard* at a rooftop reception in Park Lane to celebrate his induction into the firm. 'Dad and I have always had the greatest respect for each other. It's going to be a fantastic learning curve in every way.' Asked what he thinks he will be bringing to Single's, the young scion shows he too is not afraid to talk from the hip: 'Unashamed idealism with its head screwed on,' he replies, to her delight. 'The emerging Socialist nations need all the help, knowhow and finance we can bring to the table.' To the *Tatler* he cites yet another Single verity: 'We're offering solid long-term partnership without exploitation. Anybody hoping to make a fast rouble will be disappointed.'

*   *   *

A war party, Oliver thinks excitedly as he enters the presence. He asks nothing better. After three months of devilling in the backwaters of Alfred Winser's Legal Department he is beginning to have fears of stagnation. His professed intention of 'learning the workings of every nut and bolt in the house' has landed him in a labyrinth of offshore companies from which there seems no prospect of escape in one zealous young man's lifetime. But today Winser is in Bedfordshire buying a Malaysian glove factory, and Oliver is his own master. A dingy back staircase leads from Legal Department to the top floor. Likening it in his imagination to a secret passage in the days of the Medicis, Oliver takes it three steps at a time. Weightless, eyeless for everything but his goal, he skims through secretarial anterooms and panelled waiting rooms until he attains the famous Wedgwood double doors. He opens them and for a second the divine glow is too bright for him.

'You called, Father,' he murmurs, seeing nothing but his own smile mysteriously projected on the brilliance ahead of him.

The light clears. Six men await him and they are standing, which is not what Tiger likes, given he was born eight inches shorter than most of his opponents. They are a group photograph and Oliver is the camera, and they might as well be saying 'cheese' to order because all of them are smiling simultaneously, having apparently just risen from the conference table. But Tiger's smile is as usual the most radiant and energetic. It bestows a glow of saintly purpose over the unlikely company. Oliver loves this smile. It is the sun from which he draws his strength to grow. All through his childhood he has believed that if he can once wriggle past its rays and peek behind the doting eyes he will attain to the magic kingdom of which his father is benign and absolute ruler. *It's the Orlov brothers!* he exclaims silently in a tidal wave of excitement and anticipation. *In the flesh! Randy Massingham has hooked them at last!* For days now, Tiger has been telling Oliver to stand by, wait for orders, keep his engagement book clear, be sure to wear a decent suit. But only now has he unveiled the reason.

Tiger as team captain holds centre stage. In his latest double-breasted blue pinstripe suit by Hayward of Mount Street, his raised black brogue shoes by Lobb of St James's and haircut by Trumper's down the road, he is your perfect West End gentleman rendered in exquisite miniature, a jewel, a sparkler in the window, drawing every passing eye. Striving upward as ever, Tiger has one arm round the shoulders of a barrel-built military-looking man of sixty-plus with a cherub's double eyelashes, cropped brown hair and pumice-stone complexion. And though Oliver has never met him in his life, he recognises immediately the fabled Yevgeny Orlov, Moscow's patriarchal fixer, power broker, travelling plenipotentiary and cupbearer to the Throne of Power itself.

To Tiger's other side but free of his embrace stands a moustachioed, bandy-legged, fierce-eyed figure in a Bible-black suit that fits him nowhere, and pointed orange-coloured shoes perforated for ventilation. With his tribesman's mute glower and slouched shoulders, and his wintery hands hanging forward of him, he resembles an emaciated Cossack slumped over a slack rein. With a second leap of recognition Oliver identifies this unlikely soul as Yevgeny's younger brother Mikhail, described variously by Massingham as Yevgeny's keeper, axeman and dimmer brother Mycroft.

And posed possessively behind this trio, and looking as if he has joined them together in holy matrimony, which in effect he has, hovers Tiger's indefatigable Soviet Bloc consultant and Chief of Staff, the Honourable Ranulf alias Randy Massingham himself, lately of the Foreign Office, ex-Guardsman, ex-lobbyist and public relations whizzkid, Russian-speaker, Arabic-speaker, sometime adviser to the governments of Kuwait and Bahrain, whose primary remit in his most recent incarnation at Single's consists of whipping in new clients for a finder's fee. How one man can have had so many careers by the age of forty is a riddle Oliver has yet to solve. Nevertheless he envies Massingham his buccaneering past and today he envies him also his success, because for months now, Tiger has had the Orlov brothers obsessively and irrationally in his sights. At in-house policy conferences and focus sessions, Tiger has alternately poured scorn on Massingham, goaded and cajoled him: 'Where are my Orlovs, Randy, Heavens above? Why do I have to put up with second best?' – referring to other, inferior Russian facilitators who have been found wanting and unceremoniously tossed aside – 'If the Orlovs are the boys, why aren't they sitting here at this table talking to me?' – and then the whiplash, because when Tiger is deprived, everybody must share his discomfort – 'You're looking old, Randy. Take the day off. Come in on Monday when you're younger.'

But today, as Oliver sees at a glance, sitting at Tiger's table is exactly what the Orlovs have been doing. No longer need Massingham champ restively, waiting in vain for the summons, to fly off to Leningrad, Moscow, Tbilisi, Odessa, or wherever else the Orlovs have their itinerant being. Today the Twin Peaks have come to Mohammed, and they are accompanied – Oliver spots them immediately at either wing of the group photograph – by two men whom he correctly casts as bag-carriers: the one blond, hard-bodied and milky-skinned and Oliver's age at most, the other tubby and fifty with all three buttons of his jacket fastened.

And cigar smoke, palls of it! Improbable, impossible cigar smoke! And unfamiliar ashtrays on the conference table amid the strewn papers! To Oliver nothing in the room, not even the Orlov brothers, is as momentous as this hated, banned-to-all-eternity cigar smoke coiling through the rarefied air of the sanctum, forming itself into a mushroom-shaped cloud above the groomed head of 'Tobacco's Bitterest Foe' – *Vogue*. Tiger abominates smoking more than failure or contradiction. Each year before accounting day he donates ostentatious sums of taxable income to its banishment. Yet today on the sideboard resides a brand new silver-bound humidor by Asprey of New Bond Street containing the Most Expensive Cigars in the Universe. Yevgeny is smoking one, so is the bag-carrier with three buttons. Nothing else could have driven home to Oliver so effectively the unprecedented significance of the occasion.

Tiger's opening shot is teasing, but Oliver sees teasing as an indivisible part of his relationship with his father. If you stand five feet three in your Lobb's raised heels, and if your son is six feet three, it is only natural that you should wish to bring him down to scale in front of others – and only meet, right and Oliver's bounden duty that he should collaborate in his reduction.

'Good Heavens above, what kept you, son?' Tiger protests in a mock-serious tone put on for the company. 'Out on the town last night, I suppose. Who is she this time? I hope she's not going to cost me a fortune!'

Oliver shares the joke like the good sport he is. 'She's rather rich, actually, Father – mountainously so, in fact.'

'Is she, by God? Is she? Well, that's a change, I'll say! Perhaps this time the old man will get his money back. What?'

And with the *what*, a slippy glance to Yevgeny Orlov at his side – accompanied by a lifting and resettling of the little fist that rests daringly on Yevgeny's massive shoulder – telling him, with Oliver's connivance, that the young shaver here lives the wastrel's life these days, thanks to the munificence of his indulgent dad. But Oliver is used to this. He is practised from childhood in such scenes. If Tiger had demanded it of him, he would have done his passable imitation of Margaret Thatcher, or Humphrey Bogart in *Casablanca*, or told his funny story about the two Russians peeing in the snow. But Tiger does not demand it, or not this morning, so Oliver instead grins and shoves his hair back while Tiger belatedly introduces him to the guests.

'Oliver, allow me to present to you one of the most brilliant, fearless, far-sighted pioneers of the new Russia, a gentleman who like myself has fought life with his bare knuckles and won. They don't make many like us any more, I'm afraid –' pausing so that Randy Massingham, from his place behind them, can put this into ex-Foreign Office Russian – 'Oliver, I want you to meet Mr Yevgeny Ivanovich Orlov and his distinguished brother Mikhail. Yevgeny, this is my son, Oliver, in whom I am fairly well pleased, a man of law, a man of stature, as you see, a man of learning and intellect, a man of the future. A lousy athlete, it's true. A hopeless horseman, dances like an ox' – a lifting of the film star brows signals the familiar punchline – 'but *couples*, rumour has it, like a warrior!' Gusts of jolly laughter from Massingham and the bag-carriers suggest to Oliver that the sub-

108

ject has been aired ahead of his appearance. 'A bit short on other forms of experience, perhaps, a bit long on ethical concerns – weren't we all at his age? But a first-rate academic lawyer, well able to represent our Legal Department during the absence abroad of our revered colleague Dr Alfred Winser.' Bedfordshire is *abroad?* Oliver wonders, amused as always by Tiger's little licences. Winser a *doctor* suddenly? 'Oliver, I want you to listen extremely carefully to a summation of our morning's work. Yevgeny has come to us with three very vital, very creative and original proposals which reflect – very accurately and positively, I believe – the turning of the tide in Mr Gorbachev's new Russia.'

But first the handshakes with assorted centres. Yevgeny's cushioned fist wrestles Oliver's untested palm while the cherubic double eyelashes sparkle an impish smile. Next come Brother Mikhail's four craggy fingers and thumb. Then a spongy dab from the priestly cigar-smoker with three fastened jacket-buttons. His name it transpires is Shalva and he hails from Tbilisi in Georgia and like Oliver is a lawyer. It is the first time that the word *Georgia* is spoken, but Oliver, whose ears and eyes are open to every breeze today, at once records its significance: Georgia, and a perceptible pulling back of shoulders; Georgia, and a quickening of glances as loyal troops rally to the call.

'You have been to Georgia, Mr Oliver?' Shalva asks in the wistful tones of a true believer.

'I'm afraid not,' Oliver confesses. 'I hear it's very beautiful.'

'Georgia is very beautiful,' Shalva confirms with the authority of the pulpit. But it is Yevgeny who echoes this, in English, between long horse-like nods. '*Georgia very beautiful,*' he roars, and the egregious Mikhail nods also, in holy confirmation of his faith.

And finally a pre-fight touch of gloves with Oliver's pallid contemporary Mr Alix Hoban, of whom no description is provided, Georgian or otherwise. And there is something about this Hoban that disturbs Oliver and obliges him to place him in a separate compartment of his mind. Something cold and faithless and impatient and violent in retaliation. Something that says: *If you step on my foot just one more time...* But these thoughts are for later. With Oliver now part of the company, Tiger's snappy little hands signal everybody to sit – no longer at the conference table, but in the green leather Regency loungers reserved for the consideration of what he has called Yevgeny's three very creative and original proposals reflecting the turning of the Soviet tide. And since the Orlovs possess no English – or none today – and since Massingham is not a member of their team but Tiger's, they are presented by the unexplained Mr Alix Hoban. His voice is not at all what Oliver expects. It is neither Moscow nor Philadelphia, but a botch of both cultures. Its serrated edge is so penetrating that it seems to be wired to an amplifier. He speaks, you would suppose, at the behest of someone powerful – and no doubt he does – in brusque, pared sentences to take or leave. Only occasionally something of himself flashes like a drawn dagger at the feast.

'Mr Yevgeny and Mr Mikhail Orlov enjoy many excellent contacts in the Soviet Union. Okay?' he begins, contemptuously addressing Oliver as the newcomer. The 'okay' requires no answer. He sails straight on. 'Through his experiences in the military – and in the government service – through his connections with Georgia also – and certain other connections – Mr Yevgeny has the ear of the highest level in the land. He is therefore uniquely positioned to facilitate implementation of three specific proposals subject to appropriate commissions payable outside Soviet Union. Got it?' he asks sharply. Oliver gets it. 'These commissions are the result of prior negotiation at the highest level in the land. They are a given. You get my drift?'

Oliver gets his drift. After three months in the House of Single, he is aware that the highest level in the land does not come cheap. 'Commissions in what sort of order, actually?' he asks, parading a sophistication he does not feel.

Hoban has the answer at the fingertips of his left hand, which he grabs one by one. 'One half payable in advance of implementation of each proposal. Top-up payments at agreed intervals, contingent on the subsequent success of each proposal. Basis of computation, five per cent first billion, three per cent all future monies, non-negotiable.'

'And we're talking US dollars,' says Oliver, determined not to sound impressed by billions.

'You think we talk lira?'

A gust of rich laughter from the Orlov brothers and Shalva the lawyer as Massingham interposes himself to translate this witticism into Russian for their benefit, and Hoban directs his pseudo-American to what he calls Specific Proposal Number One.

'Soviet State property can only be disposed of by State, got it? Is axiomatic. Question. Who *owns* today the State property of the Soviet Union?'

'The Soviet State. Obviously,' says Oliver, top of the class.

'Second question. Who disposes today of Soviet State property in accordance with new economic policy?'

'The Soviet State does' – by now seriously disliking Hoban.

'Third question. Who *empowers* today disposal of State property? Okay, answer, the new Soviet State. Only new State can sell old State's property. It's axiomatic,' he repeats, liking the word. 'Got it?'

And here, to Oliver's bemusement, Hoban takes out a platinum cigarette case and lighter, extracts a fat yellow cigarette that looks as though he has been storing it since his recent childhood, closes the case and raps the cigarette on the lid to pacify it before adding billows of noxious fumes to the existing pall.

'The Soviet economy of the last decades was *command* economy, okay?' Hoban resumes. 'All machineries, plant, armaments, power stations, pipelines, railway lines, rolling stock, locomotives, turbines, generators, printing presses, all belong to State. They can be *old* State materials, they can be *very* old, no one gives a shit. Soviet Union of past decades was not interested to recycle. Yevgeny Ivanovich is in possession of blue chip estimates of these materials composed at highest level in the land. According to these estimates, he is calculating present availability of one billion tons good quality scrap ferrous metals for collection and disposal to interested buyers. All over world you got a keen demand for these metals. Follow me?'

'Particularly in South-East Asia,' Oliver puts in brightly, for he has been reading a recent technical journal on this very subject.

And saying this he catches Yevgeny's eye, as he has done several times already during Hoban's peroration, and is struck by the dependence of his stare. It is as if this old man feels ill-at-ease in his surroundings and is transmitting messages of complicity to Oliver the fellow newcomer.

'In South-East Asia, demand for high-quality scrap metals is very great,' Hoban concedes. 'Maybe we shall sell to South-East Asia. Maybe this is convenient. Right now, no one gives a fuck.' With an alarming snort Hoban clears his nose and throat simultaneously, before delivering himself of an interminable prefabricated sentence: 'Up-front investment for specific proposal regarding scrap metals will be twenty million dollars cash down-payment immediately on signature of State contract awarding to Yevgeny Ivanovich's nominee exclusive licence to collect and dispose of all scrap metals in former Soviet Union regardless of location and condition. That's a given. No messing.'

Oliver's head is reeling. He has heard of such commissions but only at second-hand. 'But who is the nominee?' he asks.

'To be determined. Nominee is irrelevant. He will be chosen by Yevgeny Ivanovich. He will be *our* nominee.'

Tiger from his throne issues a sharp warning: 'Oliver. Don't be obtuse.'

Hoban again: 'The twenty million dollars cash will be lodged in an agreed Western bank and released by telephone simultaneous to signature. Nominee must also bear cost of collection and assembly of scrap metals. Also necessary will be rental or purchase of seaport yard, forty hectares minimum. That's another overhead for the nominee. It will be necessary for him to purchase this yard privately. Yevgeny Ivanovich's organisation has contacts who can assist nominee to purchase yard.' Oliver suspects that this organisation is Hoban himself. 'Soviet State cannot provide cutting and shearing equipment. That's also for the nominee. If the State has such equipment, it's certain to be shit. Throw it on the scrap heap.'

Hoban's lips part in an ill-humoured smile as he puts down one paper and takes up another. The pause spawns another silky interpolation from Tiger.

'If we *do* have to purchase a yard, we must reckon on a few beads for the local chieftains, obviously. I think Randy made this point earlier, didn't you, Randy? Never does to get on the wrong side of the boys on the spot.'

'It's factored in,' Hoban replied indifferently. 'It's immaterial. All such matters will be resolved pragmatically by House of Single, in combination with Yevgeny Ivanovich and his organisation.'

'So *we're* the nominee!' Oliver cries, shrewdly cottoning on.

'Oliver. How very brilliant of you,' Tiger murmurs.

Hoban's Specific Proposal Number Two is oil. Azerbaijani oil, Caucasus oil, Caspian oil, Kazakhstani oil. More oil, says Hoban carelessly, than is to be found in the whole of Kuwait and Iran put together.

'The new Klondike,' Massingham purrs supportively from the wings.

This oil also is State property, Hoban explains. Okay? Many suitors have approached the highest level in the land for concessions, he says, and interesting proposals have been made regarding refinement, pipelines, dock facilities, transportation, sale to non-socialist countries and commission. No decision has been reached. 'The highest level in the land is keeping its powder dry. Got it?'

'Got it,' Oliver reports, military-style.

'In area Baku, old Soviet methods of extraction and refinement are still in place,' Hoban announces from his notes. 'These methods are complete crap. It has therefore been decided at the highest level that the interests of new Soviet market economy will be best served if responsibility for extraction is awarded to one international company.' He is holding up the index finger of his left hand in case Oliver can't count. 'One only. Okay?'

'Sure. Fine. Okay. One only.'

'Exclusive. Identity of this international company is delicate, is extremely political. This company must be a *good* company, sympathetic to needs of all Russia, also of Caucasus. It must be *expert* company. This company must have' – he speaks the words as if they are one – 'Proven-Pair-of-Hands. Not some Micky Mouse outfit from Yonkers.'

'The big battalions are simply *baying* to get their hands on it, Oliver,' Massingham explains insinuatingly. 'Chinese, Indians, the multis, Americans, Dutch, Brits, name them. Gumshoeing round the corridors, waving their chequebooks, handing out their hundred-dollar bills like confetti. It's a zoo.'

'It sounds it,' Oliver assures him keenly.

'Important for the selection of international company will be respect for many special interests of all peoples of the Caucasus region. This international company must be enjoying the confidence of such peoples. She must co-operate. She must enrich not just herself but them. She must accommodate the apparatchiks of Azerbaijan, Daghestan, Chechnya-Ingushetia, Armenia' – a glance for Yevgeny – 'She must make happy the nomenklatura of Georgia. The highest level in the land has very special relationship with Georgia, very special regard. In Moscow, goodwill of Republic of Georgia is maximum priority, ahead of all other republics. This is historical. This is axiomatic.' He consults his notes again before pronouncing the resonant cliché. 'Georgia is most precious stone in Soviet Union's crown. That's a given.'

To Oliver's surprise, Tiger hastens to confirm this. 'In *anybody's* crown, thank you, Alix,' he asserts. '*Marvellous* little country. Am I not right, Randy? Marvellous food, wine, fruit, language, beautiful women, incredible landscape, literature going back to the Flood. Nowhere like it in the world.'

Hoban ignores him. 'Yevgeny Ivanovich has lived many years in Georgia. Yevgeny and Mikhail Ivanovich were children in Georgia when their father was Red Army commandant in Senaki. They have from this time many friends in Georgia. Today these friends are very influential. The brothers spend much time in Georgia. They have *dacha* in Georgia. From Moscow, Yevgeny Ivanovich has diverted many important favours to his beloved Georgia. Therefore

114

he is most eligible to reconcile needs of the new Soviet Union with needs of the local community and traditions. His presence is a guarantee that interests of Caucasus will be respected. Okay?'

The beam is on Oliver again. The entire audience is sloped towards him, attentively observing his reactions.

'Okay,' he confirms dutifully.

'Therefore Moscow has made following informal dispositions. Disposition A. One licensee will be appointed by Moscow for all Caucasus oil. Disposition B. Yevgeny Ivanovich personally will nominate this licensee. It will be his personal decision. Disposition C. Tenders from competing oil companies will be formally and publicly solicited. *However.*' A huge suck of breath and cigarette smoke catches Oliver by surprise but he recovers. 'However, screw them. Informally and privately, Moscow will select whatever consortium is nominated by Yevgeny Ivanovich and his people. Disposition D. Terms for nominated consortium will be calculated on royalties of existing Azerbaijani oilfields on basis of average annual yield over last five years. With me?'

'With you.'

'Very important to remember is: Soviet extraction methods are horseshit. Lousy technology, lousy infrastructure, lousy transportation, shit-awful managers. Therefore calculated sum will be very modest in comparison with efficient extraction by modern Western methods. It will be based on history, not the future. It will be fraction of the future. This sum will be accepted by highest level in Moscow in full discharge of licence fee. Disposition E. All surplus revenue from future oil extraction will be property of Caucasus consortium nominated by Yevgeny Ivanovich and his organisation. Private and formal agreement will be granted on receipt of one-time payment of thirty million dollars advance commission. Public and formal agreement will follow automatically. Top-ups of original commission to be related to future actual earnings on informal basis. They will be negotiated.'

'Lucky old highest level in the land,' drawls Massingham, whose voice is permanently husky, as if he too were short of oil. 'Fifty mill for writing his name a couple of times, lovely fat top-ups to follow, not bad pickings, says I.'

Oliver's question pops out of him unbidden. Neither the surly tone nor the aggressive formulation is of his choosing. If he could un-ask it he would, but it's too late. Some half-familiar ghost has taken possession of him. It is what remains of his sense of legality after three months before the Single mast.

'Can I interrupt you here a second, Alix? Where does House of Single come into this exactly? Are we being asked to put up fifty million dollars of bribe money?'

Oliver has the feeling that he has let out a loud involuntary fart in church as the last strains of the organ die away. An incredulous silence fills the big room. The rumble of traffic in Curzon Street six floors below has ceased. It is Tiger who, as his father and senior partner, comes to his rescue. His tone is fond, congratulatory.

'A good point, Oliver, and courageously made, if I may say so. Not for the first time, I am moved to admire your integrity. House of Single does not bribe, of course. That's not what we do at all. If legitimate commissions are to be paid, they will be paid within the discretion of our correspondent in place – in this case our good friend Yevgeny – with due respect to the laws and traditions of the country in which that correspondent is operating. The details will be his concern, not ours. Obviously, if a correspondent is short of funds – not everybody can put their hands on fifty million dollars overnight – Single's will consider making a loan in order to enable him to exercise his local discretion. I think it's hugely important to make this point. And very right and proper of you, in your capacity as our legal counsellor today, to have made it. I thank you. We all do.' Massingham's hoarse 'Hear, hear' delivers the death-blow as Tiger slides smoothly into a plug for the great House of Single. 'Single's exists to say yes where others say no, Oliver. We bring vision. Knowhow. Energy. Resources. To wherever the spirit of true adventure leads. Yevgeny's not hypnotised by the old Iron Curtain – never were, were you, Yevgeny?' – out of the edge of his misted gaze, Oliver is aware of Yevgeny Orlov's cropped head shaking itself from side to side – 'He's a proxy Georgian. A lover of Georgia's beauty and culture. Georgia boasts some of the earliest Christian churches in the world. I don't expect you knew that, did you?'

'Not really.'

'He dreams of a Common Market of the Caucasus. So do I. A great new trading entity, based on fabulous natural resources. He's a pioneer, aren't you, Yevgeny? Like us. Of course he is. Randy, translate, please. Well done, Oliver. I'm proud of you. We all are.'

'Does the consortium have a name? Does it already exist?' Oliver asks while Massingham translates.

'No, Oliver, it does not,' Tiger retorts through his weatherproof smile. 'But if you will exercise a little patience I am sure it very soon will.'

Yet even while this distressing exchange goes back and forth – distressing for Oliver, if no one else – he finds himself being tugged almost by gravity in an unexpected direction. Everybody is peering at Oliver, but Yevgeny's wily old gaze is fixed to him like a ship's line, pulling at him, feeling his weight, guessing him – and guessing him, Oliver is convinced of it, correctly. Out of nothing, Yevgeny's goodwill is evident to him. Stranger still, Oliver feels he is taking part in a resumption of an old and natural friendship. He sees a small boy in Georgia in love with everything around him and the child is himself. He feels an unguarded gratitude for favours he has never consciously received. Meanwhile, Hoban is talking about blood.

Blood of all types. Common blood, uncommon, extremely rare. The shortfall between world demand and world supply. The blood of all nations. The cash value of blood, whole and retail, by category, in the medical marketplaces of Tokyo, Paris, Berlin, London and New York. How to test blood, separate good blood from bad. How to cool it, bottle it, freeze it, transport it, store it, dry it. The regulations covering its importation to the major industrialised countries of the West. Health and hygiene standards. Customs. Why is he doing this? Why is blood suddenly so attractive to him? Tiger hates blood as much as he hates smoking. It offends his notions of immortality and contradicts his passion for order. Oliver has known of this aversion all his life, sometimes seeing it as a sign of hidden sensitivity, sometimes despising it as weakness. The smallest cut, the least sight and smell of the stuff, the very mention of it, are enough to panic him. His chauffeur Gasson was nearly sacked for offering assistance at a gory accident while his master sat whey-faced in the back of the Rolls-Royce screaming at him to drive on, drive on, drive on. Yet today, judging him by his exultant expression as he listens to Hoban's droning delineation of Specific Proposal Number Three, blood is what he loves best in life. And this is blood in bucketfuls: free from the tap, thanks to generous-spirited Russian donors, ninety-nine dollars and ninety-five cents per pint retail to the American sufferer in need – and we are looking here at anything up to half a million pints a week, got it, Oliver? Hoban becomes a humanitarian. He does this by altering his voice to a reverential monotone, but also by a prudish pursing of the lips and lowering of the eyelids. The conflicts in Karabakh, Abkahzia and Tbilisi, he intones, have provided the Orlov brothers with a tragic insight into the shortcomings of Russia's run-down medical services. They do not doubt that there is worse to come. The Soviet Union possesses, alas, no national transfusion service, no programme for collecting and distributing blood to our many beleaguered capitals, none for storing it. The very notion of selling blood or buying it is foreign to finer Soviet feelings. Soviet citizens are accustomed to giving blood freely and spontaneously, in moments of particular empathy or patriotism, not – God forbid – on a commercial basis, says Hoban, in a voice now so anaemic that Oliver wonders whether he himself could do with a transfusion.

'For example, please, when Red Army is fighting at a certain front, an appeal is made over radio for donors. For example, in case of natural disaster, when whole village will stand in line to make this sacrifice. If crisis is big, Russian people will provide much blood. In new Russia will be many crisis. Also crisis can be created. It is axiomatic.' Where on earth is he going with this nonsense? Oliver wonders, but one glance round the room tells him that he is alone in his scepticism. Tiger wears a threatening smile that says, question me if you dare. Yevgeny and Mikhail are joined in prayer, their hands linked on their laps, heads down. Shalva listens with a dreamy look of reminiscence, Massingham with eyes prettily closed and elegant legs stretched towards the unlit fire. 'Policy decision has therefore been taken at highest level that national bloodbanks will immediately be established in all major cities of Soviet Union,' Hoban reports, sounding now less like a revivalist pastor than an adenoidal Radio Moscow news announcer on a chilly morning. And still Oliver doesn't catch on, even though everyone around him seems to know exactly where all this is leading.

'Great,' he murmurs defensively, conscious of their collective gaze. But no sooner has he uttered this than he finds himself exchanging stares across the circle with Yevgeny, who has tilted his head backward and to one side and, with his rock-like chin protruding, is quizzing Oliver from between the double fringes of his eyelashes.

'Consistent with state of national objective, all Republics of Soviet Union will be advised to establish separate blood facility in each designated city. This facility will contain at least' – Oliver's confusion about the project does not permit him accurately to receive the number – 'gallons of blood in each category. State funding will be available for this project, subject to certain compliances. State will also declare crisis. Also in spirit of reciprocity' – he raises one white finger demanding attention – 'each Republic will be ordered to send specified quantity of blood to central reserve bloodbank in Moscow. This is axiomatic. Any Republic not contributing specified quantity of blood to central reserve will not receive State funding.' Hoban waxes momentous, or as momentous as his misshapen voice allows: 'This central reserve will be known as Crisis Response Blood Reserve. It will be showpiece. It will be fine building. We shall select fine building. Maybe with flat roof for helicopter. In this building, paramedics will be on standby at all times to meet sudden demand that is beyond resources of local services, anywhere in Soviet Union. Example, an earthquake. Example, a major industrial accident. Example, rail crash or small war. Example, terrorist outrage by Chechnya. There will be television programme about this building. Newspaper articles. This building will be pride of all Soviet Union. Nobody will refuse to give to it, even when crisis is small, provided crisis is declared by highest level. You follow me, Oliver?'

'Of course I follow you. A child could,' Oliver blurts. But his confusion has been noticed by himself alone. Not even old Yevgeny, granite head propped in granite fist, has heard his cry.

'However,' Hoban declares – except that dropping his linguistic guard, he pronounces the initial H as hard G, which at any other time would have caused Oliver an inward grin – 'Gowever. It is already clear that operating costs of Crisis Response Blood Reserve are prohibitive to State. Soviet State has zero money. Soviet State must accept principles of market economy. So we have question for you, Oliver. How can Crisis Response Blood Reserve be financially self-supporting? How to achieve this? What is your personal specific proposal to highest level in the land, please?'

All their eyes scorching him, Tiger's scorching fiercest. Demanding his approval, his blessing, his complicity. Wanting him aboard complete with ethics and ideals. Oliver's face darkens under their collective heat. He shrugs, pulls a stubborn frown to no effect.

'Sell the surplus blood to the West, I suppose.'

'A little more volume, please, Oliver!' cries Tiger.

'I said sell the spare blood to the West' – resentfully – 'why not? It's a crop like any other. Blood, oil, old iron, what's the difference?'

To himself he sounds like someone bursting loose from his chains. But Hoban is already nodding in concurrence, Massingham is grinning like an idiot and Tiger is wearing his widest and most proprietorial smile of the day.

'An *astute* suggestion,' Hoban pronounces, pleased with his choice of adjective. 'We shall sell this blood. Officially but also secretly. Sales will be State secret, sanctioned in

120

writing at highest level in Moscow. Blood that is surplus to crisis will be transported daily by refrigerated Boeing 747 ex-Moscow Sheremetyevo airport to east coast of United States. All freight costs will be borne by contracting company.' He has a note of the terms and is consulting it as he speaks. 'Transportation will be conducted on extremely confidential basis, eliminating negative publicity. In Russia, we must not hear "They sell our Russian blood to victorious imperialists." In the States, it is not convenient to hear that American capitalists are bleeding poor nations literally. This would be counter-productive.' He licks a white fingertip and turns a page. 'Assuming mutual confidentiality can be observed, this contract also will be signed by highest in the land. Terms will be following. First term, Mr Yevgeny Ivanovich will appoint his own nominee, this will be his prerogative. Nominee can be foreigner, can be Westerner, can be American, who gives a shit? This nominee's company will not be registered in Moscow. It will be *foreign* company. Preferred will be Switzerland. Immediately on signature of contract between Soviet nominee of Mr Yevgeny Orlov, thirty million dollars in bearer bonds will be lodged at foreign bank, details will be arranged. Maybe you have suggestion for this bank?'

'Do indeed,' Tiger murmurs off stage.

'This thirty million dollars will be regarded as advance payment against down-the-line profits calculated at fifteen per cent of gross profit accruing to nominees of Mr Yevgeny Orlov. You like this, Oliver? You think it's pretty good business, I believe.'

Oliver likes it, hates it, thinks it is good business, disgusting business, not business at all but theft. But he has no time to set his revulsion into words. He lacks the age, the sureness, the address, the space.

'As you rightly say, Oliver, it's a crop like any other,' says Tiger.

'I suppose it is.'

'You sound worried. Don't be. You're among friends here. You're one of the team. Speak out.'

'I was thinking about testing and stuff,' Oliver grumbles.

'Good point. So you should. Last thing we need is a lot of do-gooders from the press telling us we're peddling tainted blood. So I'm pleased to tell you that testing, grading, selecting – all those problems – are no obstacle in these modern times. They add a few hours to shipment at most. They increase overheads, but the cost will obviously be factored in. Do it in flight is probably the answer. Save time and handling. We're looking into it. Anything else troubling you?'

'Well, there's the – well – the larger issue, I suppose.'

'Of what?'

'Well – you know – what Alix said – selling Russian blood to the rich West – capitalists living off the blood of peasants.'

'You're absolutely right again, and we'll have to watch it like hawks. The good news is, Yevgeny and his chums are as determined as we are to keep the whole thing under wraps. The bad news is, sooner or later everything leaks. Think positive, that's the trick. Hit back. Have your answers ready and slam them home.' He flings up one trim arm in the manner of a wayside preacher, and adds a tremor to his voice. ' "Better to trade blood than shed it! What finer symbol can there be of reconciliation and coexistence than a nation giving blood to its former enemy?" How's that?'

'They're not *giving* though, are they? – Well, the donors are, but that's different.'

'So would you rather we took their blood for nothing?'

'No, of course not.'

'Would you rather the Soviet Union had no national transfusion service?'

'No.'

'*We* don't know what Yevgeny's chums are doing with their commission – why should we? They could be building hospitals. Propping up an ailing health service. What could be more moral than that?'

Massingham provides what he calls the nutshell. 'Tot it all up, Ollie old lad, we're looking at an up-front sweetener of eighty mill for the three specific proposals,' he calculates with polished carelessness. 'My guess – top of my head, don't quote me – anybody asking eighty will round down to seventy-five. Even if you're the highest level in the land, seventy-five's a tidy sum. After that it's a question of who we invite to the table. Seen from this end we'll be handing out gold bars.'

* * *

Lunch at Kat's Cradle in South Audley Street, billed in the gossip columns as the private lunch club even you cannot afford. But Tiger can afford it. Tiger owns it, and owns Kat, and has owned her a little longer than Oliver is allowed to know. The weather is kind, the walk around the corner takes all of three minutes, Tiger and Yevgeny lead, Oliver and Mikhail make a second pair, the rest trail behind and Alix Hoban trails last, speaking soft Russian into a cellphone which, as Oliver is learning, is something Hoban likes to do a lot. They turn the corner, chauffeured Rolls-Royces wait like a mafia cortège along the kerbside, a closed, unmarked, black-painted front door opens as Tiger reaches for the bell. The famous round table in the bay is waiting for them, waiters in the palest sherry jackets push silver trolleys, fawn and murmur, a sprinkling of mistresses and lovers watch from the safety of their corners. Katrina, whose name the place bears, is puckish, stylish and ageless as a good mistress should be. She stands at Tiger's side, nudging her hip against his shoulder.

'No, Yevgeny, you're *not* having vodka today,' Tiger tells him down the table, 'he's having a Château Yquem with his foie gras, Kat, and a Château Palmer with his lamb, and a shoot-up of thousand-year-old Armagnac with his coffee, and no bloody vodka. I'll tame the Bear if it kills me. And shampoo cocktails while we wait.'

'So what's poor Mikhail getting?' Katrina protests, who with Massingham's connivance has mastered everybody's name ahead of their arrival. 'He looks as though he hasn't had a decent meal for years, don't you, darling?'

'Mikhail's a beef chap, bet he is,' Tiger insists while Massingham translates whatever of this he reckons appropriate. 'Tell him beef, Randy. And he's not to believe a word he reads in the newspapers. British beef's still best beef in the world. Same for Shalva. Alix, time to live a little. And put that phone away, please, Alix, rule of the house. Give him a lobster. Like lobster, Alix? How's the lobster, Kat?'

'And what's *Oliver* getting?' Kat asks, turning her sparkling ageless gaze on him, and leaving it there like a gift for him to play with as he pleases. 'Not enough,' she answers for him, to make him blush. Kat has never hidden the pleasure that she takes in Tiger's virile young son. Every time he walks into the Cradle she eyes him like an impossibly priced painting she would love to own.

Oliver is about to reply when the room explodes. Seating himself at the white piano, Yevgeny has fired off a wild prelude evoking mountains, rivers, forests, dance and – if Oliver is not mistaken – cavalry charges. In a trice Mikhail appears at the centre of the tiny dance floor, his hollowed, mystical gaze fixed upon the kitchen doors. Yevgeny starts to sing a peasant lament while Mikhail slowly swings his arms and provides a backing refrain. Spontaneously, Kat threads her arm through Mikhail's and mirrors his movements. Their song gallops up the mountain, touches the peak and mournfully descends. Indifferent to the astonished hush, the brothers resume their places at the table as Kat starts the applause.

'Was that Georgian?' Oliver asks Yevgeny shyly, through Massingham, when the clapping dies.

But Yevgeny, it turns out, has less need of an interpreter than he pretends. 'Not Georgian, Oliver. Mingrelian,' he says in a thick Russian growl that echoes all round the room. 'Mingrelian peoples are pure peoples. Other Georgians got so many invasions they don't know if their grandmothers was raped by Turks, Daghestanis or Persians. Mingrelians was smart peoples. They protect their valleys. Lock up their women. Get them pregnant first. Got brown hair, not black.'

The stately bustle of the room recovers. Tiger smoothly proposes a first toast. 'To our valleys, Yevgeny. Yours and ours. May they flourish. Separately but together. May they bring prosperity to you and your family. In partnership. In good faith.'

124

It is four o'clock. Father and son saunter arm-in-arm along the sunny pavement in the haze of after lunch while Massingham escorts the party back to the Savoy for a rest before the evening's festivities.

'Big chap for family, Yevgeny,' Tiger muses. 'As I am. As you are –' squeeze of the arm. 'The Georgians are thick as thieves in Moscow. Yevgeny's got them wired, not a door he can't open. Total charmer. Not an enemy in the world.' It is rare for father and son to touch each other for so long. Given their conflicting heights it is difficult to find a hold that works for both of them but this one does. 'Doesn't trust people much. Makes two of us. Doesn't trust *things*. Computers – phone – fax – says he only trusts what's in his head. And you.'

'*Me?*'

'The Orlovs are family men. Famous for it. They like fathers, brothers, sons. Send them your son, it's a pledge of good faith. That's why I bundled Winser off for the day. Time you moved into the spotlight where you belong.'

'But what about Massingham? They're his catch, aren't they?'

'The son's better. No skin off Randy's nose, and we'd all rather have him with us than against us.' Oliver makes to detach his arm but Tiger keeps it trapped. 'You can't blame them for being suspicious, the world they grew up in. Police state, everyone informing on everyone, firing squads – makes a chap secretive. The brothers did a spell in prison themselves, Randy tells me. Came out knowing half tomorrow's men. Better than Eton, by the sound of it. There'll be contracts to draw up, of course. Side agreements. Keep it simple, that's the message. Your basic legal English for foreigners. Yevgeny likes to understand what he's signing. You up to that?'

'I should think so.'

'He's green as a leaf about a lot of stuff, bound to be. You'll have to hand-feed him, teach him our Western ways. He hates lawyers and doesn't know banking from his elbow. Why should he, when they don't have banks?'

'No reason on earth,' Oliver replies obsequiously.

'Poor chaps have still got to learn the value of money. Privileges were the currency till now. If they played their cards right, they got everything they wanted – houses, food, schools, holidays, hospitals, cars – all privileges. Now they've got to buy the same treats with hard cash. Different ball game. Needs a different sort of player.' Oliver is smiling and there is music in his heart. 'So it's a deal?' Tiger proposes. 'You do his nuts and bolts, I'll handle the heavy stuff. Shouldn't be more than a year or so, max.'

'What happens after a year?'

Tiger laughs. A real, rare, amoral, happy, West End laugh, as he pulls his arm free of Oliver's and claps him affectionately on the shoulder. 'At twenty per cent of the gross?' – still laughing – 'What do you think's going to happen? A year from now, we'll have squeezed the old devil out of the loop.'

CHAPTER EIGHT

Oliver is in tethered flight.

If he has ever doubted the wisdom of entering his father's firm, the golden summer months of 1991 provide him with his answer. This is living. This is connecting. This is being one of the team on a scale he has only dreamed. When the Tiger leaps, the financial columnists like to say, lesser men stand clear. Now Tiger is leaping as never before. Dividing his executive staff into separate task forces, he appoints Massingham his Field Commander, Oil & Steel, which does not at all please Massingham who would prefer the lesser post of Blood. Like Tiger he has seen where the richest pickings lie, which is why Tiger has kept blood for himself. Twice, three times a month he is to be found in Washington, Philadelphia or New York, often with Oliver in attendance. With an awe tinged by apprehension Oliver looks on as his father dazzles senators, lobbyists and health officials with his persuasive powers. To listen to Tiger's pitch, you would hardly know the blood came from Russia at all. It is *European* – for does not Europe stretch from the Iberian peninsula to the Urals? – it is *Caucasian*, it is – more embarrassing still to Oliver's hard-surviving sensitivities – *white Caucasian*, it is *surplus to European requirements*. For the rest, he cannily confines himself to such uncontroversial issues as landing rights, grading, storage, customs exemptions, onward shipment and the establishment of a mobile staff of troubleshooters to oversee the operation. But if Russian blood is assured of a safe arrival, what of its departure?

'Time Yevgeny had a visit,' Tiger rules, and Oliver sets off in pursuit of his new hero.

Sheremetyevo airport, Moscow, 1991, on a perfect summer's afternoon, Oliver's first in Mother Russia. Faced with the arrival hall's sullen queues and scowling frontier guards, he succumbs to a moment's trepidation until he spots Yevgeny himself, accompanied by a squad of docile officials, wading towards him with shouts of pleasure. His huge arms lock round Oliver's back, his rough cheek presses against his own. A smell of garlic, then the taste of it, as the old man plonks a third traditional Russian kiss on Oliver's startled mouth. In a trice his passport is stamped, his luggage swept through a side door and Oliver and Yevgeny are reclining in the rear seat of a black Zil driven by none other than Yevgeny's brother Mikhail, dressed today not in a rumpled black suit, but knee-length boots, military breeches and a leather bomber jacket in which Oliver glimpses the hatched black butt of a family-sized automatic pistol. A police motorcycle rides ahead of them, two dark-haired men in a Volga follow.

'My children,' Yevgeny explains with a wink.

But Oliver knows he is not being literal, for Yevgeny to his grief has daughters and no sons. Oliver's hotel is a white wedding cake in the centre of town. He checks into it, they drive down broad, pitted streets past gigantic apartment blocks to a leafy suburb of half-hidden villas guarded by security cameras and uniformed police. Iron gates open before them, the escort peels away, they enter the gravel forecourt of an ivy-covered mansion teeming with yelling children, babushkas, cigarette smoke, ringing telephones, oversize televisions, a ping-pong table, everything in motion. Shalva the lawyer greets them in the hall. There is a blushing cousin called Olga who is 'Mr Yevgeny's personal assistant', there is a nephew called Igor who is fat and jolly, there is Yevgeny's benign and stately Georgian wife Tinatin and three – no, four – daughters, all full-bodied, married and a

128

little tired, and the prettiest and the most doomed is Zoya, whom Oliver with a kind of aching recognition takes instantly to his heart. Female neurosis is his nemesis. Add a trim waist, broad maternal hips, a large, inconsolable brown gaze and he is lost. She nurses a baby boy called Paul who shares her gravity. Their four eyes examine him with forlorn complicity.

'You are very beautiful,' Zoya declares, as sadly as if she were reporting a death. 'You have the beauty of irregularity. You are a poet?'

'Just a lawyer, I'm afraid.'

'The law is also a dream. You have come to buy our blood?'

'I've come to make you rich.'

'Welcome,' she intones with the profundity of a great tragédienne.

Oliver has brought documents for Yevgeny to sign and a personal sealed letter from Tiger, but – 'Not yet, not yet, first you will see my horse!' And of course he will! Yevgeny's horse is a brand-new BMW motorbike that stands pampered and glistening on a pink Oriental carpet at the centre of a drawing room. With his household crowding at the doorway – but Oliver sees mostly Zoya – Yevgeny kicks off his shoes, climbs onto the beast's back, lowers his rump onto the saddle and wraps his stockinged feet round the pedals while he revs the engine all the way up, then down again and shines out his delight from between matted eyelashes. 'You now, Oliver! You! You!'

Watched by an applauding audience the Heir Apparent to the House of Single hands Shalva his tailor-made jacket and silk tie and springs onto the saddle in Yevgeny's place; then demonstrates what a good chap he is by setting the building shuddering and rattling to its foundations. Zoya alone takes no pleasure in his performance. Frowning at this vision of ecological mayhem, she clutches Paul to her breast and keeps her hand protectively over his ear. She is straggle-haired and carelessly dressed and has the deep shoulders of a mother-courtesan. She is alone and lost in the big city of life, and Oliver has already appointed himself her policeman, protector and soul companion.

'In Russia we must ride fast in order to stand still,' she informs him as he reties his tie. 'It is normal.'

'And in England?' he asks with a laugh.

'You are not English. You were born in Siberia. Do not sell your blood.'

Yevgeny's office is a chapel of calm. It is a sweetly panelled annexe, roof high, perhaps formerly a stable. No sound from the villa penetrates. Sumptuous antique birchwood furniture glows with a golden-brown intensity. 'From St. Petersburg museum,' Yevgeny explains, caressing a great writing table with his palm. When the revolution came, the museum was sacked and the collection scattered across the Soviet Union. Yevgeny spent years tracking it down, he relates. Then he found an eighty-year-old ex-prisoner from Siberia to restore it. 'We are calling it *karelka*,' he says proudly. 'Was from Catherine the Great the favourite.' On the walls hang photographs of men that Oliver somehow knows are dead, and framed diplomas featuring ships at sea. Oliver and Yevgeny sit in Catherine the Great's armchairs under an Arthurian iron chandelier. With his hewn old face, gold-rimmed spectacles and Cuban cigar, Yevgeny is every man's good counsellor and powerful friend. Shalva the priestly lawyer smiles and puffs his cigarettes. Oliver has brought letters of agreement drafted by Winser and restored to plain English by himself. Massingham has provided Russian translations. From the end of the table Mikhail watches with the alertness of the deaf, his deep-sea eyes devouring words he cannot hear. Shalva addresses Yevgeny in Georgian. While he speaks the door closes, which surprises Oliver since it was not open. He glances round to see Alix Hoban standing inside the room like some beckoned henchman forbidden to advance until instructed. Yevgeny orders Shalva to be silent, removes his glasses and addresses Oliver.

'You trust me?' he demands.

'Yes.'

'Your father. He trusts me?'

'Of course.'

'Then we trust,' Yevgeny declares and, waving aside Shalva's objections, signs the documents and shoves them down the table to Mikhail to sign also. Shalva leaves his chair and stands at Mikhail's shoulder, indicating the place. Slowly, every letter a masterpiece, Mikhail laboriously carves his name. Hoban sidles forward, offering himself as witness. They sign in ink, while Oliver thinks blood.

In a flagstoned cellar with an open hearth, skewers of pork and lamb are roasting on a wood fire. Garlic mushrooms sizzle on hollowed bricks. Loaves of Georgian cheesebread are stacked on wooden plates. Oliver must call it khachapuri, says Tinatin, Yevgeny's wife. To drink there is sweet red wine that Yevgeny mysteriously proclaims to be home-made from Bethlehem. On the birchwood dining table plates of caviar, smoked sausage, spicy chicken legs, home-smoked sea trout, olives and almond cake are precariously heaped on top of each other till not a square inch of the lovingly polished surface can be seen. Yevgeny and Oliver have the head and tail of the table. Between them sit the big-chested daughters beside their taciturn husbands, all but Zoya, who languishes in becoming isolation with little Paul seated on her knee, spoon-feeding him as if he were ailing, and only rarely diverting the spoon to her own full, unpainted lips. But in Oliver's head her dark eyes are fixed eternally upon him, as are his own on her, and the child Paul is an extension of her ethereal solitude. Having cast her as Rembrandt model, then as Chekhov heroine, he is outraged to see her raise her head and frown in conjugal disapproval as Alix Hoban with his cellphone enters between a couple of hard-faced young men in suits, kisses her perfunctorily on the same shoulder on which Oliver, in his imagination, has this minute been planting his own impassioned kisses, pinches Paul's cheek so that the child snarls in pain, and dumps himself beside her while continuing his conversation on the cellphone.

'You have met my husband, Oliver?' Zoya asks.

'Of course. Several times.'

'I too,' she says enigmatically.

Down the length of the table Oliver and Yevgeny toast each other repeatedly. They have toasted Tiger, they have drunk to each other's families, their health, prosperity and, though these are still the days of Communism, the dead who are with God.

'You will call me Yevgeny, I will call you Post Boy!' Yevgeny roars. 'You mind I call you Post Boy?'

'Call me what you like, Yevgeny!'

'I am your friend. I am Yevgeny. You know what is meaning Yevgeny?'

'No.'

'Is meaning noble. Is meaning I am special people. You also are special people?'

'I would like to think so.'

Another roar. Silver-chased ram's horns are fetched and filled to the brim with home-made wine from Bethlehem.

'To special people! To Tiger and his son! We love you! You love us?'

'Very much.'

Oliver and the brothers toast their friendship by draining their horns at a draught, then turning them upside down to prove they are empty.

'Now you are true Mingrelian!' Yevgeny announces and Oliver once more feels Zoya's reproachful gaze fixed upon him. But this time Hoban is observing it, which perhaps is what she wants, for he lets out a coarse laugh and says something to her between his teeth in Russian which causes her to laugh scathingly in return.

'My husband is overjoyed that you have come to Moscow to assist us,' she explains. 'He likes very much blood. It is his métier. You say métier?'

'Not really.'

Late-night drunken billiards in the basement. Mikhail is coach and umpire, masterminding Yevgeny's shots. Shalva watches from one corner, from another the supercilious gaze of Hoban covers every move of the game while he burbles into his cellphone. Who does he talk to in such caressing terms? His mistress? His stockbroker? Oliver thinks not. He has a picture of men in shadow like Hoban himself, in dark doorways and dark clothes, waiting for their master's voice. The brass-bound cues have no tips. The yellowed balls barely fit the deeply angled pockets. The table slopes, the cloth is ripped and stretched from previous revelries, the cushions clank when struck. Whenever a player succeeds in potting a ball, which is rare, Mikhail bellows the score in Georgian and Hoban disdainfully puts it into English. When Yevgeny misses a shot, which is often, Mikhail gives vent to an oil-rich Caucasian oath against the ball, the table or the cushion, but never against the brother he adores. But Hoban's contempt grows with each demonstration of his father-in-law's incompetence: the intake of breath like a wince of pain suppressed, the ghostly sneer of the hairline lips as they continue talking into the cellphone. Tinatin appears and, with a grace that melts Oliver's heart, leads Yevgeny off to bed. A driver waits to take Oliver back to his hotel. Shalva escorts him to the Zil. About to climb into it, Oliver looks back fondly at the house and sees Zoya, childless and topless, gazing down at him from an upper window.

Next morning under a half-cloudy sky Yevgeny takes Oliver to meet some good Georgians. With Mikhail at the wheel they drive from one grey barracks to another. In the first they are marched down a mediaeval corridor smelling of old iron, or is it blood? In the next they are embraced and plied with sweet coffee by a lizard-eyed, seventy-year-old relic of the Brezhnev time who guards his great black desk as if it were a war memorial.

'You are Tiger's son?'

'Yes, sir.'

'How come such a little guy makes such big kids?'

'I hear he's got a formula, sir.'

Huge laughter.

'You know his handicap these days?'

'Twelve, they tell me.' They have told him no such thing.

'Tell him Dato is eleven. He will go crazy.'

'I'll tell him.'

'Formula! That's good!'

And the envelope that is never spoken of: the grey-blue, war-quality, foolscap-sized envelope that Yevgeny conjures from his briefcase and slides across the desk while jollier matters are aired. And Dato's oily downward glance that records the envelope's passage while refusing to acknowledge it. What does it contain? Copies of the agreement that Yevgeny signed the day before? It is too thick. A wad of money? It is too thin. And what is this place? The Ministry of Blood? And who is Dato?

'Dato is from Mingrelia,' Yevgeny declares with satisfaction.

In the car Mikhail slowly turns the pages of a pirated American comic. A doubt springs to Oliver's mind and his face does not disguise it quickly enough: *can Mikhail read?*

'Mikhail is genius,' Yevgeny growls, exactly as if Oliver had asked the question aloud.

They enter a penthouse of groomed women secretaries, like Tiger's but prettier, and rows of computers showing the stock markets of the world. They are welcomed by a svelte young man called Ivan in an Italian suit. Yevgeny hands Ivan an envelope like the last.

'So how are things in the old country these days?' Ivan enquires in a blasé remake of Oxford English from the thirties. A beautiful girl sets a tray of Campari sodas on a rosewood sideboard that looked as if it too had once resided in a St. Petersburg museum. 'Chin-chin,' says Ivan.

They are wafted to a Western-style hotel a stone's throw from Red Square. Plainclothes men guard the swing doors, pink-stained fountains play in the lobby, the lift is lit by a crystal chandelier. On the second floor, women croupiers in low-cut dresses eye them from empty roulette tables. At a door marked 222, Yevgeny presses a bell. It is answered by Hoban. In a circular drawing room filled with cigarette smoke, a bearded, bitter-faced man of thirty called Stepan sits in a gilded chair. A gilded sofa-table stands before him. Yevgeny sets his briefcase on it. Hoban watches, as he watches everything.

'Does Massingham have the fucking Jumbos yet?' Stepan asks Oliver.

'My understanding when I left London was that we're all set to go as soon as you're ready this end,' Oliver replies stiffly.

'You the son of the British Ambassador or some fucking thing?'

Yevgeny addresses Stepan in Georgian. His tone is admonishing and firm. Stepan rises reluctantly to his feet and extends his hand.

'Nice meeting you, Oliver. We are blood brothers, okay?'

'Okay,' Oliver agrees. A huge sick laugh that Oliver does not enjoy echoes in his ears all the way back to his hotel.

'Next time you come, we take you to Bethlehem,' Yevgeny promises as they once more hug each other.

Oliver goes up to his room to pack. A parcel wrapped in brown cloth-paper lies on his pillow, together with an envelope. He opens the envelope. The letter is set out like a handwriting test, and Oliver has the feeling it was written several times before an acceptable version was achieved.

> Oliver, you have pure heart. Unfortunately, you
> are pretending everything. Therefore you are noth-
> ing. I love you. Zoya.

He opens the parcel. It contains a black lacquered box of a sort on offer in every tourist trap. Inside it is a heart, cut from apricot-coloured tissue paper. No blood adheres to it.

*   *   *

To go to Bethlehem it is necessary to be whisked off your British Airways plane as soon as it has taxied to a halt at Sheremetyevo, processed at breakneck speed by yet another squad of compliant immigration officers, and transferred to a twin-engined Ilyushin with Aeroflot markings but no unfamiliar passengers, which is waiting impatiently to fly you to Tbilisi in Georgia. All Yevgeny's extended family is aboard and Oliver salutes them *en bloc*, embracing the nearest and waving to the more distant, and in the case of Zoya who is the most distant of all – being seated in the furthest corner of the fuselage with Paul while her husband sits up front with Shalva – bestowing on her a vapid half-familiar wave implying that, well, yes, now he comes to think of it, why of course, he does indeed recognise her.

At Tbilisi you are likely to arrive in a scalding hurricane that causes the wings to rock, and flings grit and smuts at you as you dash for the cover of the terminal. Otherwise, there are no formalities, unless you count half the worthy men of the city in their best suits, and a shiny albino fixer called Temur who, like everyone in Georgia, is Tinatin's cousin, nephew, godchild or the son of her closest friend at school. Coffee and brandy and a pyramid of food await you in the VIP lounge, toasts are drunk and redrunk before you can proceed. A convoy of black Zils, motorcycle outriders and a chase truck with special troops in black uniforms then spirits you at hectic speed without benefit of safety belts westward over a giddy mountain range towards the promised land of Mingrelia whose inhabitants had the wit to make their womenfolk pregnant ahead of the invader and can therefore boast the purest blood in Georgia, a claim Yevgeny happily repeats as the Zil careers over snake roads and zigzags between stray dogs, sheep, piebald pigs with triangular wooden collars, pack mules, oncoming lorries and enormous potholes. All this in a mood of childlike euphoria enhanced by frequent draughts of wine and Oliver's duty-free malt whisky, but also by the knowledge that, after months of manoeuvring, the three Specific Proposals will be signed, paid for and delivered any time within the next few days. And is this not Yevgeny's personal protectorate, the home of his youth? Does not every landmark on the perilous road to Bethlehem call for the region's perfections to be highlighted, shared and marvelled at by Yevgeny's wife Tinatin and his brother Mikhail at the wheel, and above all by Oliver himself, the sacred guest to whom everything is new?

Behind them in another car ride two of Yevgeny's daughters and one of them is Zoya, and Paul is sitting on her lap, and Zoya has her hands linked round him and her cheek against his cheek as their car bumps and swings and follows. And even with the back of his head, Oliver knows that her melancholia is for him alone, he should not have come, he should have left this work, he is pretending everything and therefore he is nothing. But her all-seeing eye cannot mar his pleasure in Yevgeny's joyous alchemy. Russia never deserved Georgia, Yevgeny insists, speaking partly his own brand of English, and partly through Hoban, who crouches spikily between Oliver and Tinatin on the back seat: every time Christian Georgia sought Russia's protection from the Muslim hordes, Russia stole her wealth and dropped her in the mire...

But this homily is interrupted by another as Yevgeny must point out the hilltop forts, and the road to Gori which boasts the accursed hovel where Joseph Stalin made his entry to the world, and the cathedral that, to believe Yevgeny, is as old as Christ himself, where Georgia's earliest kings were crowned. They pass houses with fretted balconies tottering at the edge of a great gorge, and an iron scaffold like a belltower that marks a rich boy's grave. This rich boy was an alcoholic, Yevgeny recounts earnestly through Hoban, embarking on some kind of morality tale. When the rich boy's mother came to remonstrate with him, the boy blew out his brains in front of her with a revolver, and Yevgeny's own fingers are at his temple to show how. The father, a businessman, was so stricken with grief that he had the boy's body interred in a four-ton vat of honey so that he would never decompose.

'*Honey?*' Oliver repeats incredulously.

'For preserving corpses, honey is pretty fucking good,' Hoban replies drily. 'Ask Zoya, she's a chemist. Maybe she'll preserve your corpse for you.' They drive in silence till the scaffold disappears. Hoban makes a call on his portable telephone. It is of a different breed, Oliver observes, to the type he favours in Moscow or London. It is attached by a coil to a witches' black box. One drop of your blood and it can decipher all your secrets. Three buttons and he is already murmuring. The convoy stops at a solitary petrol station to refuel. In a makeshift cage next to the reeking toilet a brown bear examines the company without favour. 'Mikhail Ivanovich says it's important to know which side bear sleeps,' Hoban translates with patent derision, lifting his mouth from the cellphone but without switching it off. 'If bear sleeps on left side, you eat the right side. Left side

137

of bear will be too hard to eat. If bear jerks off with left paw, you eat right paw. You want to eat some bear?'

'No, thank you.'

'You should have written to her. She went crazy waiting for you to come back.' Hoban returns to his telephone conversation. The sun beats onto the road's surface, making puddles of tar. The car fills with the scents of pine forest. They pass an old house set in a coppice of chestnut trees. The door stands open. 'Door closed, the husband's home,' Hoban intones, translating Yevgeny again. 'Door open, he's out at work so you can go in and fuck the wife.' They climb, and the plains to either side flatten below them. White-capped mountains glisten under an infinite sky. Ahead of them, half drowning in its own haze, lies the Black Sea. A wayside chapel marks a precarious bend in the road. Lowering his window, Mikhail tosses a handful of coins into the lap of an old man seated on the step. 'Guy's a fucking millionaire,' Hoban says wistfully. Yevgeny calls a halt at a willow tree with tags of coloured ribbon tied to its old branches. It is a dream tree, Hoban explains, once more interpreting for Yevgeny: 'Only good wishes may be attached to it. Dirty wishes rebound on the one who wishes them. You have dirty wishes?'

'None,' says Oliver.

'Personally I have dirty wishes all the time. Specially at night and first thing in the morning. Yevgeny Ivanovich was born in the city which the Soviets renamed Senaki,' Hoban resumes while Yevgeny shouts and points a thick arm into the valley. 'Mikhail Ivanovich was also born in Senaki. "Our father was commandant of military base at Senaki. We had house in military town outside Senaki. This house was very good house. My father was good man. All Mingrelians loved my father. My father was happy here."' Yevgeny's voice lifts and his arm swings towards the coastline. '"I was at kids' school in Batumi. I was at Marine School in Batumi. My wife was born in Batumi." You want any more of this shit?'

'Yes, please.'

'"Before Leningrad I was at university in Odessa. I study ships, building, marine. My spirit is on the waters of the

Black Sea. It is in the mountains of Mingrelia. I shall die in this place.'' You want me to leave my door open so you can fuck my wife?'

'No.'

Another halt. Mikhail and Yevgeny get out of the car purposefully, and make their way across the road. On an impulse Oliver goes after them. At the roadside lank men driving donkeys laden with oranges and cabbages pause to watch. Ragged gipsy children lean on sticks and stare as the brothers, trailed by Oliver, pass between them and ascend a narrow black stairway overgrown with weed. The brothers have reached a black-paved grotto. The stairway is of marble. A black marble handrail runs beside it. Set into the wall stands a statue of a bandaged Red Army officer heroically urging his troops into battle. In a misty glass case, cut into the rock, is the foxed and faded photograph of a young Russian soldier in a peaked cap. Mikhail and Yevgeny are standing shoulder to shoulder, heads bowed, hands folded in prayer. In ragged order, they take a step back and cross themselves several times.

'Our father,' Yevgeny explains gruffly.

They return to the Zil. Mikhail negotiates a hairpin bend and comes face to face with a military checkpoint. Lowering his window but not stopping, he hammers his left shoulder with his right hand, indicating high rank, but the sentries refuse to be impressed. With an oath Mikhail pulls up while Temur the fixer leaps out of the car behind them and kisses one of the men, who hugs and kisses him in return. The convoy may continue. They reach the summit. A lush land opens before them.

'He says we got another hour from here,' Hoban translates. 'On horse, he says, it would take two days. That's where he belongs. In the fucking horse-age.'

A valley field, sentries, a helicopter with its fins rotating, a mountain wall. Yevgeny, Hoban, Tinatin, Mikhail and Oliver ride in the first helicopter with a case of vodka and a painting of a sad old lady in white lace collars who has travelled with them all the way from Moscow, shedding chunks of gesso frame. The helicopter climbs a waterfall, follows a pony track, scales the mountain wall and dips between white peaks to lower itself into a green valley made in the shape of a cross. A hamlet nestles in each limb, an old stone monastery stands at the centre amid vineyards, barns, grazing cattle, forests and a lake. The party clumsily dismounts, Oliver after them. Hillsmen and children advance on them and Oliver is amused to notice that the children do indeed have brown hair. The helicopter lifts off, taking the din of its engines with it as it drops below the crest. Oliver smells pine and honey and hears the stirring of grass and the trickle of stream water. A skinned sheep hangs from a tree. Woodsmoke billows from a pit. Rich handwoven carpets of pink and crimson lie in the grass. Drinking horns and wine gourds are stacked on a table. Villagers crowd round. Yevgeny and Tinatin embrace them. Hoban sits on a rock, the telephone to his ear and the black box at his feet, embracing no one. The helicopter returns with Zoya and Paul and two more daughters and their husbands, and again departs. Mikhail and a bearded giant, armed with hunting guns, stride off into the forest. Oliver drifts with the group towards a wooden one-storey farmhouse at the centre of a sloping paddock. Inside, it is at first pitch dark. Gradually he sees a brick fireplace, a metal stove. He smells camphor, lavender and garlic. The bedrooms have bare floors and garish icons in battered frames: the hallowed Jesus as a baby, being nursed at His mother's covered breast; Jesus nailed to the Cross but stretched there so gaily that He is already flying up to Heaven, Jesus arrived safely home, sitting on the right hand of His Father.

'What Moscow forbids, Mingrelians love,' says Hoban for Yevgeny, and yawns. 'You bet,' he adds.

A cat presents itself and is made a fuss of. The old sad lady in crumbling gesso must have her place above the fire. Children are standing in the doorway waiting to see what wonders Tinatin has brought from the city. In the village, someone is playing music. In the kitchen, someone is singing and it is Zoya.

'Do you agree she sings like a goat?' Hoban enquires.

'No,' says Oliver.

'Then you are in love with her,' Hoban confirms with satisfaction.

The feast lasts two days but it is not till the end of the first that Oliver discovers he is attending a high-level business conference of the valley's elders. He learns many other things first. That when shooting bear you do best to shoot them in the eye, because on the rest of their bodies they wear a bulletproof armour of dried mud. That it is customary when feasting to pour wine onto the earth to nourish the spirits of our ancestors. That Mingrelian wines come from many different grapes, with names like Koloshi, Paneshi, Chodi and Kamuri. That to drink a toast in beer is to swear a curse on the person toasted. That Mingrelia's ancestors are none other than the fabled argonauts who under Jason's generalship built themselves a great fortress not twenty kilometres from here to house the Golden Fleece. And from a wild-eyed priest who seems never to have heard of the Russian Revolution he learns that to cross himself he must first join two fingers and his thumb – or was it only the thumb and fourth finger, his magician's fingers were too clumsy to be sure? – and point them upward to indicate the Holy Trinity, then touch the brow and afterwards the right and left sides of the belly, so that he doesn't see the Devil's cross as he looks down.

'Alternatively, you can shove clover up your ass,' Hoban advises *sotto voce* and repeats the joke in Russian for the edification of his telephone partner.

The business conference, which Oliver attends, turns out to be a consequence of Yevgeny's Great Dream, and the Great Dream is to unite the four villages of the cruciform in a single wine-growing cooperative that, by pooling land, labour and resources, and redirecting water courses, and employing the techniques of countries such as Spain, will produce the finest wine, not just in Mingrelia, not just in Georgia, but in the entire world.

'It will cost many millions,' Hoban reports laconically. 'Maybe billions. Nobody has smallest fucking idea. "We must build roads. We must build dams. We must buy machinery and make depot in the valley." Who will pay for

141

this shit?' The answer, it transpires, is Mikhail and Yevgeny Ivanovich Orlov. Yevgeny has already flown in viniculturists from Bordeaux, Rioja and Napa Valley. With one voice they have declared the vines superb. His spies have recorded temperatures and rainfall, measured the angles of hillsides, taken soil samples and pollen counts. Irrigators, roadbuilders, shippers and importers have testified to the surefire feasibility of the plan. Yevgeny will find the money, he tells the villagers, they can rest assured. 'He'll give the assholes every rouble we ever make,' Hoban confirms.

Dusk is falling fast. A furious blood-red sky proclaims itself behind the mountain tops and dies. In the trees lanterns are lit, music plays, the skinned sheep is turning on the fire. Men start singing, others make a ring and clap, a troupe of girls performs a dance. Outside the circle the elders talk among themselves, though Oliver can no longer hear them, and Hoban has given up translating. A dispute breaks out. An old man shakes his rifle at another. Eyes are on Yevgeny, who makes a joke, earns a scattered laugh and takes a step closer to his listeners. He opens his arms. He rebukes, then he promises. To judge by the applause, the promise must be substantial. The elders are appeased, Hoban leans against a cedar tree, growing larger with the dark while he murmurs lovingly into his witches' telephone.

*   *   *

In the House of Single the tension is audible. The primly clothed typists tread gingerly. The Trading Room, barometer of morale, is buzzing with rumour. Tiger has gone out there for the big one! It's boom or bust for Single's! Tiger is poised for the kill of the century.

'And Yevgeny in good heart, you say? Excellent,' says Tiger briskly, at one of the haphazard debriefings that follow Oliver's sorties to the Wild East.

'Yevgeny's terrific,' Oliver replies loyally. 'And Mikhail's right there beside him.'

'Good, good,' says Tiger and darts away into the thickets of operational costs and stock flotations.

A letter from Tinatin urges Oliver to make contact with yet another distant cousin, a girl named Nina this time, who teaches at the School of Oriental and African Studies and is the daughter of a Mingrelian violinist now dead. Taking it as a kindly hint from Zoya's mother to cast his impressionable eye elsewhere, Oliver dashes off a letter to the violinist's widow and is invited round to Bayswater for tea. The widow is a retired actress in a smock, with a habit of brushing away her fringe with the back of her hand, but her daughter Nina is black-haired with smouldering eyes. Nina agrees to teach Oliver Georgian, beginning with its beautiful but daunting alphabet, though she warns him it will take him years to learn.

'The more years the better!' Oliver cries gallantly.

Nina is of a high-minded disposition, and her Georgian and Mingrelian ties have been strengthened by exile. She is moved by Oliver's uncritical admiration of everything she holds dear, though of oil, scrap, blood and seventy-five million dollar bribes she providentially knows nothing. Oliver preserves her in her innocence. Soon she shares his bed. And if Oliver is aware that Zoya is in some devious sense the inspiration of their union, he feels no guilt – why should he? He is grateful that, by going to bed with Nina, he is able to distance himself from the predatory wife of an important business associate, whose naked body still shines provocatively at him from the upper window of the Moscow house. Under Nina's guidance he surrounds himself with works of Georgian literature and folklore. He plays Georgian music and pastes a map of the Caucasus along one wall of his disgracefully untidy prestige flat in a tower block in Chelsea Harbour built with Single-brokered finance.

And the Post Boy is happy. Not happy-happy, for Oliver does not believe in pleasure as an attainable ideal. But active-happy. Creative-happy. Happy cautiously in love, if love is what he feels for Nina. Happy also in his work – as long as work is visiting Yevgeny and Mikhail and Tinatin, and provided that the insidious shadow of Hoban does not hang too near, and Zoya continues to ignore him. For where once her unhappy eyes devoured Oliver constantly, now they refuse to acknowledge him at all. She steers clear of the kitchen when he is chopping vegetables with Tinatin. In corridors, on staircases, flitting from room to room with Paul in tow, she uses the curtains of her hair to hide her face.

'Tell your father, in one week they will sign all documents,' says Yevgeny over Stone Age billiards, when he has satisfied himself that nobody but Hoban and Mikhail and Shalva is within hearing distance. 'Tell him, when they have signed he must come to Mingrelia and shoot a bear.'

'In that case you must come to Dorset and shoot a pheasant,' Oliver counters, and they embrace.

There is no hand-carried mail this time. Oliver brings the two messages in his head. On the flight home he is so excited by them that he has half a mind to propose marriage to Nina. The date is August 18th 1991.

*   *   *

It is two nights later and Nina is weeping in Georgian. She is weeping on the telephone, she is weeping when she arrives at Oliver's flat, weeping as they sit like an old couple side by side on the sofa watching in horror as the new Russia trembles on the brink of anarchy, its daring leader is seized by the old guard risen from the grave, newspapers are closed, tanks flood the city, and people at the highest level in the land tumble from power like ninepins, taking with them their best-laid Specific Proposals for scrap metal, oil and blood.

It is summer still in Curzon Street but no birds sing. Oil, scrap and blood are as if they had never been. To acknowledge them is to acknowledge their demise. The recent history books have been tacitly rewritten, the young men and women of the Trading Room dispatched in search of other bounty. Otherwise, nothing, absolutely nothing has occurred. No precious tens of millions of investment have turned to dust, nothing has been lavished on advance commissions, there have been no sweeteners bestowed on American intermediaries and officials, no down-payments have been made on the lease of refrigerated Jumbo jets. The heat, light, rent, cars, salaries, bonuses, health insurance, educational insurance, phone and entertainment bills for five prime floors of Curzon Street and their spendthrift inhabitants are not in jeopardy. And Tiger is the least affected of everyone. His tread is lighter, his walk prouder than ever before, his vision grander, his Hayward suit crisper. Oliver alone – and perhaps Gupta, who is Tiger's Indian factotum – knows the pain that lies beneath the armour, knows how close the brittle hero is to snapping. But when Oliver in his incurable compassion chooses a moment to commiserate with his father, Tiger retaliates with a ferocity that leaves Oliver rocking with internal anger.

'I do not want your pity, thank you. I do not want your tender feelings or your safe ethical concerns. I want your respect, your loyalty, your brains for what they are, your commitment and, for as long as I am senior partner, your obedience.'

'Oh, well, sorry,' Oliver mumbles, and when Tiger does not unbend, returns to his room and telephones Nina in vain.

What has become of her? Their last encounter was not a happy one. At first he persuades himself that Zoya has launched a spoiling operation. Then grudgingly he remembers that he was drunk and while drunk let slip to Nina – out of the goodness of his lonely heart, no more – a couple of unguarded details of his transactions with her Uncle Yevgeny, as she calls him. He dimly recalls remarking in a frivolous moment that, while the Soviet Union might have lost its way, Single's had lost its shirt. When she pressed him, he had felt it incumbent on him to provide a sketchy version of how Single's, with her Uncle Yevgeny's help and inspiration, had planned to make a killing out of certain life-essential Russian substances – such as, well, yes, not to put too fine a point on it, blood. At which Nina went pale, and raged, beat her fists against his chest and stormed out of his flat swearing – not for the first time, for she has her share of Mingrelian volatility – never to return.

'She has taken new lover to revenge you, Oliver,' her distracted mother confesses over the telephone. 'She says you are too decadent, darling, worse than bloody Russian.'

But what of the brothers? What of Tinatin and the daughters? What of Bethlehem? What of Zoya?

'The brothers have been deposed,' snaps Massingham, who has been simmering with envy ever since the rôle of go-between was snatched from him and handed to the detested junior partner. 'Banished. Exiled. Sent to Siberia. Warned never to show their ugly faces in Moscow or Georgia or anywhere else.'

'How about Hoban and his friends?'

'Oh my dear chap, their lot *never* go down.'

Their lot? Whose lot? Massingham does not elaborate. 'Yevgeny's on the scrap heap, darling. Not to mention oil and blood,' he retorts nastily.

Communications with strife-torn Russia are chaotic and Oliver is forbidden by standing order to telephone Yevgeny or his outstations. A whole evening long nevertheless he crouches in an insanitary public phone booth in Chelsea, cajoling and beseeching the overseas operator. In his imagination he sees Yevgeny in his pyjamas on his motorbike revving up the engine, and the phone ringing inaudibly a few feet from him. The operator, a lady from Acton, has heard that a mob is storming the Moscow exchange.

'Give it a few days, dear, I should,' she advises, like Matron at school when he complained of an ache.

It is as if the last window upon hope has been slammed in Oliver's face. Zoya was right. Nina was right. I should have said no. If I can go along with selling the blood of poor Russians, where if anywhere will I draw the line? Yevgeny, Mikhail, Tinatin, Zoya, the white mountains and the feasts haunt him like his own broken promises. At his flat in Chelsea Harbour he takes down the map of the Caucasus and shoves it in the waste bucket of his empty white kitchen. Nina's mother recommends a substitute teacher, an elderly cavalry officer who was once her lover until he lost his powers. Oliver endures a couple of lessons from him and cancels the rest. At Single's he goes silently, keeping his door closed and ordering sandwiches for lunch. Rumour reaches him like garbled despatches from the front. Massingham has heard of a store of military electrolyte buried outside Budapest. Tiger bids him inspect it. After a wasted week, he returns with nothing. In Prague, a stable of adolescent mathematicians will repair industrial computers at a fraction of the manufacturers' charge, but they need a million dollars' worth of equipment to set them up. Massingham, our roving ambassador, flies to Prague, meets a couple of nineteen-year-old bearded geniuses and returns declaring that the proposal is a confidence trick. But with Randy – as Tiger is at pains to remind Oliver – you can never be sure. In Kazakhstan, there is a textile factory capable of producing miles of curly Wilton carpet twice as splendid as the real thing and at a quarter of the price. Having purportedly inspected a water-logged building site of rusted iron girders Massingham advises that production is some way off. Tiger is sceptical but keeps his counsel. Word has come in of a stupendous gold find in the Urals, don't tell a soul. It is Oliver this time who squats for three days in a farmhouse in the Mugodzhar hills, buffeted by imperious phonecalls from his father while he waits for a trusted intermediary who fails to materialise.

Tiger himself has chosen the path of solitude and contemplation. His gaze is remote. Twice, it is rumoured, he has been summoned to the City to explain himself. Ugly words like 'foreclose' are being whispered in the Trading Room. Mysteriously, he starts to travel. On a visit to Accounts Department Oliver happens on a statement of expenses showing that a 'Mr and Mrs T. Single' took the Royal Suite at a grand hotel in Liverpool for three nights and entertained lavishly. For Mrs Single, Oliver presumes Katrina of Kat's Cradle. Petrol vouchers rendered by Gasson the chauffeur reveal that Mr and Mrs travelled by Rolls-Royce. Liverpool is an old stamping-ground of Tiger's. It is where he earned his spurs as a defending barrister of the oppressed criminal classes. The trip is followed a week later by the appearance in Curzon Street of three wide-shouldered Turkish gentlemen in glistening suits who record their address in the janitors' book as 'Istanbul' and are appointed to see Tiger personally. Most ominously, Oliver could have sworn he heard Hoban's nasal voice alongside Massingham's issuing through the Wedgwood double doors when he calls on Pam Hawsley under a pretext, but Pam as usual is opaque:

'It's a conference, Mr Oliver. That's all I can tell you, I'm afraid.'

All morning he waits tensely for the summons that doesn't come. At lunchtime Tiger departs for Kat's Cradle with his burly guests, but they are out of the lift and into the street before Oliver can grab a sight of them. When a few days later he undertakes a second inspection of Tiger's expenses, he finds a string of entries with the one word 'Istanbul' against them. Massingham too has resumed his travels. His most frequent destinations are Brussels, northern Cyprus and the south of Spain, where an offshore Single company recently spawned a chain of disco bars, timeshare villages and casinos. And since Randy Massingham is regarded by the Trading Room as a sort of go-getting Pimpernel, there is speculation about why he seems so sunny, and what secrets he may be carrying in his black ex-Foreign Office briefcase.

Then one evening when Oliver is locking up his desk, Tiger himself appears in the doorway to suggest they pop round for a bite at the Cradle, just the two of them like old times. Kat is not in evidence. Oliver suspects Tiger told her not to be. They are tended instead by Alvaro the head waiter. Tiger's corner table, which is permanently reserved for him, is a low-lit red nest of velveteen. He has chosen duck and claret. Oliver chooses the same. Tiger orders two house salads, forgetting that Oliver detests salad. They begin as always by discussing Oliver's love-life. Reluctant to admit to the break-up of his affair with Nina, Oliver prefers to embellish it.

'You mean you're settling down at last?' Tiger cries, greatly amused. 'Good Heavens. I'd pictured you as a dashing bachelor of forty.'

'I suppose there are things you just can't plan for,' Oliver says all dewy-eyed.

'Have you told the good news to Yevgeny?'

'How can I? He's out of touch.'

Tiger pauses in mid-chew, suggesting that the duck may

not be to his liking. His eyebrows draw together to form a broken pediment. To Oliver's relief, the jaw resumes its rotation. The duck gives pleasure after all. 'You went up to that country place of his, I seem to remember,' says Tiger. 'Where he plans to grow fine wines. Yes?'

'It's not a *place*, Father. It's a bunch of villages in the mountains.'

'But a decent house, presumably?'

'I'm afraid not. Not by our standards.'

'Viable sort of project, is it? Something we ought to take an interest in?'

Oliver gives a superior laugh while a part of him turns icy cold at the thought of Tiger's shadow reaching all the way to Bethlehem.

'It's a bit of a pipe-dream, I'm afraid, quite honestly. Yevgeny's not a businessman in our sense. You'd be standing under the proverbial shower tearing up ten-pound notes.'

'Why's that?'

'He hasn't costed the infrastructure for a start' – remembering Hoban's contemptuous dismissal of the project – 'it could be a bottomless pit. Roads, water, terracing the fields, God knows what. He thinks he'll use local labour but it's not skilled, there are four villages and they're all at each other's throats.' A reflective pull of claret while he urgently thinks up other reasons. 'Yevgeny doesn't even *want* to modernise the place. He just thinks he does. It's a fantasy. He's sworn to keep the valley as it is, but also to industrialise it and make it rich. He can't do both.'

'But he's serious?'

'Oh, as the Pope. If he ever makes a few billions, that's where they'll go. Ask his family. They're terrified.'

Tiger's many doctors have advised him to drink an equal quantity of mineral water with his wine. Aware of this, Alvaro sets a second bottle of Evian on the pink damask cloth.

'And Hoban?' Tiger asks. 'He's your peer group. What sort of fellow is he? Keen? Handy at his job?'

Oliver hesitates. As a rule he is unable to dislike anyone for more than a few minutes, but Hoban is the exception. 'I haven't much to go on really. Randy knows him better than I do. He seems a bit of a lone wolf to me. A bit too much on the make. But okay. In his way.'

'Randy tells me he's married to Yevgeny's favourite daughter.'

'I don't know that Zoya is his *favourite*,' Oliver protests anxiously. 'He's just a proud dad. Loves all his children equally.' But he is watching Tiger intently, if only in the pink mirrors round the wall: he knows, Hoban's told him, he knows about the letter and the paper heart. Tiger takes a peck of duck, follows it with a sip of claret, a sip of Evian and a kiss of the napkin.

'Tell me something, Oliver. Did old Yevgeny ever chat to you about his maritime connections?'

'Only that he was at Marine School and in the Russian navy for a while. And that the sea's in his blood. As the mountains are.'

'He never mentioned to you that he once held sway over the entire Black Sea merchant fleet?'

'No. But you learn about Yevgeny in fits and starts, depending what he decides to dole out.'

An intermission while Tiger conducts one of those internal dialogues with himself that end with a decision but withhold the reasoning that leads to it. 'Yes, well, I think we'll give Randy his head for a little while yet, if you don't mind. You can take over once the show's back on the road.' Father and son stand on the pavement of South Audley Street and admire the starry sky. 'And look after that Nina of yours, old boy,' Tiger advises sternly. 'Kat thinks the world of her. So do I.'

Another month and, to Massingham's undisguised fury, the Post Boy is dispatched to Istanbul, where Yevgeny and Mikhail have pitched their tent.

CHAPTER NINE

In the gloom of a wet Turkish winter Yevgeny looks as drab
and ashy as the mosques around him. He hugs Oliver with
half his old force, reads Tiger's letter with distaste and hands
it to Mikhail with the humility of an exile. The rented house
in a new suburb on the Asian side of Istanbul is gimcrack and
unfinished, set in a puddled mess of abandoned builders'
hardware and surrounded by unfinished streets, shopping
malls, bancomats, petrol stations, fast chicken stops, all
empty, all going gently to the Devil while crooked contrac-
tors and frustrated tenants and immovable Ottoman bureau-
crats slug out their differences in some archaic courthouse
devoted to insoluble lawsuits in this sweltering, howling,
heaving, traffic-suffocated city with an uncounted population of sixteen million souls, which as Yevgeny never tires
of repeating is four times as many souls as inhabit the whole
of his beloved Georgia. The one moment of enchantment
comes as daylight dies and the friends sit drinking raki on
the balcony under an enormous Turkish sky and smell the
unlikely scents of lime and jasmine that somehow prevail
against the stench of an unfinished drainage system while
Tinatin reminds her husband, as by now she has a hundred
times, that it's the same Black Sea out there and Mingrelia
is just across the border – even if the border is eight hundred

mountainous miles away, the roads to it are impassable in times of Kurdish insurrection and Kurdish insurrection is the norm. Tinatin cooks Mingrelian food, Mikhail plays Mingrelian music on an old gramophone that takes seventy-eights, the dining table is strewn with yellowing Georgian newspapers. Mikhail carries a pistol on a lanyard under his bulky waistcoat, and a smaller one in the top of his boot. The BMW motorbike, the children and the daughters are gone – all but Zoya and her small son Paul. Hoban's movements are mysterious. He is in Vienna. He is in Odessa. He is in Liverpool. One afternoon he returns unannounced and leads Yevgeny into the street, where they are to be seen walking up and down the sliver of unfinished pavement with their jackets over their shoulders, Yevgeny bowing his head like the prisoner he used to be, and little Paul trailing after them like an undertaker's mute. Zoya is a woman waiting and she is waiting for Oliver. She is waiting with her eyes and languid, spreading body, while she derides the new super-materialist Russia, recites details of the latest wholesale robberies of State property, the names of overnight billionaires, and complains about the *lodos*, a Turkish south wind that gives her a headache every time she doesn't want to do something. Sometimes Tinatin tells her to find herself an activity, look to Paul, take herself off for a walk. She obeys, then comes home to wait, and sigh about the *lodos*.

'I shall become a Natasha,' she announces once, in a silence that she has created for herself.

'What's a Natasha?' Oliver asks Tinatin.

'A Russian prostitute,' Tinatin replies wearily. 'Natasha is the name the Turks have given to our whores.'

'Tiger tells me we're back in business,' Oliver says to Yevgeny, choosing a moment when Zoya is paying her weekly visit to the local Russian fortune teller. The statement casts Yevgeny into the depths of gloom.

'*Business*,' he repeats heavily. 'Yes, Post Boy. We do *business*.'

Oliver remembers with unease how Nina once explained to him that in both Russian and Georgian this innocent English word has become synonymous with crookery.

152

'Why doesn't Yevgeny go back to Georgia and live there?' he asks Tinatin who is filling baked aubergines with a spicy crab concoction that was once Yevgeny's favourite dish.

'Yevgeny is of the past, Oliver,' she replies. 'Those who remained in Tbilisi do not wish to share their power with an old man from Moscow who has lost his friends.'

'I was thinking of Bethlehem.'

'Yevgeny has made too many promises to Bethlehem. If he does not arrive in a gold coach, he will not be welcome.'

'Hoban will build it for him,' Zoya predicts, entering like an estranged Ophelia, and holding her hand to her brow to contain the effects of the *lodos*. 'Massingham will be the coachman.'

Hoban, Oliver thinks. Not Alix any more. Hoban my husband.

'We have also Russian ivy here,' Zoya remarks, to the long window. 'It is very passionate. It grows too fast, it achieves nothing, then it dies. It has a white flower. The scent is most elusive.'

'Oh,' says Oliver.

His hotel is big and Western and anonymous. It is after midnight on his third night when he hears a knock at the door. They've sent up a hooker, he thinks, remembering the over-friendly smile of the young concierge. But it is Zoya, which does not surprise him as it should. The room is small and overlit. They stand face to face beside the bed, blinking at each other under the fierce ceiling light.

'Do not make this trade with my father,' she tells him.

'Why not?'

'It is against life. It is worse than blood. It is sin.'

'How do you know?'

'I know Hoban. I know your father. They can possess, they cannot love, not even their children. You know them also, Oliver. If we do not escape them, we shall be dead like them. Yevgeny dreams only of paradise. Who promises him money to buy paradise commands him. Hoban promises.'

It is not clear who strikes first. Perhaps each is the initiator, for their arms collide and must be redirected before they can embrace, and on the bed they fight until they are naked, then take each other like animals until both of them are satisfied. 'You must revive what is dead inside you,' she tells him severely as she dresses. 'Very soon you will be too late for yourself. You can make love to me whenever you wish. To you it is not important. To me it is everything. I am not a Natasha.'

'What is worse than blood?' he asks her, staying her arm. 'What sin am I supposed to be committing?'

She kisses him so gently and sadly that he wishes he could begin again with her in tranquillity. 'With blood you destroyed only yourself,' she replies, holding his face in both hands. 'With this new trade, you will destroy yourself, and Paul, and many many children and their mothers and their fathers.'

'*What* trade?'

'Ask your father. I am married to Hoban.'

*   *   *

'Yevgeny's regrouped,' says Tiger approvingly next evening. 'He had a setback, he recovered. Randy breathed new life into him. With help from Hoban.' Oliver sees Yevgeny's embattled head staring across the valley at the lights, and the tracks of tears running down his wrinkled cheeks. The scent of Zoya's juices is still on him. He can smell it through his shirt. 'Still dreams of his fine wine, you'll be pleased to hear. I'm looking out some books on viniculture for him. You can take them over on your next trip.'

'What business is he into suddenly?'

'Shipping. Randy and Alix have persuaded him to revive his old naval contacts, call in a few promises.'

'Shipping what?'

A wave of the hand. The same wave that dismisses the unwanted pudding trolley. 'The spectrum. Whatever's in the right place on the right day at the right price. Flexibility, that's his watchword. It's a fast trade, it's cut-throat, but he's up to it. Given help. That's where we come in.'

'What sort of help?'

154

'Single's are *facilitators*, Oliver' – little head to one side, eyebrows sanctimoniously raised – 'you forget that – you're young. We are maximisers. Creators.' One small index finger points to God. 'Our job is to provide our clients with the tools they need and to husband the harvest when they bring it in. Single's aren't where they are today because they clip their clients' wings. We go where others fear to trade, Oliver. And we come out smiling.'

Dutifully Oliver tries his hardest to reflect his father's enthusiasm, hoping that by mouthing the words he will believe them. 'And he'll jolly well come up trumps, I know he will,' he says.

'Of course he will. He's a prince.'

'He's an old robber baron. They'll have to drag him out feet first.'

'I beg your pardon?' Tiger has risen from his desk to take Oliver by the arm. 'I'll trouble you not to use that term, thank you, Oliver. Our rôle is a sensitive one and it will need a careful use of language. Is that understood?'

'Absolutely. I'm sorry. It was just a turn of phrase.'

'If the brothers make the kind of money Randy and Alix are talking about, they're going to want our whole package: casinos, nightclubs, a chain or two of hotels, holiday villages, everything we're best at. Yevgeny once again insists on total confidentiality and, since I am similarly minded, I have no problem humouring him.' Back to his desk. 'I want you to deliver this envelope to him personally. And take a bottle of the Berry's Speyside out of the strong room with my compliments. Take two. One for Alix.'

'Father.'

'My boy.'

'I need to know what we're dealing in.'

'Finance.'

'Derived from what?'

'Our own sweat and tears. Our intuition, our flair, our flexibility. Our merit.'

'What comes after blood? What's worse?'

Tiger's wafer-thin lips have drawn together in a white crease. 'Curiosity is worse, thank you, Oliver. Idle, callow, misinformed, self-indulgent, gratuitous, moralistic problem-making. Was Adam the first man? I don't know. Was Christ born on Christmas Day? I don't know. In business, we play life as we find it. Not as it is handed down from the infant throne of the liberal newspapers.'

*   *   *

Oliver and Yevgeny sit on the balcony, drinking cuvée Bethlehem. Tinatin is in Leningrad caring for a distressed daughter. Hoban is in Vienna, Zoya and Paul are with him. Mikhail brings hardboiled eggs and salted fish.

'You are still learning the language of the gods, Post Boy?'

'Indeed I am,' Oliver answers untruthfully, afraid to cause the old man disappointment, and promises himself that he will telephone the awful cavalry officer as soon as he gets back to London.

Yevgeny accepts Tiger's letter and passes it unopened to Mikhail. In the hall, luggage and packing cases are piled to the ceiling. A new house has been found, Yevgeny explains, in the tone of someone submitting to authority. Somewhere more appropriate to future needs.

'Will you get a new motorbike?' Oliver asks, striving for a more hopeful note.

'You want me to?'

'But you must!'

'Then I get a new motorbike. Maybe I get six.'

And then to Oliver's horror, he weeps, long and silently into his clenched fists.

It is terrible that you are not a coward, Zoya writes, in a letter waiting for him at his hotel. Nothing breaks you. You will kill us with your politeness. Do not deceive yourself that you cannot know the truth.

*   *   *

It is the Eve of Christmas party at Single's. In the Trading Room everything that is movable has been pushed against

156

the walls. Modern music which Tiger at all other times of year abhors is about to howl from stereophonic loudspeakers, vintage champagne flows, there is lobster in pyramids, foie gras and a five-kilo bucket of Imperial caviar which, according to Randy Massingham's amusing speech, was 'landed informally' by clients of the House of Single 'with a line to the Caspian, where virgin sturgeons keep their legs crossed in order to produce these delicious little eggs for us'. The traders cheer, a Tiger redux cheers along with them, straightens his tie and steps onto the rostrum to deliver his annual rousing speech. Single's, he says to his excited audience, is today in a stronger position than it has been in its entire history. The music strikes, the first revellers are advancing on the table to take a frugal spoonful from the bucket as Oliver discreetly climbs the back staircase, past his native Legal Section, until he arrives at the partners' strong room to which he and Tiger alone possess the combination. Twenty minutes later he is back again, pleading a temporary sickness of the stomach. But the sickness is real, even if the stomach is the least affected part of him. It is the sickness of a nightmare realised. Of sums so vast, so sudden, so swiftly hidden that they can only have one source. From Marbella, twenty-two million dollars. From Marseilles, thirty-five. From Liverpool, a hundred and seven million pounds. From Gdansk, Hamburg, Rotterdam, a hundred and eighty million dollars cash awaiting the attentions of the Single laundering service.

*   *   *

'You love your father, Post Boy?'

It is dusk, it is philosophy time in the living room of the newly appointed twenty million dollar villa on the European bank of the Bosphorus to which the brothers have been elevated. Catherine the Great's majestic karelka furniture – the same precious gold brown sideboards, corner cupboards, dining table and chairs that in the days of Oliver's innocence graced the villa outside Moscow – stands about the ground floor waiting for a home. Russian snowscapes with horse-drawn sledges queue for places on the newly painted walls. And in the drawing room stands the most splendid, glistening BMW motorcycle that hot money can buy.

'Ride it, Post Boy! Ride it!'

But Oliver for some reason doesn't feel the urge. Neither does Yevgeny. Wet unusual snow lies on the descending garden. On the straits, freighters, ferryboats and pleasure barges spar nose to nose in a constant duel. Yes, I love my father, Oliver assures Yevgeny vaguely in reply. Zoya stands at the french window, willing Paul to sleep on her shoulder. Tinatin has lit the tiled stove and dozes thoughtfully beside it in her rocking chair. Hoban is in Vienna again, opening a new office. It is to be called Trans-Finanz. Mikhail crouches at Yevgeny's shoulder. He has grown a beard.

'He makes you laugh, your father?'

'When things are going well and he's happy – yes, Tiger can make me laugh.'

Paul grizzles and Zoya comforts him, her hand splayed on his naked back inside his shirt.

'He makes you mad, Post Boy?'

'He means American mad,' Zoya explains. 'Hoban's kind of mad. Angry.'

'Sometimes he makes me mad,' Oliver concedes, not understanding where this catechism is leading. 'But I make him mad too.'

'How you make him mad, Post Boy?'

'Well, I'm not exactly the Rolls-Royce son he wanted, am I? He's a bit mad at me all the time, if he only knew it.'

'Give him this. He will be happy.' Reaching inside his black overcoat, Yevgeny pulls out an envelope and hands it to Mikhail, who passes it silently to Oliver.

Oliver draws a breath. *Now* he thinks. *Go.* 'What's it about?' he asks. He has to repeat his question. 'The letter you just gave me – what's it got in it? – I'm beginning to worry that I'll be stopped at Customs or something.' He must have said this louder than he intended, for Zoya turns her head and Mikhail's fierce dark eyes are already staring at him. 'I don't know the first thing about your new operation. I'm on the legal side. That's all I am – legal.'

'*Legal*?' Yevgeny repeats, raising his voice in angry puzzlement. 'What is legal? How come you are *legal*, please? Oliver is *legal*? You are alone among us, I would say.'

Oliver shoots a sideways glance, intended for Zoya, but she has disappeared and it is Tinatin who is lulling Paul to sleep. 'Tiger says you're in general trade,' he stumbles on. 'What does that mean? He says you're making huge profits. How? He's going to take you into the leisure industry. All in six months. How?'

In the glow of the reading lamp beside him, Yevgeny's face is older than the mountain crags of Bethlehem. 'Do you lie to your father, Post Boy?'

'Only in small matters. To protect him. The way all of us lie.'

'This man should not lie to his son. Do I lie to you?'

'No.'

'Go back to London, Post Boy. Stay legal. Take the letter to your father. Tell him, an old Russian says he's a fool.'

Zoya is waiting for him in his hotel bed. She has brought gifts for him in small brown paper parcels: an icon that her mother Tinatin wore secretly on saints' days through the years of Communism; a scented candle; a photograph of her father Yevgeny in naval uniform; poems by a Georgian poet who is precious to her. His name is Khuta Berulava and he is a Mingrelian who writes in Georgian, her favourite combination. Oliver's desire for her is an addiction. A finger to her lips for silence, she undresses him. He is strung to bursting point. But he forces himself to lie apart from her.

'If I am going to betray my father, you've got to betray your father and your husband,' he says carefully. 'What does Yevgeny trade in?'

She turns her back on him. 'It is all bad things.'

'What's the worst thing?'

'All things.'

'What's the one worst thing? Worse than all the rest.

What's making all the money? Millions and millions of dollars?'

Flinging herself round to him, she traps him between her thighs and lunges at him with ferocity, as if by taking him inside her she will silence him.

'He laughs,' she says, panting.

'Who does?'

'Hoban' – another lunge.

'Why does Hoban laugh? What at?'

' "It is for Yevgeny," he says. "We are growing a new wine for Yevgeny. We are building him a white road to Bethlehem." '

'A white road made of what?' Oliver insists breathlessly.

'Of powder.'

'What is the powder made of?'

She screams it, loud enough for half the hotel to hear: 'It is from Afghanistan! From Kazakhstan! From Kirghizia! Hoban has arranged it! They are making the new trade. Across Russia from the East.' And her choking, abject cry of shame as she desperately assaults him.

*   *   *

Pam Hawsley, Tiger's Ice Maiden, sits at her crescent-shaped desk behind framed photographs of her three pugs, Shadrach, Meshach and Abednego, and the red telephone that links her directly to the Almighty. It is the morning of the following day. Oliver has not slept. Lying wide-eyed on his bed in Chelsea Harbour, he has tried unsuccessfully to convince himself that he is still in Zoya's arms, that he never in his life sat in a papier-mâché interviewing room at Heathrow, telling a uniformed customs officer things that till then he has not told himself. Now, standing in the huge anteroom to Tiger's state apartments, he is assailed by altitude sickness, speech loss, sexual remorse and a hangover. He clutches Yevgeny's envelope first in his left hand, then in his right. He shuffles his feet and clears his throat like an idiot. Nerve ends tingle up and down his back. When he speaks he sounds to himself like the worst actor in the world.

160

It can only be a matter of moments before Pam Hawsley closes the show for its sheer lack of verisimilitude.

'If you could just give Tiger this, Pam? Yevgeny Orlov asked me to hand it to him personally, but I reckon you're personal enough. Okay, Pam? Okay?'

And it really might have been okay if the ever-charming Randy Massingham, freshly back from Vienna, had not chosen that moment to appear in his doorway. 'If Yevvers said personal, then personal is what it's got to be, Ollie boy,' he drawls. 'Name of the game, I'm afraid' – beckoning with his head to the fatal doors crowned with Wedgwood ribbons – 'only your dad, for Christ's sake. Thump on the door and charge in, if I were you.'

Ignoring this gratuitous advice, Oliver sinks twenty fathoms into the boneless white leather sofa. The embossed S & S colophon brands him whenever he leans back. Massingham continues to loll in his doorway. Pam Hawsley's head sinks among her pugs and screens. Its silvered top reminds Oliver of Brock. Clutching the envelope to his heart, he embarks on an in-depth examination of his father's credentials. Testimonials from diploma mills nobody has heard of. Tiger in wig and gown being called to the Bar by handshake of some ghastly earl. Tiger in the fatuous habiliments of a Doctor of Whatever, clutching an engraved gold plate. Tiger in suspiciously perfect cricket gear, acknowledging applause of unseen spectators with a wave of pristine bat. Tiger in polo mode, accepting silver cup from turbanned princeling. Tiger at Third World conference, enjoying camera-conscious handshake with Central American narcotyrant. Tiger rubbing shoulders with the great at an informal German lakeside seminar for senile untouchables. One day I'll do a prosecuting counsel's job on you, starting with your date of birth.

'Mr Tiger will see you now, Mr Oliver.'

Oliver rises without oxygen from the sea bed where he has fallen into an escaper's waking sleep. Yevgeny's envelope is sodden in his hand. He raps on the Wedgwood double doors, praying Tiger will not hear. The dreadfully familiar voice calls 'Come' and he feels the love rise in him like old poison. He stoops his shoulders and urges his weight into his hips in a routine effort to reduce his height.

'Heavens above, dear boy, do you know what it costs an hour to have you sitting out there?'

'Yevgeny asked me to give you this personally, Father.'

'Did he though? Did he? Good on him' – not so much accepting the envelope as tweaking it from Oliver's fist at the same moment as Oliver hears Brock refusing to accept it: Thank you, Oliver, but I'm not quite as familiar with the Orlov brothers as you are. So what I'd suggest is that, tempting as it is, we leave this envelope just the way it was given to us, virgin and intact. Because what I'm afraid of here is our old-fashioned Biblical loyalty test.

'And he has a message for you,' Oliver tells his father, not Brock.

'Message? What message?' – selecting a ten-inch silver paperknife – 'You've given me the message.'

'A spoken message. It's not terribly polite, I'm afraid. He says to tell you, an old Russian says you're a fool. It's the first time I've heard him call himself a Russian actually. He's usually Georgian' – meekly softening the blow.

Tiger's all-weather smile is still in place. The voice is richer by an extra drop of unction as he makes the dangerous incision, draws out a single sheet of paper and unfolds it. 'But dear boy, he's so right, of *course* I am! . . . A total fool . . . Nobody else would give him the terms we're giving him . . . Nothing I like better than a fellow who thinks he's robbing me . . . Won't be taking his business round the corner, will he? What? What?' Tiger folds up the sheet of paper, replaces it in its envelope and tosses the envelope in his in-tray. Has he read it? Hardly. But Tiger rarely reads anything these days. He has armed himself with the cloudy vision of a seer. 'I expected to hear from you last night, Oliver. Where were you, if I may ask?'

Oliver's brain cells shrivel in rejection. *My bloody plane was late!* – but his plane was early – *I couldn't get a bloody cab!* – but there were cabs galore. He hears Brock's voice: *tell him you met a girl.* 'Well, I did *mean* to ring you, but I thought

I'd pop round and see Nina,' he lies, blushing and rubbing his nose.

'Did you though? Nina, eh? Old Yevgeny's grandniece once removed, or whatever she is.'

'Only she hasn't been too well. She's got this 'flu.'

'Still fancy her, do you?'

'Well, I still do quite, actually, yes.'

'Not losing your edge?'

'No – not at all – quite the reverse.'

'Good. Oliver.' Somehow they are arm in arm, standing in the great bay window. 'I've had a spot of luck this morning.'

'I'm very glad.'

'Quite a large spot. Luck in the sense that good men *make* their luck. D'you follow me?'

'Of course. Congratulations.'

'Napoleon, when he was considering an applicant, would ask his young officers –'

'"Are you lucky?"' Oliver supplied for him.

'Precisely. That piece of paper you brought me just now is the confirmation that I have made ten million pounds.'

'Splendid.'

'Cash.'

'Better still. Brilliant. Fantastic.'

'Tax free. Offshore. Arm's length. We shall not be troubling the Revenue.' The grip tighter. Oliver's arm spongy. Tiger's sinuous and strong. 'I've decided to split it. Do you follow me?'

'Not really. I'm a bit slow this morning.'

'Over-exerting yourself again, were you?'

Oliver simpers.

'Five mill for me, for the rainy day I do not propose to experience. Five mill for our first-born grandchild. What do you make of that?'

'It's incredible. I'm extremely grateful. Thank you.'

'Are you pleased?'

'Immensely.'

'Not half as pleased as I shall be when the great day comes. Just remember. Your first child, five million pounds. A done thing. Will you remember that?'

'Of course. Thanks. Really thanks.'

'It's not for your gratitude, Oliver. It's to put a third S into Single & Single.'

'Right. Great. A third S. Terrific.' Cautiously he takes back his arm and feels the blood return to it.

'Nina's a good girl. I've checked her out. Mother's a tart, never bad if you're looking for a bit of sport in bed. Small aristocrats on the father's side, a dash of eccentricity but nothing to scare, healthy brothers and sisters. Not a penny to their name but with five million for our first born, who's counting? You won't find me standing in your way.'

'Super. I'll keep it in mind.'

'And don't tell her. About the money. It could affect her aim. When the day comes, let her find out for herself. That way you'll know her heart was in the right place.'

'Good thinking. Thanks again.'

'Tell me, old boy' – confidingly, a hand on Oliver's arm – 'what are we running at these days?'

'Running at?' Oliver repeats, mystified. He racks his mind, trying to call up turnover figures, profit margins, net and gross.

'With Nina. How many times? Twice a night and once in the morning?'

'Oh my God' – smirk, wipe of the forelock – 'I'm afraid we sort of lose count.'

'Good lad. Well done. Runs in the family.'

CHAPTER TEN

In the bleak attic bedroom to which Oliver had removed himself after taking tea in the garden with Brock – and where he had remained alone ever since except for a few well-managed interruptions from the crew to ascertain his welfare – there was an iron bedstead, a pine table with a parchment-shaded lamp, and a gangrenous bathroom with kids' transfers on the mirror which Oliver in his idleness had attempted unsuccessfully to pick off. There was a telephone socket but prisoners were allowed no telephone. The crew had offered him food and company but he had declined both. Crew members occupied the rooms to either side of him: Brock's distrust of Oliver was as absolute as his affection for him. It was by now approaching midnight and Oliver, after many perambulations about the room – which included a fruitless search for a bottle of whisky he had secreted among his shirts this morning when he packed – was once more stooped in the jailbird's position on his bedstead, his tangled head lolling over his hands as they laboured at a forty-five-inch balloon. He was wearing a bath towel and expensive town socks of midnight blue silk by Turnbull & Asser. Tiger had given him thirty pairs after catching him wearing one blue woollen sock and one grey cotton one. Balloons were Oliver's sanity and Brearly was his mentor. When he could resolve nothing else in life, he could still set a box of balloons at his feet and recall Brearly on the arts of modelling, Brearly on how to inflate and knot, Brearly on Skinnies, Pencils and Doodles, how to identify a willing balloon or spot a rogue. When his marriage was falling apart he would sit over Brearly's demonstration videos all night long and Heather's tearful reproaches could not get through to him. You're on-stage at one a.m. unless there's fumble, Brock had warned. And I want you looking like a gentleman again.

Using available light from the uncurtained attic window, Oliver slightly deflated his balloon and nipped off a couple of inches to form a head before realising he had not decided what animal to make. He did a twist, measured a hand's breadth, did another and discovered that his palms were sweating. He laid down the balloon, reverently wiped his hands on a handkerchief, then dipped them in a box of Zinc Stearate powder that sat beside him on the eiderdown – Zinc Stearate to keep the fingers smooth without slippiness, Brearly never went anywhere without it – and groped under the bed for a balloon he had previously inflated. Lock-twisting the two lengths together, he held them to the window to see their shape against the night sky, selected a point and pinched. The balloon burst, but Oliver – who in the normal way held himself responsible for every natural or unnatural disaster – did not scold himself. There was not a magician on earth, he was assured by Brearly, who could beat bad luck with a balloon, and Oliver believed this. You got a duff batch or they didn't like the weather and it didn't matter who you were, you could be Brearly himself, they were exploding in your face like firecrackers and before you knew it your cheeks were cut up with tiny razor blades, your eyes were streaming and your face felt as if you'd been shoved headlong into a nettle patch. And all you'd got, if you were Oliver, was your hero's grin and Rocco's one-liners to save you from fiasco: *Well, that's one way to blow up a balloon . . . He'll be taking that one back to the shop tomorrow, won't he?*

A thump on the door and the sound of Aggie's Glasgow

voice brought him guiltily to his feet, for in another of his many heads he had been agonising over Carmen: is she in Northampton yet? – how's the sore place on her eyebrow? – does she think of me as often as I think of her? And in yet another head: Tiger, where are you? Are you hungry? Are you tired? But since Oliver's anxieties were never mutually exclusive, and he had never learned the knack of addressing each one on its own, he also worried about Yevgeny, and Mikhail, and Tinatin, and about Zoya and whether she knew she was married to a murderer. He feared she did.

'Was that a pistol shot we heard downstairs, Oliver?' Aggie was enquiring skittishly through the door. Oliver produced an unintelligible grunt, part concurrence, part embarrassment, and rubbed his nose with his wrist. 'Only I've got your fash suit here, pressed and ready to go. May I hand it over, please?' He switched on the light, secured his towel round his waist and opened the door. She was wearing a black tracksuit and sneakers and had fastened her hair in a stern knot. He took his suit from her and made to close the door again but she was looking past him in mock horror at the bedstead. 'Oliver, what in *hell* is that object? I mean should I be *seeing* that? Have you discovered a new vice or something?'

He turned and stared with her. 'It's half a giraffe,' he confessed. 'The bit that didn't bust.'

She was amazed, she was incredulous. To appease her he sat down on the bed and completed the giraffe and, because she insisted, a bird and a mouse as well. She needed to know how long they would last and would he make one for her four-year-old niece in Paisley? She was all chat and admiration and he duly acknowledged her good intentions. No one could have been nicer to him, or more appropriately dressed, while he waited to be hanged.

'The Gnat's called a war party in twenty minutes, in case there's any recent developments,' she said. 'Are those the City shoes you'll be wearing, Oliver?'

'They're fine as they are.'

'Not for the Gnat, they aren't. He'd kill me.'

A meeting of eyes – hers because the crew had orders to

befriend him, Oliver's because, as usual when a pretty girl looked at him, he was contemplating a lifelong relationship.

*   *   *

They dropped him by cab in Park Lane. Tanby drove it, Derek pretended to pay Tanby off, Derek and another boy sauntered alongside him into Curzon Street – presumably in case he thought of bolting – before wishing him a cheerful goodnight and trailing him for the remaining fifty yards. This is what happens when I die, thought Oliver. My life is a bunch of unjoined ends, there's a pair of closed doors in front of me and a bunch of kids in black urging me forward from across the street. He wished he was back home at Mrs Watmore's, watching late television with Sammy.

'There's been no arrivals or departures since Friday close of play and no outgoing phone calls,' Brock had said at the briefing. 'There's lights in the Trading Room but no one's trading. Incoming calls are taken by machine and the message says the office will be open for business 8 a.m. Monday. They're playing busy but with Winser dead and Tiger on the loose nobody's moving a finger.'

'Where's Massingham?'

'In Washington, headed for New York. Phoned in yesterday.'

'How about Gupta?' – worried about Tiger's Indian man-servant who occupied the basement flat.

'The Guptas watch television till eleven, lights out eleven-thirty. It's what they do every night and it's what they did tonight. Gupta and his wife sleep in the boiler room, his son and daughter-in-law get the bedroom, kids in the corridor. There's no alarm system in the basement. When Gupta goes downstairs he locks the steel door and it's goodbye world. He's been weeping and shaking his head all day, according to the watchers. Any more questions?'

Gupta who loved Tiger as no other, Oliver remembered sadly. Gupta whose three brothers were fitted up by the Liverpool police a hundred years ago, but as legend had it were saved by the fearless intervention of St Tiger of all

Singles. Gupta who begged only to serve, weeping and shaking his head all day. A valiant moon had risen to the twentieth floor of a monstrous hotel driven like a spike of Manhattan into the London skyline. A powdery mist was falling, half rain, half dew. Sodium streetlights shed a sticky glow over familiar landmarks: the banks of Riyadh and Qatar, Chase Asset Management and an heroic little shop called Tradition that sold model soldiers of yesteryear. Oliver used to dawdle at its window when he was stoking up his courage to enter the House of Single. He mounted the five stone steps he had sworn he would never climb again, slapped his pockets for his key and realised he was clutching it in his hand. He shuffled forward, key leading. Same pillars. Same brass tablet proclaiming farflung outposts of Single empire: Single Leisure Limited, Antigua... Banque Single & Cie... Single Resorts Monaco Ltd... Single Sun Valley of Grand Cayman... Single Marcello Land of Madrid... Single Seebold Löwe of Budapest... Single Malanski of St Petersburg... Single Rinaldo Investments of Milan... Oliver could recite the whole bogus batting order blindfold while his gaze skidded everywhere and stayed on nothing.

'What if they've changed the lock?' he had asked Brock.

'If they have, we've changed it back.'

Key in hand, Oliver stole a last look up and down the street and fancied he saw Tiger in his black overcoat with velvet tabs on the lapels charming him from each of several doorways. A man and woman stood necking in the shadow of an awning. A human bundle lay on the threshold of an estate agent's. I'm giving you a three on the street for emergencies, Brock had said. Emergency meaning the untimely return of the Tiger to his cage. He was sweating and there was sweat in his eyes. I shouldn't have worn the bloody waistcoat. His suit was one of six run up by Hayward's for the day the young master was inducted as junior partner. It had come with a dozen custom-made shirts, and a pair of gold links by Cartier with a tiger on one leaf and a cub on the other, and a maroon Mercedes sports car with quadraphonic sound and TS on the registration plates. He was sweating and his eyes were beginning to fog over, and if his waistcoat wasn't weighing him to the ground the key was. The lock yielded without a murmur, he pushed the door, it opened twelve inches and stopped. He pushed again and felt Saturday's mail slide before him. He stepped high and forward, the door closed behind him and the howling ghosts of Hell leapt forward to receive him.

Good morning, Mr Oliver! – Pat the commissionaire facetiously snapping to attention.

Mr Tiger's ringing all over for you, Oliver – Sarah the receptionist, from her switchboard.

Gave her one for breakfast, did we, Ollie boy? – Archie, cockney whizzkid of the Trading Room, having his bit of sport with the young master.

'You never left the shop,' Brock had told Oliver as they sat waiting for the quiet hours. 'Not in the Gospel According to Tiger. You never resigned your partnership, you never disappeared into thin air. You're on overseas study leave, collecting foreign qualifications, whipping up client contacts. You're paid full salary, according to the company's reports. Remunerations to full-time partners last year totalled five million eight hundred thousand. Tiger filed a tax return for three million gross, which leaves you a couple of million tucked away in some offshore account. Congratulations. You also sent the House a telegram on the occasion of its Christmas party, which was nice of you. Tiger read it out loud.'

'Where was I?'

'Djakarta. Maritime law.'

'Who believes that crap?'

'Anyone who wants to keep his job.'

Wan street light filtered through the fan window above the door. The famous gilded cage stood open to waft distinguished visitors to the top floor. 'The Single's lift goes up and never comes down!' a fawning financial correspondent had written breathlessly, after being lunched at Kat's. Tiger had had the article framed and hung beside the button panel. Oliver ignored the lift and took the staircase, stepping lightly, not feeling his feet on the carpet, wondering whether they were there at all, letting his fingers trail up the mahogany handrail but not grasping it because the patina was Mrs Gupta's pride. Reaching a half-landing he dithered. The Trading Room lay to his left behind a double swing door that banged like a bistro kitchen. Delicately he pushed it and peered inside. Boxed neon lights blazed from the ceiling. Ranks of computer screens fluttered wakefully. Dave, Fuong, Archie, Sally, Mufta, where are you? – it's me, Big Ollie the Prince Regent. No answer. They've jumped overboard. Welcome to the *Marie Celeste.*

Across the landing ran the long corridor of the Administration Department, home of embargoed secretaries in career suits and a trio of clerical accountants known as wet-nappy boys because they handled the dirty work that the super-rich expect of their paid help: cars, dogs, houses, horses, yachts, boxes at Ascot, paying off unwanted lovers and conducting whispered negotiations with disaffected menservants who have gone to earth with the Rolls, a case of whisky and the clients' chihuahua. The doyen of the wet nappies was a shy old giant called Mortimer who lived in Rickmansworth and revelled in the excesses of his awful wards. *Plus* she's humping the butler, he would murmur out of the corner of his mouth, riding his shoulder against Oliver's for extra confidentiality. *Plus* she's flogging off hubby's Renoirs and hanging up repros because the old boy's going blind. *Plus* she's cutting his children out of his Will and getting planning permission for twenty semis in his walled garden...

Ascending weightlessly to the next landing Oliver hovered long enough at the door to the Directors' Boardroom to compose a tableau of Tiger enthroned one end of the rosewood table and Oliver the other while Massingham the head waiter deals out leatherbound spurious accounts to a rabble of derelict peers, deposed government ministers, silk-shirt City editors, overpaid lawyers and rented strangers. He reached another half-landing and saw above him the castored feet of a janitors' desk and the lower half of a fisheye mirror. He was approaching what Massingham to the ribaldry of the clerks insisted on calling the Sensitive Area.

'There's a white side and a black side,' Oliver had told Brock in the papier-mâché interviewing room at Heathrow. 'The white side pays the rent, the black side starts on the third floor.' 'Which side are you on then, son?' Brock had asked. 'Both,' Oliver had replied after long thought, and from then on Brock stopped calling him son.

He heard a thump and died. A burglar. Pigeons. Tiger. A heart attack. He climbed faster, escaping forward, preparing his lines for the obligatory encounter:

It's me, Father. Oliver. I'm terribly sorry I'm four years late, only I met this girl and we got talking and one thing led to another and I overslept...

Oh hullo, Father, sorry to be a bore, only I had a crisis of conscience, you see, or I suppose it was conscience. No shining light on the road to Damascus or anything like that, I simply woke up at Heathrow after a rather taxing whistle-stop tour of major clients and decided it was about time I declared some of the contraband I had accumulated inside my head...

Father! – fab! – great to see you! – just happened to be passing, thought I'd drop by... Only I heard about poor old Alfie Winser, you see, and I naturally couldn't help wondering how you were getting along...

Oh Father, look here, thanks tons for Carmen's five million odd. She's a bit young to thank you herself but Heather and I greatly appreciate the gesture...

Oh, and by the way, Father, Nat Brock says that if by any chance you're on the run he'd very much appreciate the opportunity of cutting a deal with you. Apparently he met you once in Liverpool and was able to admire your skills at first hand...

Well, the other thing is, Father, actually, if it's all right by you I've come to smuggle you to safety. No, no, no, I'm your friend! I mean, it's true I betrayed you, but that was necessary surgery. Deep down I'm still tremendously loyal...

He was standing before an inner bailey door, uselessly studying a panel of numbers that controlled the lock. An ambulance was screaming up South Audley Street but from the din it was making it could have been coming up the stairs. A police car followed it, then a fire engine. Great, he thought, a fire's exactly what I need. 'What we are dealing

172

with here, gentlemen, is what I call our rolling combination,' a grim-jawed security consultant is explaining in his bitten-off ex-policeman's voice to the reluctantly assembled senior executives, of whom Oliver is one. 'Our first four digits are constant and we all know what they are.' We do indeed. They are 1-9-3-6, the blessed year of our Lord Tiger's birth. 'Our last two figures are what we call the rollers and these are achieved by subtracting the day's date from the number fifty. Thus if our date today is the thirteenth of the month, which my spies reliably inform me it is ha-ha, I touch in the digits three seven like thus. If our date is the first of the month, then I touch in the digits four nine like thus. Have we all absorbed that, gentlemen? I am well aware that I am addressing an above-average and extremely busy audience this morning, so I will not detain you beyond the necessary. No questions? Thank you, gentlemen, you may smoke, ha-ha.'

With a recklessness that startled him, Oliver touched in Tiger's birth year, followed it with the day's rollers and shoved the door away from him. It yelped and opened, admitting him to the Legal Department. *You are legal, Post Boy?* Yevgeny is asking him incredulously. *You are legal?* Random early English watercolours portrayed Jerusalem, Lake Windermere and the Matterhorn. Tiger once had a bankrupt client who dealt in them. A door stood ajar. Fingertips again, Oliver poked it open. My room. My cell. My Pirelli calendar, four years older. This is where our legal Post Boy learned the ropes. Ropes like trading companies that had never traded in their lives and never would. Ropes like holding companies that held nothing for longer than five minutes because it was too damn hot. Ropes like selling bum stock to the bank in order to make the bank the buyer. Then buying said stock back through other companies because the bank happens to be yours. Ropes like proposing theoretical scenarios for a client's general information, never intending, naturally, that said client should be so unprincipled as to treat the information as professional advice. Such ropes being the cherished preserve of none other than the late, murdered, penis-driven Alfie Winser in his stay-brown hair and Tiger-inspired suits; Alfie, terror of the typists' pool, unsafe in corridors, my immoral tutor:

Well, Mr Asir – smirk, and a nod across the room to our Young Master who is sitting in for the experience – let us imagine for argument's sake that you have acquired large sums of money through your flourishing cosmetics business in, well, let's just say it's multi-national. Perhaps you do not have such a cosmetics business, but let us imagine for argument's sake that you do – snigger – and let us further imagine you are helping out your much-loved younger brother in Delhi, assuming that you have such a brother and please don't tell me if you haven't, tee-hee. And this brother owns a string of hotels, let us say, and you are under an obligation as his brother to secure for him – purchase – costly and sophisticated catering equipment in Europe, machinery he is unable to obtain in India, poor fellow, and for which he has advanced you, let us say, seven and a half million dollars on an informal basis, you being his brother, which I gather in Asian circles is quite normal. And let us further suppose that, with this scenario in mind, you were to approach Mr So-and-So of the Bank of So-and-So in the agreeable city of Zug in Switzerland and indicate that you are represented by the House of Single & Single and that Mr Alfred Winser with whom he recently passed a recreational evening sends his most personal regards...

An insanitary emergency staircase, lit by blue nightlights, rose from the end of the Legal corridor by way of two fire doors and a men's lavatory to the sumptuous antechambers of the Tiger's Lair. Oliver climbed one step at a time. A panelled door appeared before him. It was curved and slender with a brass doorknob at its centre. He raised a hand and was about to knock, but caught himself in time, grasped the knob and turned it. He was standing in the fabled rotunda. A film-maker's star-strewn sky opened above him, projected through segments of a glass dome. By the fickle glow he made out shelves of perfectly bound books that no one read: law books for felons, books on Who's Rich and Whom to Con, books on contracts and how to break them, taxation and how to avoid it. New books to show that Tiger

174

is of today. Old books to show that he is trustworthy. Solemn books to show that he is sincere. Oliver was shaking and a nettlerash was crawling up his neck and over the inside of his chest and forehead. He had forgotten everything: his name, age, the time of day, whether he had been sent here or come of his own accord, what he loved except his father. To his left, the boneless sofa and the door to Massingham's office. Closed. To his right, Pam Hawsley's crescent desk and the portraits of her three pugs. And straight ahead of him, across forty feet of azure carpet, the Wedgwood curved double doors to the Tiger's tomb, closed but waiting for the robber.

Navigating by the stars, Oliver crossed the rotunda and located the right-hand of the two doors, turned the handle, crouched and, with his eyes crammed shut, as he supposed, sidled into his father's office. The air was still and sweet. Oliver sniffed it and fancied he caught a mannish whiff of Trumper's body lotion, Tiger's weapon of choice. Discovering that his eyes were after all open, he stumbled forward and halted before the sacred desk, waiting to be noticed. It was vast, and vaster in the half-darkness, though never so vast as to reduce the stature of its occupant. The throne was empty. Cautiously he straightened and allowed himself a less inhibited view of the room. The twenty-foot conference table. The ring of armchairs where customers may sit at greater ease while Tiger acquaints them with the sacred right of every citizen regardless of colour, race or creed to the best legal loopholes that illicit wealth can buy. The bay window where Tiger, like a miniature captain on his bridge, likes to strut and clutch your arm and study his reflection in the London skyline while he makes your unborn child a five-times millionaire. And where – *oh God, oh Christ Almighty!* – *where now Tiger's corpse, lengthways and wound in spectral muslin, floated in the air like a new moon on its back.* Racked. Stretched until he snapped. Tiger as spider, hanged in his own web.

Somehow Oliver edged forward but the apparition did not alter or retreat. It's a trick. Astonish your friends! Slice your partner in two before their very eyes! Send stamped addressed envelope to Magic Numbers, Post Box, Walsingham! He whispered, 'Tiger.' Nothing came back to him above the sobbing and heaving of the city. 'Father. It's Oliver. Me. I'm home. It's all right. Father. I love you.' Searching for wires, he flung out an arm and described a wild arc above the corpse, only to discover he had acquired a handful of burial shroud. Cringing, expecting dreadful things, he forced himself to keep his eyes open, looked downward and saw a fogged brown head rise to meet his gaze. And he recognised, not his father sprung from the sepulchre, but the astonished ex-ophthalmic features of the ever-loyal Gupta emerging from the depths of his hammock: Gupta tearful, joyous and bare-legged, wearing blue underpants and swathes of mosquito netting, clutching the young master by both arms and shaking them to the rhythm of his terrified delight.

'Mr Oliver, wherever in Heaven's good name have you been, sir? Overseas, overseas! Study, study! My God, sir, you must have studied your eyes out. Nobody could talk about you. You were a mystery of major proportions, to be divulged to no man! Are you married, sir? Are you blessed with children, are you happy? Four years, Mr Oliver, four years! My Lord God. Tell me only that your holy father is alive and in sound health, please. It is many long days we hear nothing.'

'He's all right,' said Oliver, forgetting everything but his relief. 'Mr Tiger's fine.'

'That is the truth, Mr Oliver?'

'It is indeed.'

'And your good self, sir?'

'Not married, but also fine. Thanks, Gupta. Thanks.'

Thanks for not being Tiger.

'Then I am doubly overjoyed, sir, and so are we all. I could not desert my post, Mr Oliver. I do not apologise. Poor Mr Winser. My God. In his second prime of life, we may say. A true gentleman. Always a laugh and a word for us little fellows and specially the ladies. And now the sinking ship is being abandoned, the passengers are departing like snow in the fire. On Wednesday three secretaries, on Thurs-

176

day two excellent young traders, and now there are rumours that our most elegant Chief of Staff is not merely on holiday but is permanently removing himself to greener pastures. Somebody must stay behind and tend the flame, I say, even if we are obliged to sit in darkness for reasons of security.'

'You're a prince, Gupta,' said Oliver.

After which there was an uncomfortable gap while each separately reappraised his pleasure in the other. Gupta had a picnic-flask of hot tea. Oliver drank from the only cup. But he was avoiding Gupta's eye. And Gupta's eager smile of expectation was coming and going like a faulty lamp.

'Mr Tiger sends his greetings, Gupta,' Oliver said, breaking the silence.

'Through *you*, sir? You have spoken to him?'

'"If old Gupta's there, kick him in the backside for me." You know how he speaks.'

'Sir, I love this man.'

'He knows that.' Oliver was putting on his partner's voice, hating himself as he listened to his own words. 'He knows the measure of your loyalty, Gupta. He expects no less of you.'

'He is most kind. Your father is a person of great and limitless heart, I would say. You are two most kind gentlemen.' Gupta's little face had turned ugly with unease. Everything he felt – love, loyalty, suspicion, fear – was written in his crumpled features. 'In what matter do you come, sir, if I may ask?' he demanded, growing bolder in his distress. 'Why do you bear messages from Mr Tiger suddenly, after four years of silence overseas? – please, sir, forgive me, I am a humble manservant.'

'My father wants me to pick up some papers from the partners' strong room. He believes they could have a bearing on the unfortunate episode of last weekend.'

'Oh sir,' said Gupta softly.

'What's the matter?'

'I am a father also, sir.'

So am I, Oliver wanted to tell him.

Gupta's tiny right hand had stolen to his breast. 'Your father is not a happy father, Mr Oliver. You are his only issue. I am a happy father, sir. I know the difference. The love Mr Tiger feels for you is not reciprocated. Such is his perception. If Mr Tiger trusts you, Mr Oliver, then well and good, I say. So be it.' He was nodding. He had seen his path and was nodding at its rightness. 'We shall witness the evidence, Mr Oliver, black on white, no ifs or buts. The challenge is not laid down by me. An act of Providence has come to our assistance. Follow me, please. Be careful where I am stepping, Mr Oliver. Do not approach the windows.' Oliver followed Gupta's shadow to a pair of mahogany doors that disguised the entrance to the partners' vault. Gupta opened them and stepped inside. Oliver joined him. Gupta closed the doors and switched on the light. They faced each other, the safe door between them. Gupta was even shorter than Tiger, which Oliver had always suspected was the reason Tiger had selected him.

'Your father was most circumspect in his personal confidences, Mr Oliver. "Who can we trust with total confidence, I ask you, Gupta?" he said to me. "Where is the gratitude for all that we have given to those we love the most, I am asking, Gupta? Where may a man look for total commitment, if not to his own flesh and blood, tell me if you will be so kind? Therefore, Gupta, I must arm myself against treachery." These were his words to me, Mr Oliver, confided on a personal basis over the midnight oil.' Tiger's words or not, they were assuredly Gupta's, delivered with tremulous accusation in the presence of the locked grey steel door on which his gaze had fixed itself with mysterious reverence.

'"Gupta," he says to me. "Take guard against your sons if they are envious. I am not blind. Certain misfortunes that have occurred to my House are not to be dismissed without a most detailed examination of all the facts. Certain correspondences known only to a certain person and myself have fallen into the hands of our implacable enemies. Who is to blame here? Who is the Judas?"'

'When did he say all this to you?'

'When the calamities began to multiply, your father became reflective. He spent many hours in that strong room you are attempting to enter, questioning the loyalty of other eyes than his, sir.'

'Then I hope he was able to clear his mind of unworthy suspicions,' Oliver replied haughtily.

'I too, sir. Most devoutly. Please, Mr Oliver, sir, help yourself at your leisure. Take your time. Let Providence decide, I say.'

It was a challenge. Observed minutely by Gupta, Oliver stooped to the dial. It was green with raised digits. Gupta placed himself belligerently the other side of it, little arms folded.

'I'm not sure you're supposed to be watching this, are you?' said Oliver.

'Sir, I am the *de facto* custodian of your father's house. I am awaiting proof of your good faith.'

The knowledge stole upon Oliver without fanfares, like knowledge already possessed. Gupta is telling me Tiger has changed the combination, and if I don't know the new combination, then Tiger hasn't given it to me. And if he hasn't given it to me, he hasn't sent me and therefore I'm lying in my teeth and Providence is about to prove it, and Providence will be bang on target.

'Gupta, I really would like you to wait outside.'

With an ill grace Gupta switched out the light, opened the door, stepped outside and closed it again. Switching the light back on, Oliver heard him delivering a eulogy of Tiger through the keyhole. Tiger as martyr to his own goodness. As defender of the weak. As the victim of a planned and devilish deception by certain persons nearest to him. As generous employer, model husband and father.

'A great man should be judged only by his friends, Mr Oliver. He should not be judged by those who are inveterately disposed against his person for reasons of envy or the smallness of their souls, sir.'

My bloody birthday, Oliver thought.

* * *

It is an evening close to Christmas. Oliver has been Brock's man for a mere few days, yet he lives in an altered state. Spying has made him dependent on stronger natures than

179

his own, more obedient than he ever was before he spied. Tonight, at Brock's behest, he plans to stay in late and continue his examination of clients' offshore bank accounts before Tiger has the chance to edit them. Seated nervously at his desk, he tinkers with a draft contract while he waits for Tiger to put his head round the door on his way out. Instead, he is summoned to the presence. When he gets there, Tiger seems, as usual, uncertain what to do with him.

'Oliver.'

'Yes, Father.'

'Oliver, it's time I initiated you into the mysteries of the partners' strong room.'

'Are you sure you really want to?' Oliver asks. And it is touch and go whether he will give his father a much-needed lecture on personal security.

Tiger is sure. Having lit upon an activity, he must now expand it into a matter of moment, for nothing Tigers do can be less than momentous. 'It's for your eyes only and no one else's, Oliver. To be shared between you and me and no one else on earth. Do you understand that?'

'Of course.'

'No little whispered confidences to our latest lady-love, not even Nina. This is for the two of us.'

'Absolutely.'

'Say, I promise.'

'I promise.'

Filled with a high sense of his own gravity, Tiger demonstrates the secret. The combination of the partners' strong room is none other than Oliver's birthdate. Tiger enters it on the dial and invites Oliver to turn the great handle. The iron door swings open.

'Father, I am moved.'

'I don't want your gratitude. Gratitude means nothing to me. What we're looking at here is a symbol of mutual trust. There's a decent whisky in the cupboard. Pour us both a glass. What is it old Yevgeny says when he wants a drink? – "Let's have a serious conference." Thought we might have a spot of dinner afterwards. Why don't I ring old Kat? Is Nina game?'

180

'Nina's tied up tonight, actually. That's why I'm at a loose end.'

*   *   *

'"When I am stabbed in the back, Gupta, tell me whose hand is on the knife!"' Gupta was yelling through the keyhole. '"Is it the hand closest to my heart, I am asking myself? Is it the hand I have fed and watered like no other? Gupta, if I told you I was today the saddest man on earth, this would be no exaggeration whatsoever of my current personal situation, regardless of the fact that self-pity does not befit a person of my stature." These were his very words, Mr Oliver. From the Tiger's mouth.'

Alone inside the strong room Oliver stared at the dial. Stay calm. This is not a good time to panic, he told himself. So when is? First, if only to confirm the hopelessness of his predicament, he entered the old combination, two left, two right, four left, four right, two left and twist the handle. It refused to budge. My birthdate is no longer operative. On the other side of the door Gupta continued his lament while Oliver desperately lectured himself. Tiger does nothing carelessly, he reasoned, nothing that does not enhance his self-esteem. Without conviction he dialled Tiger's own birthdate. Nothing budged. Commemoration Day! he thought, with greater optimism, and dialled the number 050480, this being the date of the firm's foundation, traditionally celebrated with a champagne barge-ride up the Thames. But no cheer resulted. He heard Brock: 'But *you*, you can feel him, guess him, live him, just by breathing in. You've got him *here*.' He heard Heather: 'Girls count roses, Oliver. They like to know how much they're loved.' Sickened by the dawning of his prescience, he again spun the dial with sweating fingers, three left, two right, two left, four right, two left. Grimly, stoically, no demonstrations of emotion permitted. He was entering Carmen's birthdate.

'Sir, it is not beyond my competence to call 999 and demand the appropriate service, Mr Oliver!' Gupta was screaming. 'This will be very soon my next move, you will see!'

The bolt clanged free, the door to the strong room swung open and the secret kingdom displayed itself before him, boxes, files, books and papers stacked with Tiger's obsessional precision. He switched out the light and stepped back into the office. Gupta was wringing his hands, moaning pitiful apologies. Oliver's face was on fire and his bowels were churning yet he contrived to speak snappishly, an officer of the Single Raj.

'Gupta, I need to know as a matter of urgency what my father did from the moment he received the news of Mr Winser's death.'

'Oh, he was demented, sir. How the news came to him is a matter for speculation. Office rumour maintains it was a telephone call, who from is not given to us to know, but probably a newspaper. His eyes were most wild. "Gupta," he says, "we are betrayed. A chain of events has reached its tragic culmination. Find me my brown coat." He was a stranger to reason, Mr Oliver, a man confused. "Sir, then are you going to Nightingales?" I said. Always if he is going to Nightingales he wears his brown coat. It is an emblem for him, a symbol, a gift from your sainted mother herself. Therefore when he wears it I am confident of his destination. "Yes, Gupta, I am going to Nightingales. And in Nightingales I shall seek the comfort of my dear wife and sound a bugle of distress to my only surviving son, whose assistance is imperative to me in my hour of need." At this moment Mr Massingham comes in without knocking. It is most unusual, bearing in mind the respectful demeanour of Mr Massingham at other times. "Gupta, leave us." It is your father speaking. What transpires between the two gentlemen I do not know but it is brief. Both men are white as spirits. Each has seen his vision simultaneously and now they are comparing notes. That was my impression, sir. There is talk of a Mr Bernard. Ring Bernard, Bernard must be consulted, why don't we lay this at Bernard's door? Then abruptly your father commands a silence. This Bernard must not be trusted. He is an enemy. Miss Hawsley was weeping copiously. I did not know that tears came to her except in regard to her small dogs.'

'My father made no travel arrangements that you remember? He didn't send for Gasson?'

'No, sir. He was not rational. Rationality, if it was to return, occurred later I would say.'

Oliver preserved his harsh tone for one more beat.

'Pay attention, Gupta. Mr Tiger's fortunes depend on the recovery of certain lost papers. I have engaged a team of professional investigators to assist me. You're to remain in your quarters until they leave the building. Do you understand?'

Gupta gathered up his hammock and scuttled down the stairs. Oliver waited until he heard the basement door slam shut. From Tiger's desk he telephoned the watchers across the road and blurted the fatuous codeword Brock had given him for this moment. He stormed down the stairs and pulled open the front door. First came Brock, followed by crew in dark tracksuits and backpacks for their wretched cameras, tripods, lights and whatever other junk they carried.

'Gupta's gone down to his basement,' Oliver hissed at Brock. 'Some bloody idiot didn't notice he's taken to sleeping upstairs. I'm getting out.'

Brock murmured into his jacket collar. Derek handed his backpack to his neighbour and stepped to Oliver's side. Oliver stumbled down the front steps, escorted by Derek and followed by Aggie, who grabbed his free arm in a companionable embrace while Derek held the other. A cab pulled alongside, Tanby at the wheel. Derek and Aggie whisked Oliver aboard and sat him between them on the back seat. Aggie laid a hand on his arm but he shook himself free. As they entered Park Lane he had a waking dream that he had propped his bicycle against a stationary train in India and climbed aboard, but the train refused to budge because of bodies on the line. At the safe house Aggie rang the bell while Derek handed Oliver onto the pavement and Tanby waited to catch him as he touched down. Oliver had no consciousness of going up the stairs, only of lying on his bed in his underclothes and wishing he had Aggie beside him. He woke to see morning light behind the threadbare curtains of the dormer window and Brock, not Aggie, sitting in the chair, holding a sheet of paper to him. Oliver raised himself on one elbow, rubbed his neck, accepted a photocopied letter. Printed colophon of two chain-mail gauntlets intertwined in greeting – or is it combat? The words TRANS-FINANZ VIENNA curved over the gauntlets. Electronic type with an indefinable foreign accent:

To T. Single, Esq., PERSONAL, by courier.

Dear Mr Single,

Subsequent to our negotiations with a representative of your distinguished firm, we have pleasure to advise you formally of our claim upon House of Single in sum of £200,000,000 (two hundred million pounds Sterling) such being fair and reasonable compensation for lost earnings and betrayal of confidences entrusted to you under client privilege. Payment within thirty days to the account of Trans-Finanz Istanbul Offshore, details known to you, marked attention Dr Mirsky, failing this further action will follow. Collateral is forwarded to you under separate cover to your private residence. Thanking you for your early attention.

Signed Y. I. Orlov in an ailing, elderly hand, and countersigned by Tiger's prim initials confirming that the contents had been read and duly noted.

'Remember Mirsky?' Brock enquired. 'Used to be Mirski with an i till he went to the States for two years and learned wisdom.'

'Of course I do. Polish lawyer. Some kind of trading partner of Yevgeny's. You told me to look out for him.'

'Trading partner my foot,' Brock was riding him, determined to move him forward. 'Mirsky's a crook. He was a Communist crook and now he's a capitalist crook. What's he doing playing banker to Yevgeny's two hundred million quid?'

'Why the fuck should I know?' Oliver shoved the letter back at him.

'Get up.'

Oliver sullenly heaved himself fully upright and moved his legs round till he sat on the edge of the bed.

'Are you listening?'

'Not much.'

'I'm sorry about Gupta. We're not perfect, we never will be. You managed him a treat. That was sheer genius unscrambling the strong room combination. Nobody but you could have done that. You're the best operator I've got. That's not the only letter we found by any means. Our friend Bernard is buried in there with his free villa, so are half a dozen other Bernards. Are you listening?' Oliver went to the bathroom, turned on the basin tap and sluiced water in his face. 'We found Tiger's passport too,' Brock called after him through the open doorway. 'Either he's using someone else's or he hasn't gone anywhere.'

Oliver heard this news as if it were just another death among so many. 'I need to ring Sammy,' he said, coming back to the bedroom.

'Who's Sammy?'

'I need to ring his mother, Elsie, tell her I'm all right.' Brock brought him a telephone and stood over him while he used it. 'Elsie – it's me, Oliver – how's Sammy? Good – oh right, well – see you soon' – all in one dull tone before he rang off, took a breath and, without a glance at Brock, dialled Heather's number in Northampton. 'It's me. Yes. Oliver, that me. How's Carmen?... No, I can't... *What?* Well, get the doctor... Look, go private, I'll pay... Soon...' He lifted his head and saw Brock nodding to him. 'They'll come and talk to you soon... like tomorrow or the next day...' More nods from Brock. 'And there've been no more funny people coming round?... No shiny cars or spooky phone-calls? No more roses?... Good.' He rang off. 'Carmen's cut her knee,' he complained, as if it were all Brock's fault. 'Might need stitching.'

CHAPTER ELEVEN

Aggie drove. Oliver sprawled beside her, now attacking the top of his head with sweeps of his hand, now hoisting up his long legs and with a great puff releasing them to buffet against the floor, now wondering what would happen if he took a dive at her, like putting his hand on hers while she changed gear, or running his fingers round the gap between her collar and her neck. She'd stop the car and flatten me, he decided. The olive hills of Salisbury Plain flowed to either side of them. Sheep grazed on their slopes. A low sun gilded farmhouses and churches. The car was an anonymous Ford with a toy glider on the rear ledge and a second radio secreted beneath the dashboard. Ahead of them a pick-up truck rode point, Tanby at the wheel, Derek at his side. A red streamer was tied to its aerial. Aggie doesn't like Derek, so I don't either. Two leather-clad motorcyclists rode tail, their helmets blazoned with red arrows. Sometimes the car radio crackled and a chill female voice spoke a codeword. Sometimes Aggie responded with another. Sometimes she tried to cheer him up.

'I mean, have you ever *been* to Glasgow, Oliver?' she asked. 'It's really humming.'

'So I've heard.'

'I mean you could do worse than try it when this is over, if you get my meaning.'

'Good thought. I might at that.'

She tried again. 'Do you remember Walter at all?'

'Yeah, sure, course, Walter. One of Tanby's bruisers. What about him?'

'Oh Walter, well, he just slunk off to one of these two-bit security firms up north. Thirty-five thousand a year and a fur-lined Rover, it makes you sick. Where's loyalty? Where's service?'

'Where indeed?' Oliver agreed, and smiled at fur-lined.

'I mean wasn't that *awful* for you? Discovering your own *dad* was a crook and all? – and you fresh from law school, believing that law was about protecting people and keeping society on a straight course? I mean how does a person *deal* with that, Oliver? And you're talking to someone who read philosophy for her sins.' Oliver wasn't talking to anyone, whatever they had read, but Aggie plunged on. 'I mean how do you ever *know*, in a situation like that, whether you just hate the bastard or love justice? Asking yourself day and night, "Am I being a hypocrite, all the time pretending I'm high and mighty and virtuous on my white horse, when actually I'm getting my own back on my father?" Is that how it went with you, or is it just me being vicarious?'

'Yeah. Well.'

'I mean, you're a real star for us, do you know that? The lonely decider. The idealist. The walk-in of all time. There's blokes in the Service would kill to get your autograph.' Long delay in which even the doughty Aggie might have wished she had not been quite so doughty.

'There's no white horse,' Oliver mumbled. 'More a sort of merry-go-round.'

The pick-up ahead of them signalled left. They followed it down a slip road into country lanes. The motorbike came after them. Young foliage closed above them, cutting out the sky. Sunlight danced between the tree trunks, the radio squawked static. The pick-up pulled into a layby, the motorbike behind them peeled into a side turning. The car nose-dived down a steep hill and crossed a watersplash. They reached a hilltop. A yellow barrage balloon with HARRIS painted on it was suspended over a filling station. She's been here before, he thought, watching her out of the corner of his eye. They all have. She took the left turn, they skirted the village and saw the church on the skyline and the tithe barn next to it and the pantiled bungalows that Tiger had fought tooth-and-nail to prevent. They entered Autumn Lane where fallen leaves lay dying all year round. They passed a cul-de-sac called Nightingales End and saw a parked electricity van with its ladder up and a man doing something to the wires. In the cab a woman was talking into a telephone. Aggie drove another hundred yards and pulled up beside a bus stop.

'You have lift-off,' she announced.

He got out. The sky behind the trees looked like day but in the hedgerows dusk was gathering fast. On a grass island stood a brick war memorial inscribed with the names of the Glorious Fallen. Four Harvey boys, he remembered. All from one family, all dead by the age of twenty, and their mother lived till ninety. He started walking and heard Aggie drive away. The immense gateposts rose before him. On their summits, carved tigers clutched the Single coat-of-arms. The tigers had come from a sculpture park in Putney and cost a fortune. The coat-of-arms was the work of a pedantic heraldry consultant named Potts who spent a weekend questioning Tiger about his antecedents, not realising they varied with the seasons. The results were a Hanseatic ship representing our ancient Lübeck trading connections, hitherto unknown to Oliver, a tiger rampant and two turtle doves from our Saxon side, though what doves had to do with Saxony was a riddle known only to Mr Potts.

The drive flowed like a black river over the twilit meadows. This is the grave I was born in, he thought. This is where I lived in the time before I became a child. He passed the pepperpot gatehouse where Gasson the chauffeur went to ground when Tiger decided to stay the night. No lights burned in the windows, the upper curtains were drawn. A loosebox stood in the yard, its tow-bar resting on a pile of bricks. Oliver is seven years old. It is his first pony class and he is wearing the stiff bowler and tweed jacket that Tiger from his distant place of power has decreed. Nobody else in his class is wearing a bowler so Oliver has tried to hide it, together with the silver-handled riding crop that Tiger has sent by courier for his birthday because by now Tiger's visits are rare state occasions.

'Chest out, Oliver! Don't slouch! You're nodding, Oliver! Try and look like Jeffrey more! *He* didn't nod, did he? Straight as a soldier, Jeffrey was.'

Jeffrey my elder brother by five years. Jeffrey who did everything right that I do wrong. Jeffrey who was perfect in all things and died of leukaemia before he had time to run the world. Oliver was passing the sandstone ice-house. It had arrived by magic in three green vans, gone up in a week and become his instant place of punishment – a hundred and seventy running paces to the ice-house, touch it, a hundred and seventy back, one lap for every unlearned irregular Latin verb, and more laps for not being as good as Jeffrey was, whether at Latin or running. Mr Ravilious, Oliver's tutor, is a numerist. So is Tiger. Over the long-distance telephone they deal in points, marks, distances, hours spent and punishments deserved, and what percentages are required to get him into somewhere called the Dragon School where Jeffrey got his cricket colours and his scholarship to somewhere still more terrible called Eton. Oliver hates dragons but admires Mr Ravilious for his velvet jackets and black cigarettes. When Mr Ravilious elopes with the Spanish maid, Oliver cheers for him amid the general outrage.

Preferring the long route beside the walled garden, he skirted a flattened hillock that was neither a burial mound nor a golf tee but a helipad for guests too elevated for terrestrial travel. Guests like Yevgeny and Mikhail Orlov with their plastic bags of Russian lacquerware, bottles of lemon vodka and smoked Mingrelian sausages wrapped in greaseproof paper. Guests with bodyguards. Guests with collapsible billiards cues in black carrying cases because they didn't trust Tiger's. But only Oliver knew that the helipad was a secret altar. Inspired by the story of an Indonesian tribe that laid out decoy wooden aeroplanes to attract rich tourists flying overhead, he had put out offerings of Jeffrey's favourite foods in the hope of luring him down from Heaven to complete his childhood. But the food in Heaven was evidently better, because Jeffrey never returned. And Jeffrey was not the only absentee. In the rolling mist stood jumping hurdles that were kept radiant white, and the polo field that was marked and mown all year, and the stables where every saddle and bridle and snaffle and stirrup was burnished against the never-never day when Tiger, after twenty years of being on a business trip, would roll up the drive with Gasson at the wheel and resume the hard-earned feudal English life.

The drive sank between copper beeches. Ahead lay a pair of brick and flint staff cottages. Passing them he dawdled, hoping to catch sight of Craft the butler and his wife seated over tea. He had loved the Crafts and used them as his window on the world beyond the walls of Nightingales. But Mrs Craft had died fifteen years ago and Mr Craft had returned home to Hull, where his roots were, taking with him a Fabergé box and a set of eighteenth-century miniatures of Tiger's elusive ancestors, this time Pennsylvania Dutch. Oliver descended the hill and Nightingales appeared below him, first the chimney pots, then the whole grey-stoned heap, set in weedless gravel that made his feet crunch like cracking ice as he advanced on the front porch. The bell-pull was a brass hand with its thumb and fingers stuck together. Seizing it in a monkey-grip, he tugged downward while his heart thumped with a son's inescapable longing. He was about to give a second pull when he heard a shuffle from the other side of the door, and in a panic wondered what to call her because she hated Mother, and Mummy even more. He realised he had forgotten her first name. He had forgotten his own too. He was seven years old and sitting in a police station six miles away, and he couldn't even remember the name of the house he had run away from. The door opened and a darkness came out at him. He was grinning and mumbling. His ears had blocked. He felt the fuzz of a mohair cardigan against his grin as her arms came round his neck. He folded her into his protection. He closed his eyes and tried to become a child, but it didn't work. She kissed his left cheek and he smelt peppermint and putrid breath. She kissed his other cheek and he remembered how tall she was, taller than any other woman he had kissed. He remembered her trembling and her smell of soapy lavender. He wondered whether she trembled all the time or just for him. She pulled back from him. Her eyes, like his, were flooded with tears.

'Ollie, darling.' You got it right, he thought, because sometimes she called him Jeffrey. 'Why ever didn't you warn me, Ollie? My poor heart. Whatever have you done now?'

Nadia, he remembered: don't call me Mother, Ollie darling. Call me Nadia, you make me feel so old.

*   *   *

The kitchen was low and vast. Bruised copper saucepans, bought at auction by a vanished interior designer, hung from ancient beams added during one of numberless refurbishments. The table was long enough for twenty servants. A bombé Dutch oven, never connected to the flue, filled the dark end.

'You must be ravenous,' she told him analytically, as if eating were something other people did.

'I'm really not, honestly.'

They peered into the fridge for something to satisfy him. A bottle of milk? A packet of pumpernickel bread? A tin of anchovies, perhaps? Her trembling hand was resting on his shoulder. In a minute I'll be trembling too.

'Oh dear, it's Mrs Henderson's day off,' she said. 'I bant at weekends. I always did. You've forgotten.' Their eyes met in the downlight and he saw that she was scared of him. He wondered whether she was drunk or only on the way. Sometimes she'd hardly started and already spoke girlish slur. Other times she'd have a couple of bottles inside her and be seemingly composed. 'You don't look very *well*, Ollie darling. Have you been overdoing it? You go so hard at things.'

'I'm fine. You look fine too. Incredible.'

It wasn't incredible at all. Each year before Christmas she went on what she called her little holiday and returned without a wrinkle in her face.

'Did you walk from the station, darling? I didn't hear a car arrive, nor did Jacko.' Jacko the Siamese cat. 'I'd have picked you up if you'd rung.'

You haven't driven a car for years, he thought. Not since you crashed through the barn wall in the Land Rover on New Year's Eve and Tiger burned your driving licence. 'I love the walk, honestly,' he said. 'You know I do. Even when it's raining I don't mind.' In a minute neither of us will know what to say.

'The trains don't seem to run on Sundays as a rule. Mrs Henderson has to change at Swindon if she wants to see her brother,' she complained.

'Mine was bang on time.' He sat at the table in his usual place. She remained standing, doting on him, trembling and worrying, working her lips like a baby before a feed. 'Anyone staying?' he asked.

'Just me and the pussycats, darling. Why should there be?'

'I just wondered.'

'I don't keep a dog any more. Not after Samantha pined away.'

'I know.'

'She just sat in the hall at the end, waiting for the sound of the Rolls. She wouldn't budge, not at the end, wouldn't eat, wouldn't hear me.'

'You told me.'

'She'd decided she was a one-man dog. Tiger said bury her next to the pheasantry, so we did. Me and Mrs Henderson.'

'And Gasson,' he reminded her.

'Gasson dug the hole, Mrs Henderson said the words. We weren't a very jolly party, I'm afraid.'

'Where is he, Mother?'

'Gasson, darling?'

'Tiger.'

She's forgotten her lines, he thought, watching her eyes

192

begin to flood. She's trying to remember what she's supposed to say.

'Oh Ollie, darling.'

'What is it, Mother?'

'I thought you'd come for *me.*'

'I have. I wondered where Tiger was. He's been here. Gupta told me.'

It wasn't fair. Nothing was. She was calling up a whole storm of self-pity to shelter her. '*Everyone* asks me,' she wailed. 'Massingham. Mirsky. Gupta. That creepy Hoban man from Vienna. Bernard. That ghastly Hawsley hag with her pugs. Now you. I tell them all. *I don't know.* You'd think with fax machines and cellphones and God knows what, they'd know where everyone was all the time. They don't. Information isn't knowledge, your father always says. He's right.'

'Who's Bernard?'

'Bernard, darling. You know Bernard. The big bald policeman from Liverpool that Tiger helped. Bernard Porlock. You once called him Curly and he nearly killed you.'

'I think that must have been Jeffrey,' Oliver said. 'And Mirsky, he's the lawyer.'

'Of course he is, darling. Alix's lovely bubbly Polish friend from Istanbul. Tiger only needs a bit of *privacy,*' she protested. 'It's perfectly reasonable, living in the limelight the way he does, to want to be someone *little* for a while. We all do sometimes. You did. You even changed your name so that you could. Darling, didn't you?'

'And you've heard the news, I take it. Well, you must have done.'

'What news?' – sharply – 'I'm not to talk to the newspapers, Ollie. You're not either. I'm to put the phone down on them.'

'The news about Alfred Winser. Our legal eagle.'

'*That* dreadful little man? Whatever's *he* done?'

'I'm afraid he's died, Mother. Been shot. Out in Turkey. Person or persons unknown. He was doing a job for Single's and someone shot him.'

'Oh, how horrible, darling. How perfectly disgusting. I'm

so, *so* sorry. That poor woman. She'll have to take a job. It's too cruel. Oh darling.'

You knew, he thought. You had the words ready before I finished telling you. They stood hand in hand at the centre of her snug, which she called the morning room. It was the smallest of a run of living rooms that skirted the south side of the house. Jacko the Siamese lay in an upholstered basket under the television set. Tell me what's changed since you were here last, darling, she was saying. Let's play Kim's Game, come on! He played, looking for clues. Tiger's engraved whisky glass, the imprint of his neat backside in his favourite chair, a pink newspaper, handmade chocolates from Richoux round the corner in South Audley Street, he never showed up at Nightingales without them.

'That watercolour's new,' he said.

'Ollie darling, how terribly clever of you!' – clapping her hands but making no sound. 'It's at least a hundred years old, but it's new *here*, so well done you. Auntie Bee left it me. It was done by the lady who painted birds for Queen Victoria. I never expect anything when people die.'

'So when did you last see him, Mother, actually?'

But instead of answering him, she embarked on an impassioned description of Mrs Henderson's hip operation, how the local hospital had been absolutely marvellous, just when the government was planning to close it down, which was typical: 'And our darling Dr Bill, who's been looking after all of us for aeons – he just – well, he was, well, yes' – she had lost the thread.

They moved to the boys' dayroom and contemplated wooden toys he didn't remember playing with and the rocking horse he didn't remember riding, though she swore he'd nearly rocked it off its stand, so he supposed she was thinking of Jeffrey again.

'And you're all right, aren't you, darling? The three of you? I know I shouldn't ask but I'm only a mother, I'm not stone. You're all healthy and happy and free, the way you wanted it, darling? No more bad things?'

And kept her smile on him, flickering like a home movie, and her plucked eyebrows arching while he handed her a photograph of Carmen and watched her quiz it with the folding spectacles she kept on a garnet necklace, at arm's length, the photo swaying with her arm and her head swaying with the photo.

'She's bigger than that now, and we've cut her hair,' Oliver said. 'She says new things every day.'

'Absolutely adorable, darling. Bliss' – shoving the photo back at him – 'jolly well done, both of you. What a lovely scrummy happy little girl. And Helen's well, is she? Happy and things?'

'Heather's great.'

'I *am* glad.'

'I need to know, Mother. I have to know when you last saw Tiger and what happened. Everybody's searching for him. It's important that I find him first.' It's better when we don't look at each other, he remembered, keeping his eyes on the rocking horse.

'Don't bully me, Ollie darling. You know how I am about dates. I hate clocks, I hate night, I hate bullies. I hate everything that isn't yummy and more-ish and sunny.'

'But you love Tiger. You don't wish him ill. And you love me.'

Her voice went little-girl. '*You* know your father, darling. He sweeps in, he sweeps out, you wiggle all about and when he's gone you wonder whether he was here at all. If you're poor Nadia you do.'

He was sick and tired of her, which was why he had tried to run away when he was seven. He wished she was dead like Jeffrey. 'He came here and told you Winser had been shot,' he said.

Her hand flew across her body and clutched her upper arm. She was wearing a long-sleeved blouse of tulle, with frilly cuffs to hide the veins. 'Your father's been very good to us, Oliver. Stop it. Do you hear me?'

'Where is he, Mother?'

'You're to respect him. Respect is what separates us from animals. He didn't compare you with Jeffrey. He didn't turn his back on you when you failed your exams and had to leave your schools. Other fathers would have done. He didn't mind you writing poetry or whatever else you did, even though there wasn't any money in it. He sent you to tutors and gave you Jeffrey's place in the business. That's hard for a man who believes in merit and pulled himself up by his bootlaces. You were spared Liverpool, I wasn't. If you'd known Liverpool, you'd have Jeffrey's spirit. No two marriages are the same, they can't be. He's always loved Nightingales. He's always kept me as I should be kept. It was disloyal of you, Oliver. Whatever you did to him, he didn't deserve it. You've got your own family now. Go and attend to them. And stop pretending you're in Singapore when I know perfectly well you're in Devon.'

He was dead cold, her executioner. 'You told him, didn't you?' he said flatly. 'Tiger wormed it out of you. He came and saw you, he told you about Winser, and you told him about me. Where I was. What my new name was. Where you wrote to me, care of Toogood at the bank. He must have been very grateful.' He had to hold her up because she was drooping and biting her forefinger and moaning pathetically at him from under her Princess Diana fringe. 'So what I'd like to know, please, Nadia, is what *Tiger* told *you*,' he went on brutally. 'Because if you don't tell me, I've a good notion he's going to finish up like Alfie Winser.'

She needed another different place so he led her along the corridor to the dining room with its carved white marble fireplace from Mallet's with statues of naked women possibly by Canova set into pillared alcoves. All through his puberty they had been the beloved sirens of his fantasy. One stolen peek through the half-open doorway at their celestial smiles and flawless bottoms had been enough to fire him. Above them hung a family conversation piece done by a forgotten painter of the day, with golden clouds rising over Nightingales and Tiger mounted on a prancing polo pony and Oliver in Eton jacket reaching for the bridle, and Tiger's beautiful young wife Nadia, wasp-waisted in a flowing housecoat, restraining the child's over-eager hand. And behind Tiger, and looking like a blond Italian prince, pranced the ghost of Jeffrey, brought alive from photographs, with flowing gold hair and a dashing smile as he jumps his grey pony Admiral through a sunbeam, while family retainers wave their caps.

'I'm so *bad*,' Oliver,' Nadia complained, taking the painting as a reproach of some kind. 'Tiger should never have married me. I should never have had you both.'

'Don't worry, Mother. Somebody would have had us, even if you hadn't,' he said with false cheerfulness.

He was wondering whether Jeffrey was Tiger's child. In her cups, she had once spoken of a fellow barrister of Tiger's in Liverpool, a real rough diamond with gorgeous fair hair.

They were in the billiards room. He was pressing her again: I've got to know, Mother, I have to hear what passed between the two of you. She was hiccuping and shaking her head and denying everything while she confessed herself, but her tears had ceased to come. I'm too young, too frail, too sensitive, darling, Tiger wheedled it out of me, and now you're doing the same. It was because I never went to university, my father didn't think girls should, thank God I never had a daughter. She switched pronouns and talked about herself as someone else: 'She only ever told Tiger *little* bits, darling. Never *all* of it, she wouldn't. If Ollie hadn't peached to poor Nadia in the first place, she could never have peached to Tiger, could she?' You're bloody right, he thought. It was never any use to tell you anything. I should have left you to drink and fret yourself into the grave. 'He was so *sad*, darling,' she explained through her sobs. 'Sad about Winser. Saddest about you. That Kat woman had been acting up, I expect. I'd rather have Jacko any day. All I wanted was for him to look at me, call me darling, put his arms round me and tell me I'm still pretty.'

'Where is he, Mother? What name's he sailing under?' He was clasping her and she was leaning all her weight on his arms. 'He must have told you where he was going. He tells you everything. He wouldn't leave his Nadia in the dark.'

'I'm not to trust you. Not any of you. Not Mirsky or Hoban or Massingham or anybody. And Oliver started it. Let me go.'

Leather chairs, books about horses, a headmaster's desk. They had reached the study. A questionable Stubbs thoroughbred above the fireplace. Oliver strode to the window seat and ran his hand along the top of the pelmet till he came on a dusty brass key. He lifted the questionable Stubbs from its hook and set it on the floor. Behind it, a wall-safe was positioned at Tiger height. He unlocked it and peered inside, just as he had done as a child in the days when he believed the safe was a magic henbox where a great secret would be laid.

'There's nothing there, Ollie darling, there never was. Just boring Wills and Deeds and bits of foreign money from his pockets.'

Nothing now, nothing then. He locked it, replaced the key and turned his attention to the desk drawers. A polo glove. A box of twelve-bore cartridges. Receipted tradesmen's bills. Stationery. A black notebook, nothing printed on the cover. I want notebooks, Brock had said. I want jottings, memo pads, diaries, scribbled addresses, I want names written inside book matches, screwed-up balls of paper, anything he meant to throw away and didn't. Oliver flipped open the notebook: *The After-Dinner Speaker's Guide. Jokes, aphorisms, words of wisdom, quotations.* He tossed the notebook back in the drawer. 'Any parcels arrived for him, Mother? Packages, large envelopes, registered stuff, couriers? Nothing you were keeping for him? Nothing that's arrived since he left?' *Collateral is forwarded under separate cover to your private residence, signed Y. I. Orlov.*

'Of course not, darling. Nobody writes to him here unless it's bills.' He took her back to the kitchen and made a pot of tea while she watched. 'At least you're not ugly any more, darling.' She meant it as a consolation they could share. 'He cried. I haven't seen him cry since Jeffrey. He borrowed my Polaroid. You didn't know I was a photographer, did you?'

'What on earth did he want with a Polaroid?' – thinking passports, visa applications.

'He wanted a picture of everything he loved. Me. The painting of us all, the walled garden, everything that made him happy before you made it all go wrong.'

She wanted another cuddle so he provided it. 'Old Yevgeny been down recently?'

'Last winter, darling. For the pheasants.'

'But Tiger hasn't shot a bear yet?' – joke.

'No, darling. I don't think bears are him. They're too like humans.'

'Who else came along?'

'That poor Mikhail. He shoots everything. He'd have shot Jacko if he'd had a chance. It's so sweet of Yevgeny to include him in things. And Mirsky, of course.'

'What did Mirsky do?'

'Played chess with Randy in the conservatory. Randy and Mirsky were *very* close. I wondered whether they'd got a *thing* going.'

'What sort of thing?'

'Well, Randy's hardly a lady's man, is he? And darling Dr Mirsky would get up to anything. I caught him flirting with Mrs Henderson in the kitchen, if you can believe it, asking her to come and make shepherd's pie for him in Gdansk.'

He handed her a cup. Piece of lemon, never milk. He kept his voice breezy. 'So how did Tiger get here – this time – when he came and saw you? Did Gasson bring him?'

'A taxi did, darling. From the station. He came by train like you, except it wasn't Sunday. He didn't want to be conspicuous.'

'So what did you do? Hide him in the woodshed?'

She was standing, clutching the back of a chair for support. 'We beat the bounds, just like we always do, looking at everything he loves and photographing it,' she replied defiantly. 'He was wearing the brown Raglan I gave him for his fortieth. We call it his love coat. I said, don't go, stay here. I said I'd look after him. He wouldn't listen. He had to save the ship, he said. There was still time. Yevgeny had to know the truth, then everything would be all right. "I fought them off at Christmas and I'll do it again now." I was proud of him.'

'What happened at Christmas?'

'Switzerland, darling. I thought for a minute he was going to take me, like in the old days. But it was work, work, all the way. Back and forth like a yo-yo. He never did eat his Christmas pud, although he loves it. Mrs Henderson nearly wept. But he won. He fought them off. All of them. "I've bloodied their noses," he said. "Yevgeny stood by me at the end. They won't try that one again in a hurry."'

'Who won't?'

'Whoever they were. Hoban. Mirsky. How should I know? All the people who tried to do him down. The traitors. You're one of them. He said he had to send you something. If he never had sight or sound of you again, there was something he owed you as your father although you'd done the dirty on him. Something he'd promised you. It was what his life's about. So's mine. We always taught you to keep your promises.'

'Which was when you told him about Carmen.'

'He'd decided I knew where you were. He's clever. He always was. He'd noticed I wasn't worrying about you the way I do, and why wasn't I? He's a lawyer, so you can't argue with him. I said nonsense and he shook me. Not hard, like the old days, but hard enough. I tried to go on lying for you, but then I didn't see why I should bother. You were our only son. We owned you equally. I told him he was a grandfather and he wept again. Children always think their parents are cold until they cry, then they think they're ridiculous. He said he needed you.'

'*Needed* me? What the hell for?'

'He's your father, Ollie! He's your partner! They're ganging up on him. Who's he supposed to turn to if not his own son? You owe him. It's time you stood by him.'

'Did he say that?'

'Yes! His words. Tell him he owes me!'

'*Tell* him?'

'Yes!'

'Did he have a suitcase?'

'A brown bag to match his love coat. A carry-on.'

'Where was he flying to?'

'I didn't *say* he was flying!'

'You said a carry-on.'

'I didn't. I didn't!'

'Nadia. Mother. Listen to me. The police have combed every flight list and passenger list there is. There's not a trace of him. How did he fly without them noticing?'

200

She flung round at him, breaking herself free. 'He said you were! He's right! You're in league with the *police!*'

'I have to help him, Mother. He needs me. He said so. If I don't find him and you know where he is, it'll be on our heads.'

'I don't *know* where he is! He's not like you, he doesn't tell me things I can't keep in. Stop squeezing me like that!'

Scared of himself, Oliver stepped quickly back from her. She was whimpering, 'What's the good? Tell me what you want to know and leave me in peace.' Then choking on her own words. He returned to her and took her in his arms. He put his cheek against hers and felt it stick against her tears. She was submitting to him the way she had submitted to his father and there was a side of him that triumphed and a side that hated her for her frailty. 'He hasn't been seen since, Mother. Nobody's seen him but you. How did he leave?'

'Bravely. With his chin up. The way a fighter should. He would do exactly what he'd said he'd do. You should be proud to be following in his footsteps.'

'I mean transport.'

'His taxi came back. He'd have walked to the station if he hadn't had his bag. "It's day one again, Nadia," he said. "We're in Liverpool with our backs to the wall. I said I'd never let you go and I never will." He was his old self again. He didn't wave. He just rode away. Why did you *do* it, Ollie? Why did you tell silly Nadia if you didn't want Tiger to know?'

Because I was a besotted father and Carmen was three days old, he thought hopelessly. Because I loved my daughter, and assumed you'd like to love her too. She sat stiffly at the table, clutching her cold tea mug in both hands. 'Mother.'

'No, darling. No more.'

'If the ports are being watched and he's got a carry-on and he's going off to confound his enemies, how does he propose to get around? What's he got for a passport, for instance?'

'No one's, darling. You're being theatrical again.'

'Why do you say *no one's*? Why does it have to be someone else's passport he isn't using?'

'Shut up, Ollie! You think you're a great barrister like your father. You're not.'

'Whose passport has he got, Mother? I can't help him if I don't know what name he's using, can I?'

She gave a great sigh. She shook her head and the action got her weeping again, but she recovered. 'Ask Massingham. Tiger relies on his underlings too much. Then they stab him in the back, like you.'

'Is it a British passport?'

'It's real, that's all he told me. It's not a fake. It belongs to a real person who doesn't need it. He didn't say which country and I didn't ask.'

'Did he show it to you?'

'No. He just boasted.'

'When? Not this time, was it? He wasn't in a boasting mood.'

'A year ago last March' – she who hated dates – 'he'd got some business to attend to in Russia or somewhere and didn't want people knowing who he was. So he'd got himself this passport. Randy got it for him. And the birth certificate to back it up. It makes him five years younger. It was a joke between us that he'd got a five-year rebate from the Great Taxman in the Sky.' Her voice turned deadly cold, like his. 'That's all I've got for you, Ollie. All I'll ever have. Every last drop. You ruined it for us. You always did.'

At first Oliver walked slowly down the drive. He was carrying his grey-wolf coat over his arm. Walking he pulled it over him, one arm then the other as he gathered speed. By the time he reached the gates he was running. The electricity company van was in the same place but its folding ladder was retracted and two figures sat inside the cab. He kept running until he reached the fork and saw the lights of the parked Ford wink at him, and the cheerful figure of Aggie waving at him from the driver's seat. The passenger door swung open. He clambered in beside her.

'Can you get Brock on that thing?' he shouted.

She was already holding out the phone to him.

*   *   *

'So he was never in Australia,' Heather said. 'Australia was a lie too.'

'Cover, put it that way,' Brock suggested.

He had a priestly tone for these occasions. It went with a deep-felt sense of caring. When you take on a joe, you take on his problems, he would preach to his newcomers. You're not Machiavelli, you're not James Bond, you're the over-worked welfare officer who's got to hold everybody's life together or somebody will run amok.

They sat very still in the little country police station in Northamptonshire, Brock on one side of the plain table and Heather on the other, with her head in her hand and her eyes wide but not fixed on anything, as she stared away from him into the dusky corner of the interviewing room. It was evening and the room was poorly lit. From the shadowy walls, wanted men and missing children watched them like a silent chorus of the damned. Through the partition wall came the jeering of an incarcerated drunk, the monotone of a police radio and the pat-pat of darts hitting a board. Brock wondered what Lily would make of her. With women he always did. 'A nice girl, Nat,' she would have said. 'Nothing wrong with her that a good husband couldn't put right in a week.' Lily thought everyone should have a good husband. It was her way of flattering him.

'He actually told me about the seafood in Sydney,' Heather said, marvelling. 'Said it was the best he'd had anywhere in the world. Said we'd go there one day. Eat a grand meal at all the restaurants where he'd been a waiter.'

'I don't think he's been a waiter in his life,' said Brock.

'He's been a waiter for you though, hasn't he? Still is.'

Brock didn't rise to this. 'He doesn't like what he's doing, Heather. He sees it as his duty. He needs to know we're on his side. All of us. Carmen specially. She's the world to him, is Carmen. He wants her to know he's all right as a bloke. He hopes you'll put in a good word for him now and then, while she grows up. He wouldn't want her thinking he walked out on her without a reason.'

' "Your father lied his way into my life but he's a good man" – like that?'

'Better than that, if you can.'

'So give me the spiel.'

'I don't think there is a spiel, Heather. I think it's more a case of smiling when you talk about him. And letting him be the father to her that he dreams of.'

CHAPTER TWELVE

For his visit to Pluto's Kennel, a safe flat known only to a half-dozen members of the Hydra team, Brock first took the tube south across the river, then jumped on an eastbound bus and dawdled in a sandwich bar with a good view of the pavement. Hopping on a second bus, he got out two stops early and covered the final couple of hundred yards on foot, moving with neither too much purpose nor too little, and pausing to enjoy such features of the dockland landscape as caught his fancy – a row of rusted cranes, a rotting barge, a dump for used tyres – until he arrived by stages at a row of brick arches like a viaduct, with each cave a shifty metal workshop of some kind. Selecting a pair of stout black doors numbered 8 and embellished with the encouraging message 'GONE TO SPAIN, FUCK OFF', he pressed a buzzer and announced himself into the speaker as Alf's brother come to see about the Aston Martin.

Admitted, he crossed a warehouse containing car parts, old fireplaces and a large assortment of vehicle licence plates, and climbed a rickety wooden staircase to a newly installed steel door which for decency's sake had been daubed and scratched with appropriate graffiti. There he stood, waiting for the eyehole to go black, which it duly did, and the door to be opened by a spectral man in blue jeans, trackshoes, a check shirt, and a leather shoulder holster containing a nine millimetre Smith & Wesson automatic with a piece of old sticking plaster round the butt, as if it had cut itself in some forgotten escapade. Brock stepped inside and the door closed after him.

'How's he been, Mr Mace?' he enquired. There was breathy tension in him, like a case of first night nerves.

'Depends what you're into, really, sir,' said Mace, matching his quiet to Brock's. 'Reads a bit when he's got the concentration. Plays chess, which is a help. Otherwise he's down to crosswords, the upper-class sort.'

'Still scared?'

'Shitless, sir.'

Brock moved down the corridor, passing a tiny galley, a bunkroom and a bathroom till he came face to face with a second, chubby man with long hair knotted at the nape. His holster was of canvas and rigged like a baby's Snugli round his neck.

'All well, Mr Carter?'

'Very nice, thank you, sir. Just finished a nice game of whist.'

'Who won?'

'Pluto, sir. He cheats.'

Mace and Carter because, for as long as the operation ran, Aiden Bell had arbitrarily named the two men after the discoverers of Tutankhamen's tomb. And Pluto after the king of the nether regions. Pushing open a wooden door, Brock entered a long attic room with skylights covered with iron grilles. Two corduroy-covered armchairs had been pulled up to a stove. Between them lay a packing case strewn with newspapers and playing cards. One armchair was empty and in the other sat the Honourable Ranulf alias Randy Massingham, alias Pluto, lately of the British Foreign Service and other questionable addresses, clad in a homey blue zip-up cardigan from Marks & Spencer and, instead of his customary buckskin shoes, a pair of orange bedroom slippers lined with imitation fleece. He was crouching forward and clutching the arms of his chair, but when he saw Brock he linked his hands behind his head, crossed his slippered feet on the packing case, and leaned backward in an attitude of fake ease. 'It's my Uncle Nat again,' he drawled. 'Look, have you brought me my Stay-out-of-Jail card? Because if you haven't you're wasting your time.'

Brock appeared greatly entertained by this question. 'Now come along, sir. We're both civil servants at heart. When did Ministers ever sign immunity certificates at weekends? If I push any harder I'm going to start annoying people. Who's Dr Mirsky when he's at home?' he asked, on the principle that an interrogator's best questions are those to which he already knows the answers.

'Never heard of him,' Massingham retorted sulkily. 'And I want some decent clothes from my house. I can give you a key. William's in the country. He'll stay there till I tell him not to. Just don't go on Tuesdays and Thursdays when Mrs Ambrose is scrubbing.'

Brock was once more shaking his head. 'I'm afraid that's a total no-no, sir, at present. They may be watching the house. The last thing on earth I'm having is a trail leading from there to here, thank you.' This was a small lie. In his panic to surrender, Massingham had failed to provide himself with a change of clothes. Brock, knowing his ward's fondness for fine plumage, had seized the opportunity to humble him with shapeless boiler suits and woolly trousers with elastic at the waist. 'Now then, sir,' said Brock, sitting down and opening a notebook and taking out Lily's pen. 'A little bird is telling me that you and the said Dr Mirsky played chess together at Nightingales this last November as ever is.'

'Then your little bird talkie lie,' said Massingham, who liked to fall into pidgin English when he felt threatened.

'Exchanging ribald jokes and the like, you and Dr Mirsky were, I'm told. He's not of your persuasion, is he?'

'Never met him, never heard of him, never played chess with him. And no he's not, since you ask. He's quite the other thing,' Massingham replied. He picked up a copy of the *Spectator*, shook it and pretended to read. 'And I adore it here. The boys are darling, the food's to die for, location's divine. I'm thinking of buying the place.'

'You see the trouble is, sir, with these immunity deals

always,' Brock explained, still in the friendliest of tones, 'my Minister and his cohorts have to know what they're immunising a person *from*, and therein lies the worm.'

'I've had that sermon already.'

'Then perhaps if I repeat it, you'll take it to heart. It's no good, with respect, you just picking up the phone to some grand fellow you know in the Foreign Office or wherever it was and saying, "Randy Massingham would like to trade a spot of information for a guarantee of immunity, so wave a wand for us, will you, old boy?" That doesn't answer, not in the long run. My masters are picky people. "Immunity what *from?*" they ask themselves. "Is Mr Massingham tunnelling into the Bank of England or molesting under-age schoolgirls? Is he in league with Beelzebub? Because if he is, we'd prefer he apply elsewhere." But when I ask *you* that question, I ask in vain. Because what you've told me so far, frankly, that's peanuts. We'll *protect* you if that's what you want. We're very happy to protect you. The accommodation won't be as comfortable as what it is at the moment, but you'll be protected all right. Because if you carry on like this, my masters will not only withhold their favour, but throw in a charge of obstructing the course of justice as well. Sir.' Carter came in with tea. 'Has Mr Massingham telephoned his office today, Mr Carter?'

'Seventeen forty-five, sir.'

'Where from?'

'New York.'

'Who was with him?'

'Me and Mace, sir.'

'Did he behave himself?'

Massingham slammed down his newspaper. 'Like a bloody *lamb*, he did. He gave it everything he's got, didn't I, Carter? Admit it.'

'He sounded fine, sir,' Carter said. 'A bit too camp for my taste but he always is.'

'Listen to the tape if you don't believe me. I was in *New York*, the weather was *bliss*, I'd *just* come away from breathing new hope into the hearts and minds of our wavering Wall Street investors, and I was off to do the same thing all over again in Toronto, and did *anybody* have news of our poor wandering Tiger? Answer, a tearful no. Right or wrong, Carter?'

'I'd say that was a fair depiction, sir, as far as it goes.'

'Who did he talk to?'

'Angela, his secretary, sir.'

'Do you reckon she swallowed it?'

'She *always* swallows it,' Massingham drawled. With a face of stone Carter made his exit. 'Oh dear, was I too blue?'

'Well, Mr Carter is quite a churchman, you see, sir. Very big on the boys' club and the football teams.'

Massingham was crestfallen. 'Oh Lord. Oh damn. How vulgar of me. Oh *do* tell him I'm sorry.'

Brock was back at his notebook, benignly shaking his white head like everybody's dream daddy. 'Now, sir. Can I ask you, please, a *little* more about these very threatening telephone calls you've been receiving?'

'I've told you everything I know.'

'Yes, well, we're still having a spot of difficulty in tracing them, you see. Only, when we take on a request like this we're obliged to show jeopardy. It's what I call the golden twain. There's jeopardy, and there's the tangible evidence that you're willing to cooperate with the authorities once immunity has been granted.' A pause to signal the harder tone: 'Your firm impression, as per your testimony to my officers, was that the calls came from abroad, correct?'

'There was foreign noise in the background. Trams, that sort of thing.'

'And you still can't place the voice. You've thought about it day and night, but you're stuck.'

'I'd tell you otherwise, Nat.'

'I'd like to think that, sir. And it was the same voice each time and there were four calls in quick succession and they always said the same thing. And always from abroad.'

'There were the same – atmospherics – hollowness. It's hard to describe.'

'It wasn't Dr Mirsky, for instance?'

'It could have been. If he'd shoved a handkerchief in the mouthpiece or whatever they do.'

'Hoban?' Throwing out these names, Brock was marking how each one hit the target.

'Not American enough. Alix talks as if he'd had a nose job done an hour ago.'

'Shalva? Mikhail? It wasn't Yevgeny himself, was it?'

'English too good.'

'And the old boy would have spoken Russian to you, too, I suppose – except that perhaps it mightn't have sounded so threatening.' He was reading from his notebook. ' *"You are next on the list, Mr Massingham. You cannot hide from us. We can blow up your house or shoot you any time we want."* No advance on that?'

'It wasn't as dramatic as that. You make it sound ridiculous. It wasn't ridiculous, it was terrifying.'

'It's such a shame your mysterious caller didn't ring again after you'd thrown yourself on our mercy and we'd had your phone rerouted,' Brock lamented with sweet patience. 'Four calls in as many hours, then he goes off the air the minute you come to us. It makes you wonder if he knows more than what's good for him.'

'It wasn't good for *me*, is all *I* know.'

'I'm sure it wasn't, sir. What *passport*'s Tiger using, by the by?'

'British, I assume. You asked me last time.'

'And you are aware, I take it, as a former foreign servant yourself, that it's a felony in this country to aid or abet the procurement of a false or doctored passport, of whatever nationality?'

'Of course I am.'

'And that accordingly, if I was able to demonstrate that an Honourable Mr Ranulf Massingham did knowingly and with intent *provide* such a fraudulent passport – backed up by a purloined birth certificate, what's more – you might very well find yourself changing this extremely comfortable accommodation for a prison cell.'

Massingham was sitting upright, one hand plucking at his lower lip. His eyes were turned downward and, with the frown of concentration that he wore, he might have been contemplating a crucial chess move. 'You can't put me in prison. You can't arrest me either.'

'Why can't I?'

'You'd blow your operation sky high. You're in the same boat as us. You want business as usual for as long as you can get it.'

Inwardly, Brock was not at all cheered by this accurate appraisal of his situation. Outwardly, his demeanour continued to radiate a simple decency. 'You're dead right, sir. It's in my interest to keep you out of harm's way. But I can't lie to my superiors and you mustn't lie to me. So will you kindly tell me, without further prevarication, the name that is on the false passport that you personally provided for Mr Tiger Single?'

'Smart. Tommy Smart. TS to match his rather common gold cufflinks.'

'So now let's talk a little more about the good Dr Mirsky,' Brock suggested, concealing his victory under a bureaucratic frown of hard necessity, and he managed to keep himself sitting there for another twenty minutes before rushing his news to the crew.

But to Tanby he confessed his most secret anxiety. 'He's giving me the big lie, Tanby. Everything he tells me is chickenfeed.'

*　　　*　　　*

The surveillance team had reported that Subject was home alone. The telephone monitors had confirmed that Subject had resisted two supper invitations, pleading first a bridge date, then a previous engagement. It was ten o'clock at night in Park Lane. A warm, straight rain was dancing on the pavement. Tanby had driven him here, Aggie had ridden with him in the back of Tanby's cab, chattering about Chinese nosh in Glasgow.

'We can wait till tomorrow if you're tired,' Brock had said without conviction.

'I'm fine,' Oliver the nearly-good soldier had replied.

K. Altremont, he read, shielding his eyes from the rain while he studied the illuminated bell-buttons. *Apartment 18.* He pressed the button, a light shone in his face and he heard a bisexual squawk. 'It's me,' he said into the beam. 'Oliver. Wondered if I could take a cup of coffee off you. Won't keep you long.'

A metallic voice burst through the atmospherics. 'Christ. It really *is* me. I buzz, you push. Ready?'

But he pushed too early, and had to wait and push again before the glass doors yielded. In a futuristic lobby, grey-suited earthlings manned a white space-desk. The younger wore a badge saying he was Mattie. The older, Joshua, was reading his *Mail on Sunday*.

'Centre lift,' Mattie lisped at Oliver. 'And don't touch anything because we do it *all* for you.'

The lift rose, Mattie sank into the ground. At the eighth floor the door opened by itself and she was waiting for him, an eternal thirty-something in stonewashed jeans and one of Tiger's cream silk shirts rolled to the elbows, and a tangle of tiny gold bracelets on each wrist. She stepped forward, drawing the whole length of him against her, which was how she greeted all her men, chest to chest and groin to groin, except that with Oliver's height the bits didn't mesh the way they were meant to. Her long hair was brushed out and smelt of bath.

'Oliver. Isn't it *awful*? That poor Alfie – *everything*? – Where's Tiger *gone*?'

'You tell me, Kat.'

'Where have you *been*, for God's sake? I thought he'd gone to *find* you or something.' She pushed him away, but only so that she could look at him more closely. Cracks forming at the stress points, he noticed. The same scamp's smile, but more effort to keep it there. The eye as calculating, the voice as brittle. 'Have you acquired responsibilities, darling?' she asked him when she had completed her examination.

'Not really. No, I don't think so.' Foolish giggle.

'You've acquired *something*. I rather like it. But then I always did, didn't I?' He followed her to the drawing room. A studio in search of an artist, he remembered. Cult sculpture, airport art, Kensington kilims. Property of a Liechtenstein foundation. I drew up the contract, Winser vetted it, Kat owned the foundation, mixture as before. 'How about an alcohol, darling?'

'Love one.'

'Me too.' The drinks cupboard was a refrigerator disguised as a Spanish travelling chest. She drew out a silver-chased jug of dry Martini, filled a frosted flute and half-filled another. Sun-tanned arms, Kat goes to Nassau for February. Hands rifle-steady. 'Boy's size,' she said, handing him the full glass and keeping the girl's size for herself.

He took one sip and entered an altered state. If it had been tomato juice, he would still have been drunk. He took a second sip and recovered. 'Business okay?' he asked.

'Absolutely coining it, darling. We made a profit last year which threw Tiger into a total tantrum.' She perched herself on a Bedouin saddle. He squatted at her feet on a pile of long-haired cushions. Her feet bare. Tiny toenails like spots of blood. 'Tell, darling. Omitting no detail, however sordid.'

He was lying, but with Katrina he found lying easy. He was in Hong Kong when he got the news, he said, quoting the cover story according to Brock. A fax from Pam Hawsley reported that Winser had been shot and Tiger had 'left his desk to attend to urgent matters' and perhaps Oliver should consider coming home. It was the middle of the night in London so rather than hang around he found a Cathay Pacific to Gatwick, took a cab to Curzon Street, woke Gupta, raced down to Nightingales to see Nadia.

'How *is* she, darling?' Katrina cut in, with the special concern that mistresses evince for lovers' wives.

'Bearing up remarkably well, thanks,' he replied uncomfortably. 'Surprisingly so. Yes. Very feisty.'

Her eyes, for all the time he had been talking, had not released him. 'You haven't been to our boys in blue, have you, darling?' she asked shrewdly – a bridge player, reading his face.

'Which ones?' Oliver asked, reading hers.

'I thought you might have called on darling Bernard's services. Or aren't you Bernard-friendly?'

'Are you?'

'Not as friendly as he'd like me to be, thank God. My girls won't touch him. Five grand he offered Angela to go on holiday with him to his fuck-hutch in the sun. She told him she wasn't that sort of girl which gave us all a bit of a laugh.'

'I haven't been to anyone. The firm's desperate to keep it quiet that Tiger's gone missing. They're terrified of a run on the House.'

'So why've you come to *me*, darling?'

He gave a large shrug, but could not shake off her gaze. 'Thought I'd get it from the horse's mouth,' he said.

'And I'm the horse.' Her toe prodded his flank. 'Or was it for a bit of TLC in the midst of our tribulations?'

'Well, you're his best pal, Kat, aren't you?' he replied, grinning and shifting away from her.

'Apart from you, darling.'

'Plus you were the first person he came to see when he heard the news about Alfie.'

'Was I?'

'According to Gupta, you were.'

'*Then* where did he go?'

'To see Nadia. Well, she *said* he did. I mean she wouldn't make it up. What would be the point?'

'And after Nadia? Who did he go and see then? Some special little friend I don't know about?'

'I thought he might have come back here.'

'*Darling*. Whatever for?'

'Well, he's not that bright at handling his own arrangements, is he? Not if he wants to go abroad. I'm sort of surprised he didn't take you with him.'

She lit a cigarette, which amazed him. What else does she do when Tiger isn't here? 'I was asleep,' she said, closing her eyes to exhale, 'wearing nothing but my modesty. We'd had a perfectly bloody night at the Cradle. Some air charterers brought an Arab prince and he got the hots for Vora. *You* remember Vora' – another prod of the toe, this time in the flesh of his backside – 'drop-dead gorgeous blonde, dreamy bosom, endless legs. Well, *she* remembers *you*, darling – as I do. Ahmed wanted to sweep her off to Paris in his jet but Vora's boyfriend's only just been let out and she didn't dare. There was fuss, and it was 4 a.m. before I got back here, switched off the phone, took a bomb and crashed. The next thing I know, it's lunchtime and Tiger's standing over me in his beastly brown overcoat saying, "They've shot Winser's head off for a punishment." '

'Shot his head off? How did Tiger know that?'

'Search me, darling. Turn of phrase, probably. It was certainly more than I needed in *my* frail condition. "Why on *earth* should anyone shoot Alfie, for God's sake?" I said, "Who's *they*? How do you know it wasn't a jealous husband?" No, he said, it was a plot, and they were all in it, Hoban, Yevgeny, Mirsky and the whole guards armoured. He wanted to know where I'd put the shoe-brushes. You know how he gets when he's in one of his panics. He's got to die with his boots clean.' Oliver, who did not know that his father was prone to panic, nodded wisely all the same. 'The next thing he wanted was change for the telephone. He was gibbering, so I thought at first he was telling me I'd got to change my telephone line. No, no, *money*, he said. Pound coins, 50ps, what had I got? "Don't be ridiculous," I said, "you pay the phone bill here. Use mine." Not good enough. It had to be a proper coinbox. Everywhere else was tapped by his enemies. "Get hold of Randy," I said. No good. Got to find the shillings. "Ring Bernard," I said. "If you're in trouble, that's what Bernard's for." Not from here, he said. "But darling, he's *police*," I said. "Police don't tap police." Shook his head. Did his little woman stuff. Said I couldn't see the whole picture, and he could.'

'Poor you,' said Oliver, still trying to get used to the idea of Tiger gibbering.

'So of course we couldn't *find* any bloody change, could we? My parking change was in the car. My car was in the basement. Quite honestly, I thought your revered papa was going round the twist – what is it, darling? You look as though you've eaten something.'

Oliver had eaten nothing. He was adding events together in his head and making no sense of them. He was calculating that it could only have been minutes since Tiger had received Yevgeny's letter asking him for two hundred million sterling. Yet when Gupta saw Tiger leave Curzon Street he was still apparently composed. And Oliver was wondering what could have happened between Curzon Street and Kat to panic his father and make him gibber.

'So we shlepp round the flat for ten minutes, me in my kimono, looking for loose change. Made me wish I was back in my bedsit with a tin of 10ps for the gas meter. We came up with two quid. Well, that wasn't going to be enough, was it, not for phoning abroad. But then of course he hadn't said it was abroad, not till we'd finished looking. "For God's sake," I said, "have Mattie go round to the newsagent and buy you some phonecards." That wouldn't do either. Porters weren't to be trusted. He'd rather buy them for himself. So off he went, never called me Mother. It took me absolutely *hours* to get back to sleep and dream about you.' A huge drag on the cigarette, followed by a discontented sigh. 'Oh and it's all your fault, you'll be pleased to hear, it's not just Mirsky and the Borgias. We're all in league against him, we're all betraying him, but you've betrayed him rottenest. I was rather jealous. Have you?'

'How?'

'God knows, darling. He said you left a trail behind you and he'd tracked it back to source and the source was you. First time I'd heard of trails having sources, but it's what he said.'

'He didn't say who he needed to phone?'

'Course not, darling. I'm not to be trusted, am I? He was waving his little Filofax thingy about, so he obviously didn't have the number in his head.'

'But it was abroad.'

'So he said.'

And it was lunchtime, Oliver thought. 'Where's the newsagents'?' he asked.

'Out of the door, turn right for fifty yards and it's staring at you. Are you being Hercule Poirot, darling? He *said* you were Iscariot. *I* think you're scrumptious,' she added.

'I'm just getting the picture,' he said. A picture he has never dreamed of until now: of a Tiger frenzied, irrational

216

and on the run, huddled in a phonebox in his brown Raglan and polished shoes while his mistress goes back to sleep. 'He got into a big shoot-out with somebody last Christmas,' he said. 'A bunch of people tried to do the dirty on him. He flew to Zürich and beat them off. Does that ring any bells with you?'

She yawned. 'Vaguely. He was going to sack Randy. He's always going to sack Randy. And they're all crooks, Mirsky included.'

'Yevgeny too?'

'Yevgeny wobbles. He's too much under the influence.'

'Who of?'

'God knows, darling. How's your alcohol?' He drank his Martini. Katrina smoked and watched him while one bare foot thoughtfully massaged the other. 'You're the one who slipped through his fingers, aren't you, you naughty boy,' she said reflectively. 'He never talks about you, do you know that? – only when he's roused. Well, not *roused* exactly, because that only happens on Leap Years. First you were on overseas study leave, then you were bringing in the foreign business, then you were back at studying again. He's still proud of you, in his way. He just thinks you're a traitor and a shit.'

'He'll probably show up in a few days,' Oliver said.

'Oh, if he's alone he'll come *running* back. He can't *stand* his own company, never could. That's why one rather assumes the little friend. He certainly doesn't get enough out of *me* to keep him going. Or vice versa, frankly. Perhaps he needs a change of bowling. Par for the course at his age. Par for the course at mine, come to think of it' – her toe prodded him again, this time closer to the groin – 'Have *you* got a little friend, darling? Someone who knows how to drive you mad?'

'Sort of between two stools really.'

'That nice Nina came to see me at the Cradle once. She couldn't understand why you told Tiger you were going to marry her and never told her.'

'Yeah, well, sorry about that.'

'Don't apologise to *me*, darling. What was the matter with

her? Not lively enough in the sack? She's got a dishy little body, what I could see of it. Super bum. Lovely wraparound hips. Made me wish I was a man.'

Oliver shifted further away from her. 'Nadia says Mirsky's been around a lot,' he said, changing the subject. 'Showed up at Nightingales, playing chess with Randy.' *Everything you can get on Mirsky*, Brock had ordered.

'That's not the only thing he plays, *I* can tell you, darling. He'd play *me* if he got half a chance. Not for want of trying. He's worse than Bernard. We're not allowed to call him Mirsky, by the by. His passport's temperamental. I'm not surprised.'

'What do you call him then?'

'Dr Münster from Prague. Some doctor. I'm his personal private secretary, in case you didn't know. Dr Münster needs a helicopter to Nightingales? Get old Kat on to it. Dr Münster needs the bridal suite at the Grand Ritz Palace? Old Kat'll fix it. Dr Münster needs three tarts and a blind violinist by yesterday? Kat'll pimp for him, no problem. He's too hot for the Ice Maiden to handle, I gather.'

'I thought Tiger said Mirsky was in the plot against him.'

'That was *this* month, darling. Last month he was the Angel Gabriel. Then bingo, Mirsky's joined the bad guys and Yevgeny's a soft old fool to listen to a smooth-tongued Pole and Randy's the creep who put him up to it – and for all I know you did too, didn't you? Where are you living, darling?'

'Singapore mainly.'

'I meant tonight.'

'Camden. Friend from law school.'

'A he-friend?'

'Yes.'

'Isn't that rather a waste? Unless you're a Randy, which you *definitely* aren't.' He was about to laugh when he caught her eye and saw a different, darker glow. 'There's a spare bed here if you like. Mine. Satisfaction guaranteed,' she said.

Oliver considered this proposal, and realised it did not surprise him. 'I suppose I ought to take a squiz round his pad,' he objected, as if this were a hindrance of some kind.

'Find out if there are any papers or anything. Before anyone else does.'

'You can take a squiz round *his* pad, then you can come back to *my* pad. Can't you?'

'Only I haven't got his keys,' he explained, with a shabby grin.

They stood side by side in the lift and flank against flank. Her keys were looped together with elephant hair. She took his palm and laid them on it, then folded his fingers over them. She drew him to her and kissed him and kept kissing him and fondling him until he returned her embraces. Her breasts were naked under Tiger's shirt. She feathered her tongue against his while her hands skimmed and dived around his crotch. She took his hand and opened it and selected a key which together they put into the keyhole and turned. They put in a second key. The lift rose and stopped and the doors opened onto a glazed rooftop corridor like a parked railway coach with chimney pots one side and the lights of London the other. Still without speaking she chose a long, brass-stemmed key and another key that was attached to it, and arranged them suggestively between his finger and thumb so that they were pointing outward and upward at their imaginary target. She kissed him again, and with her hand on his bottom urged him down the corridor in the direction of a mahogany door with electric coaching lamps burning to either side of it.

'Hurry,' she whispered. 'Promise?'

He waited till the lift had disappeared, then to be sure he pressed the call button and waited till it returned empty. Then he took off one sneaker and wedged the doors open to prevent the lift from going anywhere, because he knew that of the three that served the building this was the only lift to serve the penthouse, and that therefore the only person who might logically be wishing to come up here at this hour apart from Tiger was Katrina deciding after all to keep him company. Keys in hand, one-shoe-off and one-shoe-on, he hobbled down the corridor. The mahogany door yielded at once and he stepped into an eighteenth-century gentleman's London house except that it had been built fifteen years ago on a rooftop. Oliver had never slept here, never laughed here, never washed up or made love or played here. Sometimes on lonely evenings Tiger had required his attendance and they had sat watching mind-reducing television over too many nightcaps. The only other recollections he had of the place were Tiger raging against the City authorities for refusing to let him have a helicopter pad, and summer parties catered by Katrina for all the friends that Tiger didn't have:

'Oliver! Nina, over here, please! Oliver, tell us again that joke about the scorpion that wanted to get across the Nile. But slowly. His Highness wishes to write it down ...'

'Oliver! A moment of your time, dear boy, if I may detach you from your delightful companion! Describe to His Excellency once more the legal basis of the project you presented to us so fluently this morning. Since we are off the record you may wish to use a somewhat less inhibited terminology ...'

He was standing in the hall, his crotch aching from Katrina's caresses. He advanced into the house, his senses still on fire. The rooms confused him and he no longer knew his way, but that was Katrina's fault. He turned a corner and passed through a drawing room, a billiards room and a study. He returned to the hall, delved in overcoats and raincoats in search of Brock's treasured scraps of paper. Something seemed to be written in Tiger's hand on the jotting pad beside the telephone. Still lusting after Katrina, he shoved the pad into his pocket. In one room he had spotted something, but he couldn't remember which. He hovered in the drawing room, waiting for inspiration, trying to shake off memories of Katrina's breast nestling in his palm and the pressure of her mound against his thigh. Not this room, he thought, running his hands through his hair to clear his mind. Try somewhere else. He was on his way to the billiards room when he noticed a leather wastebasket nestling between a reading chair and an occasional table, and knew he had seen it before without acknowledging its significance. A padded yellow paper bag, empty but fattened by whatever it had contained, was the only thing in the basket. His gaze lifted to a pair of cupboard doors got up as bookcases. They stood ajar, revealing in vertical section a stack of audio and video and television equipment. And as he hobbled towards them with his one good shoe and one stockinged foot he caught the flash of a green pinlight winking at him from the video machine. On the lid of the video player lay a white, unmarked cassette box, also empty. Oliver's head cleared, his desires subsided. If somebody had written COLLATERAL on the box's spine and drawn an arrow pointing downward at the winking light, the connection could not have been more obvious. *Collateral is forwarded to you under separate cover. Y. I. Orlov.* The phone was ringing.

It's for Tiger.

It's Mirsky who calls himself Münster.

It's Katrina to say she's coming up and the lift is stuck.

It's bald Bernard offering to perform a service.

It's the porters to say they're on their way.

It's Brock to say you're blown, abort.

It went on ringing and he let it. No message machine intercepted it. He pressed the EJECT button on the console, extracted the cassette, put it in the white box and the box into the padded yellow bag. 'To Mister Tiger Single', ran the label. Electronically typed. BY HAND, but no courier's label and no sender's name. He hobbled to the hall and was alarmed to see a photograph of his younger self, dressed in barrister's wig and legal drag. He grabbed a leather jacket from the row of coats and slung it over his shoulder, wedging the padded bag under his arm and using the jacket to hide it. He recovered his shoe from the lift doors, put it on, stepped into the lift and after a moment's shameful hesitation pressed the button for the ground floor. The lift descended at its own stately pace. He passed the twelfth and the eleventh and by the tenth had squeezed himself into a corner so that she couldn't see him through the window as he passed the eighth landing. But in his mind's eye he had her sprawled naked and resplendent on the bed she shared with Tiger and called spare. In the lobby Mattie had appropriated Joshua's *Mail on Sunday*.

'Would you please give these to Miss Altremont,' Oliver said, handing him Kat's keys.

'In due course,' said Mattie, without looking up from his newspaper.

Emerging on the pavement, he turned right and walked briskly till he came to Mohammed's News & Smokes, Open All Hours. Not far past it, tucked against the railing, stood three phoneboxes. He heard the teasing hoot of a car horn close behind and turned quickly, half-fearing to see Katrina in her House of Single Porsche. But it was Aggie, waving to him from the wheel of a green Mini.

'Glasgow,' he breathed as he flopped gratefully onto the seat beside her. 'And step on it.'

*　　　*　　　*

The Camden house living room was a natural viewing theatre with a smell of stale sandwiches and departed bodies. Brock and Oliver sat on a prickly sofa. Brock had offered to watch on his own. Oliver had overridden him. A trail of numbers rolled down the screen. It's a blue movie, Oliver thought, remembering Kat's hands on him: just what I need. Then he saw Alfred Winser chained and kneeling on a rock-strewn hillside, and a masked angel in a white raincoat holding a glinting automatic to his head. And he heard Hoban's awful twanging voice explaining to Alfie why he had to have his head shot off. And all he could think of after that was Tiger in his brown Raglan overcoat, alone in his penthouse, seeing and hearing the same things before going to the eighth floor to wake up Kat. In the kitchen the crew listened to the drone of Hoban's voice while they drank their tea and stared at the partition wall. You lot are coming to the second house, Brock had told them. The men sat hushed and close together. Aggie sat apart from them, eyes closed and thumb knuckles driven against her teeth, remembering how she had made bird noises on blades of grass for Zach.

*　　　*　　　*

Brock took pleasure in having Massingham kicked out of bed at midnight. Hovering on the tiny landing, he was consoled to hear him shriek as Carter and Mace woke him with nearly minimum force. And when they hauled him out of his bedroom looking like a condemned man arrayed for the public amusement in his shapeless Mother Hubbard dressing gown and slippers and hideous striped pyjamas, and his dazed eyes blinking and beseeching, and a jailer either side of him, Brock thought a vicious 'serve you right' before forcing his features into an expressionless bureaucratic stare. 'My apologies for the intrusion, sir. An article of information has come to light which I feel I have to share with you. A tape recorder if you please, Mr Mace. The Minister will be wanting to hear this one personally.'

Massingham didn't budge. Carter stepped back from him. Mace went off in search of a recorder. Massingham stayed put. 'I want my solicitor,' he said. 'I'm not saying another bloody word until I get written assurance.'

'Then on present showing, sir, you had better prepare yourself for the life of a Trappist monk.'

Without drama Brock pulled open the door to the attic living room. Massingham marched ahead, ignoring him. Each sat in his usual chair. Mace brought a tape recorder and switched it on.

'If you've been persecuting William –' Massingham began.

'I haven't. Nobody has. I want to talk to you about jeopardy. You remember jeopardy?'

'Of course I bloody do.'

'Good, because the Minister's private office is giving me serious grief. They think you're hiding something.'

'Then bugger them.'

'That's not my preference, thank you, sir. Lunchtime, Tiger Single goes missing from Curzon Street. But you've already left the building. By eleven o'clock that morning you'd walked out of your office and returned to your domicile in Chelsea. Why?'

'Is that a crime?'

'Depends on the reason, sir. You remained there for a

full ten hours until nine oh-five p.m. when you asked for protection. Do you confirm this?'

'Of course I *confirm this*. It's what I told *you*.' Massingham's bold words belied his manner, which was increasingly nervous.

'What made you go home early that morning?'

'Have you *absolutely* no imagination? Winser had been murdered, the news was out, the office was bedlam, phones ringing off the hook. I'd got a *string* of people to get on to. I needed peace and quiet. Where else would I find it but at home?'

'Where you duly received your threatening telephone calls,' said Brock, reflecting that liars also sometimes told the truth. 'At two p.m. the same afternoon, you received a courier with a package. What was in that package?'

'Nothing.'

'Come again, sir?'

'I received no package. Therefore there was nothing in it. It's a lie.'

'Someone in your household received it. And signed for it.'

'Prove it. You can't. You can't find the courier service. Never signed for it, never touched it. Whole thing's a fiction. And if you think William did, you're barking up the wrong tree.'

'I never suggested it was William, sir. You did.'

'I warn you: keep William out of this. He was in Chichester since ten o'clock that morning. Rehearsing the whole bloody day.'

'What for, sir, may I ask?'

'*A Midsummer Night's Dream*. Edwardian. He's Puck.'

'What time did he get home then?'

'Not till seven o'clock. "Go, go, go," I told him. "Get out of the house, it's not safe." He didn't understand but he went.'

'Where?'

'Mind your own business.'

'Did he take anything with him?'

'Of course he did. He packed. I helped him. Then I called

224

a cab for him. He can't drive. He won't. He's had lessons galore but it's not his thing.'

'Did he take the parcel with him?'

'There was no parcel' – icy hard now – 'Your parcel is a piece of crap, Mr Brock. It doesn't exist and it never will.'

'At two p.m. exactly, a neighbour of yours saw a motorcycle courier coming up the steps to your door with a parcel in his hand and coming back down again without one. She didn't see who signed for it because the door was on the chain.'

'The neighbour's a liar.'

'She's got multiple arthritis and there's not a thing that happens in that street she doesn't notice,' Brock replied, with unearthly patience. 'And she'll make a very good witness. A prosecution witness.'

Massingham examined his fingertips disapprovingly, as if to say, look what's become of them. 'I suppose it *could* have been telephone directories or something,' he speculated, offering an explanation that would serve them both. 'Those Telecom people turn up at any odd hour. I suppose I *might* have signed for them and not realised. Given the state I was in. It's possible.'

'We're not talking telephone directories. We're talking one padded envelope, yellow, with a white adhesive label. Something approximately the size' – he looked slowly round the room, taking his time when he came to the television set and video recorder – 'the size of one of those paperback books.' Massingham turned his head to look at them. 'Or it could have been a *cassette*,' Brock went on, as if the idea were just now dawning on him. 'One of those johnnies on the shelf there. Portraying in glorious colour the murder by shooting of your late colleague Alfred Winser.' No answer, beyond the same stubborn glower that had come over him the moment Brock had mentioned William. 'With a message in it,' Brock continued. 'The film was shocking enough but the message that came with it was worse. Am I right?'

'You know you are.'

'It was so shocking that, before you sought the protection

of HM Customs, you made up a cock-and-bull story that denied the existence of the tape which you handed to William with instructions to burn it and scatter the ashes to the four winds – or words to that effect.'

Massingham rose to his feet. 'The *message* as you're pleased to call it,' he announced, digging his hands into the pockets of his shapeless dressing gown and throwing back his head, 'was not a message at all. It was a pack of lies that painted me in the foulest light. It practically made me responsible for Winser's death. It accused me of every crime under the sun, without a shred of evidence to back it up.' Theatrically, he advanced on the seated Brock and, with his knees close to Brock's face, spoke down on him. 'Do you really suppose *I* was going to arrive on *your* doorstep – my hosts, Her Majesty's Customs no less – brandishing as my ticket of entry a grossly defamatory document – tape – that portrays me as the super-shit of all time? You must be mad.'

Brock was not mad but he was beginning to appreciate his adversary. 'On the other hand, Mr Massingham, if what your detractors say is right, you'd have two good reasons for destroying the evidence instead of one, wouldn't you? He did do that, did he, your William – destroy the evidence?'

'It wasn't evidence, so he destroyed none. It was a lie, it deserved to be destroyed, and was.'

Brock and Aiden Bell sat teacup to teacup in the wardroom of the house beside the river after a late-night showing of Winser's execution. It was 2 a.m.

'Pluto knows something big that I don't,' Brock said, echoing the confession he had made to Tanby. 'It's staring me in the eye. It's like a bomb lit somewhere. I can smell burning, but I'm not going to see it till it blows me up.' Then, as seemed to happen these days, they fell to talking Porlock. His behaviour at meetings: blatant. His lavish lifestyle: blatant. His supposed prime sources in the underworld, who in reality were his trading partners: blatant. 'He's testing God's patience,' Brock said, quoting Lily. 'He's seeing how high he can fly before the gods clip his wings.'

'She means melt,' Bell objected. 'She's thinking of Icarus.'

'All right, melt. What's the difference?' Brock conceded grumpily.

CHAPTER THIRTEEN

The shotgun wedding was arranged only after prolonged debate between Brock and the planners, if not between the contracting parties. The honeymoon, it was quickly decided, must take place in Switzerland, because it was to Switzerland that Tiger Single, alias Tommy Smart, had been traced after his departure from England. Arriving at Heathrow late in the evening, Smart-Single had spent the night in the Heathrow Hilton, taken a frugal dinner in his room and caught the first plane to Zürich next morning. He had paid cash at every turn. It was to Zürich also that he had telephoned from a public phonebox in Park Lane, his interlocutor being identified as an international law firm long associated with the House of Single's offshore transactions. A six-strong support crew would shadow the couple at all times, provide counter-surveillance and communications.

The decision to join Oliver and Aggie in wedlock was not lightly taken. Brock had at first assumed that Oliver would carry on abroad as he had done at home: nominally alone, with a team to watch over him, and Brock himself on instant call to debrief him and dab away his tears. It was only when the fine print of the plan started to come under discussion – how much cash should Oliver carry? what passport? what credit cards? in what name? and should the team travel on the same planes as Oliver and share his hotels, or should they keep their distance? – that Brock went into reverse. Something had choked in him, he told Bell awkwardly. I just can't see it, Aiden. See what? I just can't see Oliver on his own, Brock said, abroad, with a funny passport and credit cards and a wad of money in his pocket, and a live telephone at his bedside. Not even with a whole regiment of minders out on the street, or in the cab behind him, or at the tables next to him, or in the bedrooms either side of him. But when Aiden Bell pressed him for his reasons, Brock was uncharacteristically lost.

'It's his bloody tricks,' he said.

Bell misunderstood him. What *tricks* had Oliver been up to, he enquired severely, that Brock had failed to report? Bell was an ex-Ireland man. A joe was a joe for him. You paid him what he was worth and dropped him down a hole when he wasn't worth it any more. If he was leading you up the garden you had a quiet word with him in a back street.

'It's his conjuring tricks,' Brock explained, sounding stupid to himself. 'It's his private puzzling all the time, never reaching a conclusion, or none he lets you know about.' He tried again. 'It's his hours and hours of sitting up there in his bedroom. Shuffling his playing cards. Juggling. Modelling his bloody balloons. I never trusted him, but now I don't know him either.' But his complaint went further. 'Why doesn't he ask me about Massingham any more?' – deriding his own inventions – '"Mending fences? Roaming the globe? Soothing customers' feathers?" What sort of a cover story is that to blind a man of Oliver's intelligence?'

Even then, Brock failed to get to the heart of his unease. Some kind of sea-change was occurring in Oliver, he wanted to say. An assurance was getting into him that hadn't been there a couple of days ago. Brock had felt it after the film-show when he'd expected Oliver to be rolling around on the floor, threatening to take himself off to a monastery or some such nonsense. Instead, he'd remained sitting sweetly on the sofa after the lights had gone up, looking as calm as if he'd been watching *Neighbours*. 'Yevgeny didn't kill him.

It was Hoban flying solo,' he had declared with a sort of heated cockiness. And this conviction was so strong in Oliver, so emboldening somehow, that when Brock proposed to run the tape a second time for the benefit of the crew – who later watched it in taut silence and departed looking pale and determined – Oliver had been half-disposed to see it round with them just to prove his point, until under Brock's admonishing eye he got up, did his stretching number and sauntered to the kitchen and made himself a hot chocolate to take up to his room.

Brock selected the conservatory for the ceremony and was conscious all the time of flowers. 'You'll be travelling as man and wife,' he told the couple. 'Which means you'll be sharing the same toothbrush and the same bedroom and the same name. That's all it means, Oliver. We're clear on that, are we? Because I don't want you coming home with both arms broken. Are you hearing me?'

Oliver was hearing him or he wasn't. First he scowled, then he turned sanctimonious and seemed to reflect on whether such an arrangement was compatible with his high moral principles. Then he pulled a silly grin which Brock put down to embarrassment and mumbled, 'Whatever you say, boss.'

And Aggie reddened, which rocked Brock to his foundations. Platonic cover-marriages were standard kit for crew members on overseas assignments. Putting girls with girls and boys with boys was just too damned conspicuous. So why this maidenly confusion? Brock decided it was because Oliver wasn't strictly crew, and chided himself for not taking her aside for a pre-marital homily. Love and its variations did not occur to him. Perhaps he was too much the victim of the belief, shared by Oliver, that any girl who fell for him had to be a basket case by definition. And Aggie – though Brock would not have told her this in a month of Sundays – far from being a basket case, was simply the best and sanest girl he had come upon in his thirty years of service.

An hour later, conducting a pair of middle-aged Hydra analysts to Oliver's room to give him a few parting words of wisdom, Brock found him, instead of packing, standing by his bed in his shirt tails juggling his thuds – stitched leather bags stuffed with sand or whatever. He'd got three going, and when the two women cheered him on he added a fourth. Then for a few glorious moments he managed the entire five-alive.

'You have just witnessed a personal best, ladies,' he intoned in his barker's voice. 'Nathaniel Brock, sir, if you can hold a five-alive for ten consecutive throws, you'll be a man, my son.' What the hell's wrong with the boy? Brock wondered once more – he's practically *happy*. 'And I want to ring Elsie Watmore,' Oliver told Brock as soon as the women had left, because Brock had ruled no calls from Switzerland. So Brock led him to the telephone and stayed with him until he was done.

The marriage decided upon, Brock gave much thought to how the couple should be named. The obvious solution was for Aggie to become Heather and for Oliver to remain Hawthorne. Credit cards, driving licences and public records would then fall into line, not to mention Oliver's notional past life in Australia. Anyone choosing to check them would come upon a wealth of corroboration and otherwise a brick wall. If they stumbled on the divorce, to hell with them: Oliver and Heather had got together again. Against this was the indisputable operational fact that the name Hawthorne must be considered blown, not only to Tiger, but to other persons unknown. Unusually, Brock went for the compromise. Oliver and Aggie would have two operational passports apiece, not one. In the first they would be Oliver and Heather Single, children's entertainer and homemaker, British, married. In the second they would be Charmian and Mark West, commercial artist and homemaker, American, resident in Britain – these latter identities having already been cleared in advance for short-term operational use outside the United States. Credit cards and driving licences and home addresses for the Wests were also available for restricted use. The decision about which passport to use would depend on the merits of each situation. Aggie would be issued with travellers' cheques in both names and would be responsible for the safekeeping of passports not in action. She would take care of all loose cash and do the paying.

'You mean you're not even trusting me with the *housekeeping*?' Oliver blubbered in mock protest. 'Then I'm not marrying her. Send back the presents.'

Aggie not liking the joke at all, Brock noticed. Squeezing her lips together and wrinkling her nose as if things were getting out of hand. Tanby drove them to the airport. The crew waved them off – all but Brock, who watched them from an upper window.

*   *   *

The castle stood on a hump of the wooded Dolder hillside where it had stood for a hundred years or more, a mediaeval keep with green-tiled turrets and striped shutters and mullioned windows and a double garage, and a comically drawn fierce dog in red with its teeth bared, and a brass plate on the granite gatepost that said, LOTHAR, STORM & CONRAD, Anwälte. And below this: *Attorneys, Legal & Financial Counsellors*. Oliver ambled up to the iron gates and pressed the bell. Glancing downward through the trees, he saw shards of Lake Zürich and a children's hospital with happy families painted on the walls and a helicopter on the roof. On a bench across the road from him sat Derek in student casuals, soaking up the sunshine and listening to a doctored Walkman. Up the hill in a parked yellow Audi with a fiery devil dangling in its rear window sat two long-haired girls, neither of them Aggie. 'You're his wife and you do what wives do when their men are doing business,' Brock had told her in Oliver's hearing when she had pressed to be included in the surveillance team. 'Mooch, read, shop, do the galleries, see a movie, get your hair done. What are *you* grinning at?' Nothing, Oliver said. The gate lock buzzed. Oliver was toting a black attaché case containing dummy files, an electronic diary, a cellphone and other grown-up toys. One of them – he was unclear which – doubled as a radio microphone.

'Mr Single, sir. *Oliver!* Five years. *My* God!' Plump Dr Conrad welcomed him with the restrained enthusiasm of a

232

fellow mourner, bustling out of his office with his chin up and podgy arms held wide, then narrowing the gesture to a handshake of commiseration, which he achieved by clamping his doughy left palm over their two right hands, and piping, 'Absolutely *shocking* – *poor* Winser – a *tragedy* actually. You are not changed, I would say. Not smaller certainly! Also not fatter from all that *excellent* Chinese food.' And with this Dr Conrad took Oliver by the arm and guided him past Frau Marty his assistant, and other assistants and other doors to other partners, into a panelled study where a sumptuous courtesan, naked but for her black stockings and gold frame, displayed herself centre stage above a gothic stone hearth. 'You like her?'

'She's great.'

'She is a little *risqué* for some of my clients actually. I have a countess who lives in the Tessin and for her I change it for a Hodler. I like very much Impressionists. But I like also women who do not grow old.' The little confidences to make you feel special, Oliver remembered. The greedy surgeon's chatter before he cuts you up. 'You have married in the meantime, Oliver?'

'Yes' – thinking of Aggie.

'She is beautiful?'

'I find her so.'

'And not old?'

'Twenty-five.'

'Brunette?'

'Sort of mousy blonde,' Oliver replied with mysterious diffidence. In his inner ear, meanwhile, Tiger is waxing fulsome on the subject of our gallant doctor: our wizard of offshore, Oliver, the biggest name in no-name companies, the only man in Switzerland who can steer you blindfold through the tax laws of twenty different countries.

'You take a coffee – filter, espresso? We have a machine now – everything by machine today! Decaffeinated also? *Zwei Filterkaffee bitte, Frau Marty,* with poison please! – sugar? – *Zucker nimmt er auch!* – soon we lawyers will also be machines. *Und kein Telefon, Frau Marty,* not even if the Queen calls, *Tschüss!*' All this while he waved Oliver to a chair across from him, extracted a pair of black-rimmed spectacles from a pocket of the cardigan that he wore to emphasise his informality, polished them with a chamois leather from a drawer, leaned forward in his chair and, raising his eyes over the black parapet of his spectacles, subjected Oliver to a second penetrating examination while he again lamented Winser's passing. 'All over the world, huh? No one is safe, not even here in Switzerland.'

'It's awful,' Oliver agreed.

'Two days ago in Rapperswil,' Dr Conrad went on, his intense gaze for some reason fixed on Oliver's tie – a new one, bought by Aggie at the airport, because I'm not having you in that soup-stained orange thing a moment longer – 'A *respectable woman* shot dead by a very normal boy, a carpenter's apprentice. The husband under-director with a bank.'

'Dreadful,' Oliver agreed again.

'Maybe it was the same with poor Winser,' Dr Conrad suggested, dropping his voice to give his theory a clandestine force. 'We have *many* Turks here in Switzerland. In restaurants, driving taxis. They are behaving *well*, actually, on the whole, *so far*. But look out, huh? One never knows.'

No, one really doesn't, Oliver echoed heartily, and set his briefcase on the desk, snapping the locks as a wishful prelude to getting down to business, and at the same time guiding the right-hand lock to transmit.

'And greetings from Dieter,' Dr Conrad said.

'Gosh, *Dieter*. How is he? Fantastic, you must give me his address!' Dieter the creamy-haired sadist who beat me twenty-one-love at ping-pong in the attic of Conrad's millionaire's gin-palace in Küsnacht while our fathers talked mistresses and money over brandy in the sun lounge, he remembered.

'Thank you, Dieter is now *twenty-five*, he is at Yale School of Management, he hopes he will *never* see his parents again, but that's a phase *actually*,' said Dr Conrad proudly. An anxious pause while Oliver forgot the name of Dr Conrad's wife, though it was clearly inscribed in Aggie's hand on the goof-sheet that she had pressed on him as he left the hotel, and was even now nestling against his heart. 'And Charlotte is also very well,' Dr Conrad volunteered, letting him off the hook. And drew a slim folder from his desk and laid it before him, then spread his elbows and set his fingertips along its two edges to make sure it didn't fly away. Which was when Oliver realised that Dr Conrad's hands were shaking and that oily little beads of sweat had appeared like an unwelcome visitation on his upper lip.

'*So*, Oliver,' said Conrad, straightening himself up and making a new beginning. 'I ask you a question, yes? An *impertinent* question, but we are old friends so you don't get angry. We are lawyers. Some questions must be asked. Not always *answered*, maybe, but asked. You don't mind?'

'Not at all,' said Oliver politely.

Conrad puffed out his sweating lips and frowned in exaggerated concentration. '*Who am I receiving today?* In what capacity? Is it Tiger's *anxious son* I am receiving? Is it Oliver the *South-East Asian representative* of the House of Single? Or the *brilliant student* of Asian languages perhaps? Is it the friend of Mr Yevgeny Orlov? Or is it a fellow lawyer discussing *legal* aspects – and if so, who is his client? With whom do I have the honour of speaking this afternoon?'

'How did my father describe me?' Oliver proposed, prevaricating. Every question a threat to you, he thought, watching Dr Conrad's fussy hands join and separate. Every gesture a decision.

'He didn't, actually. He said *only* that you would come,' Dr Conrad replied too anxiously. 'That you would come and when you came I should tell you what was necessary.'

'Necessary to what?'

Conrad tried to look amused, but fear curdled his smile. 'To his *survival*, actually.'

'He *said* that? – in those words – his survival?'

The sweat had spread to his temples. 'Maybe salvation. Salvation or survival. Otherwise he told me nothing regarding Oliver. Maybe he forgot. We had important matters to discuss.' He drew a deep breath. 'So. Who are you today, please, Oliver?' he repeated in his sing-song accent. 'Answer my question, please. I am actually *very* curious to know.'

Frau Marty brought coffee and sugar biscuits. Oliver

235

waited till she had left, then calmly, not a lie out of place, retold the Gospel according to Brock as he had related it to Kat, until he came to the point where he arrived in England. 'After I'd looked at the situation and spoken to the staff I knew that somebody had to take over the shop and it had better be me. I didn't have Winser's experience, or his legal knowhow. But I was the only other partner, I was on the spot, I knew his methods of working and I knew Tiger's. I knew where the bodies were buried.' Dr Conrad's eyes widened to register terror. 'I mean that I was conversant with the inside workings of the firm,' Oliver explained kindly. 'If I didn't step into Winser's shoes, who else was going to?' He was sitting his full height. Master of his fictions, he looked boldly down on Conrad for approval and obtained a noncommittal nod. 'My problem is, there's nobody left in the House that I can consult, and next to nothing written down. Deliberately so. Tiger's off the air. Half the staff have taken sick leave –'

'And Mr Massingham?' Dr Conrad interrupted, in a voice cleansed of all inflection.

'Massingham's on a whistle-stop tour to reassure investors. If I pull him off the job I create the exact impression we're trying to forestall. Besides, Massingham's not much use on the legal side.' Conrad's features reflected nothing but flatulent discomfort. 'Then there's the question of my father's own state of mind – health – whatever you call it' – he permitted himself a decent hesitation – 'He's been under severe stress since before Christmas.'

'Stress,' Dr Conrad repeated.

'He can take an awful lot – as you can, I'm sure – but there's such a thing as having a nervous breakdown in place. The tougher a man is, the longer he holds out. But the signs are there for those who can read them. The man ceases to function on all cylinders.'

'Please?'

'He stops performing rationally. And he's not aware of it.'

'You are a psychologist?'

'No, but I'm Tiger's son, and his partner, and his greatest fan and, as you say, he's relying on my help. And you're his lawyer.' But even this, to judge by the rigidity of Dr Conrad's expression, was more than he was prepared to own to. 'My father's desperate. I've spoken to the people who were nearest to him in the hours before he did his disappearing act. The one thing he wanted was to talk to Kaspar Conrad. You. It had to be you. Before he talked to anyone else in the world. He kept his visit here secret. Even from me.'

'Then how do you know he came to see me, Oliver?'

Oliver managed not to hear this unpleasantly perspicacious question. 'I have to get to him urgently. Give him whatever help I can. I don't know where he is. He needs me.' Get Conrad to tell you the Christmas story, Brock had said. Why did Tiger visit him nine times in December and January alone? 'Some months ago, my father was caught up in a major crisis. He wrote to me complaining of a conspiracy to unseat him. He said the only other person he could trust apart from myself was you. "Kaspar Conrad is our boy." And together you won. You fought them off, whoever they were. Tiger was cock-a-hoop. A couple of weeks ago Winser has his head blown off and again my father rushes over to see you. Then he disappears. Where's he gone? He must have said where he was going. What's his next move?'

CHAPTER FOURTEEN

It's a replay, Oliver was thinking, as Conrad began to talk. It's five years ago and Tiger is standing at this very desk and I am stationed obediently in his shadow, sated after last night's father-son dinner of chopped veal and *Rösti* and house red at the Kronenhalle followed by the more private pleasures of the minibar in my hotel suite. Tiger is giving one of his state-of-the-nation addresses and I as usual am the nation:

'Kaspar, good friend, allow me to present Oliver, my son and newly inducted partner and as of today your valued client. We have an instruction for you, Kaspar. Are you ready to receive it?'

'From you, Tiger, I am ready for anything, actually.'

'Ours is a sweetheart partnership, Kaspar. Oliver has the key to all my secrets and I to his. Agreed and understood?'

'Agreed and understood, Tiger.'

And off to lunch at Jacky's.

It is three months later and this time we are a crowd: Tiger, Mikhail, Yevgeny, Winser, Hoban, Shalva, Massingham and me. We are sharing a coffee-driven feast of friendship, to be followed by a more substantial feast at the Dolder Grand just up the road. Last night in Chelsea I made love to Nina and my left shoulder inside my Turnbull &

238

Asser shirt is lacerated with teeth marks. Yevgeny is silent and perhaps asleep. Mikhail is watching squirrels through the window, wishing he could shoot them. Massingham dreams of William, Hoban hates us all, and Dr Conrad is describing perfect harmony. We shall be one – almost. One unlimited offshore company – almost. We shall be preferred shareholders – almost, though some of us will be more preferred than others. Such trivial differences occur in the best of happy families. We shall be tax efficient – meaning we shan't pay any. We shall be Bermudian and Andorran, we shall be the almost equal beneficiaries of an archipelago of companies reaching from Guernsey to Grand Cayman to Liechtenstein, and Dr Conrad the great international lawyer will be our confessor, keeper of the company purse and chief navigator, patrolling the movement of our capital and income in accordance with hands-off, no-name instructions conveyed to him from time to time by the House of Single. And everything is going swimmingly – lunch is only a few paragraphs of Dr Conrad's brilliant working paper away – when to Oliver's stupefaction, Randy Massingham calmly inserts one elegant suède toecap into the middle of this intricate, deniable, arm's-length machinery and from his chosen place of influence between Hoban and Yevgeny drawls:

'Kaspar, I'm sure I sound as if I'm speaking against House of Single's interests here. But wouldn't it be a *teeny* bit more democratic all round if our instructions to your splendid self were thrashed out jointly by Tiger *and* Yevgeny, rather than handed down to you by my incomparable Chairman alone? Just trying to head off frictions in advance, Ollie,' Massingham explains in an outrageously relaxed aside. 'Iron out our differences now, rather than have 'em bite us in the backside later. If you follow my reasoning.'

Oliver follows it effortlessly. Massingham is playing all ends against the middle and portraying himself as Mr Nice Guy while he does it. But he is not fast enough for Tiger, who is on to him almost before he has finished speaking:

'Randy, may I thank you enormously for having the foresight, presence of mind and – dare I say it? – courage, to make an absolutely vital point ahead of time? *Yes*, we must have a democratic partnership. *Yes* to power-sharing, not just in principle but on the ground. However, we're not talking power here. We're talking one clear voice and one clear order handed down the line to Dr Conrad. Dr Conrad can't take orders from a Babel! Can you, Kaspar? He can't take orders from a committee, not even one as harmonious as ours! Kaspar, tell them I'm right. Or wrong. I don't mind.'

And of course he is right, and remains right all the way up to the Dolder Grand.

*   *   *

Dr Conrad was talking about false courtiers. Conspiring courtiers. Courtiers who banded together and turned on their benefactor. Dr Conrad's fear of them had become palpable and it was thickened by indignation. Russian courtiers. Polish courtiers. English ones. He was talking elliptically and partly in whispers, his piggy eyes were growing larger and rounder. His courtiers were no-name courtiers engaging in no-name conspiracies, he was personally absolutely not engaged in them himself, his word of honour. But the courtiers were emerging nonetheless and their ringleader this Christmas was Dr Mirsky – 'who, I may tell you in absolute confidence, has a *terrible* reputation and a *beautiful* wife with long legs, assuming she *is* his wife because with Dr Mirsky, who is a Pole, one cannot be sure'. He expelled a rush of breath, produced a blue silk handkerchief and dabbed his sweated brow. 'I shall tell you what I may tell you, Oliver. I shall not tell you *all*, but I shall tell you the maximum that I can reconcile with my professional conscience. Do you accept this?'

'I shall have to.'

'I shall not decorate, I shall not speculate, I shall accept no supplementary questions. Even if the behaviour of certain persons has been *completely* outrageous. So. We are lawyers. We are paid to respect the instruments of law. We are not paid to prove that black is black or white is white.' Another

240

mop of the brow. 'Maybe Dr Mirsky is not the *locomotive* of this train,' he suggested, in a whisper.

Mystified, Oliver gave an intelligent nod.

'Maybe the locomotive is at the *back.*'

'Maybe it is,' Oliver agreed, more mystified still.

'It is common knowledge – I am not betraying professional secrets – that for two years now, certain things have not been good.'

'For Single's?'

'For Single's, for certain clients, for certain customers. So long as the customers are making money, Single's are managing it. But what if the customers do not lay the eggs? Then Single's cannot boil them.'

'Of course not.'

'It is logical. Sometimes eggs are also smashed. That is a disaster.' A disgusting snapshot of Winser's head bursting like an egg. 'Single's customers are also my clients. These clients have many interests. Precisely I do not know which, that is not my business. If I am told it is export, so it is export. If I am told leisure, then it is leisure. If I am told precious minerals, raw materials, technical and electronic commodities – then this also I accept.' He dabbed his lips. 'We call this many-faceted. Yes?'

'Yes.' Make sense, Oliver was urging him. Spit it out, whatever it is.

'The partnership was strong, the atmosphere was good, the clients and customers were happy, also the courtiers.' *Which* courtiers? A snapshot of Massingham in the tights, yellow cross-garters and doublet of Malvolio. 'Substantial sums of money were obtained, profits accrued, the leisure industry flourished, towns, villages, hotels, also import-export, I don't know what. The structures were excellent. I am not stupid. Your father neither. We took care. We were academic but we were also practical. You accept this?'

'Absolutely.'

'*Until.*' Conrad closed his eyes, drew a breath, but kept his finger in the air. 'In the beginning it was only small embarrassments. Enquiries from *insignificant* authorities. In Spain. In Portugal. In Turkey. In Germany. In England.

241

Orchestrated? We didn't know. Where before there had been *acceptance*, now there was *suspicion*. Bank accounts frozen pending investigations. Mysteriously. Tradings unaccountably suspended. Somebody arrested – completely unfairly, in my opinion.' The pointing finger descended. 'Isolated incidents. But for certain people, not quite so isolated. Too many questions, not enough answers. Too many accidents that are not coincidence finally – please.' More staffwork with the silk handkerchief. Sweat appearing on him like dew. Sweat like tears of fear on the bags beneath his eyes. 'These are *not* my companies, Oliver. I am a lawyer, *not* a trader. I am for what is on the *page*, not what is on the *boat*. I do not *load* this boat. I do not open every banana to see whether it is a banana or something else. I do not make out the – *Manifest*?'

'Same word. Manifest.'

'Please. I sell you a box, I am not responsible for what you put in the box.' He ran the handkerchief round his neck. He was speaking faster, running low on breath. 'I provide advice, based on the information given to me. I charge a fee, goodnight. If the information is not correct, how can I be held responsible? I can be *misinformed*. To be misinformed is not a *crime*.'

'Not even at Christmas,' said Oliver, prompting him.

'So *Christmas*,' Conrad agreed, with a quick suck of air. 'Last Christmas. Five days before, actually. On December twentieth Dr Mirsky sends to me by courier out of a clear sky sixty-eight pages of ultimatum. A *fait accompli* for the immediate attention of your father my client. "Sign here and return forthwith *et cetera*, deadline January 20."'

'Demanding what?'

'Effectively, the transfer of the entire structure of companies, *intact*, into the hands of Trans-Finanz Istanbul, a *new* company, offshore naturally, but also now the *parent* company of Trans-Finanz Vienna, owing to complicated share-manoeuvring masterminded by Dr Mirsky and others, and Dr Mirsky the nominated Chairman of this company, also the Managing Director, also Chief Executive.' He was talking at breakneck speed. 'Nominated by whom? – another matter. Certain courtiers of your father – *faithless* courtiers, I would say – are also holding shares in this new company.' Shocked by his own narrative, Conrad again mopped his forehead, then ploughed on. 'It was *typical,* actually. A typical Polish mentality. At Christmas, nobody is looking, everybody is baking cakes, buying presents for the family, sign here immediately.' His voice fell to a quaver but lost none of its forward thrust. 'Dr Mirsky is *not* a reliable person, actually,' he confided. 'I have many friends in Zürich. He is not correct at all. And this Hoban –' he shook his head.

'Transfer how? It's an enormous network. You might as well transfer the London Underground.'

'That's it! *Genau.* Exactly. The London Underground is perfect.' The brave finger soared once more into the air while with the other hand Conrad grabbed a folder and pulled out a thick document bound in red cloth, guarding it close to his stomach. 'I'm glad you came, Oliver, actually. Very glad. You have many good expressions. Like your father.' He was flipping through the pages, offering a rapid-fire version of the contents: '...all shares and assets controlled by House of Single on behalf of certain clients to be transferred without delay to the control of Trans-Finanz Istanbul Offshore... that's theft actually... all offshore operations to be administered by Dr Mirsky and his wife and dog *completely* as they decide – maybe from Istanbul, I don't know, maybe from the top of the Matterhorn – why does a Pole represent a Russian in Turkey? – House of Single to relinquish *all* rights as signatories, listen, please... *all* authority over *all* company affairs to be redefined, naturally to exclude House of Single... certain delighted courtiers to replace them, the choice of such delighted courtiers to be at the sole discretion of Misters Yevgeny and Mikhail Orlov *or their nominees* who will naturally be certain delighted courtiers already clearly identified in the ultimatum... it's a putsch, actually. A palace plot, completely.'

'And if not?' Oliver asked. 'If Tiger refuses? If you do? What then?'

'You are absolutely correct to ask this, Oliver! That's a completely logical question, I would say! *If not.* It was a blackmail! *If* House of Single does *not* agree to the Mirsky masterplan, then certain no-name courtiers will immediately withhold *all* further collaboration – which will have a crippling effect, naturally – these courtiers will further regard *all* existing articles of agreement as *void* – if we sue them they will immediately file a *counter-claim* for breach of confidence, incompetent administration, malfeasance and I don't know what. *Furthermore* – it is only a hint, I would say, but it is here in the ultimatum, between the lines' – he tapped the side of his glistening nose to indicate his finely developed sense of smell while his words fell from him at ever-increasing speed – 'they regret very much that, in the event of non-compliance by House of Single, certain negative informations regarding House of Single's overseas activities may *coincidentally* be lodged with certain international authorities, also domestic. It's totally disgraceful actually. A Pole, threatening an Englishman, in Switzerland.'

'So what action did you take – you and Tiger – what did you do, in the face of this ultimatum?'

'He spoke to them.'

'My father?'

'Naturally.'

'Spoke to them *how*?'

'From where you are sitting' – indicating the telephone that lay between them – 'here, several times. At my expense. Never mind. Often for hours.'

'To Yevgeny?'

'Correct. To Orlov Senior.' He had found a slower pace. 'Your father was brilliant, I would say. Very charming, but also very firm. He swore an oath. Literally on the Bible, we have one here naturally, Frau Marty brought it to him. "Yevgeny, I give you my solemn oath, nobody has betrayed you, there has been no indiscretion on the part of House of Single, this is all a dirty fiction from Mirsky and the no-name courtiers." Mr Yevgeny is very suggestible, I believe. This way, that way, like a pendulum. Also your father made certain concessions. It was necessary. This agreement would be made, that one cancelled, it was a package. But still inside the package we had a very familiar, very fragile human situation, namely an old man who did not know which voice he should listen to. Orlov Senior puts down the telephone, whom does he see? Courtiers. Each with a dagger behind his back.' Dr Conrad thrust a fist behind his own back by way of demonstration. 'How long will the agreement last? Not long, I believe. Only till the old man's mind is changed again or the next disaster happens.'

'And it did,' Oliver suggested, when they had shared another tense silence, broken only by the words 'My God', whispered several times by a temporarily exhausted Dr Conrad. And Oliver resumed: 'The *Free Tallinn* was boarded, there was a shoot-out, a few days later Winser had his head blown off, my father panicked and rushed over here to put the fire out.'

'With this fire, it was impossible.'

'Why?'

'It was too hot. More advanced. More dangerous.'

'Why?'

'In the first place we have an *episode* – an arrested boat, confiscated materials, dead crew, maybe *captured* crew, we don't know – these were matters that could not be over-looked, even if they were not in *any way* the responsibility of your father, let alone myself, similarly the contents of the cargo –'

'And in the second place?'

'There was no answer.'

'I beg your pardon?'

'Nobody answered us. Literally.'

'From where? Who?'

'All the telephone numbers, fax machines, all the offices. In Istanbul, Moscow, St. Petersburg. Trans-Finanz here, Trans-Finanz there, the private numbers, the public numbers. Nothing responded positively.'

'You mean they were cut off?'

A weary shrug. 'There was a wall. Mr Yevgeny Orlov was *not* available, *neither* was his brother. His whereabouts were *not* known, he could *not* be contacted. We were informed that all appropriate communications with House of Single had already been *made*, it was now only necessary for House of Single to meet its financial *obligations* or face the *consequences*. Amen and thank you.'

'Who said that part? – about the consequences – who said it?'

'Mr Hoban from Vienna said it, except that he was not in Vienna. He was somewhere I don't know, speaking on a cellphone, maybe in a helicopter, maybe in a crevasse, maybe on the moon. We are calling this modern communication.'

'How about Mirsky?'

'Dr Mirsky also could not be contacted. It was the wall again, your father was convinced of it. They wished to put a wall of silence round him. Pressure and fear. It is a well-known combination. Also very effective. On me as well.' He was losing his courage before Oliver's eyes. He was dabbing his flews and shrugging and, as a conscientious lawyer, seeing the force of the other side's argument even as he protested its monstrosity. 'Listen. It's not so unreasonable. They have suffered a big loss, Single's have provided a service, the service is maybe not totally satisfactory, they hold Single's liable so they are seeking compensation. Objectively, this is normal commercial practice. Look at America. You are a worker, you break your finger on I don't know what, one hundred million dollars, please. Single's will pay, or they will not pay. Maybe they pay part. Maybe there will be a negotiation.'

'Has my father instructed you to negotiate?'

'It's impossible. You heard. No answer. How can one negotiate with a wall?' He stood up. 'I have been frank with you, Oliver, maybe too frank. You are not only a lawyer, you are your father's son. Goodbye, huh? Good luck. Break your leg and neck, as we are saying.'

Oliver remained in his chair, ignoring Conrad's extended hand. 'So what happened? He came here. He telephoned. There was no answer. What did you do?'

'He had other engagements.'

'Where was he staying? It was evening already. Did you bother to ask him? Where did he go? You've been his lawyer for twenty years. Did you just throw him into the night?'

'Please. You are being emotional. You are his son. But you are a lawyer also. Listen, please.' Oliver was listening, but he had to wait a while. And the message, when it came, was punctuated by painful, heavy breaths. 'I also have my problems. The Swiss Bar association – certain other authorities – the police also – they have spoken to me. They are not accusing me, but they are not respectful and they are coming closer.' He licked his lips, pursed them. 'Regretfully I had to inform your father that these matters were outside my professional competence. Difficulties with banks – fiscal matters – frozen accounts, perhaps – these we can discuss. But dead sailors – illegal cargoes – a dead lawyer, and maybe not the only one – they are too much. Please.'

'You mean you dumped my father as a client? Signed him off? Bye bye?'

'I was not hard with him, Oliver. Listen to me. We were not heartless. Frau Marty drove him to the bank. He wanted the bank. He must see what cards he had to play. Those were his words. I offered to lend him money. Not much, I am not rich, maybe a few hundred thousand francs. I have friends who are richer. Maybe they will help him. He was dirty. An old brown coat, dirty shirt. You are right. He was not himself. One cannot advise a man who is not himself. What are you doing, please?'

Still seated, Oliver was fidgeting with the briefcase. Having fidgeted to his satisfaction, he stood up, plodded round the desk and grabbed a handful of Conrad's cardigan and shirt front with the intention of carting him to the nearest wall and hoisting him up it by the armpits while he asked him a few more questions. But the act was easier in the imagining than in the fulfilment. As Tiger always likes to say, I lack the killer instinct. So he released Conrad and left him quaking and whining in a heap on the floor. And as a consolation he helped himself to the folder containing Mirsky's sixty-eight-page Christmas ultimatum and shoved it in the briefcase among the dummy files. While he was at it, he also took a look through the desk drawers, but the only thing that caught his eye was a cumbersome Service revolver, presumably a relic of Conrad's heroic days in the Swiss army.

He walked to the antechamber where Frau Marty was busily typing and, having closed the door behind him, leaned flirtatiously over her desk.

'I wanted to thank you for driving my father to the bank,' he said.

'Oh, you are *very* welcome.'

'He didn't by any chance mention where he was going after that, did he?'

'Alas, he did not, I am afraid.'

Briefcase in hand, he trotted down the little garden path, gained the pavement and turned down the hill. Derek fell in behind him. The afternoon was muggy. They descended a steep cobbled alley wide enough for one car. Oliver was striding out, head reeling, heels jolting on the cobble. He was passing small villas and familiar faces. In one garden he saw Carmen on a swing in her white party-dress, being pushed by Sammy Watmore. Next door to them Tiger was mowing the lawn, watched by dead Jeffrey with his flowing gold mane. From an attic window, naked Zoya waved to him. A lane opened to his left. He entered it and ran for a while, Derek following. He reached a wide road and saw the yellow Audi waiting ahead of him in a layby next to a tram stop. The back door opened, Derek jumped in after him. The girls' elected names were Pat and Mike. Pat was a brunette today. Mike, her co-driver, wore a scarf round her head.

'Why did you switch off, Ollie?' Mike demanded over her shoulder as they drove.

'I didn't.'

They were heading downhill towards the lake and town.

'You did. It was when you were about to leave.'

'Probably jogged it or something,' Oliver said, with his legendary vagueness. 'Conrad gave me a document to read,' he told Derek, handing him the briefcase.

'When did he do that?' Mike persisted from the front, holding Oliver's gaze in the mirror.

'Do what?'

'Give you the document.'

'Just shoved it at me,' said Oliver, as vague as before.

'Didn't want to admit he was doing it, most likely. He's dropped Tiger down a hole.'

'We heard that part,' said Mike.

They set him down at the lakeside where the Bahnhof-strasse begins.

CHAPTER FIFTEEN

Oliver was not entirely present for his progress through the bank. He smiled and lied, he smiled and shook hands, he sat and stood and smiled and sat again. He waited for signs of panic or aggression on the part of his hosts and encountered none. The mounting rage that had guided him through his meeting with Conrad had given way to a drugged apathy. Wafted from one teak-panelled office to another, lectured on the latest dramatic shifts by old acquaintances whom he barely remembered – Herr Somebody had taken over Loans Department but sends his regards, Frau Dr Somebody Else is now regional director for Glarus and will be sad not to have met him – Oliver floated in a state of intermittent consciousness that reminded him of the recovery room after his appendix operation. He was nobody, doing everybody's bidding. He was an understudy who hadn't learned his lines.

From the bank's lobby he had ascended in a satin-steel lift with no controls. He was greeted by a carrot-haired man called Herr Albrecht, whom he at first sight mistook for one of his several headmasters: 'We are so pleased to see you here again, Mr Single, after all these years, and so soon after your good father,' said Herr Albrecht as they shook hands. So how was my good father or did you drop him down a hole like that bastard Conrad? Oliver replied. But it was evident that he had only asked these questions in his head, because the next thing he knew was that he was being wafted down a river of blue carpet at the side of a kind matron on his way to see a Herr Dr Lilienfeld who will take a photocopy of your passport in view of the new regulations. – 'How new?' – 'Oh *very* new. Also it is a long time since you were here. We have to be sure you are the same person.' So do I, Oliver thought.

Herr Dr Lilienfeld required a sample of Oliver's new signature after the rounder, younger version of five years ago. If he had asked for a blood sample, Oliver would have provided it. But when the kind matron returned him to Headmaster Albrecht, there sat Tiger in the very rosewood chair Oliver had occupied minutes before. He was looking much as Oliver expected, unwashed and wearing his brown love coat. But it was Oliver, not Tiger, whom Herr Albrecht addressed while the world's prices rallied and collapsed on monitors along the wall behind him. And it was a round-eyed pixie called Herr Stämpfli, not Tiger, who stepped forward out of the shadows to present himself as the official now responsible for the extended family of Single accounts. Everything was satisfactory, Herr Stämpfli assured Oliver. The original authorisation was still valid – it was in perpetuity – and of course – sycophantic smirk – Oliver required no authorisation to examine his own *personal* account which, Herr Albrecht was pleased to report, was in excellent health.

'Fine. Great. Thank you. Excellent.'

'There is however one small *snag*,' Herr Albrecht the Headmaster confessed over Herr Stämpfli's balding head, pronouncing it 'sneg'. 'You asked for copies of all correspondences. I regret very much that the authorisation does not permit you to take copies. No bank correspondences may leave the bank except by hand of Mr Single Senior in person. This is written expressly in the instructions and we must accept this limitation.'

'I shall expect to be able to take notes.'

'That is what your father was expecting you to expect,' Herr Albrecht said gravely.

So it's ordained, Oliver thought. I don't have to worry.

The river of carpet was this time orange. Herr Stämpfli waded at Oliver's side, a jailer jangling his keys.

'Did my father take papers away with him?' Oliver asked.

'Your father has an excellently developed instinct for security. But he would have been permitted, naturally.'

'Naturally.'

The room was a chapel of remembrance. Only Tiger's corpse was missing. Wax flowers, a polished table for the dear departed. Trays of perforated printouts from the loved one's private papers. Stacks of account sheets in imitation leather folders clamped together by brass rods. A stapler, a plastic dispenser of pins, paperclips and elastic bands and crisply bonded notepads. And a stack of complimentary picture postcards showing a peasant of the Engadine waving the Swiss flag from the top of a green mountain that reminded Oliver of Bethlehem.

'You like coffee, Mr Oliver?' Herr Stämpfli intoned, offering him his last meal on earth.

Herr Stämpfli lived in Solothurn. He was divorced, which he regretted, but his wife had decided she preferred solitude to his company, so what could he do? He had a daughter named Alouette who lived with him, a little fat at present but she was only twelve and with exercise she would grow thinner. It was five o'clock and the bank was closing but Herr Stämpfli would be honoured to remain till eight o'clock if Oliver required him, he had nothing particular to do and the evenings hung heavy on him.

'Won't Alouette mind your being late?'

Alouette is playing basketball, Herr Stämpfli rejoined. On Tuesdays, she has always basketball till nine o'clock.

Oliver was writing and reading and drinking too much coffee all at once. He was Brock. I want bald Bernard and his nasty companies. He was Tiger, landlord of the 'satellite accounts', which were in turn attached by drip-feed to the parent account of Single Holdings Offshore. He was Oliver again, authorised in perpetuity to exercise all powers invested in his partner and father. He was bald Bernard, owner of a Liechtenstein foundation called Dervish, worth thirty-one million pounds sterling, and a company called

Skyblue Holdings of Antigua. Bernard thinks he's bullet-proof, Brock is saying. Bernard thinks he can walk on the bloody water, and if I have my way he'll go under for the rest of his dirty little life. He was Skyblue Holdings and the holdings were not one villa but fourteen, each the property of a separate owning company with a silly name like Janus, Plexus, or Mentor. Bernard is the paymaster, Brock had said, Bernard is the Hydra's biggest head. He was Brock again, talking about less-than-perfect civil servants signing up for their second pensions. He was Oliver son of Tiger, writing patiently and legibly under the sobering eye of Herr Stämpfli. He was twelve years old and sitting an examination and Mr Ravilious, not Herr Stämpfli, was invigilating. He was Alouette in Solothurn, playing basketball till nine o'clock for her figure. He was in Antigua on one page, Liechtenstein the next and Grand Cayman a page after that. He was in Spain, Portugal, Andorra and northern Cyprus, writing. He was the owner of a chain of casinos, hotels, holiday villages and discothèques. He was Tiger, totting up his personal assets and seeing by how much they fell short of two hundred million sterling. Answer, off the top of Tiger's head, by one hundred and nineteen million pounds. 'Liquid Account', he read. No heading, just a six-figure number and the letters TS at the top of the page. Current value seventeen million pounds in various currencies. Two debits recorded in last two weeks: one of five million and thirty pounds sterling marked *Transfer*, the other of fifty thousand pounds sterling, dated and marked *Bearer*.

'Did my father withdraw this sum in cash?'

Cash, Herr Stämpfli confirmed. Herr Stämpfli had personally assisted him to load the money into his airbag.

'In what currency?'

'Swiss francs, dollars, Turkish lira,' Herr Stämpfli replied like a Swiss speaking clock, and added proudly, 'I fetched them for him personally.'

'Can you fetch some for me too?'

The question, which surprised Oliver, turned out to have been forced on him by two external factors. The first, that he had stumbled upon his own numbered account and discovered it was worth three million pounds. The second, that he resented the fact that Brock had forbidden him money of his own while he was abroad, with the insulting implication that he might make an unscripted dash for freedom – a course of action he had contemplated repeatedly over the last three days.

Herr Stämpfli was not permitted to leave Oliver alone with the papers. With tremendous circumstance, he therefore telephoned the night cashier and placed an order on Oliver's behalf for thirty thousand US dollars in hundreds, a couple of thousand Swiss francs, oh and some Turkish like my father. A vestal appeared, armed with a wad of notes and a receipt. Oliver signed the receipt and distributed the notes among the copious pockets of his Hayward suit. No magician could have done it more discreetly. By way of celebration, he helped himself to one of the bank's postcards of a flag-swinger, scribbled a jolly message to Sammy and slipped that also into his pocket. He returned to the figures. Seven o'clock chimed before his courage ran out.

'I just can't bear to keep Alouette waiting,' he confessed to Herr Stämpfli with a shy laugh. Carefully he pulled his precious handwritten pages from the notepad, Herr Stämpfli produced a stout envelope and held it open while Oliver fed them into it. Then Herr Stämpfli escorted Oliver down the main staircase as far as the front doors.

'Did my father mention where he was going from here?'

Herr Stämpfli shook his head. 'With the lira, maybe Turkey.'

Outside in the half-darkness, Derek was waiting. 'You're changing hats,' he announced as they strolled towards a parked cab. 'Nat's orders. You're Mr and Mrs West and you're staying in a commercial travellers' love-nest on the other side of town.'

'Why?'

'Ferrets.'

'Whose ferrets?'

'Not known. Could be Swiss, could be Hoban's lot, could be Hydra. Maybe Conrad bubbled you.'

'What did they do?'

'Tailed Aggie, quizzed the hotel, sniffed your underpants. It's orders. You lie low, stay clear of the bright lights and you're on the first plane home in the morning.'

'To *London?*'

'The Gnat's calling time out. What do you expect him to do? Tie you to a tree and wait for the wolves?'

Seated at Derek's side in the cab, Oliver watched the lights along the lake. In the lobby of a dingy highrise that smelt of old soup, Derek spoke to room 509 on the house telephone while Pat and Mike studied the noticeboard. Seizing his moment, Oliver magicked Sammy's postcard from his pocket, scribbled 'charge to 509' where the stamp should have been and dropped it in the hotel mailbox.

'She's waiting for you,' Derek murmured, pointing Oliver at the lift. 'Sooner you than me, mate.'

*   *   *

It was a double bed in a very small bedroom. The bed was small even for small lovers and out of the question for two tall married strangers intent on not touching one another. There was a minibar and a television set. Two tiny armchairs were crammed at the foot of the bed, and there was a slot in the bedhead that for two francs provided you with a therapeutic massage. She had unpacked for both of them. His spare suit hung in the wardrobe. She was wearing a rather nice scent. He had never associated her with scent, more with outdoors. All this he established before sitting himself on the edge of the bed with his back to her while she stood at the basin in the bathroom adding finishing touches to her make-up. He had brought Rocco the raccoon with him and was passing him round his shoulders, and keeping his jacket on because of the money in the pockets.

'Is it all right to talk in here?' he asked.

'Unless you're paranoid,' she retorted through the open doorway, while he discreetly unloaded the cash from his jacket, unbuttoned his shirt and set to work wedging the notes inside his waistband.

'Everyone's ganged up on him. Only Yevgeny's on his

side. Even I'm not,' he complained, shoving a wad of hundreds into the small of his back.

'So?'

'I owe him.'

'Owe him *what*?' He guessed she was biting in her lipstick or something, because she sounded a bit like Heather. 'Oliver, we can *not* owe ourselves to everybody.'

'You do,' he said. The money was all inside his shirt. He took off his jacket and put Rocco back to work. 'I've seen you. You're like a nurse on her rounds. Everyone's your patient.'

'That is total crap.' But she lost the p because of whatever she was doing with her lips. 'And stop wiggling that animal at me, because you're just putting yourself down, and it pisses me off.'

Our first marital row, Oliver thought, rubbing Rocco's snout and pulling faces at him. She came out of the bathroom. He went in, closed the door behind him and locked it. He took the money from round his waist and wedged it behind the cistern. He flushed, and ran the taps. He returned to the bedroom and poked around for a clean shirt. She pulled open a drawer and handed him a new one that went with the tie she'd bought him at Heathrow.

'When did you get this?'

'What else was I meant to do all day?'

He remembered the ferrets and supposed that was what was annoying her. 'So who's been following you?' he asked solicitously.

'I don't know, Oliver, and I didn't see them to ask. The crew saw them. It is not my part to act surveillance conscious.'

'Oh, right. Yes. Of course. Sorry.' It seemed silly to go back to the bathroom to put a new shirt on. Besides, it was always good to show the audience you'd nothing up your sleeve when you hadn't. He peeled off his old shirt and held his stomach in while he tore off the cellophane and groped inexpertly for the pins that held the new shirt to the cardboard inside. 'They ought to print it on the packet how many you're supposed to look for,' he groused, when she took the shirt from him and finished the job. 'You could impale yourself, just pulling it over your head.'

256

'It's plain cuffs,' she said. 'They're what you like.'

'I'm not very fond of the links,' he explained.

'You don't need to tell me. I'm aware.'

He put the shirt on and turned his back to her while he unzipped his fly to tuck in the tails. He'd always tied his tie badly and remembered how Heather had insisted on retying it in a Windsor knot, a trick that the great magician had never mastered. Then he wondered how many men it had taken Heather to teach her the knack, and whether Nadia tied Tiger's tie, or Kat did, and whether Tiger was wearing one at the moment, or whether for instance he had hanged himself with it, or been strangled with it, or had his head blown off while he was wearing it, because Oliver's mind was bouncing around inside his head like a rubber ball and there was absolutely nothing he could do about it except act naturally and be his charming self and get hold of one of those air and railway timetables that he'd spotted peeping out of the rack beside the reception desk.

Their table was a lovers' niche with cowbells hanging over it. In the rest of the dining room interchangeable men in grey suits ate without expression. Pat and Mike sat alone against a wall being covertly undressed by a hundred lonely male eyes. Aggie ordered US beef and chips. Same for me, please. If she'd ordered tripe and onions, he would have said same for me. Small decisions were eluding him. He ordered half a litre of Dôle but Aggie would drink only mineral water: sparkling, she told the waiter, but don't let me stop you, Oliver.

'Is that because you're on duty?' he asked.

'Is what?'

'Staying on the wagon.' She answered but he didn't notice what she said. You're beautiful, he was telling her with his eyes. Even in this sickly white light, you're absurdly, healthily, radiantly beautiful. 'It's a bit of a tall order,' he complained.

'What is?'

'Being one person all day and somebody else in the evening. I'm not sure who to be any more.'

'Be yourself, Oliver. Just for once.'

He rubbed his head. 'Yeah, well, there's not that much left to be, really. Not after Tiger and Brock have finished with me.'

'Oliver, if you're going to talk like that, I think I'll eat alone.'

He gave it a rest for a while, then tried again, asking the questions the young master used to ask Single's female staff at the all-ranks Christmas bash: what her larger ambitions were, how she'd like to see herself five years from now, whether she wanted babies or a career or both.

'Actually, Oliver, I don't have the least fucking idea,' she said.

The meal dragged to an end, she signed the bill and he watched her: Charmian West. He proposed a nightcap in the bar – the bar being the other side of the reception desk. One brush past it and I'm home free, he was thinking. All right, she agreed, let's have a nightcap in the bar. Perhaps she was grateful for a delay before returning to the room.

'What the hell are you looking for?' she asked.

'Your coat.' Heather had always worn a coat when they went out. She liked him to sweep her in and out of it, and hang it up for her between acts.

'Why on earth should I wear a coat to go from the bedroom to the dining room and back?'

Of course not. Silly of me. At the reception desk Aggie asked the concierge whether there were any messages for West. There were none, but by the time they had resumed their passage to the bar Oliver had a bunch of timetables in the left pocket of his jacket and the audience hadn't seen a thing. Love is what you can get away with. In the bar he ordered brandy and she another mineral water, and this time when she signed the bill he made an ambiguous joke about being a kept man, but she didn't smile. In the lift, which they had to themselves, she remained distant: no Katrina she. In the bedroom, which she entered ahead of him, she had it all worked out. He was larger than she was so he got the bed, she said. The two armchairs would suit her fine. She would have the duvet and two pillows, Oliver the blanket and the quilted bedspread and first use of the bathroom. He thought he caught a glimpse of disappointment in her eye and wondered whether, if he'd managed to bring his act down instead of pursuing an agenda of his own, the sleeping arrangements might have been more conciliatory. He took off his shirt but kept his shoes and trousers on. He hung his jacket in the wardrobe, extracted the timetables, wedged them under his arm, slung a bathrobe over his shoulder, collected his spongebag and, mumbling something about taking a bath in the morning, shuffled into the bathroom and locked the door. He sat on the lavatory, studying the timetables. He fished the money from behind the cistern and put it in his spongebag and made a show of sloshing water and brushing his teeth while he added the last touches to his plan. Through the door he heard the martial fanfares of American television news.

'If that's Larry King, turn the bastard off,' he called in a show of bravura.

He rinsed his face, cleaned the handbasin, knocked on the door, heard 'Come in' and returned to the bedroom to find her shrouded to the neck in a bathrobe with her hair packed into a shower cap. She entered the bathroom, closed the door and locked it. The television was showing disasters in black Africa, brought to us courtesy of a well made-up woman in a flak-jacket. Oliver waited for the sound of water but heard none. The door opened and without a glance at him she fetched her hairbrush and comb, returned to the bathroom and relocked the door. He heard the shower running. He put his shirt back on, dropped his spongebag into a canvas grip, threw in Rocco, socks, underpants, a couple more shirts, his thuds and Brearly on balloons. The shower was still running. Reassured, he slipped on his jacket, took up the grip and tiptoed towards the door. Passing the bed he paused to scribble a message to her on the telephone pad: *Sorry I have to do this. Love you, O.* Feeling better, he put his hand on the doorknob and turned it, relying on disaster in the African jungle to cover the sound. The door yielded, he turned round to take a last look at the room and saw Aggie, without her shower cap, watching him from the doorway.

259

'Shut the door. Gently.'

He shut it.

'Where the fuck do you think you're going? Keep your voice down.'

'To Istanbul.'

'By air or rail? Decided yet?'

'Not really.' Anxious to escape her glare, he peered at his watch. 'There's a twenty-two thirty-three from Zürich station gets to Vienna around eight in the morning. I could make the Vienna–Istanbul flight at ten-thirty.'

'Otherwise?'

'Twenty-three hundred to Paris and nine fifty-five from Charles de Gaulle.'

'How are you reckoning to get to the station?'

'Tram or walk.'

'Why not a cab?'

'Well, a cab if I find one. Depends.'

'Why not fly from Zürich?'

'I thought trains were more anonymous, sort of thing. Fly from somewhere different. Anyway I'd have to wait till morning.'

'Bloody brilliant. You've Derek across the corridor and Pat and Mike between our bedroom and the lift. Have you thought of that?'

'I thought they'd be asleep.'

'And you think the hotel will be happy, do you, with you sneaking past reception with a suitcase in your hand at this hour of night?'

'Well, they'll still have you to pay the bill, won't they?'

'What do you think you're going to use for money?' – and before he could answer – 'Don't tell me. You drew some from the bank. That's what you hid in the bathroom.'

Oliver scratched the top of his head. 'I'm going anyway.' He had his hand on the doorhandle still, and he was standing his full height, and he hoped he looked as determined as he felt because he knew that if she made an attempt to stop him – by raising Derek and the girls, for instance – he was going to prevent her somehow. Turning her back to him she slipped off her robe and, for a moment splendidly naked, began dressing. And it dawned on Oliver, too late as ever, that a girl who is proposing to spend a chaste night on two armchairs would take her pyjamas or nightdress to the bathroom in order to emerge decent, but Aggie hadn't done that.

'What are you doing?' he asked her, gawping at her like an idiot.

'Coming with you. What d'you think I'm doing? You're not safe crossing the fucking road.'

'What about Brock?'

'I'm not married to Brock. Put that bag on the bed and let me pack it properly.'

He watched her pack it properly. He watched her add things of her own, not everything, so that they had one suitcase between them. He watched her put the rest of her stuff into a second bag so that it would be 'all ready for Derek in the morning when he wakes up' – under her breath – and he noted that causing Derek embarrassment was not going to upset her unduly. He padded uselessly round the tiny room while she returned to the bathroom, and he heard her through the paper-thin wall ordering a cab in a low voice on the bathroom telephone, and at the same time asking the desk to have the room bill ready because they had to check out immediately. She came back and murmured to him that he was to follow her and bring the suitcase and not thump about. She turned the doorhandle and lifted it and it opened silently, which it hadn't done for him. There was a door marked 'Service' straight across the passage. She opened it and beckoned to him and he followed her down an evil stone staircase that reminded him of the back staircase in Curzon Street. He watched her pay the bill at the desk, and she did that unconscious thing with her hips that he'd seen her do in the garden in Camden, weight on one leg and cocking the other somehow. He noticed that she still had her hair down, and that even under the awful overhead lighting he could imagine her riding horses and climbing glens and looking like an advertisement for rainwear while she fly-fished for the salmon.

'Is the cab out there, Mark?' she asked over her shoulder

while she signed. And Oliver, because he was still dreaming, looked round helpfully for Mark before remembering who he was.

They rode in silence to the station. When they got there, he stood guard over the suitcase and checked their platform number several times because he kept forgetting it while she bought the tickets. And suddenly, there they were, just another Mr and Mrs West, pushing their his-and-hers suitcase down the platform, looking for their berth.

CHAPTER SIXTEEN

Until that evening Brock had relied on the long game to keep Massingham at the table, dropping in on him unannounced at any odd moment of day or night, firing off a few cryptic questions and leaving others pregnantly unasked while he kept his promises on the boil – yes, sir, your immunity is in the pipeline – no, sir, we will not be hounding William – and meanwhile can you help us with the following little problem? Anything to keep him talking, he told Aiden Bell, anything to keep the chemistry working in him while the information comes in.

'Why don't you have him walk into a door and save yourself the time?' Bell argued.

Because he's afraid of bigger things than us, Brock replied. Because he loves William and knows where the bomb is hidden. Because he's a turncoat with loyalties, and they're the worst. Because I don't understand why he came to us, or what he's hiding from. Or why the pragmatic Orlovs have taken up ritual killing in their old age.

Tonight, however, Brock knew he was a step ahead of Massingham and made his dispositions accordingly, though still with that mysterious lack of confidence that had bedevilled their previous encounters: something was out of joint, something was missing. He had listened to Oliver's interview with Dr Conrad, digitally encrypted by the British Consulate in Zürich that same afternoon. He had cut a grateful path through Oliver's notes from the bank and, though he knew it would be months before the analysts had squeezed the last drop out of them, he had seen with Oliver's eyes the living proof, if he had ever doubted it, that Single's were paying huge retainers to the Hydra and that Porlock was its treasurer and comptroller of the purse. Under his arm he was carrying Dr Mirsky's sixty-eight-page ultimatum, spirited back to London on the last plane of the day and now residing in a brown official envelope sealed in HM Customs tape. He led off briskly, as he had planned to do, firing his first question before he had sat down.

'Where did you spend last Christmas, sir?' he demanded, wielding the word 'sir' like a meat cleaver.

'Skiing in the Rockies.'

'With William?'

'Naturally.'

'Where was Hoban?'

'What's he got to do with it? With his family, I should imagine.'

'Which family?'

'His in-laws, probably. I'm not sure he's got parents of his own. I rather think of him as an orphan-chil', don't you?' Massingham responded lethargically, in deliberate counterpoint to Brock's haste.

'So Hoban was in Istanbul. With the Orlovs. Hoban was in Istanbul for Christmas. Yes?'

'I assume so. One never quite knows for certain with Alix. He's a bit of still water, if that's the expression. Runs deep.'

'Dr Mirsky was also in Istanbul over Christmas,' Brock suggested.

'What an amazing coincidence. Population twice the size of London, they must have been falling over one another's feet.'

'Does it surprise you to learn that Dr Mirsky and Alix Hoban are old buddies from way back?'

'Not particularly.'

264

'What do you think was the nature of their relationship – way back?'

'Well, they weren't lovers, darling, if that's what you're suggesting.'

'I'm not. I'm suggesting they were bonded by other factors, and I'm asking you what those factors were.'

Doesn't like it, Brock recorded, his spirits rising. Buying time. Eyes to the envelope on the table. Back again. Moistens lips. Wondering how much the little bastard knows, and how much do I need to tell him?

'Hoban was a high-flying Soviet apparatchik,' Massingham conceded, after deliberation. 'Mirsky was the same sort of creature in Poland. They did business together.'

'When you say apparatchik, what type of apparatus are you referring to?'

Massingham gave a disdainful shrug. 'A little of this and that. I'm just wondering whether you've been cleared for this stuff,' he added insolently.

'So Intelligence. They were in their countries' respective Intelligence services. One Soviet, one Polish.'

'Let's just call them technocrats,' Massingham proposed, attempting once again to put Brock in his place.

'During your tour in Moscow with the British Embassy, weren't you one of the people who had side-door dealings with Soviet Intelligence?'

'We took a few soundings. It was *very* informal and *rather* romantic and *terribly* secret. We were looking for common ground. Targets of potential interest. How we might go forward, hand in hand. That's all I'm allowed to tell you, I'm afraid.'

'What sort of targets?'

'Terror. Where the Russians weren't financing it, of course.' Massingham was enjoying himself.

'Crime?'

'Where they weren't involved in it.'

'Drugs?'

'Isn't that a crime?'

'*You tell me*,' Brock shot back, and to his pleasure fancied he had scored a hit, for Massingham had set his fingers to his lips to hide his mouth, and his gaze had slipped away to the bookshelves. 'And wasn't Alix Hoban one of the people on the Soviet side you took soundings from?' he asked.

'This really isn't your business at all. I shall have to clear this with my former masters, I'm afraid. I'm sorry. I can't go on.'

'Your former masters wouldn't speak to you if you paid them. Ask Aiden Bell. Was Hoban on the Soviet team or wasn't he?'

'You know bloody well he was.'

'What was his expertise?'

'Crime.'

'*Organised* crime?'

'Oxymoron, darling. It's *disorganised* by definition.'

'And he was involved with Soviet criminal gangs?'

'He was *covering* them.'

'You mean he was on their payroll.'

'Don't be such a prude. You know very well how that game is played. It's give and take between poacher and game-keeper. Everybody has to get something or there's no deal.'

'Was Mirsky around at that time?'

'Around what?'

'You and Hoban.' It was an inspired gesture on Brock's part. He hadn't planned it, hadn't even thought to do it till that moment. He picked up the envelope and tore it open. He pulled out the red-bound document and dumped it back on the packing case. Then he scrumpled up the envelope and tossed it with perfect accuracy into a wastepaper basket on the other side of the attic. And for a while the red book smouldered like a fire in a dark room. 'I was asking you whether you made the acquaintance of Dr Mirsky during your tour in Moscow in the late eighties,' Brock reminded Massingham.

'I met him a couple of times.'

'A couple.'

'You're being too Gothic. Mirsky went to the conferences. I went to the conferences. That doesn't mean we played doctors during lunch hour.'

'And Mirsky was representing Polish Intelligence.'

'If you want to make it sound bigger than it was, yes.'

'What was Polish Intelligence doing at side-door conferences between British and Russian intelligence officers?'

'Talking about talking about collaboration. Putting the Polish view. We had Czechs and Hungarians and Bulgarians' – appealing to him now – 'we *encouraged* all that, Nat. There was no point in taking our case to the Satellites unless the Sovs had given them the green light, was there now? So why not short-circuit the system and have the Sats aboard from the start?'

'How did you meet the Orlov brothers?'

Massingham let out a silly shriek of derision. 'That was bloody *years* later, you dunce!'

'Six. You were pimping for Single's. Tiger wanted the Orlov connection so you pimped that too. How? Through Mirsky or Hoban?'

Massingham's questing eye again took in the red book on the packing case, then returned to Brock.

'Hoban.'

'Was Hoban married to Zoya by then?'

'He may have been' – sulkily – 'who believes in marriage these days? Alix had targeted Yevgeny's daughters and wasn't fussy which one he got. The son-in-law also rises,' he added with an uneasy giggle.

'And it was Hoban who introduced Mirsky to the brothers.'

'Probably.'

'Did Tiger object to Mirsky being let into the act?'

'Why should he? Mirsky's bright as hell, he was a fatcat Polish lawyer, knew all the angles, had a first-class organisation. If the brothers were looking for openings further west, Mirsky was their man. He knew the boys in the ports. He was a Gdansk man, a door-opener. What more could Yevgeny ask?'

'You mean Hoban, don't you?'

'Why? It was still the Orlovs' operation.'

'But Hoban was running it. It was the Hoban–Mirsky show when you got down to it. Yevgeny was the figurehead by then. It was Hoban, *Massingham* and Mirsky,' Brock ended, stabbing his finger at the red book. 'You're a villain, Mr Massingham. You're in it up to your ears. You're not just a money-launderer. You're a frontline player in the dirtiest game on the planet. Sir.'

Massingham's manicured hands were twitching where they lay. For the second time in as many minutes he cleared his throat. 'That's not true at all. That's an absolute travesty. It was Tiger to Yevgeny on the money and Hoban to Mirsky on the shipments. The whole thing was conducted by hand-delivered letters and I never saw them. Tiger's eyes only.'

'Can I ask you something, Randy?'

'Not if you're trying to pin the whole business on me.'

'Did you ever – let's say at the very start of it all – for example, when Hoban took you up onto the high hill – or Mirsky did – or you took them – and you showed each other the kingdom – and you took Tiger aside and did the same to him – or he took you, I'm not point-scoring – did you ever, any of you, once mention, aloud, to one another, just on a one-to-one basis, the word *drugs*?' Massingham gave a sneering shrug, implying that the question was ridiculous. 'Warheads? Nuclear and otherwise? Fissile materials? Also not?' Massingham was shaking his head at each of them. 'Heroin?'

'Good God no!'

'Cocaine? So how did we get round this tricky problem of vocabulary, may I ask? What figleaf, if I may be so vulgar, disguised our shame, sir?'

'I've told you and I've told you. Our job was to bring the Orlov operation from the black side to the white side. We came in after the fact. Not before. That was the deal.'

Brock leaned very near to Massingham and, almost as a favour, begged him: 'Then what are we *doing* here, sir? If you're so legit, why are you so anxious to cut a deal?'

'You know bloody well why. You've seen what they do. They'll do it to me.'

'*You*. Not Tiger. You. Why *you*? What have you done that Tiger hasn't? What do you know that Tiger doesn't know?

What's so *bad* about you that you're so afraid?' No answer. Brock waited and still no answer. The anger in him acquired a deadly edge. If Massingham was terrified, let him be more terrified. Let him see his whole life rotting away before his eyes. 'I want the black book,' Brock said. 'Tiger's list of people in high places. Not bent Poles in Gdansk or bent Germans in Bremen or bent Dutch in Rotterdam. I like them but they don't make me horny. I want bent Brits. Home-bred, with lots of power to abuse. People like you. The higher they are, the more I want them. And what you're going to tell me is, Tiger knew about those people and you never did. And what I'm going to tell you is, I don't believe a word of you. I think you're being economical with the *vérité* and hoping I'll be generous with the immunity. I won't. That's not my nature. I'm not taking one more step down Immunity Lane until you give me those names and telephone numbers.'

In a fresh convulsion of fear and anger, Massingham broke free of Brock's taunting gaze. 'Tiger's the streetwise one, not me! Tiger's the defender of crooks, the befriender of police. Where did he cut his milk teeth? In Liverpool, down among the immigrants and druggies. How did he make his first million? In property, bribing council officials. It's no good shaking your head at me, Nat! It's the truth!'

But Brock had already changed his ground. 'You see, what I keep asking myself is, Mr Massingham: *why*?'

'Why what?'

'Why did Mr Massingham come to me? Who sent him to me? Who's the puppetmaster behind his act? And then a little bird leans over his twig and says to me: Tiger is. Tiger wants to know what I know and how I know it. And who from. So he sends his highly impressive Chief of Staff to me posing as a frightened British subject while he suns himself in some nice tax haven where there's no extradition. You're the fall guy, Mr Massingham. Because if I can't have Tiger, I'm having you!' But Massingham had found his balance again. A smile of disbelief had spread across his tight lips. 'And if Tiger Single didn't plant you on me, the brothers did,' Brock went on, trying to sound triumphant. 'Those pseudo-Georgian horse-traders were never short of a trick or two, that's for sure.' But the smile on Massingham's face only widened. 'Why did Mirsky move to Istanbul?' Brock demanded, giving the red document an irritable shove so that it slid to the other side of the packing case.

'For his health, darling. The Berlin Wall was coming down. He didn't want to be hit by a falling brick.'

'I heard there was talk of putting him on trial.'

'Let's just say the Turkish climate became him.'

'Do you own shares in Trans-Finanz Istanbul, by any chance?' Brock asked. 'You or any company on or offshore that you have an interest in?'

'I'm pleading the Fifth,' Massingham said.

'We haven't got one,' Brock replied, and with this exchange there occurred between the interrogator and his subject one of those mysterious truces which are followed later by renewed and intensified combat. 'You see, I can understand your two-timing Tiger, Randy, I have no difficulty with that. If *I* was working for Tiger, I'd two-time him right and left. I can understand your getting into a cabal with a couple of badmen from the ex-Soviet Intelligence world. None of that bothers me. I can understand Hoban and Mirsky bullying Yevgeny into cutting Tiger out of the loop and you lending a helping hand, to say the least. But when *that* failed, and there was no Father Christmas after all – *what the hell happened next*?' He was so warm! He could feel it! It was here in the room. It was across the packing case from him. It was inside Massingham's skull and begging to come out – till at the very last second it turned and scurried back to safety. 'All right, the *Free Tallinn* was nabbed,' Brock conceded, pressing forward in his mystification. 'Tough luck. The Orlovs lost a few tons of dope, and a few men besides. These things happen. And face was lost. There'd been too many *Free Tallinns*. Somebody had to be punished. Reparation had to be demanded. But where are *you* in this, Mr Massingham? Whose side are you on, apart from your own? And what the hell is keeping you sitting here, putting up with my insults?'

But though Brock went back and forth with this question,

put it to Massingham in a dozen different ways, though he shoved the sixty-eight-page document at him and made him read in black and white the evidence of his villainy, and though Massingham, now churlishly, now pertly, answered a string of less pressing questions arising from Oliver's visits to Dr Conrad and the bank, Brock returned to his office in the Strand with a deeper sense of failure and frustration than before. The promised land is still out there and it's unconquered, he told Tanby bitterly, and Tanby said maybe get some sleep. But Brock didn't. He rang Bell and went over old ground with him. He rang a couple of his whisperers in far-off places. He rang his wife and listened gratefully to her insane opinions about what to do with the Northern Irish. None of these dialogues brought him nearer to breaking Massingham's code. He dozed and woke abruptly with the telephone already to his ear.

'Open line call from Derek in Zürich, sir,' Tanby was saying in his lugubrious West Country drawl. 'The bridal pair have flown the coop. No forwarding address.'

CHAPTER SEVENTEEN

The hilltop was an enchanted sea above the smog. Domes
of mosques floated on it like basking tortoises. The minarets
were stand-up targets on the shooting range at Swindon.
Aggie switched off the engine of the rented Ford and
listened to the dying wheeze of the airconditioning. Somewhere below her lay the Bosphorus but she couldn't see it
through the smog. She lowered her window for a bit of air.
A wave of heat leapt at her from the tarmac, though it was
by now early evening. The stench of smog mingled with
scents of wet spring grass. She raised the window and
resumed her vigil. Grey cumulus collected purposefully
above her. Rain fell. She switched on the engine and ran
the wipers. The rain stopped, the cumulus turned pink,
the pine trees around her blackened until their fir cones
resembled plump flies caught in the tracery of the foliage.
Again she lowered the window and this time the car filled
with the scents of lime and jasmine. She heard cicadas and
the burping of a frog or toad. She saw crows with grey
chests sitting to attention on an overhead cable. A celestial
explosion blasted her out of her seat. Sparks burst above
her and wandered into the valley before she realised that a
nearby house was throwing a firework party. The sparks
vanished and the dusk deepened.

She was wearing jeans and a leather jacket which was what she had eloped in. She had no gun because she had made no contact with Brock's family. No gift-wrapped parcel had been delivered to her hotel, no thick envelope shoved at her under the Visa Section grille with a gruff 'Sign here, Mrs West.' Nobody in the world except Oliver knew where she was, and the stillness up here on the hilltop was like the stillness that had descended on her life. She was unarmed and in love and in danger, and she was staring down a lonely Turkish hillside at a pair of iron gates set into a shellproof wall a hundred yards below her. Behind the wall lay the flat roof of Dr Mirsky's very modern brick fortress and to Aggie's travelled eye it was just another dope lawyer's pad, with bougainvillaea and intruder lights and fountains and video cameras and Alsatian dogs and statues, and two burly men in black trousers and white shirts and black waistcoats who were doing nothing very particular in the forecourt. And somewhere inside the fortress was her lover.

They had arrived here after a fruitless visit to Dr Mirsky's very legal offices in the centre of the city. 'The Doctor is not here today,' a beautiful girl informed them from behind a mauve reception desk. 'Maybe you leave your name and come back tomorrow, please.' They left no name but once on the pavement Oliver hammered at his pockets till he found a bit of paper with Mirsky's home address on it, memorised from a sneak view of the file he had stolen from Dr Conrad's office. Together they stopped a venerable gentleman who thought they were German and kept shouting '*Dahin, dahin*' while he pointed them in the general direction. On the hillside more venerable gentlemen directed them, till out of nowhere they were in the right private road and driving past the right fortress and drawing the attention of the right dogs, bodyguards and cameras.

Aggie would have given anything to go into the house with Oliver but it wasn't what he wanted. He wanted a lawyers' one-to-one, he said. He wanted her to park a hundred yards away and wait. He reminded her that it was his father they were looking for, not hers. And anyway what use can you be, with or without a gun, sitting there like a wallflower?

273

Much better to wait and see whether I come out, and if I don't, holler. He's taking over his own life, she thought. Mine too. She didn't know whether she was alarmed or proud or both.

She was parked on a deserted building lot alongside a pink lorry with a lemonade bottle painted on it, and half a dozen Volkswagen beetles, all empty. It would take a pretty sophisticated surveillance camera, she reckoned, or a very smart bodyguard, to spot her at that distance. Anyway, who was interested in one woman in a small brown car without aerials, talking on a cellphone in the twilight? Not that she was talking, absolutely not. She was listening to Brock's messages one by one. Nat, steady as a good Merseyside sea-captain in a storm, no reproaches, no fuss: 'Charmian, this is your dad again, we'd like you to give us a call as soon as you receive this message, please... Charmian, we need to hear from you, please... Charmian, if you can't get through to us for some reason, then please contact your uncle... Charmian, we want you both to come home as soon as possible, please.' For uncle read local British representative.

While she listened, her quick gaze scanned the iron gates and trees and hedges of the surrounding gardens, and the lights pricking through the blue-grey smog. And when she had stopped listening to Brock, she listened to the conflicting voices of her complexity while she tried to fathom what she owed to him and what she owed to Oliver and to herself, though the last two were in reality a single debt, because every time she thought of Oliver he was back in her arms laughing, and shaking his head in disbelief, with the sweat running off him from the overheated sleeping car, and looking altogether so light-hearted and enthusiastic that she felt her entire life had been spent trying to get him out of prison, and to rat on him was to put him back inside with no remission. The Service had an operational message desk and Aggie had the number in her head. The compromiser in her considered ringing it and saying that Oliver and Aggie were alive and well and not to worry. A stronger side of her knew that the smallest message was betrayal.

The night was gathering in earnest, the smog was lifting,

the intruder lights were casting a white cone over the fortress, and the car lights on the bridges over the Bosphorus were like moving necklaces against the blackness of the water. Aggie discovered she was praying, and that prayer did not affect her powers of observation. She braced herself. The gates were parting, one black waistcoat to each. A pair of headlights was coming up the hill at her. She saw them dip and heard a distant fanfare of a car horn. The car turned into the gateway and she identified a silver Mercedes before the gates closed on it. It was chauffeur-driven. One bulky man sat in the back, but he was too far away, and the sight of him too brief, for her to recognise Mirsky from the photographs she had been shown in London a million miles away.

*   *   *

Oliver pressed the bell and to his confusion heard a woman's voice, which reminded him that when you are obsessed by one woman, all other women become unconscious ducts to her. She spoke to him first in Turkish, but as soon as he spoke English she switched to Euro-American and said her husband was out right now but why not try him down at the office? To which Oliver replied that he had tried the office without success, it had taken him more than an hour to find the house, he was a friend of Dr Conrad's, he had confidential messages for Dr Mirsky, his chauffeur had run out of petrol and could Mrs Mirsky perhaps suggest a time when her husband might return? And he reckoned that something in his voice as he said all this must have communicated itself to her, some blend of authority and flirtation left over from his lovemaking with Aggie, because her next question was 'Are you American or English?' spoken in a relaxed, almost post-coital purr.

'English to the core. Does that disqualify me?'

'And you are a client of my husband?'

'Not yet, but I intend to be, just as soon as he'll have me,' he replied heartily, at which she went off the air for a few seconds.

'So why don't you come on in and have a lemon juice till Adam shows up?' she suggested.

And soon a man in a black waistcoat was rolling back an iron gate far enough to admit one pedestrian, while a second man bellowed in Turkish at the two Alsatian dogs to shut up. And to judge by the men's expressions Oliver might have landed from outer space, for they first scowled up and down the road in puzzlement, then at his dust-free shoes. So Oliver jabbed his thumb down the hill and laughed and said, 'Driver's gone to get petrol,' hoping that if they didn't understand him they would at least accept that an explanation had been given. The front door was open by the time he reached it. A prizefighter in a full black suit was guarding it. He was glossy and unfriendly and Oliver's height, and he kept his hands curled at his sides while he frisked Oliver with his eyes.

'Welcome,' he said finally, and led Oliver through an outer bailey to a second door which in turn led to a courtyard with an illuminated swimming pool and a fairy-lit paved patio with trumpet flowers growing over it and, in the patio, rattan swing-chairs suspended from rafters. In one chair sat a small girl who looked as Carmen might when she attained the ripe age of six, with plaits, and a double gap where her top teeth should be. Squeezed in beside her was a sloe-eyed Romeo two years her senior, whose features were mysteriously known to him. The little girl was spooning ice cream from a common plate. Drawing-books, paper scissors, crayons and bits of pop-together warriors were strewn around the tiled floor. Opposite the children sat a blonde, long-legged woman in the last weeks of pregnancy. And Dr Conrad was right, she was beautiful. A volume of Beatrix Potter's *Peter Rabbit* in English lay open at her side.

'Children, this is Mr West from England,' she announced with mock portent while she shook his hand. 'Meet Friedi and Paul. Friedi is our daughter, Paul is our friend. We have just discovered that lettuces are soporific, haven't we, children? – and I am Mrs Mirsky – Paul, what does soporific mean?'

Oliver guessed she was Swedish and bored, and he

276

remembered how Heather had flirted with any male over the age of ten from her fifth month onward. Friedi who was Carmen aged six grinned and spooned ice cream while Paul stared at Oliver and the stare continued to accuse him. But of what crime? Against whom? Where? The black-suited prizefighter brought iced lemon juice.

'Sleepy,' Paul replied at long last, when everyone had forgotten the question, and too late the penny dropped: *Paul, for God's sake! Zoya's Paul! That Paul!*

'You arrived today?' Mrs Mirsky asked.

'From Vienna.'

'You had business there?'

'Sort of.'

'Paul's father also has a business in Vienna,' she said, articulating slowly and clearly for the children's benefit, but keeping her large eyes appreciatively on Oliver. 'He *lives* in Istanbul but he *works* in Vienna, yes, Paul? He is a *big* trader. Today everybody is a trader. Alix is our *great* friend, isn't he, Paul? We admire him *very* much. Are you also a trader, Mr West?' – languidly drawing her wrap across her bosom.

'That kind of thing.'

'In any particular commodity, Mr West?'

'Money mostly.'

'Mr West trades in *money*. Now Paul, tell Mr West what languages you speak – Russian naturally, Turkish, a bit of Georgian, English? The ice cream does not make you *soporific*, Paul?'

Paul the party's clouded child, Oliver thought empathetically as the recognition took wing. Inconsolable like his mother. Paul the bereaved one, the divorced one, the eternal stepchild, the one you want to beg a smile from, the one whose smudged eyes brighten when you walk into the room, and stay on you reproachfully when it's time to pack up your tricks and leave. Paul the troubled eight-year-old memory, trying to retrieve a misty encounter with a mad monster called Post Boy, from the days when Grandpa and Grandma lived in a leafy castle outside Moscow and had a motorbike which the Post Boy rode while Mummy hugged me to her breast and kept her hand over my ear.

277

Bending abruptly double in his chair, Oliver swooped and grabbed a drawing book and a pair of paper scissors from the floor and – when he had secured Paul's nodded consent – whipped a double page from the drawing book. Having swiftly folded and refolded it, he cut and fretted with the scissors until he had produced a string of happy rabbits nose to tail.

'But that's fantastic!' cried Mrs Mirsky, the first to speak. 'You have children, Mr West? But if you have no children how can you be so expert? You are a genius! Paul and Friedi, what do you say to Mr West?'

But it was what Mr West would say to Dr Mirsky that was causing Oliver the greater concern. And what he would say to Zoya and Hoban when they called by to pick up their little boy. He made aeroplanes and to the common delight they really flew. One landed on the water so they sent a rescue plane to fetch it, then fished them both to dry land with a pole. He made a bird and Friedi refused to let it fly because it was too precious. He magicked a Swiss five-franc piece out of Friedi's ear and was about to produce another from Paul's mouth when a two-toned view-halloo of a car horn, and a joyous yell of 'Papa!' from Friedi announced that the good Doctor had come home.

Commotion in the forecourt, a clatter of running servants, a slamming of car doors, a throaty howl of happy dogs and a soothing roar of Polish greeting, as a bustling, boisterous, black-haired man with a widow's peak bursts into the courtyard, wrenches off his necktie, jacket, shoes, then everything, and with a bellow of relief dives hairy-naked into the pool and swims two lengths underwater. Emerging like a half-shaven bear to seize a multi-coloured robe from the prizefighter, he wraps it round himself, embraces first his wife, then his daughter, calls 'Hi, Pauli!' and bestows a friendly scrabble on Paul's hair before inclining once more to his wife, and only then, with visible displeasure, to Oliver.

'I'm *terribly* sorry to barge in like this,' Oliver said in his most disarming upper-class voice. 'I'm an old friend of Yevgeny's and I bring greetings from Dr Conrad.' No answer but the straight stare, older than Paul's by several centuries, and cushioned between plump eyelids. 'If I could talk to you alone,' Oliver said.

Oliver followed Dr Mirsky's multi-coloured backside and bare heels. The black-suited prizefighter followed Oliver. They crossed a corridor, climbed a few steps, entered a low study with scenic Polaroid windows looking at dusky hilltops prickling with restless lights. The prizefighter closed the door and leaned against it, one hand tucked against his heart.

'Okay,' said Mirsky. 'What the fuck do you want?' His voice beat on one bass level, like a salvo of artillery.

'I'm Oliver, Tiger Single's son. I'm the junior partner of the house of Single & Single of Curzon Street and I'm looking for my father.'

Mirsky growled something in Polish. The prizefighter put his hands affectionately under Oliver's armpits, explored them, then his breasts and waistband. He turned Oliver round and, instead of kissing him, or wrestling him to the bed like Zoya, felt his crotch like Kat, and continued the caress all the way to his ankles. He removed Oliver's wallet and handed it to Mirsky, then the passport in the name of West, then the junk from Oliver's pockets which as usual would have disgraced a twelve-year-old schoolboy. Cupping his hands, Mirsky took the whole lot to the desk, and put on a pair of dainty spectacles. A couple of thousand Swiss francs – he had left the rest of his money in the suitcase – some loose coins, a photograph of Carmen sitting on a beach donkey, a cutting, still unread, from a weekly magazine called *Abracadabra*, offering 'tricks new and newly slanted', one freshly laundered handkerchief forced on him by Aggie. Mirsky was holding the passport to the light.

'Where the fuck you get this?'

'Massingham,' Oliver said, remembering Nadia at Nightingales and wishing for a moment he was there.

'You a friend of Massingham?'

'We're colleagues.'

'Massingham send you here?'

'No.'

'British police send you?'

'I came for myself, to find my father.'

Mirsky spoke in Polish again. The prizefighter replied. A staccato conversation followed in which the manner of Oliver's arrival appeared to be discussed, and the prize-fighter was rebuked and sent from the room.

'You're a danger to my wife and family, you understand? You got no business coming here. You understand?'

'I hear you.'

'I want you out of my house. Now. You ever come back, God help you. Take this shit. I don't want it. Who brought you here?'

'A taxi.'

'A fucking woman drives a taxi in Istanbul?'

They spotted her, Oliver thought, impressed. 'I got her from the car hire people at the airport. We took an hour to find the house. She had another job and she was out of petrol.' Mirsky watched with distaste as Oliver loaded his junk back into his pockets. 'I've got to find him,' Oliver said, stuffing his wallet into his jacket. 'If you don't know where he is, tell me someone who does. He's in over his head. I need to help him. He's my father.'

From across the courtyard they heard the jolly chatter of Mrs Mirsky and the children as she turned them over to a maid to be put to bed. The prizefighter returned and seemed to be reporting that what was ordered had been done. Reluctantly, Mirsky appeared to give him a different order. The prizefighter demurred and Mirsky roared at him. The prizefighter departed and returned with jeans, a checked shirt and sandals. Mirsky threw off his bathrobe, stood naked, pulled on the trousers and shirt, stepped into the sandals, said 'Jesus H. Christ' and, with the prizefighter bringing up the tail, marched ahead of Oliver down a back corridor to the forecourt. A silver Mercedes stood facing the closed gates, chauffeur at the wheel. Mirsky opened the chauffeur's door, yanked him out and barked another order. The prizefighter pulled a pistol from his left armpit and handed it to Mirsky, who with a disapproving shake of his head jammed it butt-forward into his waistband. The prizefighter escorted Oliver to the passenger door, one hand on his arm, and sat him smartly in the passenger seat. The gates opened. Mirsky drove into the road and slewed left down the hill towards the city lights. Oliver wanted to turn round and look for Aggie but didn't dare.

'You a big friend of Massingham?'

'He's a bastard,' said Oliver, feeling this was no time for half-truths. 'He shafted my father.'

'So what? We're all bastards. Some bastards, they don't even play chess.'

Mirsky drew the car to a sickening halt in the middle of the road, lowered the window and waited. A snake-track to their right zigzagged towards a cluster of winking antennae on the hill's crest. The sky was drenched with stars, a brilliant moon had cleared the black saddle of the horizon, the Bosphorus twinkled below them. Still Mirsky waited, watching his mirrors, but no Aggie came down the hill behind them. With a muttered expletive, Mirsky slammed the car into gear, lurched off the road and onto the track, rounded a bend at speed, bumped five hundred yards over grass and rubble and stopped in a layby out of sight of the main road. Tall tree trunks rose around them. Oliver remembered his own secret place on the hilltop at Abbots Quay and wondered whether this was Mirsky's.

'I don't know where your fucking father is, okay?' Mirsky said, in a voice of grudging complicity. 'That's the truth. I tell you the truth, then you get the hell out of my life, you stay away from my house, my wife, my kids, you go back to fucking England, I don't give a shit where you go. I'm a family man. I've got family values. I liked your father, okay? Sorry he's dead, okay? Sorry about that. So fuck off home and found a new dynasty and forget you ever knew him. I'm a respectable lawyer. It's what I like to be. Not a crook any more, not unless it's necessary.'

'Who killed him?'

'Maybe they didn't do it yet. Maybe they kill him tomorrow, tonight, what's the difference? You find him, he'll be dead. Then you'll be dead too.'

'Who will have killed him?'

'All of them. The whole family. Yevgeny, Tinatin, Hoban, every cousin, uncle, nephew, what do I know who kills him? Yevgeny's reinvented the blood feud, declared war on the whole fucking human race with no dispensations. He's a Caucasus man. Everyone's got to pay. Tiger, Tiger's son, his son's dog, his fucking canary.'

'All because of the *Free Tallinn*?'

'The *Free Tallinn* screwed everything. Till Christmas – okay, we do some things. Massingham, me, Hoban – we got a little tired of everybody else's mistakes, thought it was time to reorganise, improve security, go modern.'

'Get rid of the old men,' Oliver suggested. 'Take over the shop.'

'Sure,' said Mirsky generously. 'Screw them all ways up. That's business, what's new? We try to pull a takeover. A bloodless coup. Why not? By peaceful means. I'm a peaceful guy. I made a long journey. Lousy little flea-kid from Lvov, studies to be a good Communist, learns to fuck in four languages at the age of fourteen, *magna cum laude* in law, gets to be a big Party guy, nice operation going, lot of influence, sees the way the wind is blowing, gets churchy a little bit, gets baptised, big champagne party, joins Solidarity but the cure is not a hundred per cent, the new guys think they ought to put me in jail so I come to Turkey. I'm happy here. I build a new practice, I marry a goddess. Maybe I'm getting a little tired of the Holy Trinity. Maybe one day I convert to Islam. I'm flexible, and I'm *peaceful*,' he repeated emphatically. 'Peaceful today, it's the only way to go, till some crazy Russian decides he'll start the third fucking world war.'

'Where have they taken him?'

'Where they took him. How should I know? Where's Yevgeny? Where they took the corpse. Where's Alix? Where Yevgeny went. Where's Tiger? Where Alix took him.'

'Whose corpse?'

'Mikhail's fucking corpse! Who do you think? Yevgeny's brother Mikhail. You got rocks in your head or something? Mikhail, who was killed on the *Free Tallinn*, for Christ's sake. Why else do you think Yevgeny needs to start a war? All he wanted was the body. Paid a fortune for it. "Get me my brother's body. In a steel coffin, lots of fucking ice. Then I kill the world."' Oliver noticed a lot of things concurrently. That his eyes were seeing negative instead of positive, so that for several seconds the moon shone black in a white sky. That he was under water, deprived of speech and hearing. That Aggie was reaching for him but he was drowning. When he recovered his faculties, Mirsky was talking about Massingham again. 'Alix tells Randy about the load, Randy snitches to his old employers, the fucking British Secret Service. His old employers snitch to Moscow. Moscow calls out the whole fucking Russian navy, they make a new Pearl Harbor, kill four guys, seize the boat, three tons of best shit go back to Odessa for the Customs boys to make themselves a fortune. Yevgeny goes crazy, has Winser's head shot off. That's for openers. Now they get down to business.'

Oliver spoke stiffly ahead of him, through the trees to the city. 'What was Mikhail doing on the *Free Tallinn* when it was boarded?'

'Riding with the load. Protecting it. Doing his brother a favour. I told you. They'd been losing too much stuff. Too many mistakes around the place, too many accounts frozen, too much money going down the toilet. Everyone was pissed off. Everyone was blaming everyone. Mikhail wants to be a hero for his brother, so he goes on the boat, takes his Kalashnikov along with him. The Russian navy boards the ship, Mikhail shoots a couple of them, creates a bad atmosphere. They shoot him back, so everybody has to pay. It's logical.'

'Tiger came to see you,' Oliver said, in the same mechanical tone.

'The fuck he did.'

'He came here to Istanbul just days ago.'

'Maybe he did, maybe he didn't. He called me. At my office. That's all I know. Didn't sound like a normal telephone. Didn't sound like a normal man. Like he'd got an onion in his mouth. Maybe it was a pistol. Listen, I'm sorry, okay? He's your fucking father.'

'What did he want?'

'He insulted me. Said I'd tried to rob him last Christmas. "Rob you, I don't know," I said. "At that time we had a bad feeling you were robbing us. Anyway, you won, so who gives a shit?" Then he tells me I should call off this crazy demand for two hundred million pounds. Talk to Yevgeny, I tell him. Talk to Hoban. The demand is not my idea. Yell at the client, not me, I tell him. Those two guys together, they went off the reservation. Then he tells me, "If my son Oliver shows up, don't talk to him, he's a fucking lunatic. Tell him not to come any further, tell him not to follow me. Tell him to get the fuck out of Istanbul and go hide in a hole. Tell him the joke's over."'

'That doesn't sound like my father speaking.'

'It's his message. In my words. It's my message too. I'm a lawyer. I give the essence. *Get the fuck out now*. You want to go somewhere? The airport? The train station? You got money? I take you to a cab rank.' He started the engine.

'Who told you Massingham was a traitor?'

'Hoban. Alix knows stuff. He's got his people in Russia still, guys in the system. Spooks.' Without putting on his headlights, Mirsky released the handbrake and eased the car towards the road, letting the moon show him the way.

'Why did Hoban tell you it was Massingham who betrayed the *Free Tallinn*?'

'He told me, that's why. Like we're friends. Like we did stuff together in the bad times, pair of spooks, doing our best for Communism and making a buck on the side.'

'Where's Zoya?'

'Off her screwball head. Don't mess with her, hear me? Russian women are crazy. Alix has to come back to Istanbul, put her in a clinic or something. Alix is neglecting his marital duties.' He had reached the bottom of the hill. He was watching his mirrors all the way. Oliver was watching them too. He saw the Volkswagen come up behind them, and as Mirsky pulled up he saw Aggie, jaw set and both hands firmly on the top of the wheel as she rolled past them. 'You're a nice guy. I hope I never see your fucking face again.' He pulled the pistol out of his waistband. 'You want one of these?'

'No thanks,' said Oliver.

Mirsky parked just short of a roundabout. Oliver stepped out and waited on the kerb. Mirsky circled the roundabout at racing speed and headed for home, not another glance for Oliver. He was succeeded after a suitable intermission by Aggie.

'Mikhail was Yevgeny's Sammy,' Oliver said, staring blindly ahead of him. They had parked close to the water. Oliver had debriefed himself while Aggie listened.

'Who's Sammy?' – already calling Brock on her cellphone.

'Boy I knew. Helped me with my magic.'

*   *   *

Elsie Watmore heard the doorbell in her sleep, and after the doorbell she heard her late husband Jack telling her Oliver was wanted down at the bank again. After that it wasn't Jack but Sammy in his dressing gown with the landing light on, saying two plainclothes policemen were standing on the doorstep, somebody must have been murdered and one of them was bald. Sammy's thoughts had taken a gory turn recently. Death and disaster, he couldn't get enough of them.

'If they're plainclothes, how can you be so sure they're policemen?' she asked him while she pulled on her house-coat. 'Whatever time is it?'

'They've got a police car,' Sammy replied, following her down the stairs. 'With POLICE on it.'

'I don't want you round me, Sammy, so don't be. You're to stay upstairs, it's better.'

'I won't,' Sammy said, which was another thing that worried her: his rebelliousness, just in the few days since Oliver had left. It went with his bedwetting and wanting everybody killed in disasters. She looked through the fish-eye. The near one wore a trilby hat. The other was bare-headed and bald like a wrestler and Elsie had never seen a stone-bald copper before. His scalp glistened in the lamp-light of the porch and she had a notion he rubbed it with a special oil. Behind them, parked bang next to Oliver's magic van, stood their white Rover car. She opened the door but kept it on the chain.

'It's quarter past one in the morning,' she said through the gap.

'Very sorry, Mrs Watmore, I'm sure. You *are* Mrs Watmore, aren't you?'

The one with the hat talking, the bald one watching. A London voice, educated, but not as much as he'd like. 'What if I am?' she said.

'I'm Detective Sergeant Jennings, this is Detective Constable Ames.' He waved a cellophane-backed card at her but it could have been his bus pass. 'We're acting on information regarding a person we'd like to talk to before they commit another felony. We think you may be able to help us with our enquiries.'

'It's about *Oliver*, Mum!' Sammy croaked in a gravelly whisper from her left elbow, and Elsie almost rounded on him and told him to shut his stupid mouth. She unchained the door and the policemen stepped into the hall, one close behind the other. It's that ex-wife of his, she's put the law on him for his maintenance, she thought. He's been on one of his benders and belted somebody. She had a vision of Oliver curled on his side, the way she had found him on his bedroom floor that time, staring at a prison wall.

The policeman with the hat took it off. Leaky eyes like a drinker. Ashamed of himself somehow. But the shiny bald one wasn't ashamed of anything. He had spotted the Rest registration book and was stooped over it and flipping through the pages as if he owned them. Bully-boy shoulders. Arse too small for the rest of you.

'Name of West,' said the bald constable, licking his thumb and flipping another page. 'Know a West at all?'

'I expect we've had one here and there. It's a common enough name.'

'Show her,' the constable said, and went on turning pages while the sergeant with the hat extracted a greaseproof paper envelope from his wallet and presented her with a photograph of Oliver looking like Elvis Presley with his hair marcelled and his eyelids fatty from the time when he was doing whatever he had run away from. Sammy was standing on his toes trying to get a look and saying, 'Me, me.'

'First name Mark,' said the sergeant. 'Mark West. Six foot, dark hair.'

Elsie Watmore had only instinct, and the memory of Oliver's stifled phone calls coming in like SOS messages from a sinking ship: *How are you, Elsie, how's Sammy? I'm all right, Elsie, don't worry about me, I'll be back to see you soon.* Sammy had changed his plea to 'Show me, Show me,' and was snapping his fingers under her nose.

'It's not him,' she said hoarsely, like a formal declaration she had rehearsed too often.

'Not *who?*' said the bald constable, straightening and barging round on her at the same time. '*Who's* not who?'

His eyes were water-pale and empty, and it was the emptiness that scared her: the knowledge that whatever amount of kindness anyone poured into them it was wasted. He could be watching his own mother dying, he wouldn't look any different, she thought.

'I don't know the man in the photograph, so it's not him, is it?' she said, handing back the photograph. 'You ought to be ashamed of yourselves, waking decent people up like this.'

Sammy could bear his exclusion no longer. Emerging from her skirts, he marched up to the sergeant and boldly struck out his arm.

'Sammy, go up to bed, please. I'm serious. You've got school tomorrow.'

'Show it to him,' the constable commanded, though his lips never moved. A constable, giving orders to a sergeant.

The sergeant handed Sammy the photograph and Sammy made a show of examining it, first one eye, then both.

'No Mark West here,' he pronounced, and shoved it back into the man's hand as if it were a dud, before stomping upstairs to bed, not looking back.

'How about Hawthorne?' the bald constable asked, back at the registration book. 'O. Hawthorne. Who's he?'

'That's Oliver,' she said.

'What is?'

'Oliver Hawthorne. He's a lodger here. He's an entertainer. For children. Uncle Ollie.'

'Is he here now?'

'No.'

'Where is he?'

'Gone to London.'

'What for?'

'To entertain. He had an engagement. An old customer. A special.'

'How about Single?'

'You just say "how about" all the time. I don't know what you're asking. Single rooms? They're all double.' She had found her anger. The clear strong kind that served her best. 'You've no right. You've no warrant. Get out.'

She pulled open the door and held it for them and she thought she could feel her tongue swelling the way her father always said it would if she lied. The bald constable had come up close to her and was breathing whisky and ginger straight into her face.

'Has anybody from this establishment, a male, recently gone abroad to Switzerland, either on business or on holiday?'

'Not that I know of.'

'Then why should someone write a picture postcard of a Swiss peasant swinging a flag on a mountain top to your son Samuel saying he'll be back home shortly, and why should the stamp on the said postcard be charged to the room account of Mr Mark West?'

'I don't know. I've not seen a postcard, have I?'

The empty eyes closer, the whisky fumes stronger and warmer. 'If you're lying to me, madam, which I think you are, you and that big-mouth son of yours will wish you'd never been born,' said the constable. Then he put his cap on and smiled goodnight to her before walking with his colleague to the car.

Sammy was waiting in her bed.

'I did all right, didn't I, Mum?' he said.

'They was more frightened than what we ever was, Sammy,' she assured him, forgetting her grammar, and began to shiver.

CHAPTER EIGHTEEN

Once long ago, in the fire of youth, Nat Brock had beaten a man until he cried. The tears, so unexpected, had disconcerted Brock and shamed him. Entering Pluto's Kennel less than an hour after his conversation with Aggie, he remembered this incident, as he always did whenever the temptation returned, and swore that he would abide by its lessons. Carter opened the steel door and saw from Brock's face that something was afoot. Mace, trapped in the corridor, pressed himself respectfully against the wall to let Brock sweep past. Down in the street, Tanby was waiting in his tame cab, with his meter running and his operational radio on receive. It was ten o'clock at night and Massingham was seated in an armchair eating Chinese take-in with a plastic fork and watching a bunch of sniggering television journalists congratulating one another on their wit. Brock unplugged the set at the door and ordered Massingham to stand, which he did. The weakness in Massingham's face was like a stain that in the last days had deepened with each interrogation. Brock locked the door and put the key in his pocket. Why he did this he could never afterwards explain.

'Here's the situation, Mr Massingham,' he said, sweet and calm, which was what he was determined to be. 'Mikhail

Ivanovich Orlov was shot dead on the *Free Tallinn*. You knew that, but you didn't see fit to tell us.' The pause he made was not intended as an invitation to Massingham to speak, but rather to let the accusation sink in. 'Why not, I wonder?' And receiving no reply beyond an unconvincing shrug: 'It is also my information that Yevgeny Orlov blames you and Tiger Single jointly for his brother's death. Is that your information also?'

'Hoban did it.'

'I beg your pardon?'

'Hoban pinned it on me.'

'Did he then? And how did that information reach you, may I ask?'

A protracted silence, ended by the muttered words, 'My business.'

'Was it something that was said to you in your personalised version of the video tape of Alfred Winser's killing, by any chance? Some tailored message or PS that made you aware of the danger you were in?'

'They told me I was next on the list. Mikhail was dead, I'd betrayed him. I and those I loved but William in particular would pay for it in blood,' Massingham said in a parched voice. 'It was a set-up. Hoban two-timed me.'

'Three-timed, wasn't it? You were already two-timing Tiger.'

No answer, but no denial either.

'You had played an enthusiastic part in an earlier plan, round about last Christmas, to strip your employer Single of his assets and create a new entity controlled by Hoban, Mirsky and yourself. Is that a nod, Mr Massingham? Will you say *yes*, please?'

'Yes.'

'Thank you. In a minute I shall ask Mr Mace and Mr Carter to come in here and I shall formally charge you with a number of criminal offences. They will include obstructing the course of justice by withholding information and destroying evidence, and conspiring with persons known and unknown to import proscribed substances. If you collaborate with me now, I shall go into the witness box at your trial and plead for a reduction in the draconian sentence that awaits you. If you don't collaborate with me now, I shall so represent your part in this matter as to obtain maximum sentences on all charges, and I'll put William in the dock beside you as an accessory before and after and during the fact. I shall also deny under oath that I said what I just said. Which is it to be, Mr Massingham? Yes, I collaborate or no, I don't?'

'Yes.'

'Yes what?'

'Yes, I collaborate.'

'Where is Tiger Single?'

'I don't know.'

'Where is Alix Hoban?'

'I don't know.'

'Do I see William in the dock beside you?'

'No, you bloody well don't. It's the truth.'

'Who betrayed the *Free Tallinn* to the Russian authorities? Be very careful how you answer, please, because you will not have a later opportunity to correct your story.'

A whisper. 'The bastard dropped me in it.'

'The bastard in this case being who?'

'I told you, damn you. Hoban.'

'I'd like the reasoning behind this, please. I'm not seeing everything as clearly as I should tonight. What was to be gained, from the point of view of Hoban and yourself, from the seizure of the *Free Tallinn* and a few tons of best refined heroin by the Russian authorities – not to mention the killing of Mikhail?'

'I didn't know Mikhail was *on* the bloody boat! Hoban never told me. If I'd known Mikhail was going to be aboard I'd never have dreamed of playing along with him!'

'Playing along with him in what way?'

'He wanted a last straw. A last spectacular failure of a long line. Hoban did.'

'But you did too.'

'All right, we both did! He suggested it, I saw the logic of the idea. I went along with it. I was a fool. Does that satisfy you? If the *Free Tallinn* was seized, that would be the clincher and Hoban would be able to deliver Yevgeny.'

'Deliver in what sense? Speak up, if you please. I'm having trouble hearing you.'

'Deliver like persuade. Don't you know English? Hoban's got some hold on Yevgeny. He's married to Zoya. He's the father of Yevgeny's only grandson. He can play on him. If the *Free Tallinn* was blown, there'd be no more resistance, no more last-minute changes of heart from Yevgeny. Not even Tiger would be able to sweet-talk him round.'

'Then for good measure Hoban put Mikhail on the boat and didn't tell you. You're going all faint again, I'm afraid.'

'Put him there, I don't know. Mikhail decided to go on the boat. Hoban knew in advance the cargo was betrayed but didn't stop him going.'

'So Mikhail was killed, and instead of a paper putsch you had a five-star Georgian blood feud on your hands.'

'It was a trick. I'm the traitor, so I'm the prime target. The way Hoban spins it to Yevgeny, Tiger put me up to being the traitor, so he goes with me.'

'You're losing me again. *Why* are you the traitor? How did you get yourself in that position? Why didn't Hoban blow the whistle on the *Free Tallinn* for himself? Why couldn't Hoban do his own dirty work?'

'The tip-off had to come from England. If it came from Hoban, his old pals in the business would tumble to it and Yevgeny would find out.'

'That was the logic as purveyed to you by Hoban?'

'Yes! And it made sense. If the tip-off came from England, then by inference it came from Tiger. If I did it, I did it on Tiger's orders. Tiger was double-crossing Yevgeny. It was part of the plot to finger Tiger.'

'But it fingered you as well.'

'In the event – turned round – yes. Played Hoban's way – yes. Played my way – no.' He had recovered his voice and with it a kind of self-righteous indignation.

'So you went along with him?'

No answer. Brock took half a step towards him, and the half-step was enough.

'Yes. I went along with him. But I didn't know Mikhail

was aboard. I didn't know Hoban would turn the tables on us. How could I?'

Brock appeared lost in thought. He was nodding, holding his chin, vaguely agreeing. 'So you agreed to snitch,' he mused. 'Snitch *how*?' No answer. 'Let me guess. Mr Massingham went to his old friends in the what-we-call the Foreign Office.' Still no answer. 'Anyone I know? I said: anyone I know?' Massingham was shaking his head. 'Why not?'

'How the hell was I supposed to have found out what the *Free Tallinn* was carrying out of Odessa? Overheard it in a pub? Picked up a crossed line on the telephone? They'd have had me under the bright lights in seconds.'

'Yes, they would,' Brock conceded, after due reflection. 'They'd be more curious about *you* than about the *Free Tallinn*. That wouldn't do at all, would it? You wanted a no-questions-asked passive ally, not a thinking Intelligence officer. So who did we go to, Mr Massingham?' Brock was so close to him by now, and his demeanour so thoughtful, that it was neither necessary nor appropriate for either man to speak above a murmur. His sudden shout was therefore all the more shocking. '*Mr Mace! Mr Carter! In here, if you please! At the double!*' And they must have been hovering the other side of the door, for finding it locked, and suspecting Brock was under threat, they smashed it down and were standing to either side of Massingham almost before Brock had finished speaking the command. 'Mr Massingham,' Brock resumed. 'I wish you, please, to tell me, in front of these two gentlemen: which British enforcement agency did you advise – in great secrecy – of the illegal cargo that was to be found aboard SS *Free Tallinn* departing Odessa?'

'Porlock,' Massingham whispered, between breathy gaps. 'Tiger said ... if I ever needed anything from the police, go to Porlock ... Porlock had a network ... it could fix anything ... if I'd raped someone ... if William was caught snorting ... if somebody was blackmailing somebody or I needed someone out of the way ... whatever it was, Porlock would cooperate, Porlock was his man.'

Then to the common embarrassment he began weeping, accusing Brock with his tears. But Brock had no time for remorse. Tanby was hovering in the doorway with a message to impart, and Aiden Bell was on standby at Northolt airport with a bunch of very hard men.

*   *   *

They had crossed a long bridge over water and were exploring, to Oliver's conflicting instructions, another set of hills – 'left here, no right... hang on a minute, left *here*!' – but Aggie was not objecting, she was doing her best to give his intuition its head as he craned forward in his seat like a great bloodhound, scenting and frowning and trying to remember. It was past midnight and there were no venerable old gentlemen any more. There were villages and hilltop restaurants and night revellers in fast cars who swept down on them like attacking fighter-planes and peeled away into the valley. There were black bowls of empty field, and puffs of sudden mist that enveloped and released them.

'A blue tile,' he told her. 'A sort of Muslim tile with squirly calligraphy on it, and three five in white.'

He had written down several approximations of the address, and he and Aggie had sat shoulder to shoulder in laybys, poring over a road map, then a street map, hunting through the gazetteer – could it be this one, Oliver? how about that one, Oliver? and she had barely used their new intimacy except to guide his finger on the map occasionally and, once, to kiss his temple which was damp and shivery with cold sweat. From a phonebox she had fought and failed to find an English-speaking enquiries operator who could give them the address and telephone number of Orlov, Yevgeny Ivanovich or Hoban, Alix, patronymic unknown. But it must have been a holiday or a birthday or just another early night for Istanbul telephone operators, because all she got was promises in broken English, and courteous requests to call again tomorrow.

'Try the view from the french windows,' she urged him, pulling up at a tourists' lookout spot and switching off the engine. 'Something you saw, a landmark. It was on the European side. You looked at Asia. What did you see?'

He was so remote from her, so inward. He was Oliver on the day she first saw him march into the Camden house in his grey-wolf overcoat, hurt, fierce-eyed and trusting nobody.

'Snow,' he said. 'It was snowy. Palaces on the opposite shore. Boats, fairy lights. There was a gate,' he said as the images began forming for him. 'A gatehouse,' he corrected himself. 'At the bottom of the garden. There were terraces, and at the bottom of the garden there was a stone wall with a gate, and this gatehouse above it. And a narrow street the other side. Cobbled. We walked there.'

'Who did?'

'Yevgeny and me and Mikhail.' A pause for Mikhail. 'We took a turn round the garden. Mikhail was proud of it. He enjoyed having a big spread. "Like Bethlehem," he kept saying. There was a light in the gatehouse. Someone lived there. Hoban's people. Guards or whatever. Mikhail didn't care for them. Scowled and spat when he caught sight of them in the window.'

'What shape?'

'I didn't see them.'

'Not the people, Oliver. The gatehouse.'

'Crenellated.'

'What on earth does *that* mean?' – jocular, hoping to bump him out of himself.

'Turrets. Stone teeth.' Vaguely, he sketched the shape in the moisture on the windscreen. 'Crenellated,' he repeated.

'And the cobbled street,' she said.

'What about it?'

'Was it in a village maybe? Cobble sounds village to me. Were there streetlights the other side of the gatehouse, when you looked down the garden in the snow?'

'Traffic lights,' he conceded, his mind still far away. 'Bottom left of the gatehouse. The villa in an angle between two roads. Cobbled lane at the bottom, serious road to one side, traffic lights where the lane met the road. Why did he say he talked as if he had an onion in his mouth?' he mused while she searched the map. 'Why did he think I'd come after him? I suppose he knew I'd go to Nadia.' Stick to the job in hand, she advised. He was consulting his memory meanwhile: 'There were two roads. A coast road and a hill road. Mikhail liked the hill road because he could show off his driving. There was a china shop and a supermarket. And a lighted beer ad.'

'What beer?'

'Efes. Turkish. And a mosque. With an old minaret with an aerial on it. We heard the muezzin.'

'And saw the aerial,' she said, starting the car. 'At night. Stuck above a wall with an inhabited gatehouse and a cobbled street and a village and the Bosphorus below it and Asia across the way and it's number thirty-five. Come on with you, Oliver. I need your eyes. Don't die on me, it's not the time.'

'The china shop,' he said.

'What about it?'

'It was called Jumbo Jumbo Jumbo. I had this mental picture of three elephants in a china shop.'

In another phonebox they found a tattered directory and an address for Jumbo Jumbo Jumbo but when they looked at the map the street didn't exist, or if it did, it had changed its name. They quartered the hillside, weaving between pot-holes, until Oliver's head jerked forward and his hand grabbed her shoulder. They had reached a junction. A cobbled street faced them. Along its left side ran a brick wall. Halfway down it, the pointed black teeth of an ancient turret bit into the starry sky. To their right rose a mosque. There was even an aerial on the minaret, except that Aggie wondered whether it was a lightning conductor. Ahead of them down the lane a pair of traffic lights glowed red. Using sidelights only, Aggie advanced on them under the shadow of the crenellated gatehouse. No light shone in the arched window. At the traffic lights she turned left up the hill, passing a signpost to Ankara.

'Left again here,' Oliver ordered. 'Now stop. We've got a hundred yards, then there's a pair of high gates and a fore-court. Where the trees are. The house is below the trees.'

She parked gingerly on a sand verge, avoiding tin cans and bottles. She switched out the lights. They were two lovers looking for privacy. The Bosphorus once more lay below them.

'I'm going in alone,' Oliver said.

'Me too,' said Aggie. She had her shoulder bag on her lap and was delving in it. She took out her cellphone and stowed it under the driving seat. 'Give me your Turkish money.'

He handed her a wad and she gave him back half and put the rest under the seat together with the Single passports. She took the ignition key out of the lock and freed it from its ring and hirer's tag. She got out of the car. He did the same. She opened the bonnet, took out the toolkit and, from the toolkit, a wheelbrace which she stuffed jemmy-end first into her belt. She closed the bonnet and set to work searching the ground with a pinlight handtorch.

'I've got my Swiss army knife if you want it,' he said.

'Shut up, Oliver.' She stooped and came up with a rusted can with no lid. She locked the car and held up the key and the rusted can. 'See this? If we get split up or hit trouble, the first to reach the car takes it. No waiting.' She laid the key in the can, and the can against the inside wall of the front left wheel. 'Rendezvous, the base of the minaret. Fall-back, the main railway station concourse every two hours starting at six a.m. They did train you, Oliver.'

'I'm all right. I'm fine.'

'Assuming we're separated. Whoever gets to the car first, as soon as he can, he reports to Nat on the hot line. Press one and send. Switch on the power first, okay? Are you following me, Oliver? I've a feeling I'm talking to myself. Come here.' She cupped his ear with her hands. 'This is an operational instruction. Kindly bear it in mind throughout all that follows. Most people, when they do the wrong thing, they think they're heroes when in fact they're total pricks. Whereas *you* – you do all the right things, and you think you're a total prick. That's a major error. Are you hearing me, Oliver? You go first, you're on home ground. Mush.'

He led, she followed. The track was of beaten mud with rain holes. From behind him, the pen-torch lit the way. He smelt fox or badger and falling dew. Her hand was on his shoulder. He stopped and turned to her, unable to see her clearly in the darkness, but sensing the caring in her eyes. It's in mine too, he thought. He heard an owl, then a cat, then dance music. An opulent villa appeared high up on the hill to his right, all its lights on and a flock of cars parked around its drive. Shadows of revellers danced in the windows.

'Who's that?' she whispered.

'Crooked millionaires.'

He wanted her terribly. He wished they could take the Orient-Express from the old railway station in Istanbul and make love all the way to Paris. Then he remembered that the Orient-Express no longer came to Istanbul. A white-winged owl clattered out of the elaeagnus bushes, scaring him out of his wits. He was approaching the gates, Aggie close behind him. The gates were set fifteen yards from the track at the foot of a steep tarmac ramp. A sentry box stood one side of them. Security lights shone on them, heavy chains bound them, razor wire capped them. On each gate-post the figures 35 gleamed large and white against a swirling Moorish background. Scurrying across the ramp with Aggie on his heels, Oliver came to a second, humbler entrance for staff and deliveries. Two steel-panel gates, six feet high and mounted with spikes for impaling Christian martyrs, barred their way. Behind them lay the back of the villa, a mess of drainpipes, chimney pots and gargoyles. Not a light showed in any of the windows. Aggie inspected the lock with her pen-torch, then inserted the jemmy end of the wheelbrace into the gap between the gates, tested it, and cautiously withdrew it. An electric wire was protruding from a small hole beside the lock. She licked her finger, put it to the wire and shook her head. She shoved the wheelbrace into Oliver's waistband, placed her back against the wall and linked her hands, palms upward, across her stomach.

'Like this,' she whispered.

He did as she ordered, she stepped into his hands but spent no time there. He felt a brief pressure as she ascended, saw her fly over the martyrs' spikes and into the stars. He heard a scuffle as she landed and panic seized him. How do I follow her? How does she get back? A man-gate squeaked and opened. He slipped through the gap. Suddenly he knew the way. A flagstoned alley took them between the villa and the wall. He had played chase games here with Yevgeny's granddaughters. A flying buttress made an arch against the sky, huge drainpipes lay like old cannon along the path. The children had used them as stepping stones. Oliver led, keeping one hand on the wall for balance. He remembered the glazed corridor to Tiger's penthouse, and limping on one shoe. They had reached the front of the villa. In the moonlight, the descending terraces of the garden lay flat as playing cards. At their foot, the wall and gatehouse resembled cut-out ramparts of a children's fort.

Aggie put her arms round him and gently recovered the wheelbrace. 'Wait here,' she signalled. He had no choice. She was already sidling along the front of the villa, peering in at the french windows one by one, darting in cat-like bounds, peeking and moving, then freezing again before she peeked. She beckoned, so he began following her, conscious of his clumsiness. The moonlight was like day in black-and-white. The first window was not familiar to him. The room was bare. Dead flowers were strewn over the floor: old roses, carnations, orchids, bits of silver foil. A pair of battens, nailed crosswise, were propped in one corner. He noticed an extra batten lower down the upright and remembered the Orthodox cross. A painter's narrow trestle stood at the centre but he saw no brushes or pots. She was signalling come on.

He moved to the second window, saw a child's bed and bedside table, reading light, a heap of books and a small dressing gown hanging from a hook. He moved to the third and nearly laughed out loud. Pieces of Yevgeny's precious birchwood furniture stood shoved against the walls. At the centre of the floorboards, in pride of place, the BMW motorbike, like a shrouded Shetland pony, stood sleeping under a dustsheet. Wanting to draw this amusing sight to Aggie's attention he swung round and saw that she had frozen with her back against the wall and her hands splayed while she repeatedly tipped her head at the window nearest to her, the last. He crept towards her and, remaining on the near side of the same window, peered in. Zoya was sitting in Tinatin's rocking chair. She was wearing a long black dress like an evening gown, and black Russian boots. Her hair was taken up in an untidy bun, and her face was an icon of herself, haggard and wide-eyed. She was staring out of the long french window but with a look so grim and faraway that Oliver doubted whether she saw anything at all, except the demons of her own mind. She had a guttering candle on a table next to her, and a Kalashnikov across her knees. Her right forefinger was curled round the trigger.

*　　　*　　　*

At first Aggie didn't understand what Oliver was trying to tell her, and he had to mime it several times, first underarm, then overarm, before she dragged the wheelbrace from her belt, sank into a crouch and signed to him to do the same. She held out her arms and made a cradle of them and Oliver copied her. She tossed the brace the five feet or so across the window and he caught it with one hand, not at all the way she meant him to. In a series of gestures he tried to tell her other things. He tapped his chest and pointed in Zoya's direction and nodded and stuck his thumb in the air at Aggie in reassurance: we're old buddies. He made slowing-down gestures with his palms: we take this softly softly. He pointed at himself again: it's *my* show this time, not yours, *I'm* going in, you're not. He tapped the side of his head, diffidently, to indicate Zoya's possible mental disturbance, then frowned in doubt, tipping his head to right and left, questioning his own vulgar diagnosis. Reverently, he made to embrace himself: I was her lover, she is my responsibility. How much Aggie followed of all this he didn't know, but he guessed by her docility quite a lot because, having watched him closely, she kissed the tips of her fingers and blew the kiss in his direction.

Oliver clambered to his feet and knew that if he had been alone he would have been afraid, and probably at a loss, but thanks to Aggie he saw things clearly and had no doubt of what to do. He knew that the french windows were of armoured glass because Mikhail had demonstrated their weight to him, gleefully displaying the reinforced hinges that were needed to bear them and the locks to hold them. Therefore the improvised jemmy was not by any means his first recourse but more probably his last. What was indisputable was that, by handing him the jemmy, Aggie was handing him the job, which was what he wanted. The idea of sending Aggie into battle for him, of Aggie taking a salvo of Kalashnikov bullets for her trouble and becoming another body on his wrecker's path was more than he could handle. Armoured glass was one thing. A burst from a high-velocity sub-machine gun at a range of six feet was another.

So he wedged the wheelbrace, Aggie-style, into his own waistband and in stiff, sideways movements edged himself to the centre of the window, then a little past the centre so that Zoya could see his face complete in one pane rather than split in two. He rapped on the armoured glass, gently then vigorously. When her head lifted and her eyes appeared to focus on him, he pulled a winning smile of some sort and called out, 'Zoya. It's Oliver. Let me in,' loudly enough, he hoped, to penetrate the glass.

Slowly she opened her eyes to stretching point, then in a rush of activity began to fuss with the gun on her lap as a prelude to pointing it at him. He slammed his palms on the window and put his face as close to it as he could without becoming a funny man.

'Zoya! Let me in! I'm Oliver, your lover!' he shouted – without, it must be said, any awareness at that moment of Aggie's presence, but he'd have said it anyway. And clearly Aggie would have wished him to say it because, out of the corner of his eye, he saw her emphatically nodding her support at him. But Zoya's response was like an animal's when it hears a half-remembered sound: I recognise it – nearly – but is it friend or enemy? She had stood up, uncertainly – he guessed she was short of food – but she was still holding the gun. And having stared at Oliver for a time, she peered sternly around the room, apparently suspecting an ambush from behind while her attention was being taken up with what was happening out there in front of her. 'Can you open the door for me, please, Zoya? I need to come in, you see. Is there a key in the lock? Otherwise we could go round to the front and you could let us in from there. It's just me, Zoya. Me and a girl. You'll like her. No one else, I promise. Can you try turning the key, perhaps? It's one of those little brass wheels, I seem to remember. It takes three or four turns.'

But Zoya still had the gun and she had brought the barrel round to point it at Oliver's groin, and there was such lethargy in her movement, such despair in her face, such an utter indifference to life or death, that it seemed as likely she might loose it off as not. So there was a long pause while he remained firmly standing, with Aggie watching him from the wings, and Zoya trying to come to terms with the idea of him again, after all the years of whatever life had done to her in the meantime. At last, with the gun still aimed at him, she took a step forward, then another, till they were standing man to woman either side of the glass, and she was able to examine his eyes and decide what she saw in them. Holding the gun in place with her right hand, she reached out her left and tried to turn the lock, but her wrist was so thin it hadn't the power. Finally she set down the gun and, having straightened her hair in order to receive him, used both hands to let him in – and Aggie straight after him and past him, scooping up the Kalashnikov and tucking it under her arm.

'Will you tell me, please, who else is in the house?' she asked Zoya calmly, as if they'd known each other all their lives.

Zoya shook her head.

'Nobody?'

No response.

'Where's Hoban?' Oliver asked.

She closed her eyes in renunciation.

Oliver put his hands under her elbows and drew her towards him. He extended her arms and laid them round his shoulders, then he gathered her into an embrace, holding her cold body against him, patting her back and rocking her while Aggie, having checked that the Kalashnikov was loaded, cocked it and, holding it across her body, stole into the hall on the first leg of her inspection of the premises. For a long while after Aggie had gone, Oliver kept Zoya in his arms, waiting for her to thaw and soften and grow warm against him, and her fists to unclasp from the lapels of his jacket, and her head to lift and find his cheek. He felt her heart beating against him, and the trembling in her emaciated back, then the heaving of her ribs as she began to weep in long exhalations, emptying her breast of wave after wave of grief. Her thinness shocked him but he guessed it was not new to her. Her face was hollowed and as he lifted her chin and pressed her temple against his cheek he felt her skin slipping like an old woman's across the bone.

'How's Paul?' he asked, hoping that, if he could persuade her to talk about her son, he would open the door for other things.

'Paul is Paul.'

'Where is he?'

'Paul has *friends*,' she explained, as if this phenomenon distinguished Paul from other children. 'They will protect him. They will give him food. They will let him sleep. There will be no funerals for Paul. You wish to see the body?'

'Whose body?'

'Maybe it is gone.'

'Whose body, Zoya? My father's body? Have they killed him?'

'I will show you.'

The front rooms of the villa were linked by connecting doors. Clutching his arm with both of hers, she led him past Catherine the Great's furniture and the shrouded motorbike, through Paul's empty bedroom to the room with flowers strewn over the floor and the trestle table at its centre and the builders' battens nailed in an Orthodox cross.

'It is our tradition,' she said, placing herself beside the table.

'What is?'

'First we put him in an open coffin. He is prepared by villagers. Here we have no villagers so we prepare him ourselves. It is hard to dress a body with many bullet holes. Also the face was affected. However, this was accomplished.'

'Whose face?'

'With the body we place his favourite objects. His umbrella. His watch. His waistcoat. His pistols. But we keep also his bed for him upstairs. We make also a place for him at table. We eat for him beside a candle. When neighbours come to say goodbye to him we greet them and we drink for him. But we have no neighbours. We are exiles. It is our tradition to leave a window open so that the soul can depart like a bird. Maybe his soul did this, but the weather was very hot. When the body leaves the house, the clocks are turned three times against their natural inclination, the table is turned upside down, all flowers are removed and the coffin is struck three times against the door before it makes its journey.'

'Mikhail's body,' Oliver suggested, and she confirmed this with a series of long, ominous nods.

'Maybe we should do that, then,' he said, covering his relief with a determined brightness.

'Please?'

'Turn the table upside down.'

'It was not possible. After they have gone, I was not strong enough.'

'We're strong enough together. Here. Let me do it. Why don't I just collapse it?'

'I remember you are very kind,' she said, and smiled admiringly as he folded the legs under the table, pressed them home and laid the table face downwards on the floorboards.

'Maybe we should clear up the flowers too. Where's a broom? We want a broom and a dustpan, that's the best thing. Where do you keep your brushes?' The kitchens reminded him of Nightingales: high and raftered and a smell of cold stone. 'Show me,' he said.

Like Nadia she pulled open several cupboards before finding what she was looking for. Like Nadia she muttered about absent servants. They returned to the front room and she swept vaguely at the flowers while he held the dustpan for her. Then he took the broom from her and leaned it against the wall and held her because her weeping had started again, and this time it seemed to Oliver that the companionship between them had revived her, and her tears were cathartic. And he gave everything he had to tending her – all his feelings and empathy and willpower were beamed at her. It was an essential discipline to think of nothing except gentling her out of her catatonic state and back to life: because to have done otherwise would have been to shove her aside and abandon her to her tears and convulsions, and race back to the second kitchen cupboard from the left, where a brown bag to match his coat – a carry-on, Nadia had called it – boldly labelled Mr Tommy Smart in Tiger's handwriting, leaned exhausted among mildewed boots, rubber overshoes and back numbers of Russian-language newspapers.

'My father was betrayed by time,' Zoya announced, breaking free of him. 'Also by Hoban.'

'How did that happen?'

'Hoban loves nobody therefore he has betrayed nobody. When he betrays, he is being loyal to himself.'

'Who has he betrayed, apart from you?'

'He has betrayed God. When he returns, I shall kill him. It will be necessary.'

'How has he betrayed God?'

'It is irrelevant. No one may know. Paul likes very much football.'

'Mikhail liked football too,' Oliver said, remembering kickabouts on the lawn, and Mikhail with his gun still in his boot, leaping for the ball. 'How has Hoban betrayed God?'

'It is irrelevant.'

'But you're going to kill him for it.'

'He betrayed God at the football match. I was present. I do not like football.'

'But you went.'

'Paul and Mikhail will go to the football match, it is arranged. Hoban has obtained the tickets. He has bought too many.'

'Here in Istanbul?'

'It was night. There was a full moon at the Inönü stadium.' Her gaze drifted to the window. She was shivering again so he gathered her into him. 'Hoban has obtained four tickets, therefore there is a problem. Mikhail does not like Hoban. He does not wish Hoban to be in attendance. But if I come also, Mikhail cannot resist because he loves me. This also Hoban knew. I have never been to a football. I was afraid. The Inönü stadium holds thirty-five thousand people. One cannot know them all. At football there is a half-time. In this half-time, the teams withdraw and discuss. We also discussed. We had bread and some sausage. Also for Mikhail vodka. Yevgeny does not permit Mikhail very much vodka, but Hoban has brought a bottle. I am at the edge of the group. Beside me is Paul and after him Mikhail. After Mikhail is Hoban. The lights are too bright. I did not like the lights.'

'And you discussed,' Oliver said softly, leading her.

'With Paul we discuss football. He is explaining to me the subtleties. He is happy. It is rare that his father and mother attend such an occasion together. Also the *Free Tallinn* is discussed. Hoban is proposing that Mikhail takes a boat ride on the *Free Tallinn*. He is tempting him like the Devil. It will be a beautiful journey. From Odessa through the Bosphorus is beautiful. Mikhail will be so happy. It will be a secret from Yevgeny. A gift, to surprise him.'

'And Mikhail agreed to go?'

'Hoban was very subtle with him. Devils are always subtle. He placed the idea in Mikhail's head, he promoted it, but in his conversation he made sure that the idea proceeded from Mikhail. He congratulated Mikhail on his good idea. He turned to me. Mikhail has this great idea. He will sail with the *Free Tallinn*. Hoban is wicked. It is normal. That night, he was more wicked than normal.'

'Have you told this to Yevgeny or Tinatin?'

'Hoban is the father of Paul.'

They had returned to the drawing room and it was evident that Aggie somewhere in her training had acquired nursing skills, because she had made a broth from bouillon cubes, and stirred two eggs into it, and now she was sitting at Zoya's arm feeding soup to her, and taking her pulse and chaffing her wrists and dabbing her face with eau de cologne from the bathroom. And it was inevitable that Oliver should remember Heather on the occasions when he had one of his galloping temperatures and the shivers, but whereas Heather had always got some kind of power-kick out of ministering to him, Aggie just seemed to feel responsible for the whole universe, which was pleasing to Oliver, if disconcerting, because until now he had always assumed that he was alone in this regard. He had fetched Tiger's bag and it had told him nothing except that, wherever Tiger was or wasn't, he lacked a change of clothes. Aggie had disarmed the Kalashnikov and propped it in a corner and she had brought fresh candles because like Oliver she had an instinct for preserving atmosphere and didn't want to startle Zoya with the harshness of electric light.

'Who are you?' Zoya asked her.

'Me? I'm just Oliver's new squeeze,' she replied with a cheerful laugh.

'What does that mean, please?'

'I'm in love with her,' Oliver explained, and looked on while Aggie put a blanket over her, and puffed up the pillows she had brought from upstairs, and patted more cologne on her brow. 'Where's my father?'

A long silence followed in which Zoya appeared to recompose her memory. Suddenly, to Oliver's astonishment, she laughed. 'It was preposterous,' she replied, shaking her head in amusement.

'Why?'

'They had brought us Mikhail. From Odessa. First they take him to Odessa. Then Yevgeny gives them money so they send him here to Istanbul. The coffin was of steel. It was like a bomb. We bought ice. Yevgeny made a cross. He was demented. We laid him on the table in his coffin in the ice.'

'Was my father here already?'

'He was not here.'

'But he came here.'

She laughed again. 'It was a theatre. It was ridiculous.

The doorbell rang. There were no maids. Hoban opened the door, he thought it was more ice. It was not ice, it was Mr Tiger Single in an overcoat. Hoban was very pleased. He brought him to the room and said to Yevgeny, "See. A neighbour has called after all. Mr Tiger Single wishes to pay his respects to the man he has murdered." Yevgeny's head was too heavy for him. He could not lift it. Hoban had to bring your father to him before he would believe.'

'How? – bring how?'

She put her arm behind her back, as high as it would go. Then she raised her chin and grimaced in empathetic pain. 'So,' she said.

'Then?'

'Then Hoban said, "Shall I take him into the garden and shoot him?"'

'Where was Paul?' Oliver asked, as an extraneous wave of anxiety for the child seized him.

'Thank God he was with Mirsky. When Mikhail's body came I sent him to Mirsky.'

'So they took my father into the garden.'

'No. Yevgeny says no, don't shoot him. If we are in the presence of the dead, we are also in the presence of God. So they tied him.'

'Who did?'

'Hoban has people. Russians from Russia, Russians from Turkey. Bad people. I do not know their names. Sometimes Yevgeny sends them away, but then he forgets or he is sorry.'

'And after they'd tied him? Then what did they do with him?'

'They made him look at Mikhail on the table. They showed him the bullet holes. He did not like to look. They forced him. Then they gave him a guard, and put him in a room.'

'There's a single bed in the attic,' Aggie said. 'It's soaked.'

'With blood?'

She shook her head and wrinkled her nose.

'How long did they keep him in the room?' Oliver asked Zoya.

'Maybe one night, maybe longer. Maybe six, I do not

know. Hoban is like Macbeth. He has murdered sleep.'

'Where is he now?' – he meant, his father.

'Hoban is saying all the time: I will kill him, let me kill him, he is a traitor. But Yevgeny has no will. He is destroyed. "Better we take him with us. I will speak to him." They bring him down. Somebody has beaten him, maybe Hoban. I put some bandages on him. He is so small. Yevgeny spoke to his honour. We shall take you on a journey, we have chartered a plane, we have to bury Mikhail, his body is not sanitary, you must not resist, you are our prisoner, you must go with us like a man, otherwise Hoban will shoot you or throw you out of the plane. I did not hear it. It is what Hoban told me. Maybe it is a lie.'

'Where was the plane going?'

'To Senaki in Georgia. It is a secret. They will bury him in Bethlehem. Temur from Tbilisi arranges it. It will be a double funeral. When Hoban killed Mikhail, he killed also Yevgeny. It is normal.'

'I thought Yevgeny wasn't welcome in Georgia.'

'It is precarious. If he is quiet, if he does not compete with the mafias, he is tolerated. If he sends much money, he is tolerated. Recently he has not been able to send much money. Therefore it is precarious.' She gave a great sigh and closed her eyes for a time, then slowly opened them. 'Soon Yevgeny will be dead and Hoban will be the king of everything. But he will not be content. As long as there is one innocent man on earth he will not be content.' She gave a beautiful smile. 'So take care, Oliver. You are the last innocent.'

Responding to this easing of the atmosphere, Oliver stood up, and grinned, and stretched, and scratched his head and worked his arms around, and arched his back, and generally did the things he did when he had been sitting in one position for too long, or was thinking of so many things at once that the motors in his body needed to let off a bit of steam. He asked a few questions – carelessly – like what was Temur's other name, and which day exactly did they fly on, did she remember? And while he was wandering around, and taking mental note of her answers, he couldn't resist a little pilgrimage to the BMW in the adjoining room, where he lifted its shroud and smiled at its glistening contours – at the same time establishing, by way of the connecting doorway, that Aggie with her unflagging solicitude was making use of his absence to get more soup into her patient.

Escaping from her eyeline, he stepped nimbly to the french windows, grabbed the brass knob and, as softly as he dared, turned it until the doors were unlocked. Then he pushed them an inch, proving to his satisfaction that, like the windows in the drawing room, they opened outwards into the garden. And here he was seized by an almost unbearable sense of guilt, which nearly drove him back to the drawing room, either to confess to what he had done or invite Aggie to come with him. But he couldn't do either of those things because, if he did, he would no longer be protecting her, which, given the dangers of his undertaking, he considered the decent thing to do. Stealthily therefore, like a schoolboy playing truant, he took another look through the connecting doors and, having confirmed that Zoya and Aggie were engaged in a conversation of their own, opened the french windows, stole the dustsheet from the motorbike's back, bumped the bike off its stand, mounted it, turned the ignition, pushed the starter button and with a roar that seemed to rise from the very entrails of his being, flew into the starlit night and across the Conqueror's Bridge on his way to Bethlehem.

CHAPTER NINETEEN

Oliver had loved motorbikes ever since Tiger had decreed them lower class. In his sleep he had ridden away on them, awarded them wings and other magic powers; in the village next to Nightingales he had ridden behind farmers' boys and tasted the elixir of speed; in adolescence he had dreamed of barelegged girls riding pillion behind him. But though the ride to Ankara answered many of his most exotic expectations – a resplendent moon, the night firmament, the empty winding road to anywhere – it was haunted by the perils ahead of him, and by those he had left in his wake.

He had paused at the Volkswagen only long enough to collect money from the suitcase and scribble a note and wedge it in the wiper blade: *Sorry, didn't feel I could drag you into this, Oliver.* This text now struck him as so inadequate that he yearned for some way to pick up the telephone to her, or turn back and explain himself more fully. Their clothes, her cellphone, the Single passports, the rest of the money – he had left them undisturbed. He had taken the road to Ankara because he had seen the signpost and he guessed that the first thing Brock would do when he heard the news was slap a watch on flights from Istanbul. But that did not mean that Ankara was safe, or that he was free to grab a flight from Ankara to Tbilisi. Also Mr West had no Georgian visa and Oliver had a hunch he needed one. But all these cares together were as nothing beside the image he had fixed in his head of Tiger with his arm twisted up his back, being frogmarched by Alix Hoban – of Tiger beaten, Tiger bleeding, Tiger forced to look at Mikhail's mangled body, Tiger wetting himself in terror while he waited to be carted off to Bethlehem and shot. He is so small, Zoya had said.

At first he kept to the motorway, he had no choice. He rode fast but the potholes were a constant fear to him. To either side of him flowed black hills punctuated with satellite highrise towns like lighted oil-rigs. A tunnel had him. He raced through it and emerged to see a horizontal blue beam with white lights and numbers spring towards him at head height. It was a tollgate. Somehow he braked in time, tossed a fifty million lira note at an astonished man in a window and raced on. Twice, perhaps more often, he was stopped at police checkpoints by men in plastic yellow smocks with silver glitterbands across their chests. Armed with torches, they studied his face and passport for signs of Kurdishness or some similar disorder. Once, flying blind, he hit a huge pothole and the bike nearly bucked him off. Once he found himself skidding to a halt at the very lip of an immense ravine. Running out of fuel, he cadged a lift, only to discover a filling station five hundred yards away, around a corner. But these travails passed by him in a dream, and when he woke he was standing at the information desk at Ankara airport being told that the only way to fly to Tbilisi was to return to Istanbul and pick up a plane that left at eight p.m. tonight, which was fourteen hours away. But Istanbul was where he had left Aggie, and by eight o'clock tonight Hoban might have put Tiger out of his misery.

Then Oliver remembered that he was rich, and had brought some of his riches with him, and that money, Tiger liked to say, was the best general purpose tool in the world. So he wandered away into the airport's administrative catacombs and, with five one-hundred dollar bills lying on the table between them, spoke slow English to a fat gentleman with worry-beads who finally opened a door and yelled at a menial who returned with a haggard man in grimy green overalls with wings on the pocket whose name was Farouk, and Farouk owned and flew a transport plane that was currently under repair in the hangar, but would be ready in one hour, which became three. And Farouk would accept the charter for a mere ten thousand dollars provided Oliver would not be sick in his plane or tell anybody Farouk had flown him to Tbilisi. Oliver trailed the idea of Senaki but Farouk would not be tempted by Senaki, even for an extra five thousand dollars.

'Senaki too forbidden. Too much militaries. Abkhazia make big trouble.'

With the contract struck, the fat gentleman with worry beads became unhappy. Some deep-rooted bureaucratic instinct told him that things had gone too smoothly and too fast. 'You must write paper,' he told Oliver, offering him a bunch of aged forms in Turkish. Oliver declined. The fat gentleman hunted for other reasons to detain him, but in the end gave up.

They flew and bumped and scraped over the mountain tops and for the second part of the journey Oliver providentially slept, and perhaps Farouk did too, for they landed with such a bang at Tbilisi, and taxied for such a short distance, that it was as if the pilot had pulled out of a sound sleep at the last minute. At Tbilisi airport a valid entry visa was mandatory and the law was not to be trifled with. Neither the Field Marshal of Immigration, nor his colleague the Admiral of Security, nor any of their many aides-de-camp, adjutants and fellow mariners could consider allowing Oliver into the country for less than five hundred dollars cash, large bills not accepted. It was by then evening. Oliver took a taxi to Temur's address, which was a doorway with ten bell-buttons to press and no names in the panels beside the buttons. He pressed one, then another, then pressed all of them at once, but though there were lights in some of the windows nobody came down to him and when he shouted 'Temur' some of the lights went out. He telephoned from a café, but in vain. He walked. An arctic north wind was whipping off the Caucasus and tearing through the town. The wooden houses creaked and rattled like old ships. In side streets men and women in topcoats and balaclavas huddled round burning car tyres for warmth. He returned to Temur's house and pressed the bell-buttons again. Nothing. Again he walked, keeping to the centre of the narrow streets because in the pitch darkness he was suddenly, unreasonably scared. He descended a hill and to his relief recognised an illuminated gold mosaic doorway that marked the ancient mineral baths. An old woman took his money and showed him to an empty white-tiled room. A skinny man in jockey shorts dunked him in a sulphur bath, stretched him naked on a meat counter and scoured him with a loofah until he was raw from neck to toe. Burning all over, he went to a discothèque and, having again failed to raise Temur on the telephone, had himself directed to a boarding house that had no name. Though it was only two blocks away, the streets were so dark he nearly lost the way. He passed a line of ghostly trolley buses and remembered that in Tbilisi trolley buses stopped dead whenever there was a power cut, which happened for large parts of each day. He beat on the door and waited, listening to the unfastening of locks. An old man in a dressing gown and hairnet appeared and spoke to him in Georgian but Nina's lessons were too long ago. The old man switched to Russian which was worse, so Oliver laid his hands together, and his head on them in simulated sleep. The old man showed him to an attic cell with an army cot in it, and a parchment lampshade with cavorting nymphs, and a piece of army soap and a handbasin, and either a very large face-flannel or a very small bath towel. All night long the sirens rose and fell. A fire? A coup? An assassination? Or a little girl killed in a car smash and her name is Carmen? Somehow nonetheless he slept, with his shirt and pants and socks on, and the rest of his clothes heaped on the bed for extra warmth, and his barked skin aching and itching, and the wind cracking in the wooden eaves while he longed for Aggie and feared terribly for Tiger, and in his dreams watched him being led whimpering from one corner of

Bethlehem to another while Hoban and Yevgeny argued about the best place to blow his head off. He woke and discovered he was freezing. He woke again and he was sweating sulphur. He woke a third time and rang Temur's number and he answered immediately, the soul of efficiency. A taxi and a helicopter? No problem, Oliver. Three thousand dollars cash, come round at ten.

'Those guys expect you up there?' Temur enquired.

'No.'

'Maybe I tell them. That way they don't get nervous.'

*   *   *

Of all the things Brock might have ordered Aggie to do at that moment, the absolute total worst, she decided, was to sit tight and wait for further instructions. If he had told her to jump in the Bosphorus, if he had uttered one solid word of rebuke, if he had ordered her to present herself, shaven-headed in disgrace and forthwith, at the Embassy back door for immediate transportation back to Britain, she might at least have felt some easing of her humiliation. But all she got in wise, even-tempered Scouse accents was: 'Where are you, Charmian? Are you free to talk to us? So what time did this happen, d'you remember? Well, stay exactly where you are, please, Charmian, and don't do anything further till you hear from your mother or me...' Which was why she had been caged these last two hours in a tin-roofed café with empty benches and bare-necked chickens and a scrofulous yellow dog called Apollo who rested his chin on her knee and made eyes at her until she bought him another beefburger.

And it's all my own stupid fault, she kept telling herself. It was an accident waiting to happen, in slow motion, with my consent, so it did. She'd spotted the motorbike, she'd recognised the signs in him, she'd watched him being solicitous with Zoya but she knew he was broody. And when she watched him lolloping away like a big silver hare across the moonlit lawn, onto the drive and out of her sight behind the house, her first thought was you impatient bastard, if

316

you'd waited a moment I'd have been on there with you.

But it was a crisis, and Aggie had risen to it as she always did. She did everything she was supposed to do, meticulously and conscientiously, as if she were about to set off on her longest journey ever, which for some reason was how she felt. She ran to the car and read Oliver's note, which duly drove her mad till she remembered his voice at its least affected, telling Zoya, 'I'm in love with her.' She phoned Brock's direct number, got Tanby and gave him the stark minimum in her most dispassionate tones: 'Primo's stolen a motorbike and is believed to be heading for Georgia. Further information in two hours. Over and out.' She ran back to Zoya, whose mood appeared to have been lightened by Oliver's departure, for she was smiling to herself in a self-congratulatory way that in other circumstances could have annoyed Aggie considerably. But Aggie had work to do and promises to keep, if only to herself. She marched Zoya upstairs, stood over her while she washed, and together they found her a nightdress and a change of clothes for the morning. Busying herself on Zoya's behalf in this way, Aggie was also obliged to listen to snatches of questionable wisdom about Oliver and herself, which Zoya imparted with the authority of the deranged. Promising to take her advice to heart, Aggie pondered what more she should do for her. A daubed note of Mirsky's home number on the wall beside the telephone provided her with an answer. She dialled and got the Mirsky message machine. She described herself as a friend of Zoya's from New Zealand who happened to have dropped by, and though she didn't wish to interfere, would it be possible for the Mirskys to give Zoya some fairly urgent attention? – like getting her to a doctor, and taking her away for a few days? She took the bolt out of the Kalashnikov and put it in her shoulder bag, she went back upstairs to make sure Zoya was in bed, to her pleasure found her asleep. She jogged back to the Volkswagen.

Driving to Istanbul airport she had been tormented by a fresh nightmare. Had Oliver simply headed east into Turkey's mountainous badland? She put nothing beyond him. At the departures terminal, having returned the Volkswagen to the hire company, she threw a calculated force-twelve tantrum of remorse and despair. She put her whole heart into it, which wasn't difficult. She was Charmian West and she was in hell, she told the sensitive-eyed young clerk behind the desk at Turkish Airlines. She showed him her passport and her most appealing smile. She and Mark had been married exactly *six days*, and last night they'd had this *awful* row about nothing, their *first*, and when she woke up this morning, there was this note saying he was getting out of her life for*ever*... Tenderly tapping the keys of his computer, the clerk told her what she had feared to be the case: no flightlist of this morning showed a West departing from Istanbul for anywhere. No reservations list had him leaving later in the day.

'All right,' said Aggie, meaning, not all right at all. 'Suppose he took a bus to Ankara and flew from there?'

But here the clerk regretted, rather severely, that Ankara's flightlists were outside the scope of his romanticism. So Aggie withdrew herself from the precincts of the airport to this last-chance café where, with Apollo's participation, she made her promised call to Brock on her cellphone. After which there was nothing to do but wait, and go on waiting to hear from your mother or me, which was what she was doing now.

So what would my real mother say – she who is never happy unless her own interests are being ignored? *Do whatever you want with him, Mary Agnes, as long as you don't cause him any harm...*

And my father, the paragon Scottish schoolmaster? *You're a strong girl, Mary Agnes. You'll have to tone down your act a wee bit for Mr Right...*

Her phone was ringing. It was neither her mother nor her father but the central message exchange in the person of a 15 rpm woman with social pretensions:

'Following for Archangel.'

That's me.

'You have a seat booked for you on the flight to Toytown.'

That's Tbilisi.

'You will be met on arrival. Fallback, your local uncle.'

Allelujah! That's a reprieve!

Leaping to her feet, Aggie tossed a wad of money on the table, gave Apollo a last fond embrace, and with joy in her heart set course for the departures terminal. On her way she remembered the bolt from the Kalashnikov and the clip of ammunition and just summoned enough common sense to drop them in a rubbish bin before she passed through the X-ray check.

*   *   *

Brock stepped into the camouflaged military transport plane at Northolt airport feeling he had done all the unimportant things in his life well and all the important things badly. He had arrested Massingham but Massingham had never been his primary target. He had identified Porlock as the rottenest apple but lacked the court-proof evidence that would send him down. For that he needed Tiger and he reckoned that his chances of obtaining him were next to nil. When Brock had cut his deal with Russian and Georgian liaison that morning, it had been agreed that he could have Tiger if the Russians could have Hoban and Yevgeny. Yet the chances of Tiger being alive by the time Brock got to him were in his private judgment zero, and what gnawed at his entrails was the knowledge that, in his determination to nail the father, he had sent the son to his destruction too. I should never have put him on a long rein, he told himself. I should have been there myself, on the spot, round the clock.

As usual he blamed no one but himself. Like Aggie he felt he had been shown the obvious signs and drawn none of the obvious conclusions. I was pushing him, but Tiger was pulling him, and Tiger's pull was harder than my push. Only the imminence of battle consoled him, the prospect that after all the weaving and ducking and backroom calculation, a date and place had been set, the seconds had been appointed and the choice of weapons agreed. As to the risk he was taking on his own account, he and Lily had discussed this in their devious way, and had agreed that he had no choice in the matter:

319

'There's this young man,' he had told Lily on the telephone an hour ago. 'And I've put him to a lot of trouble, you see, and I'm not sure that I did right.'

'Oh yes? So what's happened to him, Nat?'

'Well, he's taken himself for a bit of walk, you see, and fallen into some bad company on my account.'

'Then you must go and get him, mustn't you, Nat? That won't do at all, not a young man.'

'Yes, well, I thought you'd see it that way, Lily, and I'm grateful,' he replied. 'Because it's not a pushover, if you follow me.'

'Of course it isn't. Nothing worth doing is. You've always done the right thing, Nat, ever since I've known you. You can't stop now, not if you're wanting to stay who you are. So you just go off and do it.'

But she had more pressing matters to discuss with him, for which he loved her dearly. That flighty daughter of the postmistress had run off with Palmer the builder, leaving his poor wife with all those children to cope with. Lily was going to have a word with young Palmer the next time she saw him. She'd a good mind to make a special journey to his yard, and tell him what she thought of him. And as for that postmistress, throwing her daughter at the richest man in the village and then sitting there behind her bulletproof counter thinking nothing can touch her...

'Well, you take care now, Lily,' Brock warned her. 'Young people aren't respectful like they used to be.'

The snatch team was eight strong. Aiden Bell said any more would be a crowd, given the liaison problems when they got the other end. 'If the Russians bring a howitzer, I shan't be surprised,' he predicted grimly. They sat three and four down the fuselage, dressed in light battle gear and warpaint and black trackshoes and black balaclavas. 'We take the last man aboard when we change ships at Tbilisi,' Bell had told them, omitting to mention that the last man was a woman. Brock and Bell sat apart, a high command of two. Brock wore black denims and a flak jacket with H.M. CUS-TOMS like a medal ribbon over his heart. He had refused a handgun. Better dead than face an internal enquiry about why he'd shot one of his own men. Bell wore flashes of glitterpaint on his tunic to mark him as leader, but you only saw them if you were wearing the right goggles. The plane shook and grunted but seemed to make no progress until they were above the cloud in no man's land.

'We'll do the dirty work,' Bell growled at Brock. 'You handle the social side.'

CHAPTER TWENTY

The first thing Oliver noticed as he took his place between the two hard-eyed young men in jeans who were waiting at the helicopter pad was tractors. Yellow agricultural tractors. If I'm ever short of a yellow tractor or two, I can always borrow them from Bethlehem and they'll never notice, he thought jauntily. He was forcing his thoughts outward. He had sworn to do that. On the approach he had admired the majesty of the mountains. Landing he had admired the four hamlets, the cruciform of the valley, the rim of gold on the snowcaps. Walking, it was the tractors. Look at anything you like, he was telling himself, as long as you look out, not in.

Abandoned tractors. Tractors to build new roads that had suddenly stopped being roads and turned into fields again. Tractors to flatten land for housing, lay out irrigation and drainage pipes, break fields, tow away cut timber, except that there were no new houses, the pipes were stacked but not laid, and the timber was lying where it fell. Tractors sticking like slugs to their smear-trails. Tractors peering wistfully upward at the glistening peaks. But idle. Not one of them moving, anywhere, not by a tremor. Relinquished at a stroke to the half-planted vineyards, half-completed pipelines. Crashed against invisible buffers, and not a driver anywhere.

They crossed a railroad track. Weeds poked from the wheels of deserted dump trucks. Goats ambled between the sleepers. It is precarious, Zoya is saying. If he sends much money, he is tolerated. Recently he has not been able to send much money. Therefore it is precarious. From the doorways of stone cottages the occupants eyed him malevolently. His escorts were no more friendly. The boy to his left was scarred and elderly in manner. The boy to his right had a limp and was grunting to the rhythm of it. Both carried automatic rifles. Both had the air of belonging to a secret order. They were leading him to the farmhouse, but by an unfamiliar route. Trenches, waterlogged foundations and a collapsed walkway blocked the old path. Cows and donkeys grazed amid a colony of silent cement-mixers. But the farmhouse when they came upon it was much as he remembered it: the fretted steps, the oak verandah, the wide-open doors and the same darkness inside. The boy with the limp gestured him up the steps. Oliver climbed to the balcony, listening to the clump of his feet echoing in the evening air. He knocked on the open door but no one answered. He stepped into the darkness and stood still. Not a sound, no smells of Tinatin's cooking. Only a musty sweetness, testifying to the recent presence of the dead. He made out Tinatin's rocking chair, the drinking horns, the metal stove. Then the brick fireplace and the painting of the sad old woman in her battered gesso frame. He swung round. A young cat had sprung from the rocking chair and was arching its back at him, reminding him of Jacko, Nadia's Siamese.

He called out: 'Tinatin?' He waited: 'Yevgeny?'

Slowly a door opened at the back of the room and a shaft of evening sunlight spread along the floor. At the centre of the shaft he made out the crooked shadow of a goblin. It was followed in the fullness of time by Yevgeny, frail beyond Oliver's worst expectation, wearing bedroom slippers and a fleecy cardigan and leaning on a stick. White stubble grew where his brown hair had been, and it had spread over his cheeks and jaw in a downy silver dust. The wily old eyes that four years ago had twinkled from between double fringes were slashed cavities of dark. And behind Yevgeny, part manservant, part devil, loomed the bland unblemished figure of Alix Hoban in a white summer jacket and dark blue trousers and the witches' black box of his portable telephone dangling like a handbag from his wrist. And perhaps, as Zoya insisted, he was indeed the Devil for, like the Devil, he cast no shadow, until belatedly it placed itself beside Yevgeny's goblin.

Yevgeny spoke first and his voice was as firm and fierce as it had ever been. 'What are you doing here, Post Boy? Do not come here. You are mistaken. Go home.' And he turned to repeat the order angrily to Hoban, but had no time because Oliver was speaking.

'I came to find my father, Yevgeny. My other father. Is he here?'

'He is here.'

'Alive?'

'He is alive. Nobody has shot him. Not yet.'

'Then may I greet you?' He moved bravely forward, arms lifted for the embrace. And Yevgeny was about to reciprocate, for he whispered 'Welcome' and raised his hands before catching Hoban's eye and lowering them again. His head dropped, he shuffled backwards until there was room for Oliver to pass. Which Oliver did, briskly, refusing to acknowledge the slight and, in his relief at knowing that Tiger was alive, he peered happily and nostalgically around the room until, much later than was somehow natural, his gaze fell on Tinatin thirty years older, seated in a tall rush chair, with her hands folded on her lap in a cross, and another cross at her throat, and an icon of the Christchild above her, suckling Himself at the covered bosom of His mother. Oliver knelt beside her and took her hand. Her face, he noticed, as he moved to kiss her, had been redrawn. New lines ran vertically and diagonally across her forehead and down her cheeks.

'Where have you been, Oliver?'

'Hiding.'

'From whom?'

'Myself.'

'We cannot,' she said.

324

He heard a click and peered round. Sauntering to a rear door, Hoban had pushed it open with his fingertips and, tilting his head to Oliver, was inviting him to follow.

'You will go to him,' Yevgeny ordered.

On Hoban's heels, Oliver crossed a courtyard to a low stone stable guarded by two armed boys of the same unlovely stamp as those who had brought him to the farmhouse. The door was barred with wooden beams dropped into iron brackets.

'Too bad you missed the funeral,' Hoban remarked. 'How did you find this place? Zoya send you?'

'No one sent me.'

'That woman can't hold her tongue for five minutes. Did you invite anybody else to join you?'

'No.'

'If you did, we kill your father, then we kill you also. I shall be personally involved in that operation.'

'I'm sure you will.'

'Did you fuck her?'

'No.'

'Not this time, huh?' He banged on the door. 'Anyone home? Mr Tiger, sir, we brought you a visitor.'

But by then Oliver had pushed past Hoban and the guards and was himself manhandling the wooden bars from their housings. He hammered on the door, then kicked it till it yielded. He called 'Father' and strode in, smelling sweet hay and horse. He heard a plaintive call, like an invalid waking, and it was followed by a rustle of straw. There were three stalls. All had straw in them. From a nail beside the third hung Tiger's brown Raglan coat, and in the straw lay his father, half naked on his side, the way Oliver himself lay when he was sad, in black City socks and white underpants and a filthy blue Turnbull & Asser shirt with what had once been a white collar, his knees to his chest and his arms round them, and his face blackened with bruises, and his puffy eyes pink from fear of the world into which he had been so recently reborn. He was bound with one chain. It joined his feet, then his hands, then passed to an iron ring embedded in a wooden pillar. He was trying to stand up as

Oliver approached, and not quite managing it, and going down again, and on the point of having another try. So Oliver, instead of keeping a respectful distance for fear of towering over him, put his hands under his arms and lifted him the rest of the way, remarking, as Zoya had done, what a lightly made little creature he was, and how skinny under the Turnbull & Asser shirt. He looked into his father's bashed face and was reminded of Mrs Watmore's drowned husband Jack though he knew him only from photographs and hearsay: in the water for ten days, she had once confessed to him, and me having to go to Plymouth to identify him. He thought about giving the kiss of life to people you didn't want to kiss. He thought about dead Jeffrey, and he wondered how a man who owned Nightingales and a penthouse and a Rolls-Royce coped with being chained hand and foot in a stable with no view and no secretary.

'I've seen Nadia,' he said, feeling he ought to be bringing news of some kind. 'She sends her love.'

And he had no idea why he selected this particular item of news, except that Tiger was embracing him with a fervour that was unprecedented and some kind of fudged kiss was taking place at an angle between their cautiously averted cheeks – except that no sooner had they achieved it than Tiger pushed him away again, and said, with a hasty practicality designed for Hoban's hearing:

'And they reached you all right, wherever you were, did they – Hong Kong or somewhere?'

'Yes. They did. Hong Kong. Understood.'

'I wasn't quite sure where you'd be, d'you see? You flit about so. I never know whether you're studying or drumming up business. I suppose that's the prerogative of the young: to be elusive. What?'

'I should have kept in touch more,' Oliver agreed. And to Hoban: 'Take this chain off. My father is coming with us to the house.' Seeing that Hoban was smirking contemptuously, Oliver grasped him by the elbow and, watched by the guards, guided him out of earshot. 'You're dead in the water, Alix,' he told him, on the strength of little except bluff and supposition. 'Conrad's going public with the Swiss police,

326

Mirsky's cutting a deal with the Turks, Massingham's retired to his deep shelter and your face is on every wanted list as the man who shot Alfred Winser. I don't think it's a very good time for you to get fresh blood on your hands. It could be that my father and I are the only bargaining chips you've got left to play with.'

'Who are you in this comedy, Post Boy?'

'I'm a dirty informant. I betrayed you to the British authorities four years ago. I betrayed my father, and Yevgeny, and the whole shooting match. My masters are just a bit slow about sharpening the knife. But they'll get to you very soon, I promise.'

There was a delay while Hoban conferred with Yevgeny's household. He returned and gave an order to the guards, who unlocked the chain and looked on while Oliver first sponged his father down with water from a bucket, trying to remember when Tiger had last done this to him when he was a child, then deciding he never had. He dragged Tiger's suit from the hayrack where it had been tossed, and made the best of it before helping him to put it on, leg by leg, arm by arm, then doing up his shoes.

In the farmhouse a kind of wakening was under way, or perhaps it was a going back to sleep, a restoration of life's comforting routines in the aftermath of death. Under Hoban's sceptical eye, Oliver sat his father in a chair across the fire from Yevgeny's and poured each a glass of cuvée Bethlehem from a flagon on the table. And though Yevgeny refused to acknowledge Tiger's presence, preferring to set his gaze firmly at the flames, some tacit complicity obliged them to take their first sip in unison and, by ignoring one another so intently, to accord each other mutual recognition. And Oliver, observing them, bent every fibre to foster this atmosphere of conviviality, however artificially arrived at. Acting the part that came most naturally to him – the adopted prodigal returned – he lent a hand to Tinatin with paring vegetables, shifted saucepans on and off the flame for her, found candles, matches, set plates and cutlery on the table and generally deported himself, if not with levity, then with an insistent busyness that was like a spell –

'Yevgeny, can I top this up for you?' – he could, and earned a muttered 'Thank you, Post Boy' for his trouble – 'It won't be long now, Father, how about a bit of sausage to keep you going?' – and Tiger, though he was ashamed of his grimy fingernails, woke from his daze and took a piece, and chewed at it with his bruised mouth, and declared it the best, while he pulled jerky, self-congratulatory smiles and, in the relief of his partial liberation, began to preen himself, and follow Oliver round the room with his bruised eyes.

'This place is very clearly Yevgeny's Nightingales,' he called out, above the clatter. He had a front tooth missing, which made him lisp.

'Yes, indeed,' Oliver agreed, setting knives.

'You could have told me. I didn't realise. You should have given me advance warning.'

'I thought I did, actually.'

'I like to be informed. Couple of holiday villages wouldn't do it any harm. Four, come to think of it. One in each valley.'

'Might go very well. Four's a good idea.'

'Hotel in the middle, disco and nightclub, Olympic-sized pool.'

'Made for it.'

'You've tried the wine, I take it?' – sternly, despite the missing tooth.

'Any amount of it.'

'Good. What do you make of it?'

'I like it. I'm fond of it.'

'You should be. It's palatable. I see an opening for us here, Oliver. I'm surprised you didn't spot it. You know I've always been interested in food and beverages. It's a natural adjunct to our leisure interests. You've seen all those tractors out there, busily doing nothing?'

'Of course –' cutting up flat bread with an ancient guillotine.

'What did you think when you saw them?'

'I suppose I was a bit sad.'

'You should have thought of your father. It's the type of situation where I excel. Bankrupt stock, a defunct enterprise. Everything waiting for the creative flair. Buy the plant for a song, apply modern methods, rationalise the infrastructure, quarter the workforce, turn the whole thing round in three years.'

'Brilliant,' said Oliver.

'The banks will love it.'

'Bound to.'

'Good food, good wine, good service. The simple pleasures of life. It's what the next millennium is about. Is that not so, Yevgeny?' No answer while Tiger allowed himself another appreciative pull of his cuvée Bethlehem. 'I'm going to tell old Kat to add this one to the list,' he announced once more to Oliver. 'A perfectly acceptable Cabernet. Little heavy on the tannin.' Sips. 'A few more years in the bottle would help. But up there with the greats, no question.' Swallows. Ruminates. 'A blind tasting, that's the trick. Kat'll do it superbly. There'll be a few red faces I don't mind betting you. I can think of one or two names right now who rather fancy themselves as connoisseurs. Always good to see the mighty tumble.' Another long sip. Rinse the wine round the teeth. Swallow. Smack the lips. 'We'll need a designer. Have a word with Randy. Get a clever label done, stylise the bottle. Those long necks always look good. Château Argonaut, how's that? The Spaniards won't like it, I'll tell you that for a start.' He chuckled. 'Oh dear me, no.'

'The Spaniards can do the other thing,' Oliver said over his shoulder while he set the table; at which Tiger burst out clapping in a crazed exhilaration.

'Spoken like a true Englishman, sir! I was telling Gupta only the other day. There's no more arrogant fellow on earth than a Spaniard when he's above himself. You can have your German, your Frenchman, your Italian. Is that not so, Yevgeny?' – no answer. 'Caused us a lot of aggravation, the Spaniards have, down the centuries, I can tell you.' He drank again, bravely setting his little jaw for combat as his faltering gaze once more sought out Yevgeny, but without success. Undaunted, he slapped a hand on his own knee in inspiration. 'My goodness me, Yevgeny, I nearly forgot! – Tinatin, dear lady, this will delight you no end! – too much bad news about sometimes, one forgets the *good* news – Oliver's a father. A very beautiful young lady by the name of Carmen – raise a glass with us, Yevgeny – Alix, you cut a gloomy figure this evening – Tinatin, my dear – to Carmen Single – long life and health and happiness – and prosperity – Oliver, I congratulate you. Fatherhood becomes you. You're a bigger man than you were. Carmen.'

And you've shrunk, thought Oliver, briefly furious to have his daughter taken over and paraded in this way. You have revealed the full scale of your immense, infinite nothingness. At the brink of death, you have nothing to plead but your stupefying triviality.

But none of this was detectable in Oliver's behaviour. Agreeing, encouraging, raising his glass to Tinatin, though not to Hoban, stepping blithely between the kitchen and the table and the two old men seated at the fire, he was bent solely upon creating a mood of circumspect good fellowship. Only Hoban, nursing his witches' telephone and seated on a bench between two sullen cohorts, showed no sign of entering the spirit of the party. But his embittered, brooding presence could not discourage Oliver. Nothing could. The magician was coming alive. The illusionist, the eternal pacifier and deflector of ridicule, the dancer on eggshells and creator of impossible *karma* was answering the call of the footlights. The Oliver of the rainswept bus shelters, children's hospitals and Salvation Army hostels was performing for his life and Tiger's, while Tinatin cooked, and Yevgeny half-listened and counted his misfortunes in the flames, and Hoban and his fellow devils dreamed their sour mischief and pondered their dwindling options. And Oliver knew his audience. He empathised with its disarray, its stunned senses and confused allegiances. He knew how often in his own life, at its absolutely lowest moments, he would have given everything he had for one lousy conjuror with a stuffed raccoon.

Even Yevgeny, little by little, was unable to withstand his magic: 'Why did you not write to us, Post Boy?' he called reproachfully from beside the fire when the prodigal had once more replenished his glass. And another time: 'Why

did you give up our beloved Georgian?' To both of which
questions Oliver replied disarmingly that he was but flesh,
he had been unfaithful, but he had learned the error of his
ways. And from these seemingly innocent exchanges, a kind
of madness grew, a shared illusion of normality. The food
ready, Oliver summoned everyone to table, and placed Yevgeny unprotesting at its head. For a while the old man sat
there, head down, lowering at the food. Then as if the sight
had restored him, he hauled himself upright, and clenched
his fists and braced his broad chest, and bellowed for more
wine. And it was Hoban, not Oliver, whom Tinatin dispatched to fetch it.

'What must I do with you, Post Boy?' Yevgeny demanded,
as tears appeared at the corners of his nearly vanished eyes.
'Your father killed my brother. Tell me!'

But Oliver with perilous sincerity contradicted him: 'Yevgeny, I am truly sorry that Mikhail died. But my father didn't
kill him. My father's not a traitor and I'm not the son of
one. I don't understand why you're treating him like an
animal.' He shot a covert glance at Hoban, seated impassively between his uneasy protectors. And Oliver noticed that
his telephone was nowhere in sight, which led him to the
happy thought that Hoban had run out of friends or spells.
'Yevgeny, I think we should enjoy your hospitality and leave
with your blessing as soon as it's light,' he said.

And Yevgeny seemed disposed to sympathise with this
suggestion – until Tiger, unable to resist hogging the conversation, ruined the moment: 'Let me handle this one, if you
don't mind, Oliver. Our hosts – largely I suspect encouraged
by our friend Alix Hoban here – take a rather different view
– no, don't interrupt me, please – their position being that
since I have delivered myself into their hands, they are in a
twofold position of advantage. *One* – not while I'm speaking,
Oliver, thank you – *one*, to persuade me to sign everything
over to them, which is what they have been demanding for
months. *Two*, to take vengeance for the killing of Mikhail
on the totally erroneous grounds that I, with the connivance
of Randy Massingham of all people, am the author of it.
Nobody – no member of my House or family – is in the

remotest way guilty of such an act. However, as you see for yourself, my denials have so far fallen on deaf ears.'

Which in turn prompted Hoban to restate the charge, even if his awful voice lacked something of its customary arrogance. 'Your father fucked us all ways up,' he declared. 'He cut a side-deal with Massingham. He cut a deal with your British secret police. Killing Mikhail was part of the deal. Yevgeny Ivanovich wants vengeance and he wants his money.'

Yet again Tiger blundered recklessly into the gap, using Oliver as his jury. 'That is the most utter nonsense, Oliver. You know as well as I do that I have long regarded Randy Massingham as a bad apple, and if I am at fault at all in this matter, which I contest, it is because I have been too soft on Randy for too long. The axis of conspiracy is not between Massingham and myself, but between Massingham and Hoban. Yevgeny, I beg you to assert your authority here –'

But Oliver the grown man had already cut him short: 'Tell us, Alix,' he suggested, with no more emphasis than if he were seeking enlightenment on some semantic point. 'When did you last watch a game of football?'

Yet Oliver felt no enmity towards Hoban as he asked this. He did not see himself as some shining knight or great detective unmasking the evildoer. He was a performer, and for a performer the only enemy is the one who doesn't clap. His overriding aim was to magic his father out of here and say sorry to him if he felt it, though he wasn't sure he did. He needed to dab the bruises from his father's face and get him a tooth job and put a pressed suit on him and shave him and deliver him to Brock, and after Brock to sit him behind his half-acre desk in Curzon Street; to set him on his feet but say, 'There you are, you're on your own, we're quits.' Beside these concerns, Hoban was an incidental nastiness, the consequence and not the origin of his father's folly. So he told it without histrionics, calmly, much in the way Zoya herself had told it to him, right down to the sausage and the vodka at half-time, and little Paul's pride at having both his parents there, and Mikhail's mistrust of Alix which Zoya's presence fatally overcame. He spoke reasonably, never lifting his voice or pointing a finger, but preserving with all the vocal tricks he knew the glass-like delicacy of the illusion. And as he spoke he was able to watch the truth gradually descend on them: on Hoban, white-faced, immobile and calculating, and on Hoban's uneasy consorts; on Yevgeny, made strong again by Oliver's ministrations; on Tinatin, as she rose to her feet and glided away to the darkness, trailing her hand along her husband's shoulders to reassure him as she passed; and on Tiger who was hearing him from within a cocoon of faked superiority while his fingers absently explored the outlines of his battered face, reassuring himself of his restored identity. And when Oliver had completed his account of the football match, and given time for its significance to resonate in Yevgeny's memory, he was so moved by his own call to honesty that he was halfway to tossing aside all strategy and confessing to his own betrayals also, to the assembly at large and not just Hoban. But mercifully a number of extraneous happenings were on hand to deflect him from this rash course.

First came the unexpected drone of a helicopter passing overhead – the distinctive gub-gubbing noise of twin rotaries. It faded, and nothing more was heard until a second followed. And though nowhere in the world is silent any more, and helicopters and other powered aircraft are nightly visitors to the mysterious Caucasus, Oliver felt enough hope stir him at the sound of them to be disappointed by their passing. Hoban was protesting, of course – ranting was a better word – but he was protesting in Georgian and Yevgeny was gainsaying him. Also Tinatin had returned from whatever corner of the house she had retired to and she was carrying a handgun of the same design, it appeared to Oliver, as the one that Mirsky had offered him in Istanbul. But this event was in turn overtaken by the rush of Hoban's two companions to escape the room – one by the main door to the verandah and the other by way of a window between the fireplace and the kitchen. Both skidded and collapsed on the floor before they reached their goals. Immediately after these events, the reason for them became apparent: namely that dark figures had been entering the room at the same time as the two men were trying to leave it, with the result that the dark figures, with their dark instruments, won the day.

But still nobody had spoken or fired an audible shot, until the room lit up and exploded to one finite and incontrovertible bang, not of a thunderflash or a stun grenade, but of Tinatin's handgun, which she was directing at Hoban with great competence, using both hands in a golf professional's grip. And the effect of this piece of home magic was that Hoban was now wearing a big bright ruby at the centre of his forehead and his eyes were wide open in surprise. And while this was going on Brock was taking Tiger into a corner and advising him, in the simplest and most energetic Merseyside phrases, of the unhappy course his life would follow if he did not pledge his unstinted cooperation. And Tiger was hearing him, as he would say. Hearing him with respectful attention, with his hands to his sides and his shoulders dropped, and his eyebrows raised for greater receptivity.

What am I seeing? Oliver wondered. What am I understanding now that I didn't understand before? The answer was as clear to him as the question. That he had found it, and it didn't exist. He had arrived at the last, most hidden room of his search, he had prised open the most top-secret box, and it was empty. Tiger's secret was that he had no secret.

More men were pouring through the windows, and clearly they were not Brock's because they were Russian, and shouting in Russian, and they were led by a bearded Russian, and it was this bearded leader who, to Oliver's disgust, hit Yevgeny across the side of the head with some kind of blackjack, causing copious bleeding. But the old man seemed scarcely to notice or care. He was on his feet, his hands bound behind him with some kind of instant tourniquet, and it was Tinatin who was screaming at them to leave her husband alone, although Tinatin couldn't do much to help either, because they had disarmed her, and thrown her face downward to the ground, and she was seeing everything sideways, from boot level, where, to his astonishment, Oliver now joined her. Stepping forward to remonstrate with Yevgeny's bearded assailant, he felt his feet being kicked from under him. His head flew over his feet, and the next thing he knew he was lying on his back on the floor and a steel-hard heel was being driven so viciously into his stomach that the lights went out and he thought he was dead. But he wasn't, because when the lights came on again, the man who had kicked him was lying on the ground, clutching his groin and groaning, and he had been put there, as Oliver quickly deduced, by Aggie, brandishing a submachine gun and wearing a panther suit and Apache warpaint.

Indeed, he might not have recognised her, had it not been for her rich Glaswegian accent delivered with schoolmarmish emphasis: 'Oliver, on your feet, please, stand up, Oliver, *now*!' And when that had no effect on him she flung down her weapon and part-hauled him and part-willed him to his feet, where he stood swaying and worrying about Carmen and whether all the shouting was going to wake her up.

ACKNOWLEDGEMENTS

My special thanks to Alan Austin, magician and entertainer, of Torquay, Devon; to Sükrü Yarcan of the Tourism Administration Programme, Boğaçi University, Istanbul; to Temur and Giorgi Barklaia of Mingrelia; to the distinguished Phil Connelly latterly of Her Majesty's Customs and Excise Investigations Service; and to a Swiss banker whom I may only call Peter. George Hewitt, Professor of Caucasian Languages at the School of Oriental and African Studies since 1996, has once more spared me many blushes.

John le Carré
July 1998
Cornwall